Totally Bound Publishing books by C.J. Burright

Music, Love and Other Miseries
Every Kiss
Every Minute
Every Breath
Every Step

I0691665

Music, Love
and
Other Miseries

EVERY STEP

C.J. BURRIGHT

Every Step
ISBN # 978-1-83943-884-4
©Copyright C.J. Burright 2020
Cover Art by Erin Dameron-Hill ©Copyright May 2020
Interior text design by Claire Siemaszkiewicz
Totally Bound Publishing

EVERY STEP

Dedication

To Brittany, for your unwavering
belief in me and never giving up.

Chapter One

Kat had signed the divorce papers before dawn. She'd wadded up the envelope the documents had arrived in and tossed it on the floorboard of her SUV before getting out. She'd let Vic, aka scumsack dogface — and not a cute pooch like a beagle or husky, but more of a Mexican hairless — have everything he'd asked for, including the house, the bank account, the twenty-year old Taylor Swift lookalike and her thigh-high boots. Dragging around someone else's dirty laundry wasn't her MO.

An hour of blowing holes in innocent targets beat reflecting on her miserable past, and guns were preferable to marriage. Her Colt Python had never betrayed her.

She stepped over the railroad tie that served as a curb and swung open the door leading into the firing range office with more force than necessary. A bell cheerfully announced her entry into the emptiness. *Screw Vic.* Screw his loyal sidekicks who she'd thought were her friends too. Screw the required leave of absence from her badge and gun. She didn't need extra time to reflect on an error that would never be repeated. After a lifetime of being subtly criticized, she was fully aware of her every single flaw and knew exactly how to deal with them. Proving that didn't require time off.

The case in her hand bumped her thigh, a reminder that she wasn't taking leave of *all* guns. Her firearms collection was the one personal possession Vic hadn't dared to touch or request in the split. During her obligatory absence, she'd accepted a temp job as firearms instructor for the local authorities of Graywood, a tiny town with an even tinier police force. A temporary stint in a backwoods village should be demonstration enough that she could handle anything.

The small-time outdoor range was nothing like the indoor luxury she was used to at home, and she liked it more because of the simplicity. A coded, automatic gate allowed members entry into the rural acreage miles from town and citizens, offering both privacy and safety. Beyond the one-room office that was presently unoccupied, a gravel road led to the dozen or so tin-shed shooting bays. It was basic, rustic and minimal.

But minimal was phenomenal. She was absolutely done with big-city pretenses and all the underlying dredges that went with it—the stuff only discovered after it was too late to prevent being slimed.

Kat lowered her gun case to the floor and grabbed the pen beside the login sheet. She scribbled her name and membership number, ready to use her new club benefits for the first time, long overdue for shooting off some steam. It was a shame she'd already destroyed the targets her sister Gia had made specially for her—all blown-up pictures of Vic's face. Gia was the best sister on the planet.

The *ding* of another member entering the office echoed as she tossed the pen aside. She grabbed her case, pivoted toward the door and paused.

Son of a jerkface. The man blocking the exit was unfortunately familiar. *Roman Farkos.* Both times she'd crossed paths with Roman, bad things had happened — first a blow-up with her sister, then the aftermath of a shootout where Gia had been the victim. The fact that he was friends with Gia's shady fiancé said it all.

Roman had a tendency to get on her nerves simply by breathing. The way he looked at her... It was as if his midnight eyes could see right into her soul and pluck every string that made her want to snap and snarl. *No one* needed to see her depths.

"Good morning, Katerina." He slung his holster with his Desert Eagle over his arm. He was wearing all black.

Unsurprising — shady people, shady colors.

"Nice day to shoot something, isn't it?"

"Is that a rhetorical question?" Kat narrowed her eyes. "Every day is a good day to shoot something."

"Imagine that. We actually agree on a subject." Roman leaned one shoulder against the doorjamb, clearly not going anywhere until he was good and ready.

"It *was* a nice day a few seconds ago, before you showed up — and don't let our minimal agreement fool you into thinking I'm going soft." She flipped her long ponytail behind her shoulder and sniffed. "The only thing I like about you is your gun."

He twitched one black eyebrow and his eyes glittered like a crow's when spying a shiny jewel in the grass. It didn't take much imagination to follow where his mind had gone — straight into the gutter.

Typical man.

"I'm referring to the Desert Eagle in your holster, scumbag—not your *little* gun." She waved at his crotch.

"How dare you objectify me," he said in a monotone. "I'm deeply offended."

"And I'm deeply annoyed. Move aside. I need to shoot until I'm out of ammo."

"Bad day already?" If he were the smirking type, she suspected he'd be wearing one. From what she'd seen of Roman so far, he strictly controlled his expressions, as if he got a personal thrill from making people guess at his emotions. "It's barely dawn."

"Affirmative. It started out bad and has become progressively worse." She stared at him so he'd have no misunderstanding about the fact that the 'worse' applied to him currently bothering her.

"What did you bring?" He jerked his chin at the long, unmarked case in her hand.

"Oh, this and that." Her favorite Beretta, because it always shot true and brightened her mood. Then there was her Colt Python. Every girl could use a power trip from time to time and there was nothing like the smell of gunpowder and the kick in her hands as bullets pierced the bullseye until only a ragged hole remained.

That was a picture-perfect vision of her life.

Kat clenched her jaw. It was nothing a hard round of perfect shooting couldn't cure, and today she needed a pick-me-up. If she had to be honest with herself, her marriage had been crumbling before lil' miss thigh-highs had shown up. Kat simply hadn't noticed until it was too far gone, and that felt like a personal failure.

Failure was the worst.

But not noticing the state of her marriage was also a big fat sign that maybe it hadn't been all that amazing to begin with. Before he'd walked out, Vic had made sure she knew beyond any doubt that she was the main ingredient in that non-amazingness.

What was I thinking, getting married at the idiot age of eighteen? Ten years wasted – poof! – gone, see ya, wouldn't wanna be ya.

"You brought your Python. There's no need to deny it," Roman murmured, his gravelly voice bringing her back to the problem at hand — aka, *him.* He was a marginally more palatable problem than her prior marriage. That glitter in his eyes grew and he straightened from his sexy lean. "May I?"

"Absolutely not." She sniffed. His lean was irritating, not sexy. "Don't you Graywood hicks have any manners? Asking to handle a girl's gun is like asking if you can fondle her boobs."

He was smart enough not to even glance at her chest, but the tiny twist of his mouth told her enough.

Holding his gaze, she strolled nearer, adding a saucy swing to her hips. She stopped right beside him, leaned near his ear and said in a breathy voice, "That's also a no."

"A shame." He turned his head slightly, his mouth too close to hers for comfort, but she refused to surrender further ground. She'd given enough to the male cause today. "I'll let you handle mine any time you ask and, as a bonus, I won't make you feel awkward about it."

"Keep it in your pants, Farkos." She hadn't noticed before that Roman was a handful of inches taller than her five-foot-ten, and being so near to him now made his height impossible to miss. She had to lift her chin to stay at eye level, and if he hadn't lowered his, she would have been out of luck.

11

It was almost refreshing. Vic had whined on the rare occasion she'd worn heels. Apparently, being shorter than his wife had threatened his ego.

And Roman Farkos was *not* refreshing.

"I was referring to my baby Eagle, of course." Roman stroked the handle of the gun in his shoulder holster. "The questionable paths your mind takes disturb my delicate sensibilities."

"You wish." Katerina snorted and brushed by him, getting a mild whiff of some spice. Cinnamon? Cloves? *Doesn't matter.*

"How about a wager, Hellman?"

Kat paused, her hand on the door. Technically, her last name wasn't cut to Hellman until the judge signed on the dotted line, but she wasn't in the mood to correct him or explain. Besides, Hellman was easier to say than Hellman-Patterson and was certainly less time-consuming to write. "Excuse me?"

"A wager." He rocked back on his heels, and with his black T-shirt, jeans and scuffed boots, he resembled some secret agent who was off the clock but ready to jump into action at the first whisper of trouble. "Bet I hit the bullseye with my bird more than you do with your snake."

She almost laughed. Since the tender age of five, she'd been shooting with her dad and older brothers. The walls of her room back home were lined with ribbons, awards and sharpshooting trophies. On the days off from her public-servant job — protecting, serving and everything in between — she'd taught firearms at the police academy. She'd been sent to the top sniper school in the country on the city's dime and had returned with honors and the nickname Oakley — as in Annie Oakley.

Vic had probably found that emasculating too.

"And after you lose," he continued, "I'll allow you to buy me coffee."

Kat killed her laughter and stared at him, adding a touch of menace. Did he believe he could outshoot her because she was a woman? As tempting as it was to prove how woefully incomparable his shooting skills were to hers, the range was her sacred place. She needed alone time to burn off the last traces of her failed relationship, a decade wasted.

And to remind herself that her ex-husband, legal papers and the opinion of an annoying small-city badge had zero impact on her identity.

"I already had my caffeine intake this morning and I never waste my personal bullet stash on idiots, but if you lurk around in the office long enough, I'm sure someone closer to your competitive level will show up." She gave him a quick once-over, ignoring the long lines of his legs and how nicely he filled out his short-sleeved T-shirt. "I'd suggest returning next week on novice training day."

Laughter shimmered in his eyes, an unusual disparity from his sober expression. "I understand why you'd be intimidated by all this breathtaking awesomeness." He gestured at his face. "I've been known to move a woman to distraction, but in all fairness, it's usually my dance moves that do the trick more than my stunning charm and glowing good looks."

"I'll take your word for it." She tugged the door open and cool morning air drifted in, not yet baked by the late July heat.

"See you on Monday," he called after her.

Kat let the door slam shut between them, muffling the hint of humor in his tone. Roman could think what he wanted. Monday was her first day as the Graywood

Police Department temporary firearms instructor. After getting appropriate approval from the brass back home, Police Chief Clifton had offered her the job. Since she had another six weeks of leave and Gia had graciously offered her couch for as long as she wanted, she'd accepted.

She needed *something* to keep herself occupied. She could only watch so many redeye movies while feeling sorry for herself without getting soft, and since her bank account had slipped to pennies with the divorce, she couldn't single-handedly keep the local potato chip company in business anymore.

As gravel crunched beneath her boots along the way to the closest firing bay and air scented with country dust from the field nearby curled around her, she allowed herself a small smile. On Monday, she'd be back in her element. She'd show the Graywood blue all a girl with a gun could do and reaffirm that she didn't need time, reflection or anything else to be at full throttle on the job, at the range or on the streets.

And Roman Farkos could suck it.

* * * *

Roman waited until the door shut behind Katerina before signing in. He neatly wrote his name on the range register and set the pen down, dawdling in the office long enough for Kat to choose her shooting bay and get situated. He had no intention of being accused of stalking.

She wouldn't have a problem taking out any fool dumb enough to stalk her.

Leaning against the wall, he sipped his hazelnut-infused mocha and gazed out of the window at the golden hayfield beyond. Maybe there was something wrong with him that he'd thoroughly enjoyed the last few minutes, letting Katerina Hellman disparage him. Perhaps it was simply a need to distract her from the lingering shadows that turned the beauty into a beast. Since her arrival to Graywood, she'd been in a growly mood on every occasion he'd run into her, and instead of inspiring a survival instinct to stay back, her snarls had lit an unexpected spark of challenge — his weakness. He never could resist the potential payoff of a hard-won contest or bet.

And he suspected winning over Katerina Hellman would be worth the claw marks and bruises. He wanted to dig into her darkness and find out who she was beneath — not simply Gia's protective older sister, calloused cop or sharpshooter cover girl, but the woman entangled in it all.

Katerina's unexpected appearance in Graywood had been a slice of personal serendipity in different ways. The chief had initially wanted *him* to be the firearms instructor, an extra responsibility that would have a significant impact on his extracurricular commitment to the floundering afterschool club. A subtle mention of Katerina's accomplishments and current leave of absence were all it had taken to set the wheels in motion.

More notably, her arrival had stirred a forge to life inside him, so fierce he'd forgotten to breathe. The moment he'd first seen her remained a permanent portrait in his memory — a natural beauty parting the glitz and glamour at a charity masquerade party, dressed in Converse, skinny jeans that molded to her long legs and a strappy baby doll that had made his gut clench. He hadn't stopped thinking about her. He hadn't stopped wondering when she'd last smiled.

He wanted to see her smile — more, he wanted to be the reason for it. Next in line would be a laugh — not one a villain used to strike fear into victims, but one of joy. He needed to know if the spark Katerina had awakened would flare into something more, something significant and life-altering. Lose or win, he'd be selling himself short if he didn't try.

Personal challenge accepted.

Roman straightened from the wall, adjusted his holster and made for the door. He'd better intensify his self-defense skills along with his shooting. Surviving Katerina without losing an eye — or a particular manly appendage — might depend on it.

Chapter Two

Supervising only two gunmen at once was a new experience for Kat. She breathed in fresh country air laced with a metallic hint of gunpowder and made the best of the tiny firing range the department had reserved for her use. At home base, she'd usually take a dozen or more officers at a time to qualify them as capable and efficient with their weapons. The Graywood police force didn't have enough officers to spare from daily duties for a large group, and only two was almost too easy, too personal — especially since one of them happened to be Roman.

"Am I holding the weapon correctly, Miss Hellman?" Roman's tone was serious, and any observer would believe he was being sincere, not patronizing. He'd been like this the entire hour, asking for her advice, demanding that she supervise him, even though he obviously knew exactly what he was doing — both with and without the duty firearm in his hands.

If she were anywhere else, she'd rip him a new one. That was one of the problems with being employed by the police department—she had to behave herself, watch her words and act accordingly instead of smacking him on the back of the head.

Kat stood at his side and carefully studied him as Boyd, the other officer, waited his turn. She wished she could find even a tiny criticism, but Roman held the gun in a perfect 'push-pull'—pushing out with his strong hand, support hand pulling back to create a solid base. His stance was flawless, his large hands clearly practiced at carrying a weapon. His gaze was fixed on the target down the range, unwavering. A slight breeze ruffled his short, ebony hair and carried a trace of spice—*cloves, definitely. Maybe cinnamon. Could be nutmeg.* He smelled like the best holiday.

It doesn't matter.

"I suppose that will work," she finally said.

"Your approval warms my heart," he said, deadpan.

"As it should, since I'm the one who decides whether or not to qualify you. There's always the chance of FTQ, Farkos." *FTQ*—failure to qualify, an embarrassment to any respectable cop. Roman didn't need to worry about failing, but putting him at ease wasn't her job.

His gaze briefly flicked from the target to her, black and glittering behind protective glasses. "I'll take as long as you need."

Kat ignored the way his voice dropped an octave, the underlying suggestion in his words. If he was trying to distract her, he'd be disappointed.

Boyd folded his arms, his expression sour, and rested his hip against the counter that served as a barrier between the target area and the covered firing bay. When it came to FTQ, he *should* worry. "As much fun as it is to review safety protocol and pretend like we're in awe of having you demonstrate how to hold our weapons, as if we didn't know how, can we get on with it? I have actual duties waiting for me."

Roman relaxed and set his gun down, as if in agreement.

"Your tolerance is appreciated." Adding some ice to her tone, Kate held Boyd's narrowed gaze. "Right now, *this* is your duty, and it's my job to make sure that if you're required to use your weapon, you'll know how to do it correctly. The only way to do it correctly when under fire is to practice until it becomes as natural as breathing." She lifted Boyd's last target and jabbed her finger at the paper center, where there were zero bullet holes. "You're not quite there."

"Maybe it's the instruction." The saccharine sweetness in Boyd's smile snapped a tight wire inside her. "My last qualification was fine."

Roman lifted his own target and aimed it at Boyd. Only a speck of red remained of the bullseye. "I don't seem to be having any problems with Miss Hellman's guidance."

Boyd kept his stare on Kat, his hazel eyes gleaming a challenge.

Forcing her hands to remain relaxed instead of balling into fists took more effort than she wanted. She'd had to face the same tests when she'd started the force at home — proving herself to the boys. Again, when she'd started teaching at the academy, she'd been pushed until her reputation preceded her. It was like being the substitute teacher at a grade school where none of the students listened because they didn't think they had to, that she wasn't worth the respect. And it was ninety-nine percent men who pressed the issue.

"Remember that bet from the range last weekend, Farkos?" she asked, never breaking Boyd's stare.

"Python versus Eagle?" An edge of excitement slipped into Roman's tone, and Boyd's attention switched to him. "Winner buys coffee?"

She decided that ignoring Boyd was more productive than showing him she wasn't intimidated by him in any manner. Jerking her chin at the gun cases neatly lined on the counter, she kept her expression neutral. "Care to do it right now?"

Roman paused, lifted his gaze skyward and mouthed 'thank you'. "All this time I thought you'd brought your Python out of the kindness of your heart, to share it with us."

She snorted.

"Or to make us jealous."

Kat shrugged. *Maybe.*

His mouth twitched, as if he'd read her mind. "To prepare you, I prefer a hazelnut macchiato from Growlers and Grounds, iced with almond milk."

"Your preferences make no difference in this instance." She turned and strode for her Python case. "And only a monster would ruin coffee with hazelnut. Disgusting."

"Don't change the subject." Roman slid up beside her, where his Desert Eagle rested, cartridge out and empty. He quickly filled it with bullets, almost as fast as she filled her revolver, his long, capable fingers flying.

Kat ignored the warmth coiling in her stomach and the idle thought that flashed to mind, contemplating what else he could do with his hands. *Wrong place, wrong time, most definitely wrong man.*

"A first-year double action Python?" Boyd gave a low whistle. "How did you get your hands on that beauty?"

All the warmth bled away as she brushed past both Boyd and Roman. While she could appreciate the reverence, she didn't miss the underlying meaning in his words. He didn't believe she was worthy of possessing such a gun, let alone using it — which made him undeserving of knowing how she'd gotten it.

"How she got it makes no difference," Roman said. "Only that she has it. Stop asking stupid questions before she puts it away again."

She hid a tiny smile, glad her back was to them, and managed to keep her tone icy. "Need a warmup first?"

"I've been warmed up for some time now." The way Roman watched her, she wasn't entirely sure if he referenced shooting…or something else entirely.

She studied him for a moment and that warmth returned, spiraling higher. It had nothing to do with the man and everything to do with the familiar weapon in her hand, of course. Guns made sense. Men didn't. "You want to go first?"

His dark eyes danced.

"Make it a speed round." Boyd leaned on the counter, his sour expression back. "I've already been here longer than necessary and have no desire to be stuck here while Roman does his usual thing."

"His usual thing?" Kat hated that she had to ask. She didn't want to know, didn't care and didn't want Roman to think she held any curiosity where he was concerned — because she didn't.

"When it comes to any sort of shooting contest, Farkos gets all persnickety."

"That's an exaggeration," Roman said mildly.

Boyd barked a laugh and folded his arms, accentuating his protruding belly over the tight duty belt. "I was there when the chief challenged you last year. You demanded to go through it all—the moving targets, the short range, the rifle range. It only ended because we ran out of daylight."

"Correction. It ended because I won." He shrugged. "And a seafood platter was on the line. I never mess around when seafood is involved, especially if pie is also part of the deal." His eyes gleamed. "Which it was. The fact that the chief paid for it made it all the more delicious."

"Don't worry." Kat clicked the cylinder of her Python into place. "We won't be here more than a few minutes. Speed round, Farkos. Aim, shoot and see what's still standing after the dust settles."

Roman studied her and one side of his mouth ticked up, the closest thing he'd come to a full-out smile, causing that coiled warmth in her gut to expand. "Coffee *and* pie."

"It doesn't matter what you want."

That crooked smile widened slightly and his eyes sparked with heat. "Time will tell."

She had a sneaking suspicion that he referred to more than the showdown between snake and bird, and she had no desire to delve deeper into his meaning. "Boyd, keep him honest. I'll give him the advantage of a larger bullet." *He'll need it.*

"Six shots each. Farkos keeps one bullet in the cartridge since the eagle carries seven." Boyd nodded and pivoted to face the range. "Got it."

Kat slipped her electronic ear protection on. Two fresh targets hung on stands at fifty yards out, and as Roman got into position a few feet away, square with his own target, she fought to hold back a grin. Sure, it would have been smug, but this was one of those moments where she had to make a stand, to defend her place and prove she was absolutely worthy of her position and the respect that went with it. Humor could wait until after the win, at home and in private. Over the years, she'd found most men didn't appreciate being beaten by a woman, let alone a smiling woman. Laughing had a tendency to get their shorts in a twist.

So many men were such delicate pansies.

Assuming her shooting stance, she took a breath in, released it and lifted her Python. Beside her, Roman did the same with his Desert Eagle. She had to admit that he looked good doing it—confident and natural, the long, lean line of his body set, those big hands ready, his expression coolly determined. When was the last time she'd ever noticed so many small details about a man during training? And why the hell was she noticing them now?

"Ready." Boyd's voice snapped her attention back to the target. "Aim."

She drew another breath and held it, finger in the trigger.

"Fire."

The weapon shuddered in her steady hands, the crack of shots dulled by her earmuffs, the mild, burnt scent of powder dusting the air. Her Python was empty in less than five seconds and, in the sudden quiet, she freed the breath she'd been holding.

Roman discharged the mag from his Eagle, flashed her a view of the last bullet, checked to make sure the gun was clear and set it on the counter.

Good boy.

Kat followed suit and removed her ear protection as Boyd trudged out to collect the targets.

Roman's dark eyes gleamed as he hooked his thumbs in his leather duty belt and pivoted to face her.

"You're not as mysterious as you think you are," she said, leaning a hip against the counter.

"That's a mean thing to say. I'm an enigma."

Right. "You might like to keep people guessing by controlling your expressions, but newsflash—your eyes don't hide anything."

He cocked his head. "What an interesting tidbit to notice, Katerina. It's almost as if you've been studying me, trying to figure me out."

She snorted and folded her arms. "Like that's hard."

"So, you freely admit it. You have been studying me. That's unsurprising, considering my powerful intrigue factor." That tiny, crooked grin was back, and this time her stomach fluttered.

Son of a jerkface. Her body was suddenly in cahoots against her. "You're like one of those weird circus acts where no matter how much you want to look away, it's too horrifying. You can't help staring and wondering how in the hell such a thing exists."

"It's true," he said with a hint of drawl. "I'm one of a kind." He winked.

Kat's eye twitched.

Frowning at the two targets in his hands, Boyd returned from down range. He laid the paper targets on the counter. "Bird wins."

Impossible. "Give me those." Kat jerked the targets around and bent over them. Both bullseyes were blown out and it was clear which one belonged to her and which one was Roman's. His bullets were larger, an advantage she'd let him have—a handicap to herself that she'd never imagined would have any impact. But it had. One of her bullets had hit outside the bullseye, leaving an edge of red.

24

No way. Her stomach clenched. She'd freakin' missed. She hadn't missed in years.

"Nice shooting, Hellman." Roman watched her and none of the glee she expected filtered into his voice.

But she couldn't tear her gaze from the symbol of failure, a chill winding through her veins. First her marriage, then her job, now the one talent she'd always counted on... The world seemed to drop out beneath her combat boots.

"I don't have much of a social life," he said. "I practice at the range. A lot."

He'd basically described her own life, minus the chips, ice cream and sappy movies as of late. Steeling herself, she lifted her gaze to his and swallowed the fist-sized lump in her throat. "Coffee and pie will be delivered later."

"I don't want delivery." If he felt any triumph or humor, he hid it well. Maybe she'd spoken too soon about reading him easily. "It's not a victory if you're not there to participate in the celebration."

"My attendance wasn't part of the deal." She resisted the urge to crumple the accusing target. "You can both go. You qualify for today."

Carefully, she set her Python in its case and began gathering up the equipment, anything to avoid looking at the evidence of her unexpected defeat and stop the lead ball in her stomach from rolling over and over.

Instead of leaving, Roman set about collecting empty rounds and boxes.

"I've got it, Farkos." She didn't care that her words were snarled. "Go save the world. Keep Graywood streets safe from all the speeders and littering offenders."

"It's my day off, training notwithstanding."

25

"Let's go, Farkos," Boyd called from the doorway. "Afternoon beers on me for your contribution in revealing who should and shouldn't be instructing in our department."

Kat stiffened. *Oh no he didn't.* Heat rushed into her face.

Roman paused. Straightening, he pivoted toward Boyd. "Hellman could outperform you blindfolded with one wrist handcuffed to her belt." A darkness entered his voice, completely erasing his customary cool. "Lay off, Boyd."

Her heart contracting, Kat whirled on Roman, her teeth bared. "I don't need you to defend me or fight my battles." She swiped up her Python case and strode for the door. "I've changed my mind. You can clean up."

At the door, she paused and gave Boyd her ice-queen glare. "I suggest you start spending more time at the range than the buffet." She flicked a contemptuous glance at his beer belly. "The odds of you needing to shoot someone in Graywood are *slim* — pun intended — but a barely passing seventy percent qualification in your file isn't going to do you any favors." She leaned in his face. "And, to be clear, I don't freakin' care what you or any of your other buddies in blue say about me or my qualifications. I can kick your ass to sunset and back again, on and off the range."

She shouldered past him. It wasn't her fault that he was standing in the doorway, too close to avoid her swinging gun case.

"Watch it, Hellman." Whatever else he muttered beneath his breath was indecipherable, but she didn't need to hear it. She could guess well enough. Over the years, she'd heard it all while trying to prove she belonged in a career mostly occupied by men.

Making it back to her SUV, she hit the keyless entry, completely forgetting in her fury that it had stopped working during the past week. She fumbled with the keys, and after jerking the door open, she carefully laid her gun case on the passenger's seat then flung her ear and eye protection beside it. She climbed in and closed her eyes.

Crap, crap, crap. Her hands were shaking, her breath too rough and all she could see was the police department building in her rearview mirror as she'd driven away. Her identity seemed to be falling apart, slipping through her fingers until only a blank slate remained. If she lost her trademark shooting skills too...

At the rap on the window, she snarled and opened her eyes. Roman was close enough that his breath fogged up the glass. Why couldn't he stay out of her business? She opened the door fast, annoyed that he jumped back before it hit him. "What?"

He stepped into the empty space between the door and the SUV, hooked his hands on the frame and loomed down, invading her personal bubble with his big body and annoying holiday scent. "I was thinking."

There were so many snarky responses she could make to that open-ended statement, but she figured that was why he'd said it — to get a response out of her. Instead, she stared at him, waiting.

The sparkle in his black eyes confirmed her guess. "I volunteer at the afterschool club for low-income kids in my meager spare time."

"I don't hand out the citizen-of-the-year awards, Farkos."

"So, I have a chance, then," he said, without missing a beat. "But, more to the point — since you'll be in Graywood for a while, you should check it out. You'd be a great role model to the girls and we could really use another female on the co-ed softball team. Valerie would be psyched to no longer be the sole girl with a mitt out there."

Kat drummed her fingers on the steering wheel. If she refused, he'd know it was because of him and read something more into it. He'd know that losing the shooting match had shaken her confidence. "I'll think about it."

"If you're not up to the challenge, I understand." His expression was utterly serious. "There's no shame in sucking at softball. At least you're good at shooting."

"Shut your face." She curled her lip and stared him down. She wasn't *good* at shooting—she was freakin' phenomenal. The leave of absence had been forced on her by her captain with the intent of it being an adjustment period, an opportunity for her to be away to regroup and relax, and if she couldn't handle the small Graywood force—and cope with Roman and all the buttons he so easily pushed—that would only prove that Cap had been right in requiring a vacation to deal with her demons...aka defying the need to booby trap Vic's new love nest and seeing how many times she could make him jump and yelp like a child. Bonus if she scared off his new Barbie doll in the process.

"Better idea." Roman's rough voice lowered. "Since you're here for six weeks, that's plenty of time to redeem yourself."

She narrowed her eyes, which was met with a reappearance of his tiny, mischievous almost-smile.

"It's possible I merely got lucky today beating you—unlikely, but not impossible." He continued over her growl, "But daily shooting matches might become tedious and boring, so how about we make it more exciting?" He cocked his head and wriggled his eyebrows. "What do you say to a six-week challenge with a bet to sweeten the deal?"

All the buttons — *push, push, push*. Redeeming herself was exactly what she wanted, what she needed — and she had no intention of sharing that with him. Her marriage to Vic hadn't defined her, and there were far more terrible things than being divorced from a man who hadn't held her hand or her heart. But being cheated on and left behind seriously bruised a girl's ego. Then being put on leave...

She could do this. She *had* to do this — work with Roman without letting him affect her. Prove to herself and everyone else that she could handle whatever life threw at her, that she could rise to any challenge and conquer it. If she didn't, another piece of herself might crumble and she wasn't sure she could afford to lose any more of what remained.

"Come on, Katerina. Live a little."

"Don't pressure me." She released the steering wheel and angled to partly face him, ignoring how close he was, how the muscles in his arms flexed as he hung on to the SUV frame, how a slight wind ruffled his short, raven hair. "Let's say I'm considering this challenge. What are the rules and what's at stake?"

"Besides pride, honor and bragging rights?" He studied her, as if trying to figure out what she cared about most. "First, the rules. At least one challenge per week and it can be anything — ping-pong, chess, basket weaving, whatever."

"I rock at basket weaving." She gave him an evil smile.

"I'm not surprised." For a second, his gaze dropped to her mouth, and that unwanted flutter in her stomach made a comeback. "We switch off choosing the challenge every other week—three weeks each, with the option of making additional challenges upon mutual agreement."

"Is that so when you find yourself losing hard, you can try to bridge the gap by making extra-frivolous challenges?" She took a move from her sister Gia's playbook and curled the end of her ponytail around her finger, trying to look innocent.

Roman didn't seem to be fooled. He nodded. "Exactly."

"What if I challenge you to a pickled rocky mountain oyster eating contest and you refuse?"

"When it comes to a bet, I'll do whatever the rules require." His attention drifted again to her mouth and he paused for a heartbeat before meeting her gaze. "To prevent future arguments, any refusal to participate is considered a forfeit."

She bit the inside of her cheek to keep from letting out a real smile. Her family made competition a daily routine, and jockeying for position with her brothers had molded her into a fierce competitor, no matter what the game might be. Backing down wasn't in her genetic makeup. "There have to be some ground rules. No challenge can be something that's physically impossible for the other."

"Such as?"

"Like seeing who can grow a mustache or chest hair faster." Her brothers had totally tried to pull that over on her.

A rumble of laughter rose from him like a distant earthquake, soft and trembling. "I acquiesce to that rule. I'll add that no trial shall include breaking any laws."

She lifted her chin. "Of course."

"And every contest has to be a face-to-face event, no online trivia contest or some lame long-distance battle of intellect or test of useless information."

She smirked. "Scared that you're both outmatched and unarmed in the wits category, Farkos?"

"Marginally, but the rule stands. There isn't as much room for accusations of cheating if we're both present."

"Is cheating a concern?" All humor vanished, turning her tone frosty. "I don't tolerate dishonesty." *Or infidelity, disloyalty and omitting the truth to further one's own benefit.*

"Have you seen this angelic face?" Roman motioned to his expressionless features. "I'm the worst liar, which is why I don't do compliments unless I mean them. And I never answer when I suspect someone doesn't want to hear the brutal truth."

His dark eyes seemed clear and guileless, and the slight lift of his eyebrows gave him an offended edge, as if he found it insulting that she dared to question his integrity. Her gut told her to believe him. Her heart? Not so much. She'd trusted Vic too.

"You in, Hellman?"

She drummed her fingertips on her arm. "What's in it for me?"

"Besides the exclusive opportunity of basking in my presence and a chance to redeem your reputation?"

Kat leveled her blackest stare on him. Redeeming herself was enough of an incentive to play his game — and thoroughly thrash him in the process — but she had no intention of letting him discover how important that was to her, how important it was to prove to herself that she could still win at *something*.

"Feel free to name a potential prize for yourself, but if I win," he said in a low purr, "I want to shoot your Python."

The velvet in his words sent tingles over her skin, and it took her a moment to shove back an irrational urge to close her eyes and simply listen to his gravelly voice. *Hell.* She could really use a good night's sleep instead of staying up until she was too exhausted to drag herself off the couch in the hopes she wouldn't dream.

"No one outside of family shoots my Python."

"Then I suggest you bring your A-game, but fair warning, Katerina..." Once more, he dropped his gaze to her mouth, and this time it stayed there. "I'm in it to win. First challenge — meet me at the afterschool club at three." His mouth twitched as he straightened. "*If* you think you can handle it."

She watched him walk away through narrowed eyes until he disappeared around the corner of the range building. Handling whatever game or contest he dreamed up wasn't a problem. She could just as easily ignore his challenge as accept it. Impressing Roman Farkos wasn't one of her life goals. In six weeks, Graywood would be in her memory, left behind.

Kat shut the door and started the engine. After this morning, she could use a pick-me-up, a finish line to aim for, an objective to accomplish and remind her that she didn't need anyone's approval, support or love to make an impact. She backed up her SUV in a spray of gravel. And until she finished her leave of absence, kicked ass at her temp job and hit the road, she'd make sure Roman never had a chance to wrap his big, capable, annoying hands around her Python.

Chapter Three

Cutting across the parking lot behind Kaito's, the solo local sushi bar in Graywood, Roman checked his watch. He was two minutes late to his lunch appointment with Ian, his close friend and fellow conspirator, and as much as he hated to be late, he couldn't regret the extra few minutes he'd taken to convince Kat to play.

His mouth twitched. As his father had loved to say, *holy shiznit*. The woman had a vicious glare and he couldn't help but speculate how that passion panned out when her settings turned from ice to heat. He suspected she didn't let many people beneath her skin on her best day and getting divorced hadn't helped on that front.

But that wouldn't stop him from weaseling his way in and discovering the woman Katerina Hellman hid from the rest of the world.

He found Ian already at their usual table beside the koi pond on the back patio, basking in the sun and sipping an iced tea, sunglasses on, a beast disguised in suit and tie. At Roman's approach, he looked up.

"Dude, you're late, which means you're paying for lunch."

"Tightwad." Roman sank into an empty cushioned chair and planted his elbows on the table. Ian must have been waiting longer than two minutes and ordered already. Two plates of sushi and an iced coffee waited. "In a rare moment of inspiration, I might have done something stupid." He paused. "Correction. I might have done two somethings stupid."

"Are we talking more stupid than the sentence you just spewed? Or is it more on the level of the time you decided wrangling racoons after a six-pack sounded like a fun idea?" Ian arched one of his manscaped eyebrows, just enough to peek above the rim of his sunglasses. "Either way, I can't wait to hear what disaster you've instigated."

"Have a bad morning in court and need some entertainment to distract you from your litigation woes?" Roman made a quick sweep of his buddy's posture and expression. Reading people was one of his superpowers, and while he used it to advance his own purposes from time to time—especially if he could score some cash or food through a wager, innocent or not—he most often used it to keep an eye on those he cared about. Not long ago, Ian's cool expression and relaxed position had been a veneer to hide a simmering volcano. Since Gia had inspired him to crack open the safe to all his deep, dark secrets, the relaxed posture was no longer an act. The fact that his emotionally scarred and cynical friend had found someone to love made Roman all warm and gooey inside—like apple pie straight out of the oven.

The thought of pie reminded him that he was starving. He picked up a California roll with his fingers and stuffed half of it into his mouth.

"I don't need a reason to be entertained by your reckless decisions, Baconbits." Ian smirked.

Roman pointed the other half of the roll at him. "Boy Wonder, you're under a misapprehension. Nothing I do is reckless." *At least half of the time.*

"Today was your first day at the range with Katerina, wasn't it?" Wearing a wicked grin, Ian leaned forward. "What did you do?"

"Outshot her."

"Did you now?" Ian said in a low, approving tone, his smile going malevolent. "That's payback, not stupidity."

"Depends on perspective." Roman squinted up at the brilliant blue sky.

"Damn." Ian laughed. "I wish I could have witnessed that."

Roman wolfed down the remaining half of the sushi still in his hand. He didn't doubt for a second that Ian would've loved to watch Kat fall. Katerina and Ian held opposite ideas about who was the right man for Gia and neither one of them liked to lose. The fact that Gia had stuck with Ian hadn't improved Kat's opinion, but at least she hadn't threatened to kick anyone's testicles up to their throat lately. An attitude improvement— even a small one—was a hopeful sign.

But he'd intended to challenge her with the shooting wager, not hurt her. He hadn't missed the flash of devastation in her gorgeous brown eyes when she'd examined their targets and judged herself the loser. It had been bad enough that he'd been the one to cause that emotion, even worse that Boyd had witnessed it. Yet if he hadn't given everything he had, he had a suspicion Katerina would have sensed it and respected him even less for it. He was the same way. Any victory had to be legit and won with sweat and full-out effort, or it didn't count.

He'd make it up to her for causing any pain, if she let him. He clenched his jaw. She *would* let him.

"What's that?" Ian casually waved at Roman's face.

"What's what?"

"That look on your mug." He pulled off his sunglasses and stared at Roman, his eyes narrowed. "Don't tell me you have a hot itch for our mean Kitty-Kat? You wouldn't do anything *that* stupid. She has claws and isn't afraid to use them on whoever gets in her way."

"She has teeth too." Roman rubbed his lower lip. White, straight teeth he wanted nibbling on his neck. When she'd smiled at him with all sorts of evil instead of the contempt she'd always used before, he'd nearly popped. He'd always had a soft spot for the misunderstood villain. "Not to mention she's an expert at tongue lashing."

"And not in the good way." Ian shook his head. "Dude, don't do it. Whatever it is you're thinking where Kat is concerned, run the opposite direction."

"Too late," he said without any resignation or regret. "Not only did I outshoot her, I went a step farther. I challenged her to play with me while she's in town."

"Play?" Ian repeated the word as if it was poison. "Katerina Hellman doesn't *play*. She seeks, destroys and picks her teeth with the bones of her enemies. That's Gia's description of her own sister—and they're siblings who actually love each other."

"As I suspected. She's perfect." Roman couldn't stop his mouth from twitching at Ian's look of horror. "You know how I can't resist a challenge."

"You're confusing the thrill of a dare with risking your stones in a completely avoidable disaster."

"Possibly." Slowly, Roman shook his head, all humor draining away. "I can't stop thinking about her. That...doesn't happen to me. *Ever.*"

"She's beautiful. No one will contest that," Ian said, as if her looks alone explained that persistent, undeniable tug on his gut where Katerina was concerned.

"Legs that go for miles." Roman gazed past Ian's shoulder, reliving the first time he'd seen Katerina, a dark, impervious queen standing firm among a sea of color and glitter. "Curves that make everything hard for a man."

Ian made a strangled noise.

"Hard not to touch," Roman continued. "Hard not to discover if her pouty mouth tastes as good as it looks. Hard not to trace my fingertips over every soft inch of —"

"Stop." Ian sliced a hand in the air. "It's a classic moth versus flame. To be clear, you're the brainless insect flinging yourself into a hellish death by shrew."

"It's not just the physical attributes that keep me fluttering near her fire, though," he said, going with the symbolism Ian had used. "I respect that she unapologetically protected Gia with all she had, even if she went about it in a hostile manner." While he'd visited Gia from time to time in the hospital during her recovery, he'd lost count of how many menacing statements Katerina had snarled at him simply for being Ian's unapologetic friend and daring to breathe the same air. The rest of her family had been perfectly civil.

"Some define it as being obnoxiously over-protective." Ian ate his sushi with a meaningful look, as if he'd already won the argument. "And she was completely off-base. I'd never hurt Gia."

"Cross-fire doesn't count, of course," Roman agreed, sipping his coffee. "As much as I disagree with her methods, I get why she lashed out at both of us. You're...*you*, so no explanation necessary."

Ian made an affirmative noise.

"And since her douchebag ex-husband is also a cop, she's probably reflecting any negativity of that situation onto me simply for being the combination of a man and officer. That will change once she gets to know me. I'm irresistibly sexy, after all."

Ian shook his head, smirking. "While that all may be true in some version, there's one huge flaw in your theory, Baconbits. You're assuming you'll survive her claws that long." He tapped his glass in an uneven beat. "I don't question your dedication to the cause, and I've always supported whatever you pursue. This would be no different if Kat didn't have a warning tag stuck to her forehead."

"There's just something exhilarating about jumping into a dangerous situation," Roman said in a monotone.

"It's clear you have no intention of heeding wise counsel. Don't come limping to me when you're burnt toast while Kat's eating your heart and laughing."

"I'd never waste time going to you. I'll run straight to Gia." He managed not to grin at Ian's possessive growl. "She'll understand."

"Don't drag Gia into your schemes. It's hard enough for her being engaged to me." Ian lowered his sunglasses long enough to glare. "Gia's happiness trumps yours, dude. Make even a hairline crack in it and I'll have to kick your ass."

Roman gave his friend a semi-smile. "I'd let you try, just so you could feel better about yourself, Boy

Wonder." He leaned back in his chair. "Keep your gloves on the shelf for now. Katerina hasn't even accepted my challenge." *Yet.*

Ian stared at him a moment longer, enough to give him the impression that he was expected to squirm — which he didn't. "You do know the ink on any divorce papers hasn't had time to dry, right? Even if she gives you a chance, you'll be the rebound guy, which I wouldn't usually discourage." His mouth twisted as if he had a bad taste on his tongue. "But you're exhibiting disturbing behavior when it comes to Kat. It's like she's hypnotized you with her bad attitude and arsenal, which means you're the victim in this scenario. Are you sure you want to deal with being used and dumped? Because that's what will happen if she doesn't destroy you first."

Roman rubbed his lower lip. He could think of far worse things than being used by Kat — and, despite the wisdom in Ian's words, he couldn't bring himself to believe she was the type of woman who'd surrender to temporary pleasure only to sober up later and cast him aside like trash. She'd either play or not, and whichever her choice, she'd be all in.

"Thanks for the advice," he said, grabbing the last *uramaki* as he stood. "And for lunch." He shoved the sushi into his mouth and walked away over Ian's mild protest about paying the bill, headed for the afterschool club.

Whether or not Kat showed up, he had promises to keep at the club — but *holy shiznit.* If she didn't accept his challenge, the next six weeks might be harder than he could take, in more ways than one.

* * * *

As Kat plopped onto Gia's couch and kicked her feet out on the cushions, her baby sister emerged from the kitchen with a precious bag of potato chips in her clutches.

"How'd your first day go?" Gia asked, leaning a hip on the back of the couch.

"Stupendous." Kat grabbed the bag from her sister, crammed a chip into her mouth and basked in the temporary joy of salted crunchiness. "Assigned to your slimy fiancé's buddy Roman on day one. What could be better?"

"You promised you'd be nice to Ian *and* his friends." Gia swiped the chips back and held them out of reach. "No respect, no chips."

"Fine. I'll rephrase." Kat made a monster face. "Day one with Roman was a real treat. Better?" She made grabby hands.

"Acceptable, since you left Ian out of the sentence." Gia had mercy on her and tossed the bag of chips onto the couch. "I don't know what your deal is with Roman. He's never done anything to you."

She dug for another chip. "He's annoying."

"He's great." Gia rested her elbows on the couch, studying her. "Any guy who gets pedicures during his lunch hour is okay in my book."

Kat paused mid-crunch, her hand in the bag, and tried to imagine Roman with his black duty pants rolled up to his knees and wriggling his bare toes in a warm foot bath scented with rose water. "Seriously?"

"Would I joke about the salon?" Gia grinned. "Roman's full of surprises."

"Full of something, anyway." Kat snorted. "What are you doing home so early?"

"I took a personal half day to fill out my college application and other various paperwork." She scrunched her delicate nose. "I forgot how much fun going to school can be."

"You'll rock it, sis." As much as Kat distrusted Ian, she couldn't deny he'd been a shockingly good influence on her sister. Gia had always flitted through life, not knowing where she belonged, who she wanted to be, what she wanted to do. After her brush with death and danger—thanks to an assignment as Ian O'Connor's partner in an unusual case at the law firm she'd worked at for several years—she'd figured out she wanted to be a lawyer specializing in domestic abuse. Kat couldn't have been prouder of her.

But choosing Ian as her romantic partner was a different story—and none of her business, as Gia reminded her daily. Backing off was hard, especially when she was accustomed to looking out for her sister. For Gia's sake, she'd try harder. She understood intimately what it was like to have her choices questioned at every turn, as if she didn't have a clue.

Kat took the last handful of chips and tossed the empty bag on the coffee table. "Signed the divorce papers this morning," she said between chips, as if the crunching might minimize the end of an era. "And Roman challenged me to a mystery pentathlon of sorts, minus a few events. What do you call a competition with six events? A sextathlon?"

"Ooh, you're having a sextathlon with Roman?" Gia jumped up and down, clapping. "You go, sis! Good for you, diving back into the game and not letting any unworthy, scumbag, cheating jerkface hold you back. I always suspected Roman had a hint of wild behind his serious side." Her blue eyes glittered, playful. "I bet he knows all sorts of *events* to keep you occupied during your sextathlon—or should I say 'sextath*long*'?"

"It has nothing to do with sex," Kat growled, sacrificing a chip to throw at Gia's head and ignoring the sudden heat in her face. "Or anything long."

"Sure it doesn't," Gia said, grinning like a fool. Her smile faded at the edges. "I'm sorry about Vic and the divorce — all of it."

Shrugging, Kat focused on her remaining potato chips. "This might sound weird, but after being royally pissed off, I'm actually relieved. When I got married at the age of stupid and naïve, I imagined it would be like mom and dad's relationship. You know, fun in between the fighting, a partnership based on love, respect and loyalty. Forever." She made a face and cracked a chip in two. "Obviously, I was an idiot."

Gia circled the couch and pushed Kat over enough to snuggle up beside her. "There was only one idiot in that relationship and it wasn't you." She laid her head on Kat's shoulder like she used to do when they were little. The only difference was that it had always been Gia who'd been upset and seeking comfort, not the other way around. "You deserve the forever, Kitty-Kat. Don't give up on it."

Gushing about her emotions and problems wasn't Kat's usual MO, but she rested her cheek on the top of her sister's head and released a little sigh. "The worst part — I mean besides the cheating itself — was that almost everyone at the department knew about the affair before I did." Her throat tightened, making her voice rasp. "It was humiliating."

"Crap," Gia murmured, wrapping her arms around Kat. "And I added to your pain by keeping my relationship with Ian from you, and you found out by default when everyone else around us already knew." She squeezed harder. "I'm really, really sorry."

"I get why you didn't tell me, G." She sniffed. "*Now.*" Before she'd ripped out of town to visit Gia in Graywood while on leave—and avoid Vic and his girlfriend before she did something irreparable to her career—Gia had been assisting Ian with a hush-hush case. Pretending to be Ian's fiancé had turned into the real deal later, and due to confidentiality, Gia hadn't been at liberty to explain the full truth to her.

Being left out of such an important detail of Gia's life had hurt...a lot. And she'd made sure everyone present had experienced a piece of that hurt. It hadn't been one of her proudest moments. "I'm sorry I was such a jackass to you."

"You apologized. Remember? With ice cream, chips and a promise to not tell the rest of the Hellman fleet about my engagement for a week."

"Yeah, well. I'll try to my best to avoid more jackass moments while in Graywood."

Gia laughed and let her go. "Don't go making promises you can't keep."

As Kat pushed her off the couch into a giggling heap on the floor, the doorbell rang.

"I'll get it." Kat leaped off the couch and made it to the door before Gia could scramble up. Gia might no longer be in danger from any shady politician or his cronies, but she was far too easygoing when it came to preventative measures. As a Hellman, she failed, big time.

Kat looked through the peephole and froze. The woman standing on the front step was dressed in a carnation pink jacket and skirt, elegant pearls around her neck, her golden hair perfectly styled and blue eyes narrowed slightly, as if already set on judge mode and ready to find everything unworthy.

Caroline Hellman, aka *mother.*

Her blood going cold, she seriously considered not answering the door and sneaking out of the back while she still had a shot at escape.

The doorbell rang again and the knob rattled as Caroline tried it. Thank God their father had taught them to always lock doors behind them.

"Who is it?" Gia came up behind her and tried to look around her into the peephole.

"Mom," Kat mouthed the word.

"What? Why?" Gia's eyes went wide. "What do we do?"

"I heard you in there, dear." The door did nothing to muffle their mother's crisp tone, all prim and proper expectancy. "Don't make your mother stand on the doorstep like a stranger."

"Crap," Kat said beneath her breath.

"We have to let her in." Gia looked like she'd rather crawl away and hide under the bed.

If there were any real choice, Kat would have done the same, but no one defied Caroline Hellman and survived without scars, and some battles weren't worth the cost. Sighing, she turned the deadbolt and opened the door.

"Mom!" Wearing her favorite daughter mask, Gia pushed past Kat and embraced their mother in a warm hug. "What are you doing here?"

Kat did her best not to snarl. Gia was always so good at schmoozing every member of their family, a skill Kat hadn't chosen to learn. She hated to pretend she was something she wasn't, even when it would make some situations easier.

"Didn't you receive my text message?" Caroline asked as she released Gia and came in for Kat. She gave Kat's army green T-shirt, cargo pants and combat boots a disdainful sweep before hugging her lightly. "How are you holding up, Katerina?"

She never called her 'Kat', 'Kitty-Kat' or 'Oakley' like the rest of her family or her co-workers. She always used the formal name, as if that might recreate her into the daughter she'd always envisioned her to be and Kat never was.

"I'm fine." She smiled tightly as she slipped free and prayed Caroline would focus on Gia's engagement to Ian instead of her separation from Vic.

"No one is fine on the day of their divorce." Caroline skewered her with a knowing look, her mouth set in an expression Kat unfortunately recognized. Escape was impossible, resistance futile. "That's why I'm here."

Kat didn't bother asking how in the world her mother had known she'd signed divorce papers only that morning. Caroline Hellman knew *everything*. And dealing with her mother on top of all the other ongoing joy wasn't her idea of a good therapy session.

"My phone's still on the fritz," Gia said, looping her arm through Caroline's and sidestepping the suitcase on the porch. "I can't believe you texted me, not to mention came all the way across the continent just to check on us."

A spear of cold shot through Kat as her attention fell again on the waiting luggage. That wasn't an afternoon bag or even a dreaded overnight duffel, but a full-sized, staying-for-at-least-a-week monstrosity.

Hells bells and whistles. Their mother intended to stay for a while. *This is a nightmare.*

"It was no trouble. First-class is always so comfortable. I finished the book club's monthly selection, took a quick nap and woke up quite refreshed." Caroline looked over her shoulder as Gia led her into the house. "Be a dear and bring in my suitcase, Katerina."

"Sure," she mumbled and somehow managed not to grimace as she wrangled the heavy valise inside. It was clear who would be sleeping on the couch all week, and it wouldn't be queen Caroline Hellman.

"Since your father and I are no longer together, I have enough free time not only to practice texting but to spend a week with my favorite girls. Isn't that a delight?"

A lot of words came to mind, none of which were 'delight'. Kat dragged the suitcase to Gia's spare room as her mom and sister made small talk. Handling her divorce, forced vacation, a fresh round of proving herself after an unimaginable failure, working with a man who effortlessly pushed her buttons—none of those trials could compare to a week trapped in the same house with her mom. She'd self-combust.

Inside the spare room, her shoulders slumped beneath a wave of weariness. Her clothes scattered the floor, her unmade bed and chair in the corner. The book she'd been reading when she couldn't find anything on television to watch and still couldn't sleep lay spread and face down on the nightstand. Any story with a hot, immortal warrior with blue hair and black blades to fight *demonii* was made for late, restless nights, but she didn't have the patience to endure her mother's disdainful sniff at her reading choices—or her lack of cleanliness and order.

Sighing, she trudged to her duffel bag and set to gathering her meager wardrobe. Vic had asked what she'd wanted done with the rest of the shoes and clothing that she'd left in their closet. He hadn't mentioned the furniture they'd bought together, the Death Star waffle iron he'd given her for her birthday one year or the photo albums commemorating a decade of life now broken.

She'd told him to burn everything. Her only regret was that she hadn't been there to witness the bonfire and dance around it, cackling.

Setting the book on top of her clothes, she zipped up her duffel and shouldered it back into the living room. As she dropped it beside the couch, both her mom and Gia stopped talking and looked at her.

At the twin expressions of concern and pity, as if she might crumble at any moment, a tightness wrenched in her chest. As much as she knew that they were merely worried about her, she loathed that sort of attention aimed at her. She didn't want to be anyone's idea of a burden or project in need of repair, and if she didn't get out of here, she might break open and say something she couldn't take back.

"I have to go," she said, striding toward the door and swiping her keys from the coffee table.

"Don't be rude, Katerina." Caroline smoothed her skirt as she settled onto the couch, clearly intending to stay for as long as she wished. "I just arrived."

"Sorry, mom, but I got a temp job in Graywood during my leave." She halted at the door and glanced at Gia, hoping her sister could read the apology in her eyes for ditching her to handle their mother alone.

"Oh?" Her mother's expression brightened, hopeful. "Doing what?"

Somehow, she managed to rein in her evil smile as she opened the door to escape. "Firearms instructor at the rinky-dink Graywood Police Department."

Kat walked out before she could see her mother's disappointment. She'd had enough of that for one lifetime.

Chapter Four

As Kat strode toward her SUV, a sports car pulled up to the curb, and if it hadn't been a recognizable, retina-scarring red, she probably wouldn't have paid it any attention. If she hadn't been plotting how to avoid her mother, instinct would have kicked in and she would have kept on going, even if the world exploded into a war zone around her. It was too late to salvage that fantasy, but maybe she could still escape without looking like a coward.

Before she could pivot, a familiar voice belonging to a face she'd prefer to never see again called her to another halt. "Hey, Kitty-Kat. I was hoping to find you at Gia's."

She briefly closed her eyes. First the Roman range personal defeat, then dealing with her mother, and now Vic? Whoever had her voodoo doll was making excellent use of it today.

Gritting her teeth, she faced her ex. Vic climbed out of the convertible, tossed his ballcap onto the seat and shut the door. He ran his fingers through his thick chestnut hair, tousling it in a way she used to find sexy. Now, it only made her sick. There was no evidence of the bruises on his face that had been there the last time she'd seen him and his nose wasn't swollen. It was almost as if the...*incident* after he'd confessed his affair had never happened at all.

"What do you want?" Really, she didn't want to know. Whatever reason he'd had to drive hundreds of miles in his quarter-century crisis car to see her rather than text or email couldn't be good.

Vic circled his car and leaned on the fender. He slipped his fingers into his jeans pockets, an indication that he was slightly nervous—not that anyone who didn't know him intimately would detect it. From his eyes to his straight back, he exuded confidence. "We need to talk."

"I signed and mailed the divorce papers this morning. I let you have everything you wanted." She folded her arms, prepared for whatever battle he brought now, although she couldn't imagine what it could possibly be about. Only space remained between them with no more details to settle. "There's nothing left to talk about. You have your life. I have mine."

"That's what we need to talk about," he said in a low, velvet rumble that once upon a time had melted her.

She wasn't that naïve, starry-eyed girl anymore.

"What, you want my blood now too?" She bared her teeth. "To harvest my organs? Don't tell me your new Barbie needs a kidney and I'm the only match."

For once, he had enough sense to look sheepish. "I never meant to hurt you, Kat."

Funny how words sometimes destroyed and in other moments held zero power. If that was his idea of an apology, it slid off her like oil, slick and ineffective. "I have someplace to be, so whatever you came here to say, get on with it."

He released a long breath. "I haven't signed the divorce papers."

"Whyever the hell not?" What was his angle? The divorce gave him all their assets with the exception of the items in her duffel bag by Gia's couch, her decades-old SUV in the driveway, her retirement account — and her gun collection. Her temperature dipped then blazed. *Does the jerkface want to take my firearms too?*

"I think I made a mistake," he said, his voice rough. "Leaving you."

Kat blinked, going numb. She couldn't have possibly heard him right. He wouldn't have put her through hell for no reason, destroyed their life together on a whim, only to change his mind.

He watched her with green eyes that had inspired such a wide range of emotions over the years — amazing, ugly, furious and the whole spectrum in between. At that moment, none of those feelings fit quite right.

"I miss you." He straightened and took a single step toward her, apparently taking her silence as a signal to continue. "I woke up yesterday and I just — " He cleared his throat and took another step closer. "I didn't feel *right*."

While her brain was stuck on blank, it took her a moment to process his meaning, to connect the dots between the affair everyone had known about except her, the ruthless way Vic had walked out on her, every brutal hammer strike of the divorce.

I *made a mistake.*

I *miss you.*

I *didn't feel right.*

I-I-I-I-I. While he'd been tipping her life over, smirking at the office with the people she'd considered her second family, taking, taking, taking, not once had he expressed regret or sorrow or even a simple 'I'm sorry'. It was always about him—what he wanted or believed he was missing while shackled to her. And now he wanted takebacks.

"You didn't feel right." She repeated the phrase slowly, testing its weight, finding it wanting. "So, you're saying you *felt right* the first time you kissed another woman while married to me? You *felt right* while lying to me, being unfaithful to me for weeks, months?" With each word, her voice snapped, growing louder. "You *felt right* ripping my life apart beneath my feet and watching me fall and it's only now that you *don't feel right?*"

Vic lifted his hands, whether in a warning, surrender or in self-defense, she didn't know or care. "Kitty-Kat—"

"Did you tell your new girlfriend that you didn't feel right before coming here? Or does she even know where you are?" His guilty expression was enough of an answer, and an icy calm washed through her, honing her fury into a cold, sharp edge. "I have no idea why it took me a decade to see who you really are." She laughed, humorless. "You're a selfish prick, but you know what? I'm grateful for my freedom. Since I've been away from you, I've discovered that going solo has its benefits—namely, I don't have to waste my breath dealing with you." Stepping into his space, she held his gaze and, with an effort, leashed the violent urge burning beneath her skin. "Keep our stuff, the money, the house and most certainly yourself. My singledom is a gift I have no plan to return or refund."

He shook his head and every ounce of tenderness drained away as if it hadn't ever been there, as if it had disappeared years ago and she'd chosen not to notice. "And there she is, the Katerina I fell madly out of love with. I thought, for the sake of our years together, the happy times, that we could try to restart, but I guess that was just my warped memories talking."

Kat curled her lip. "While your backup girl waits unknowingly in the wings. How noble of you."

"Do you know why I found Melinda so charming, why I couldn't even talk myself into resisting her?" He didn't wait for her to respond, his eyes as hot and unforgiving as coals. "She's the opposite of you — warm, caring, understanding. Curling up beside an iceberg every night got old after the honeymoon, which made it easier to choose the graveyard shift, swing shift, whichever one that would require less time with you. It's probably a smart idea to stay single, because you're incapable of being happy with yourself, let alone making anyone else happy. No one wants an unfeeling witch."

Vic stormed back to his convertible with impeccable timing. Another second and she wouldn't have been able to control her fist from flying — which had probably been his ultimate plan. For once, she appreciated that his ego exceeded hers. Her entire arm trembled with restrained fury, her keys digging painfully into her palm. Instead of watching him leave, she stalked toward her SUV waiting in the driveway.

His convertible's engine purred to life behind her and, with a peeling of rubber, Vic's car squealed away from the curb and screeched around the corner. In the distance, another angry shriek of tires drifted to her before peace descended over the neighborhood again.

Planting her hands on the SUV door, she leaned her head down, breathing hard, her stomach hurting as if she'd been physically punched. Apparently, not only was it her fault he'd cheated on her, but she'd been a failure in the role of wife too. Vic's description of her had been savagely accurate. She'd never been the type of person whose personality had others flocking to her. That had always been Gia's gig. She had no illusions that others believed she was uncaring, because she didn't stand for crap and wasn't much of a hugger or sharer of sappy feelings. Most people didn't want brutal honesty, and once they realized her outward beauty was nothing more than a natural disguise, it wasn't hard to chase them off. It was easier that way. It saved everyone a big, fat round of disappointment.

Knowing that didn't stop her heart from battering at her ribs or ease the sick coil writhing in her gut. She'd come to terms with the fact that she'd never fit into a proper box with a neat, pretty label, so she'd poured all her efforts and passion into what she knew she'd rock at—not only marksmanship but a career in law enforcement—and she'd kicked ass. Winning a popularity contest had nothing on helping a victim or making the world safer, arresting one dirtbag at a time. What she did *mattered* and it had been enough—at least, she'd thought it had. Vic clearly hadn't agreed.

Maybe nothing she did would ever be enough.

Kat straightened and jerked her SUV door open. She didn't need to answer to anyone, not anymore. Vic could think what he wanted about her, because what she'd told him was absolute truth. She didn't need to waste another ounce of herself on him.

Driving to the afterschool club didn't take Kat long, even with forcing herself to obey the speed limit when she wanted to peel out from Gia's house, pretend she was on a car chase and rip through town, hit the highway and keep on going until she found a place where no one knew her and she could just *be*, without the accompanying nametags of 'divorced', 'disappointment' or 'frosty she-devil'.

She entered through the front door and took a moment to take it all in. The building reminded her of a converted grade school — a single hallway with doors on both sides leading into what had probably once been classrooms. Popcorn scented the air. At the end of the hall, double doors were propped open wide, spilling the squeak of tennis shoes on wood flooring, high-pitched voices of children in mid-play and shouts of a competitive game in full swing. School might be out of session, but some kids still needed a place to go in the summer.

Coming here and taking Roman up on his challenge hadn't been the particular destination on her mind when she'd escaped the unexpected arrival of both her mother and Vic. She could have gone to the range and shot until her ammo stores were dangerously low or to the tiny bookstore to see if anything new or interesting had been added to the shelves. There were other options, and even though it was a respite she needed, she found herself driving to take up the banner of competition.

And she had no intention of figuring out why it was Roman who had come to mind instead of a cup of coffee and a book or her Python kicking in her hands and destroying a bullseye.

Kat strode straight for the gymnasium and halted in the doorway. In one corner, a handful of six-year-old girls played hopscotch between two boys bouncing a rubber ball to each other. A juvenile basketball game was happening at the far end, and on the sidelines more children chased each other, laughing. Several adults and teenagers supervised, but Roman wasn't among them. Then again, it wasn't three o'clock yet—which meant she still had time to reconsider.

"I knew you'd show up, Katerina." Roman's gravelly voice came from behind her, too close.

A shiver rolled through her and she hid a grimace. She was truly off her game if she hadn't kept an eye on the door behind her, leaving her back exposed, let alone being so distracted that she hadn't heard him enter and approach. Maybe it had been the right thing to do, taking a break. A mistake like that on the job could get someone killed. She pivoted halfway to face him.

"It's about time you got here." She made a quick sweep of him—his black T-shirt, nylon basketball shorts and tennis shoes instead of his usual boots—and ignored the unwarranted fluttering in her belly. The reaction was probably due to the disturbing realization that she hadn't noticed him first, nothing more. *No biggie, I'm losing my mind along with everything else.* "You call that a uniform?"

"I call it my day off to wear whatever I want, but feel free to use any creative adjective you wish to describe this full meal deal of deliciousness." He swept a hand down his long, lean body, and the fact he said that with an utterly sober expression was the only thing that prevented her from walking out.

And she wasn't willing to forfeit their challenge on round one due to his overblown regard for his own person.

She arched a disdainful eyebrow, a skill perfected from the look her mother faithfully aimed her way. "Yawn."

His sharp, black eyes sparkled. "Pretend all you want, Hellman. I know you like me. After all, what's not to like?"

She snorted. "How about your inflated ego? Your persistence in annoying me? Your overestimation of what you call 'charm'?"

"I understand why you'd be jealous." His mouth quirked. "But if we stand here and list all my amazing qualities, we'll be here forever." He handed her one of the softball mitts he had tucked under his arm. "This was my sister's. I figured you wouldn't have one of your own, and since I suspected you aren't the type of person to bail, I came prepared."

For some reason she couldn't define, knowing that he had a sister added a sprinkle of irresistible curiosity and she spoke before she could reconsider. "Does your sister live in Graywood too?"

"Not the particular sister who's the owner of that glove. Two of my sisters decided to stay in Graywood, but Nadia attends college a few towns away."

"If you have sisters close by, why didn't you convince one of them to be a female presence on the afterschool softball team instead of me?"

"I prefer to have a solid reason to look at you longer." Before she could process that admission said in such a serious tone, he brushed by her in a draft of holiday spicy-sweet and entered the gym. "Come on in. I'll introduce you around."

At least half of the kids stopped what they were doing and surrounded Roman, obliging Kat to hang back as he worked through them and offering her an opportunity to silently observe the man she'd agreed to spend time with on a weekly basis.

'Yawn' hadn't been an accurate or honest description of him. Even in casual civilian clothes, Roman carried himself like a natural born cop — watchful, alert and subtly dangerous, as if he could jump from play to attack without any notice. Her dad and brother had instantly liked him when they'd met during Gia's stay in the hospital, and for that sole reason, she should walk away, whether or not her pride was bruised in the process. The law enforcement side of her family had embraced Vic with open arms, and even if her mom and Gia hadn't been crazy about Vic, they'd liked him well enough.

The approval of her family was obviously the kiss of death.

And she really needed to figure out how to hang with normal people, not another officer. *Who am I kidding?* She didn't even know *how* to be normal.

Forcing her gaze from Roman, she studied the other people who weren't greeting him. The basketball game had continued, consisting of a handful of teenagers who seemed more interested in making hoops than whoever had come in. By the side door, a knot of tweens waited, some sitting on the floor, others leaning against the wall, all either holding or near to a softball mitt. One girl stood in a typical teenage slouch, hand on her waist, one hip cocked at an impatient angle — truly, creating such a pose was an art in itself — and her stare aimed at Roman dripped with annoyance. She chomped bubblegum as if the angry snap between her teeth might hurry him along from his adoring fans.

Kat bit her lip to hide a grin. That must be Valerie, the solo female on the otherwise all-boy softball team. She liked the girl already.

After enduring a whirlwind round of introductions with kids and staff members, pounded by dozens of names she'd never remember, she followed Roman to the side door and the waiting team.

"Don't tell me you're the coach," she said, slipping the mitt on. The leather was soft, worn from use, molded by his sister's hand. "I'm not playing if you're not."

"Assistant coach, and it disturbs me that you're already searching for ways to forfeit our six-week challenge." His tone held no emotion, but when he glanced at her, one side of his mouth twitched up. "Worry not, my snarling sharpshooter. I'm playing. Today's just practice, so you'll be fine."

She narrowed her eyes at him. "I wasn't worried about that, Farkos. I can handle a softball game, and I may be a snarling sharpshooter, but I'm not yours."

That thing on his mouth that barely counted as a smile spread. "You are today." He paused before the handful of kids. "Hey, everyone. This is Katerina." He landed a heavy hand on her shoulder and squeezed just enough to hold her there, as if she might run—or deck him. The heat from his palm and fingers seeped through her shirt to sear her skin, and it took an effort not to move. "She has accepted a Roman Farkos personal challenge."

"Sucker," someone said. A few of the kids groaned. Others shook their heads and some gave her sympathetic looks. Valerie merely stared and popped her gum.

"This is her first test, to see how long she lasts playing with all of you." He gave a sweep of his mitt at the team.

"I give her half an inning before she falls on her face," one rangy, freckle-faced kid piped up, looking her over as if she didn't amount to much.

Roman canted his head to the side, as if considering the merits of the insulting statement, then turned his gaze on her. "You might be right on that one, Derick."

Kat gave them both a cool look.

"Or not." Laughter danced in his eyes. "You willing to bet laps on that, D-Man?"

Derick scrunched his nose and studied Kat again. "Two innings." The amendment was made with a confident nod. "If she makes more than two, I'll do the laps. If she doesn't, you're buying us all ice cream after practice."

Valerie huffed, rolled her eyes and headed for the side door. "Are you pansies going to play or talk about it all day?"

Roman gave Derick a high-five. "You're on, buddy."

As the rest of the kids trailed outside, Roman gave her an elbow nudge. "Good job wearing combat boots to softball practice. It completely threw Derick off."

"Teaching sleazy betting skills to impressionable teenagers? Impressive."

"You've got it all wrong, Katerina. I learned everything I know from Derick."

"I'm sure." She punched the mitt with her free hand. "I may not have any mentoring skills, but I can handle a demonstration of girl power, no problem."

"I never doubted it."

Ignoring the vote of confidence, Kat followed him outdoors into the afternoon heat. A field that had seen better days spread out behind the building. A chain-link backstop marked the catcher's position. Neon green chalk made up the batter's box and the pitching mound was nothing more than a dusty rubber doormat. The infield appeared to have been plowed and raked at some point in the past, but weeds sprouted among the dirt in spots that were less traveled, making the diamond shape around the bases look more like a trail. The outfield lawn had at least been cut recently. An aroma of freshly mown grass floated in the warm air.

"It may not be as pretty as the city parks and recs fields, but it works." Roman knelt beside a plastic trunk bolted down by the players' bench. "I hope you aren't too picky about what position you play," he said as he opened the trunk and rummaged through it. "Most of the team are set in their positions, but right field is open." He pulled out a catcher's mask and tossed it to Derick, who waited by the backstop.

"That's not fair." Derick caught the mask and frowned at Roman. "Nothing happens in right field. Everyone knows that." He pointed a finger at Roman, accusing. "You're setting me up to fail the bet."

"You didn't set any ground rules prior to sealing the deal." Roman stood, a stained softball in his grip, and his eyes gleamed. "It's not my fault you flubbed up and forgot. Or maybe it was Katerina's intimidating presence that threw you off."

"Not." Derick snorted. "The pretty ones are never that smart. If you find her so intimidating, man up and put her at shortstop."

Kat grinned, unoffended by the kid's initial assessment of her intelligence. She'd make sure he figured out her looks had nothing to do with her mind or status as a competitor. "Yeah, Roman. Man up—unless you're afraid to lose? Buying everyone ice cream would put a terrible dent in your future firearm fund. It's a definite risk, banking on me."

Derick nodded in approval.

Roman turned to her. Heat made his dark eyes glitter and the slow, subtle curl at the corner of his mouth made her stomach clench. For some reason she didn't want to examine closely, prickles shivered over her skin. "I have no guarantee that you won't purposely fall on your face simply so I'll lose."

She shrugged, surprised at the sudden lightness, how easy and natural it was to tease him. "I could do that in right field just as easily. So many blades of grass to trip me up." She twisted the end of her braid around her finger, doing her best to make her expression vapid. "And these heavy boots make me *so* clumsy."

"Clumsy enough to fall before the second inning is done, right?" Derick tossed the catcher's mask in the air and caught it by the strap.

Kat flashed them both her evil smile.

"I may have seriously underestimated the consequences of introducing you two." Roman's tone was cool, unaffected.

"Are you ladies through discussing the weather and trading recipes?" Valerie glared at them through the chain-link fence from the field side, her fingers hooked in the mesh. "Time's wasting, fools."

"Right?" Kat punched the palm of her glove again. "Less talk and more action, pansies. Where do you want me, Farkos?"

For a second, his gaze went distant, as if he was imagining a place far from the softball field and activities that had nothing to do with bats, mitts or fields. His Adam's apple bobbed in his pale throat and, when he focused on her again, the fire in his eyes made her heartbeat stutter.

Kat swallowed, her mouth suddenly dry as a desert, the afternoon heat shimmering through her veins. *Hell's bells. What is it about this guy?* She should reconsider this six-week challenge. The fruits of victory might not be worth the price. It had been a very long time since she'd noticed a man, let alone been physically affected by one — Vic included, sadly enough. But being attracted to Roman came as a shock. She'd been separated from Vic for almost a month, which didn't seem particularly long after ten years of marriage, and yet it felt like a lifetime. She might have been married on paper and on occasional holidays and required social gatherings, but she'd been emotionally single for years.

Maybe her subconscious had recognized the cracks in her marriage while she'd refused to acknowledge them and she'd compensated by investing in her job instead, something she knew would endure. Date nights and dinners had been replaced with swing-shift duty and sometimes seeing each other only in passing until kissing him goodbye had been more of an afterthought than a pleasure.

Kissing Roman... She shook herself. Kissing Roman would not be happening. Crap, she didn't even know how to date in the new age of social media and digital hookups. When she'd arrived to Graywood, fired up and furious, she'd asked Gia to show her how to be single again. Now, the thought made her want to lock herself in a room with her books.

"Why don't you try second base?" Roman's voice was husky, rougher than usual, and he cleared his throat. "It's a compromise, but I'll be watching you, Hellman."

I'll be watching you. Kat turned toward the field. Being observed by Roman was the last thing her flipped-over life needed.

But she certainly wasn't going to let that little fact break her — or affect the outcome of any challenge.

As she set up between first and second base, she caught Valerie studying her from first base with narrowed eyes. Tough words and a bad attitude were things Kat understood completely. She gave Valerie a chin jerk of acknowledgment.

"I hope you play ball better than you make bets, Beauty Pageant," Valerie said with a sniff.

"That all depends."

Valerie gave her a long, scathing look and popped her gum a few times. She rolled her eyes when Kat made no response. "Depends on what?"

"Whether or not I want Roman to buy everyone ice cream after the game." Kat let her wicked smile free to counteract her sweet tone. "Or maybe Derick could use a few laps. I haven't decided yet which way to go."

Valerie stopped chewing her gum for a moment and stared at her. "You'd make a fool of yourself for ice cream?"

"No one said anything about making a fool of myself, Gherig Girl."

Her eyebrows rose, and Kat suspected it was due to the nickname. Every first baseman respected Lou Gherig, and the fact that she knew enough about baseball to throw his name around might earn her some points.

"I can fall on my face diving for a hard grounder, no problem, and if you're worried that I'll embarrass the female population, relax." Kat drew herself up to her full height. "The real question is who deserves to win the bet more, Roman or Derick? I don't know Derick at all, so I have no idea. Help me out."

"That's a hard one." Her brown eyes narrowed, Valerie's gaze turned first on Roman then to Derick, where her attention remained. "Roman's devious, but if you lay out all the rules, he sticks to them. He never tries to cheat, not like Derick. Derick will try to weasel his way out of any loss." A hint of admiration entered her tone, as if being dishonest was a good quality.

But the way she looked at Derick, who was slipping his catcher's mask on and oblivious to their conversation, it wasn't hard to figure out she was crushing on the boy. Her eyes shone and the defiant line of her full mouth had softened.

"Don't let feelings affect bets." Kat adjusted her mitt and dragged her boot over an uneven rut, going for casual. Mentioning that she knew Valerie was sweet on Derick would probably earn her a sneer. "It messes everything up."

"What feelings? Derick annoys me."

Kat grinned. "That's a natural state of being for boys, no matter the age."

"And Roman is here because he's sick in the head and doesn't have a life." The girl straightened her cut-off shorts. "Nothing to feel."

"So, what's it going to be—ice cream or laps?"

Valerie bared her teeth, sharp white against her brown skin, a smile almost as wicked as Kat's. "Ice cream. Definitely."

Chapter Five

When Kat slid into a dramatic dive in the dirt to intercept a grounder that she probably could have caught before it rolled past her, leaped back up and threw Roman out at first, he managed not to smile. The fact that the play made the third out of the second inning wasn't lost on him. She'd managed to save Derick's bacon and force Roman to buy them all ice cream, doing it with the grace and elegance of a home run queen accepting her trophy.

Derick whooped and threw his catcher's mask in the air.

Her lovely face smudged, dust streaking her T-shirt and cargo pants, Kat approached him and made a sad face that wasn't even close to convincing. "Dang. Did you see how I tripped over that rock between first and second? Clumsy me."

"And still magically recovered enough to throw me out." He crossed his arms and pretended that the sparks in her eyes didn't make his blood heat.

Something about the grime on her perfect skin and her sleek hair being mussed added a savage edge to her beauty. A girl who didn't mind getting dirty or playing hard, no matter the sport, had always been a turn on. He'd already suspected Katerina would participate with a one hundred percent effort and whatever might be left over in her tank after that.

He hadn't known it would make him want her even more. And even though she'd technically taken the fall so Derick wouldn't have to do laps, she'd done it in a way that wouldn't earn any disrespect from her teammates, Derick included.

"Nice going, Beauty Pageant." Valerie gave Kat a high-five. "Way to not embarrass all of womanhood, but there's still time."

"Thanks for the vote of confidence, girlfriend," Kat said, her tone flat.

"No prob."

As the teams switched sides, Roman walked with her off the field. He had to fight the urge to wipe a smudge of dirt from her cheekbone or tug her ponytail, the need to touch her making his fingers itch. "I would have bought you ice cream anyway, if you asked nicely."

"Haven't you heard? I don't do nice."

"So, I have a chance." He met her questioning look directly. "I'm only nice when I want to be. I can be" — he lowered his gaze to her mouth for a lingering moment—"bad in certain scenarios. Very, *very* bad."

Kat blinked, as if surprised. "The only reason I'm still here is to take your ego down a few pegs and give Valerie some girl power support in the meantime."

"What a terrible thing to do, Katerina. I hardly know what to make of your actions, being nice and not-nice simultaneously. It must be another one of your superpowers."

"And beating you." She smiled sweetly and sauntered to the opposite bench with the rest of her teammates.

But he hadn't missed how her pupils had dilated at the mention of him being bad. She might not want to admit it, would probably deny it if pressed, but Kat felt *something* for him beyond irritation. Roman hid a smile. Making this challenge with her had been one of his most inspired bets to date, and he'd do whatever bad thing that might be required to convince her to give him a chance.

They played ball for another hour before taking an ice cream break, which Roman paid for, grumbling all the way, even though he didn't mind in the least. When it came to the kids at the club, spending his hard-earned, limited funds came easy. Some of the kids belonged to single parents who worked full-time or more and still struggled to provide for their families. Others had no parents at all, living with whatever relatives were able to take them in, and still others had no family whatsoever and filtered through the foster system.

Valerie was one of the latter.

A pang of guilt tumbled through him. In so many ways, she echoed Irini—the tough pretense, the indifferent attitude, never letting on that she wanted or needed help. He'd failed Irini. Valerie's story would be different. He'd make sure of it.

And as soon as he found Irini—which he would, he refused to believe otherwise—he'd do everything in his power to give her story a happy ending too.

Valerie tossed the last bat into the trunk and frowned at him. "You here tomorrow? Or are you scheduled to be out stirring up hate and discontent on the streets?"

Roman closed the trunk lid and locked it before standing. The sun made a golden strip along the tree line, slowly stealing the light. After ice cream, several of the kids had left with their parents or guardians and the ones who remained had resumed playing with half-teams. One by one, the kids had trickled out until it was impossible to conduct a proper game, but without light, they couldn't have played for much longer anyway. The club didn't have enough funds to provide a proper playing field, let alone lighting. And Valerie rarely left before closing.

He met Valerie's insistent gaze. "I do my best to stir up hate and discontent, whether or not I get paid for it. You know that."

She stuffed a fresh wad of pink gum into her mouth and popped it. "Yeah, but are you doing it here or out there tomorrow?"

"Haven't you figured out his schedule yet, Poppy?" Derick tossed a ball into the air and caught it. "Today is his second day off, so he works tomorrow, has training on Wednesday and Friday and his secret mission on Saturday. He'll be here tomorrow morning for a couple hours, tops."

"Don't call me Poppy, D-bag."

"That's D-*man*, Popster," he said without looking at her, tossing the ball again.

"What disturbs me is that you know my schedule better than I do." Roman gave Derick's sleeve a meaningful tug and started walking toward the club building, where Kat had gone a few minutes before. "What do you think of my new recruit?"

"Eh." Derick shrugged. "Guess she's all right."

Valerie snorted. "Lame. Kat threw you out every time. You just can't admit she's awesome because she's a girl, even though she totally cut the bet your way so we'd get ice cream when you would've been running laps instead."

"Are you suggesting Katerina fell on purpose?" Roman asked in a monotone. "I'm appalled that she'd cheat. I might require her to run laps."

"Good luck with that." Valerie blew a huge bubble until it broke with a sigh.

"She your girlfriend or something?" Derick asked, slouching along beside him.

"No, but I'm hopeful." Roman elbowed Derick. "You could help me out and tell her what a great couple we'd make. You too, Vee. She'll listen to you more than she will to me."

"If you can't win a girlfriend on your own, that's your problem, Blue." Valerie sniffed and finger-combed the end of her tight French braid, her sleek black hair still mostly in its original weave, despite the hours of playing. Every morning, as soon as she showed up at the club, she'd braid her own hair before doing anything else. "You should probably handcuff her and lock her up until she breaks. That's the only way you're going to get someone like Kat."

"Thanks for the support...and the idea." Handcuffs and Katerina would be stimulating.

"I don't know why you want a girlfriend, anyway. All they do is take your money and complain that you don't take them out enough." Derick nodded sagely.

"You don't know anything." Valerie reached behind Roman and punched Derick in the arm, hard enough that the boy winced. "Boyfriends are the worst. They sit around, expecting you to wait on them hand and foot while they watch television, burping and farting."

It took a valiant effort of willpower for Roman to keep a straight face.

"Better burping and farting than spending hours in front of the mirror to look like a clown," Derick said, his smile all snark, "Poppy."

Fireworks erupted in Valerie's dark eyes. "Call me Poppy again and I'll—"

"Sorry, I forgot you didn't like that name, Popster." Derick burst into a run as Vee swung at him again and he narrowly missed being clobbered. He kept going when she screeched and chased him.

Roman watched them race across the field toward the club building until Derick made it safely inside, Valerie a few seconds behind. Luckily for Derick, he could run fast. The door shut behind them, leaving Roman alone in the cool quiet of twilight. He had a huge soft spot for all the kids at the club, and while he tried not to play favorites, he harbored a special space for those two.

True, he'd wanted Kat here for other reasons, but he'd meant it when he'd said Valerie needed a positive female role model. She'd been passed from foster home to foster home, never finding the right fit, never being wanted enough, loved enough to be fought for. Never belonging twisted a person, and even though she was still a girl, he knew firsthand the hardened woman she could become if nothing changed. Sometimes, it was less about the belonging and more about the continual loss.

Derick's situation was different. He had parents and a home—technically. His mother went from one loser boyfriend to the next and his father wasn't much better, an alcoholic living off the system. They were currently in a custody battle over Derick, and while they both professed to care deeply about the boy, Roman suspected that care had more to do with the financial benefits of collecting welfare for a child in the household than anything emotional.

When did it become so hard to be a kid in this world?

He shoved his hands into his pockets, the spring of grass beneath his feet and the distant chirp of crickets reminding him of his own childhood, summer days playing tag with his sisters by the lake while their father fished. His mother had died while he'd been too young to remember more than impressions of her, leaving his father to care for a boy and three girls on his own, yet never once had Roman felt unwanted, unloved. It was hard to imagine what drove a person to allow a child to feel otherwise—his chest tightened, squeezed by a vengeful fist—or why a child would want to leave a safe and stable home with the people who loved them.

Roman opened the clubhouse door and slid quietly inside, his attention immediately focusing on Katerina. Even though the gymnasium was clear of kids, he suspected it wouldn't have mattered if an entire crowd had filled the emptiness. He'd still be able to find her, as if she held a cord tied to his ribs that tugged whenever she was close.

He leaned against the wall for a moment to observe her from afar while she spoke to Clay, the club's director. His blood warmed a degree or two. She made cargo pants and a T-shirt look like the latest fashion craze. The leather belt accentuated her slender waist and the pants clung to her shapely hips and long legs, the T-shirt just tight enough to remind everyone that while she might dress like one of the guys, she definitely didn't possess the same components. She could have easily chosen to ignore his challenge, going with the cold shoulder routine and ignoring whatever barbs Boyd stirred up at the department regarding their shooting match and her loss. He'd banked on her pride and the warrior queen he suspected she was, the hint of vulnerability beneath the steel she tried so hard to conceal.

Thank God his risky plan had succeeded. If he'd had to spend the next six weeks figuring out ways to convince Katerina to get to know him, he suspected he'd be stalled at the *Go* square the entire time.

"You in there, Roman, or are you daydreaming again?" Clay's voice echoed in the gym, loud enough to disrupt Roman's musings. He found both Kat and Clay staring at him, as if they'd been at it for more than a handful of seconds and he hadn't noticed.

"Daydreaming. It's a nice place to be." He pushed away from the wall and headed their way.

"Since you weren't listening the first time, I'll repeat my question." Clay smoothed his blue polo shirt, a nervous habit that made him seem like he was always running behind. "Can you lock up? I promised Lindsey I'd be on time for dinner tonight and I'm already fifteen minutes late." He grimaced and pushed his glasses up. "Again. Derick's mom was waiting for him, Valerie walked home and that was the last of the kids. If you clean up, I'll buy you pizza later."

"Free pizza? Done." Roman caught the keys Clay tossed his way. "Next time start out with free food and you won't have to do any convincing. And Katerina is here to keep me safe."

Kat snorted and folded her arms, the papers in her grip crinkling.

"If you plan to stick around," Clay called to her, walking backward to the door, "don't forget to fill out all the paperwork. We can't be liable for volunteers who don't go through the background process."

"I'm a cop." Her tone was flat, unamused. "I'm sure I've already passed the background check."

As the door shut behind Clay, Roman sidled up beside her and kept any emotion out of his voice. "So, you're coming back?"

"Unconfirmed."

"Admit it. You had fun today." He planted his butt on the edge of the cleared snack table. "When was the last time you let the rest of the world slide away enough to do that?"

"I have fun all the time." Defiant, she lifted her chin, a challenge sparkling in her eyes. "I don't need you to orchestrate my extracurricular activities."

"Maybe not, but I promise to make them more memorable." He wriggled his eyebrows, enjoying her disdainful expression. She might be practiced at being dismissive, but he was an expert at seeing through acts, and no matter what she said, she *had* liked playing softball today with the kids — playing with him. With any luck, she'd continue to play until she trusted him enough to confess that she liked it. That was just the first step in his master plan when it came to Katerina.

"Keep telling yourself that." She waved the paperwork at him. "Whatever the case, I clearly won our weekly challenge and if that's all you've got, you might as well concede now."

"A Farkos never surrenders, Katerina, and today was merely a testing of the waters, to see what you're made of."

Her smile was as lovely as it was wicked. "Your mistake. A Hellman shows no mercy."

"I don't recall asking for mercy, merely an equal opportunity." He held her stare so she'd understand his meaning. He wasn't looking for a chance to lose for six weeks straight, but a key, no matter how small, to grant him access to her inner workings.

Surprisingly, instead of a sly remark or contemptuous curl of her mouth, she pivoted and leaned on the table beside him, close enough that the scent of her mild herbal soap drifted near — lavender and a trace of mint. A long pause stretched before she spoke. "What's the deal with the lame softball field? You're lucky no one has tripped and broken an ankle."

He suspected that whatever topic she'd been thinking on had little to do with the softball field, but she was talking to him civilly, so he'd take it. "I mowed yesterday after going to the range. I didn't have time to rake the diamond since I was scheduled for firearms training on my day off, but with the heat and no rain, it could use a good tilling. It's too late to blame the rough terrain on your fumble. You already got your ice cream." *And oh, what a vision she was, licking that chocolate ice cream cone.* His imaginings had taken over, and while they'd included Kat and ice cream, the cone had been completely, carnally different. He cleared his throat. "The club doesn't get a lot of community support, not with the low-income clientele. Clay does his best with government grants and fundraising, campaigning for volunteers. It's never enough."

The weight of her gaze slid over his face, and he made a point to brush some dirt off his shorts rather than look at her. Until she trusted him, if Katerina wanted to discuss anything important, it had to be her decision, not something he pushed on her. Gia had told him enough about her sister while in the hospital to get that. From a young age, Kat had been pressured to follow one path by her mother and had chosen instead to get into the law enforcement line behind her father and brothers. From what Gia had shared, that decision had caused a lot of tension for the whole family, created a rift between Kat and her mother, her mother and father. That was a lot to put on any girl.

"So, this is what you do with your free time?" She gestured at the empty gym with her papers. "Play with underprivileged kids?"

"Some." He stopped pretending that he cared about his dusty shorts. "And since you accepted my challenge by showing up today, now I get to play with my Kat too."

"You'd better not be referring to me, Farkos. I don't play well with others."

"It's clear you haven't figured out yet that I'm not like anyone else." He leaned nearer. "I'm limited edition and an acquired taste. I'll grow on you."

"Like a fungus, no doubt." She straightened as if preparing to go.

"You made an impression on Valerie." He wasn't above using a kid to encourage Katerina to stick around, both right now and long term. If she agreed, it would be a win-win for him and the club. "I think she might even like you."

"Did you pick that out of the teenager attitude she threw my way? Or was it the smacking of bubble gum rather than talking that revealed this imaginary tidbit?" She paused and lifted her finger in the air. "Although, she did sneer at me once. Maybe that's what you saw."

"If she acknowledges you at all, it's a step in the right direction. Valerie doesn't let anyone get too close to her — and no one can blame her. She's been passed through so many foster homes that she's lost count. I'd imagine she doesn't think personal relationships are worth the effort, when they're just going to end." Even with him and Derick she kept her guard up, and he'd been very careful never to give her any reason to distrust him.

Kat's expression softened. "That...sucks."

"Which is why having you around would be huge. You'd be a strong, solid female presence to show her without going into lecture mode on the potential of the woman she could be, that it's possible to be whoever she wants to be if she's willing to fight for it."

She pursed her lips, but he didn't miss the faint flush in her cheeks. The steely sharpshooter wasn't immune to flattery. *Good to know.* And hopefully he'd struck a chord with the subtle kid's choice in their future career pursuits. "I'm only here for six weeks. Even if we connected, I'd be another person who left her behind."

"With the beauty of virtual interaction?" He shook his head. "You'd figure it out." And he didn't want to think about her leaving in six weeks when he was just getting started with her.

The door squeaked open before she could respond, and the burly man standing in the entryway brought Roman to immediate attention. It was Derick's father, and from the glassy state of his eyes, he'd already had a long date with his bottle. Even without that visible factor, Roman would have known he was drunk. He'd already been trespassed twice from the club after showing up and claiming he had permission to pick up Derick. The entire staff was aware of the temporary order preventing him from taking custody of the boy.

"Where's my son?" he asked, moving inside. "I have visitation rights and Derick's with me this weekend." At least he hadn't slurred his words. Maybe he'd be reasonable this time—and when it came to a dude who was six-foot-five and three hundred pounds, reasonable was always a bonus.

"Do you now have a court order confirming that, Mr. Peters?" Roman asked, keeping his focus on the man coming straight at them.

Mr. Peters paused. "I must've left the paper in my car."

"You know we can't let Derick leave if you don't have it," Roman said, keeping his voice low and calm. "And the trespass notice is still in place. Until that's resolved, you should call ahead so someone can meet you on the street with Derick."

"Sure. Whatever." He looked around the gym, as if suddenly realizing there weren't any kids around. "Where's Derick?"

"He left with his mother earlier." He wasn't about to reveal any more detail than that. If Mr. Peters discovered his wife and son had departed a mere five minutes ago, who knew what he might do?

Shockingly fast, the man's face went a brilliant shade of red beneath carrot-top hair the same shade as Derick's. All his freckles seemed to vanish in the flood.

"I realize you're in a difficult and frustrating situation and I'm sorry for that," Roman continued calmly. "If you leave now without a scene and assure me you won't return until you have authorization from the court, I won't press the trespass issue."

Beside him, Kat smoothly straightened, a panther ready to spring into action if needed, her hand on her waist as if instinctively going for the duty weapon that should be there and wasn't, the papers curled in her grip. Even with the distraction of Mr. Peters, he couldn't help the heat spiraling through him. *Holy shiznit*, she was sexy. He'd take her as backup any day.

"Go ahead. Trespass me again. You think I care about that? My *son* has been taken from me because of the lies that stupid cow convinced the judge to be true." His blue eyes blazed in his flushed face, his breath coming fast and hard. "I'm forced to pay child support for a kid I'm not allowed to see and I'm sick of everyone telling me I can't have him."

"Mr. Peters, I won't say it again." Roman stepped slowly toward him, holding his gaze. Weapons weren't allowed at the club, but that didn't prevent an outsider from coming in with one. They were at a distinct disadvantage on that end. "You need to leave before I have you arrested."

Mr. Peters laughed, and the harsh noise echoed loudly in the gym. "Great, another follower fooled into believing I'm the bad parent and Renee is mother of the year." He pointed a finger at Roman. "You know what you can do with your trespass notice and your threats?"

"I have a good idea of what you think I should do with them," Roman said with his usual dispassion. "We can leave it at that."

Kat snorted softly.

Mr. Peters squinted, as if he couldn't decide if Roman was being serious or snarky. "You think this is funny?"

"I'm not smiling, sir."

His hands fisting, he stared at Roman for a moment, the tendons in his neck standing out.

Roman tensed. *Hell, here it comes.*

Without a word, Derick's father turned and stalked out of the gym. When the door banged shut behind him, Kat released a breath and relaxed.

"Talk about a time bomb set on countdown. The explosion is inevitable." She glanced at him, her brown eyes wide. "I can't decide if you're a genius or an imbecile, joking with him like that."

"That's not even worth pondering." He pretended to examine his fingernails. "Obviously, I'm a genius."

A tiny furrow appeared between her eyebrows. "What is it with scumbags who use their kids as pawns against each other and pretend it's some noble form of love? Or twist love into being about themselves? Those people *suck.*"

The cut of her tone made it clear she wasn't only referencing Derick and his father, and Roman's heart thudded faster. He'd known winning Kat over so soon after her divorce would take time and patience. That was a given. Rebuilding her faith in love, showing her that not every relationship was based on selfishness or another's needs might take even longer. But the bitterness beneath her words hinted at a wound deeper, older than the distrust created by her ex-husband.

What are you afraid of, Katerina?

"If he had possessed a weapon, we'd be toast," she continued, "and you know as well as I do that he won't honor the no trespassing notice. He'll be back. Next time, he might not be emptyhanded." She glanced at his belt, where a holster could be. "You should be carrying."

He eased nearer to her, unable to resist. "Worried about me, Katerina?"

Kat blinked, as if suddenly realizing he was invading her personal space and refusing to surrender ground no matter how uncomfortable she might be. She cocked her head and gave him a look of disdain. "Hardly. Self-appointed geniuses can take care of themselves."

"But every genius can always use a partner." Her lavender-mint soap teased him closer and only a cold-blooded man could have resisted a glance at her lush mouth, temptingly within kissing distance. "Back-up." His voice, always rough, dropped an octave. "A guardian angel who only misses on a rare occasion when distracted by a worthy competitor."

She had to know how beautiful she was, couldn't miss how men noticed her, and whether she was used to it or chose to ignore it, he couldn't help but respect her more for not using her beauty to manipulate others. She most definitely could, and he had no doubt that magic would work on him — a secret he would keep to himself, for now. He was already at a disadvantage when it came to her.

Whether or not she meant to, her gaze dipped to his mouth for the briefest second, so fast he might have missed it if he hadn't been watching her. And *damn*. The fact that she did was like diesel to his blood.

"You honestly believe you have the power to distract me?" She laughed. "Not even."

"I know this morning was a fluke." He kept his voice soft, compelling, as if she might fly away if he spoke too loudly or made a sudden move. "I had a really, really good day and you had a minorly bad one, but there's a word a pal of mine uses that fits the situation perfectly.

Serendipitous. Even though I suspect you hate losing with a passion, if you had won our little shooting challenge, you wouldn't be here now. This might surprise you, but I like having you here."

Kat looked at him as if she expected he'd sprout horns at any second. "You seriously need a new life, Farkos."

"Maybe I need some gentle claws and snuggle time with a certain Kat. I'm sure I have a ball of yarn hiding somewhere in my house." He tilted his head and surrendered to the urge to look at her mouth again. "I'd keep you entertained for hours. I promise."

"As tempting as that is — Oh wait, that isn't tempting at all, since I have yarn of my own." She smiled evilly and turned away. "I'm sure you can handle closing up alone, genius."

"Two players are always more fun than one, Katerina."

"Not true. One can entertain herself without all the BS." She stopped and pivoted to face him, giving him a superior look. "Multiple times."

Heat spun through him as he imagined all the ways she might find to distract herself — more than once. That was one daydream he wouldn't mind staying in for a while. As she turned toward the door, he smiled at her back. She might not realize it, but she'd already entered the game, and he had every intention of making their play time so satisfying that the thought of being alone paled in comparison.

"Since I lost our first match, I'm invoking the right to a makeup challenge," he called after her.

Kat opened the door and paused. "I'm not going to give you open-ended opportunities to try to even the score, not that you're capable of keeping up with me.

The rule was that additional challenges had to be by mutual agreement—and I don't agree."

He choked back a laugh. Provoking her into a challenge was a cakewalk, but if he pushed her too hard, she might figure him out and balk on principle alone. "Refusing a challenge to avoid me, Katerina?" He *tsk*ed. "I'm flattered that your attraction to me is so intense that you have to hide behind a refusal, but there's no need to be a chicken. Bonus challenges are only worth a quarter point. I'll be gentle, even when you lose."

"Hell's bells." Her hand on her hip, she threw her head back and muttered something to the ceiling. "Have you been talking to my brother again?"

"Not since Gia was in the hospital." Most of the Hellman family had flown out to Graywood when Gia had been injured, and Roman had spent hours trading stories with her brother Bryan, a fellow officer. There was nothing like being a brother in blue to make an instant connection, and sharing scars and experiences had made the time pass while they'd all waited for Gia to recover.

Katerina had not been pleased, and he'd never been sure if it was because she felt they should be hovering over Gia rather than bonding, if she was just testy due to the combination of worry for her sister and divorce, or if it had been the fact that it was *him*—a friend of Ian's—who was befriending her brother. He hadn't talked to Bryan about that particular issue, but he had discussed it with Gia at their mutual pedicure appointments. She'd offered some helpful tidbits when it came to dealing with her sister.

"Fine." She scrunched her nose, as if catching the whiff of a nasty smell. "What's the challenge?"

82

"All will be revealed at the appointed hour—which is seven p.m. tomorrow at Franny's Diner, by the way."

Even with the space between them, he didn't miss the sudden sparkle in her eyes. Clearly, she thought she had him and his challenge pegged. "Oh, I'll be there, Farkos. Prepare to fall farther behind on the scoreboard."

He waited until she'd walked out before allowing himself a small smile. Falling for her wasn't an issue, and no matter the game, he intended to be the ultimate winner.

Chapter Six

As Kat stepped out beneath a clear sky purple with twilight and the first sprinkling of stars, she drew a deep breath. Someone was barbecuing nearby and the smell of roasting meat filled the warm air. Kids laughing echoed from a distance, a reminder of when summer days had been long and lazy, filled with popsicles and iced tea, and the biggest worry was a bikini top coming untied while swimming.

With everything that had happened today, she should be on the verge of popping her buttons. Instead, the hard knot in her shoulders had eased and the concrete weight in her stomach had dissolved. Although she'd never admit it to Roman, playing an informal softball game had been exactly what she'd needed — simple fun without pressure. Sure, there had been an edge of competition, but just enough to make it exciting. While she'd played, all the sucky parts of her life had faded into the background.

She kept her pace unhurried as she strode across the parking lot. Her SUV waited in the far corner beneath the overhanging branches of the oak next door, the only spot that had offered shade earlier. The air conditioning had called it quits on the drive to Graywood and since she'd had no idea how long she'd be at the club, finding shade had felt like a tiny slip in her bad luck streak.

Truthfully, that had been the catalyst to a break she'd needed, not that she'd admit it aloud. Or maybe Roman and his ridiculous challenge were responsible for the change. When he'd acknowledged her failure at the range and provided a viable excuse for her miss, the burn of shame hadn't even made a halfhearted sputter, as if the fact *he* said it rendered any indignity magically mute and ineffective.

What is it about him? When she'd first met Roman, she'd dismissed him as just another arrogant badge, then something worse—Ian O'Connor's unabashed accomplice in Gia's accident. Every time she'd gotten into his face at the hospital, he hadn't even blinked. She couldn't decide if he believed she was all talk and no action and therefore not worth a sharp response, or if he was simply incapable of being offended. Never losing his cool was freakin' annoying.

And the way he looked at her mouth as if he thought she tasted like cream and honey? That was even more irritating. Kat flipped her hair over her shoulder and tried to forget how her lips had tingled beneath his heated gaze—how they *still* prickled and throbbed— and he hadn't even touched her, let alone kissed her.

Something's wrong with me. It was the only explanation. Her breakup with Vic had altered her state of reality. Being on leave had messed with her head. Submerging herself in a small town confused her emotions and made her think *things*. Stupid things. Ridiculous things. Things she had no business thinking. Whatever it was, there had to be a logical reason for her body's response to a man who annoyed the hell out of her. It couldn't be that his gravelly voice danced along her nerves and awakened her senses...or the mischief in his barely-there smile that made her wonder what schemes he had planned to get inside her defenses. It surely wasn't his dry sense of humor, used at inappropriate times, such as when dealing with an irate noncustodial father demanding his son.

Kat reached her SUV, unlocked the door with her key and slid inside. She tossed the crumpled volunteer paperwork on the seat and paused with her hands on the steering wheel, gazing out of the windshield at the faded wooden fence separating the club property from the seedy apartment complex next door. In a strange way, the incident with Derick's dad had echoed Vic's earlier visit and cemented a truth she hadn't fully accepted before. It had been so easy to detect the stain of selfishness in Mr. Peters' push for custody of his son. If Vic had split with his girlfriend before coming to see her, if he'd had some solid explanation for his actions, had apologized with any number of heartfelt words, she would have at least listened to what he had to say for the sake of their years together. But there was no going back to a relationship founded on expectations she couldn't meet.

There was a damn good reason she guarded her heart. Not even the closest friend or family member could be trusted not to hurt the ones they claimed to love.

She put the keys in the ignition, only to freeze. *Mom is at Gia's.* Groaning, she laid her head back and considered spending the night in her SUV. It hadn't made sense to rent an apartment or house when she was only going to be in Graywood for a month and a half, not to mention that she didn't have the funds. But it was tempting to scrape up as much cash as she could and buy a tent, just to have somewhere else to go.

Entering a building prepared to shoot, she didn't even break a sweat. Stopping a potential criminal went with the routine. Facing her mother's disapproval? All her bravery slithered out of reach. But maybe she'd misread the situation. Maybe her mother intended to rent a hotel room for the duration of her visit. It was possible. Caroline liked her luxuries and preferred to keep the lifestyle she was accustomed to.

Reaching for her phone to text Gia and hopefully continue her streak of good luck, she found only an empty pocket. *Hell.* She must have set it down on the table while speaking to either Clay or Roman, and, with the distraction of Mr. Peters, forgotten it — which meant she had to deal with Roman again.

Get in, grab my phone, get out. No problem. I can do this.

Kat squared her shoulders and pocketed her keys. Before she could consider how peaceful life would be without a cell phone, she leaped out of her SUV, hit the locks and marched back toward the club.

Roman Farkos wasn't charming and he certainly wasn't sexy or funny. He was just an overconfident competitor who wrongly believed he could win her over through some warped series of challenges meant to... She didn't even know. But she knew why she'd accepted — to prove to herself that not only could she handle whatever ridiculous contest he thought up but also that she'd overcome everything he threw at her. And Roman, with all his civil service, softness for underprivileged kids and ways of making her failures seem insignificant wouldn't change that.

As she entered the front door, voices drifted from the gym, loud enough to filter through the closed doors, and the argumentative undertone made the hairs on her arms stand on end. Gently, she closed the door without a sound and made her steps light. For the second time that day, she reached for her duty gun and came up empty. She could return to her SUV, where she'd stowed all her firearms in the space a spare tire should be. There was no way Vic was getting her collection, and since Gia didn't have a gun safe, it was the best place she could think of to hide them while she was in transition. But sometimes bringing a weapon into the game made a situation even worse. Besides, she had other methods of defusing an argument that got out of hand.

Sidling up to the closed gymnasium door, Kat peeked through the window. Roman faced the door, his hands in the air, as if surrendering. Mr. Peters had his back to her, a baseball bat in his meaty grip.

Crap.

Her pulse kicked up the pace as she carefully squeezed the latch of one door, having no idea how well-oiled the hinges might be or if the metal would squeak when she opened it. If anything, the noise would offer a distraction Roman could use to his advantage — provided he was quick-witted enough. She had no guarantee that would be the case. Small-town cops usually didn't see a lot of action, and without regular training, instinct often failed.

Kat gritted her teeth and inched the door open, alert to every noise. The door creaked softly, and she winced.

If Mr. Peters heard it, his voice made no indication of it, continuing loud and strong. "I may not be able to do anything to that idiot judge who ruled against me or my wife's sleazeball attorney, but *you* —" The word trembled, even with his slurring. "I don't have to take disrespect from my kid's babysitter."

What he thought he'd prove coming back to threaten Roman, she had no idea, but she understood how he might feel like he needed to control something, anything, when every other facet of his life slipped beyond his reach.

"I prefer to call it 'glorified child attendee'," Roman said, his tone cool. He didn't look at her to give her away as she crept inside, but he couldn't miss her, even with Mr. Peter's bulk blocking his view. "Derick doesn't really need to be watched. He's old enough to understand responsibility. What he could use is a sober father who is there when he needs him. Even if that's not possible right now, practice makes perfect. I suggest you start right away."

Hell, Roman could use some verbal judo lessons. Even though his voice was soft and calm, his word choices sucked. She eased the door shut, her focus all on the big man standing between them. Mr. Peters could do some serious damage if he landed a hit with that bat. Even if Roman deflected it, he'd pay for it with a broken bone or worse.

"That's rich." Mr. Peters' fingers made white strips on the bat. "Do you even have kids, boy?"

"Grew up the oldest of three sisters, with my mother dead. My dad did his best to raise four children on a single income, and I can tell you this —"

Don't do it, Farkos. End it there.

89

"His children *always* came first." Roman's dark eyes gleamed, hard and sharp as obsidian. "Not once did he drown his anger and sorrows in the contents of a bottle or take out his frustrations on another person."

Mr. Peters paused, as if he needed a moment to process whether or not Roman's words were meant as an insult. The moment passed and, bellowing, he raised the bat and charged.

But Kat was already there. Using a football move first learned from her brothers in her rough-and-tumble childhood and honed to perfection in the academy, she dove for his legs and took him down hard. He grunted beneath her and flailed. Something hit her in the temple—whether his fist or the bat, she wasn't sure. She barely felt it through the rush of adrenaline burning in her veins. Before he could land another strike, she rolled up, her knee digging mercilessly into his back, twisting one arm behind him in a restraint hold. He might be big, but being smashed made him clumsy, and she had a lot of experience taking down men of all sizes.

Roman jerked the bat from Mr. Peters' loosened grip and tossed it behind him before assisting her in restraining him. "Well done, Angel. I knew you'd be back."

"Shut up, Farkos." She grimaced as the brute beneath her bucked and tried to roll. "Do something useful and call one of your buddies to take him in."

"Did that the second he walked in the front door." He had the nerve to wink. "Boyd should be here any—" The wail of a siren broke through the grunts and slurred cursing. "Perfect timing. I'll be sure he knows about every detail of your magnificent tackle." One corner of his mouth curled. "What a beauty."

As Boyd hustled in and took over with handcuffs and Taser at the ready, Kat stepped back and pushed a few escaped strands of hair from her face. She caught her breath, but her heart refused to calm. *What a beauty.* Roman hadn't been referencing her looks and...*hell.* It was the best compliment anyone had given her in a long time.

"Katerina..." Roman loomed in her face and before she could jerk away, he had her head between his big hands. Frowning, he focused on a spot above her eye. "You're hurt." He traced his thumb along her eyebrow, and she hissed.

"Just a flesh wound." She should really push his warm, gentle hands away, step beyond his reach, but she seemed trapped by his nearness. Her body refused to listen to common sense, confused by his spicy-sweet holiday scent.

Roman's features, usually so expressionless, took on a darkness as he examined her injury, and the fierceness, the protectiveness — for *her* — made her pulse pitter-patter. She didn't need protecting or defending. They both knew that. So why was it making her melt instead of pissing her off?

"Boyd," Roman barked, not looking away from her face, "add assault to his charges."

"Unnecessary." Even her voice betrayed her, all soft and breathless. "It wasn't intentional, and he has enough problems."

He lowered his gaze to hers, and the banked fury in his eyes sent an electric jolt through her. "He hurt you, Angel. That's unacceptable."

"He already paid the consequences." She managed a small smile instead of surrendering to the horrifying urge to lean into his hand and close her eyes. Clearly, the adrenaline rush had faded, affecting her judgment, making her soft. "I have very bony knees. There are endless visits to the chiropractor in his future. Trust me."

"Even so." He grabbed her hand and tugged her relentlessly toward the bathroom as Boyd hauled a shaky Mr. Peters onto his feet. "Got it under control?" Roman asked in passing.

Mr. Peters' nose was bent at an unnatural angle, and the hate-filled look he gave them both made the fine hair on the back of her neck prickle. They hadn't seen the last of him...guaranteed.

"Affirmative." Boyd glanced at her. "You gonna survive, Hellman?"

She curled her lip at him, but Roman dragged her onward so fast she wasn't sure he saw it. *A contemptuous expression not reaching its target. What a waste of energy.*

I'm absolutely losing my mind.

Before she could process his intentions, Roman wrapped his hands around her waist, lifted her as if she weighed no more than a doll and set her on the sink, her back to the mirror. Her self-defense instincts hadn't even twitched. Maybe the hit to her head had been harder than she'd initially thought.

Keeping one hand on her hip and his body pressed against her knees as if she might try to escape, he tore off a paper towel and dampened it with water. He frowned slightly at her—a warning—as he folded the material and gently pressed it against her temple.

"Easy with that thing, Farkos." With the adrenaline high all but gone, her head ached like the wicked witch in possession of her voodoo doll was jabbing her repeatedly with a sharp, poisoned needle.

"Suck it up, Angel."

She protested with a weak huff and stayed put. With his focus set on her minor injury, she took the opportunity to study him openly, with no judgment. While not classically handsome, he wasn't exactly hard to look at, and the fact that he wasn't male model material made him more appealing and certainly less suspicious. A lot of guys who knew they were good-looking expected to get whatever they wanted, and she hated any sense of entitlement, especially for a detail so trivial as outward appearance. They never seemed to appreciate her opinion on that subject when she offered it.

But Roman was physically appealing in his own unique manner. The way his ebony hair had drifted over his forehead gave her an insane urge to brush it back and read the faint lines of care beneath. Stubble shadowed his clean-shaven jaw line, adding an edge of danger, as if he were a ruffian hiding beneath the disguise of a cop. His nose was a smidge too big to be called Greek, but its straight line claimed that it had never been broken and fit perfectly with his perfectly kissable mouth.

Not that she'd be kissing him, ever. It was almost a shame that he didn't use such a weapon in his facial features. His mouth was so full of expression waiting to happen and yet he rarely released it. She couldn't recall even seeing his teeth in a full smile.

"Katerina," he said in a low, hypnotic lull, "if you keep looking at my mouth like you're imagining lovely, wicked things happening between us, I can't be held accountable for my actions."

She flicked her gaze up. He watched her, his dark eyes burning, and heat flared in her face.

"Why don't you smile?" she asked, needing his focus away from her, especially now that he'd switched his attention from her head to her lips, making them tingle.

"I smile." He used that monotone that he loved so much. "All the time. See?" One side of his mouth twitched.

Maybe it was due to her off-the-rocker day or the throbbing in her head, but she grabbed his face between her hands and pinched his cheeks, stretching his mouth to force a full smile. It was so out of character for her of late, so playful, that she froze.

The friction of his stubble beneath her fingers scraped deliciously, and the intensity in his eyes, as if the contact had set fire to his veins, made her own blood sing with swift, savage awareness. Their faces were mere inches away, so close his breath drifted over her mouth, warm and intimate. Somewhere along the way, he'd dropped his hands and planted them on each side of her, bracing himself on the sink.

"If I smiled for you, Angel, I might scare you off," he murmured. His throat worked as he swallowed. "I'm not willing to take that risk...yet." His gaze lifted to her temple. "You're bleeding again."

Kat released him as he set the cool towel on her head again, unwanted curiosity swirling through her, carried on the current of an even less wanted but undeniable attraction. Why would he be afraid to flash a full smile? She'd discover the answer. Focusing on that was far preferable to examining the desire still thrumming through her. That anomaly would be leashed and extinguished before it got out of control...as soon as she could think clearly again.

"I told you Mr. Peters would come back." She winced as he applied more pressure to her head. "You should have listened to me."

"I did listen to you." He was back to using his monotone, and she couldn't decide if it was his natural way of speaking or some sort of self-defense mechanism he used to deflect or annoy people—her in particular. "But when I saw you creeping in like an assassin, all stealth and sexy, excuse me if I got distracted."

He hadn't appeared distracted at all.

"I knew you cared about my welfare." His mischievous almost-smirk had returned. "I'm hungry. Want to catch some dinner?"

"Hard negative." Kat pushed his hand away and slid off the counter, needing some distance. If he stayed close, with her head not quite right, she might do something she'd regret later—like jump on him. "I came back for my phone. You got lucky. Period."

His smile made it to both corners. "I got lucky weeks ago, the second you showed up at the senior center masquerade ball without a mask, decked out in purple Converse and jeans, ready to rip Ian and anyone else who stood between you and your sister to pieces." He tossed the towel in the trash. "Since you don't want to eat, I'll see you at seven o'clock tomorrow, Angel. Don't be late, or it will cost you a quarter-point."

The best she could do was watch him leave, stunned mute. First, her mortifying loss at the range, now a past incident where her actions had been less than admirable, to say the least... She'd been horrible that day, mean to Gia and unforgivably rude to people who hadn't deserved it—including Roman. How could someone take some of her worst moments and give them an edge of beauty? And if he had the power to do *that* — on the first freakin' day of their challenge?

Son of a jerkface. Win or lose, she might have seriously underestimated both the competitor and the potential consequences.

Chapter Seven

Roman tossed his duffel bag beside the couch and sighed into the shadows of his house. His police radio, always on, crackled from the kitchen, relaying messages between dispatch and the officers on duty. Boyd's assigned number went twelve-two at the county jail, indicating that he was delivering Mr. Peters to the two-star motel room he'd earned for at least one night—clean, but nowhere close to comfortable.

Without the radio, the quiet would have been complete. He scrubbed his fingers through his short hair and wandered to his father's old record player nestled between the sagging couch and a hideous floor lamp his sister Nadia had created as a school project. She'd laughed so hard when he'd unwrapped it at Christmas that he thought she'd break a rib. Their father had passed on a few years back, enough that the grief had faded, but even now the space he left behind ached at unexpected times—and he wouldn't trade those pangs for anything. They were a reminder of the man who had molded his life and how so many others weren't as lucky as he'd been growing up.

He flipped through the collection of vinyl records, waiting for inspiration to strike. It wasn't that he couldn't bear the silence or didn't appreciate a peaceful moment every so often, but the emptiness reminded him of the life that had once filled this house, the family now scattered and separated.

Irini. He'd trade it all to hear her voice, to know she was okay, to have even one of his many contacts come up with the smallest information on her whereabouts.

Gently pushing the thought aside, he resumed his record search. He'd hoped Katerina would accept his spur-of-the-moment invitation to dinner so she could have filled some of the space. He would have even cooked for her. Everyone liked toasted peanut butter and banana sandwiches—and if she didn't, he might have to reconsider what his gut said about her, loud and clear.

Katerina belongs beside me.

He'd dated occasionally, casually—when he had free time and criminals were scarce. He'd even once had a steady relationship that had ended when she'd realized that she'd have to share him with his duties, that plans would sometimes be broken and he couldn't promise to make every social event. No other woman had ever come close to Katerina Hellman. No other woman had sparked him to life, ignited a wildfire that threatened to devour him, body and soul.

He lifted a record free. *Grease. Perfect.* As Frankie Valli's croon filled the corners, he pulled his dirty shirt over his head and tossed it on a chair before venturing into the kitchen. He opened the refrigerator and grimaced at the moldy smell that drifted out. An expired carton of milk and two shriveled apples weren't much of an incentive to coax a woman into staying for any length of time, and despite how much he talked, his mediocre looks and charm only went so far. With the Katerina potential...he needed to go grocery shopping.

Pizza it is. He should have collected on Clay's offer, and any other day he would have—when it came to promises of free food, he didn't trust anyone fully until he had the grub in his hands—but with Katerina so close, dinner had taken a back seat. That alone indicated how bad he had it for her. Their challenge had only started and he was already setting aside his deep love affair with his stomach.

It *had* to be fate.

As he freed his phone from his pocket, it buzzed with a text from Lars at the office.

All set for tomorrow. Equipment will be there by six-thirty. You owe me one.

At the thought of the quarter-point make-up night with Katerina, a thrill of anticipation coasted through him, hard and undeniable. The challenge might only be worth a nominal amount, but it was the game and getting her to play that mattered. Every careful step with her felt like a risk, as if it had an equal chance to either blow up in his face or bring him another day closer to persuading her to relax with him, to give him a chance to prove that he wasn't her ex and would never pressure her to be anything more than she wanted to be. Earning her trust was vital, betraying it fatal.

There was an element of vulnerability beneath her layers, a shard hidden so deep and camouflaged with such practiced expertise that he wondered if she even knew it was there, waiting for someone to both acknowledge and protect it.

Not *someone* — him — and he had no illusions about the delicate nature of the road to his Angel's heart. He'd have to tread softly to avoid tripping the land mines.

Angel. It was the word that had slipped through his mind when she'd snuck inside the club behind Mr. Peters' back, ringing with an element of truth he hadn't been capable of holding back. Whether guardian or avenging, 'Angel' fit, and the fact that she hadn't reprimanded him for the nickname merely confirmed the rightness.

The doorbell chirped and he spun, automatically reaching for the duty belt and gun that weren't there. He was home so little other than to sleep that someone ringing the doorbell was suspicious — not that he expected a criminal to ring before breaking and entering, but anything was possible.

After picking up his Taser along the way, Roman sidled along the wall on silent feet. He snuck up to the door peephole and slowly leaned in, holding his breath.

Katerina.

Seeing her on his doorstep sent all the air rushing out, replaced by a wild heartbeat hammering against his ribs. She was here, as if his thoughts had drawn her. If that wasn't a sign, he'd offer up his arsenal to the next thug.

The locks and alarm were disabled in seconds and he swung open the door as fast as he could. He had no idea why she was at his home, but he wouldn't give her any time to change her mind.

"Katerina," he said, half-surprised his voice didn't crack. "To what do I owe the unexpected pleasure?"

She still wore her cargo pants and shirt, dusty and crumpled from the afternoon game and her takedown of Mr. Peters, and her long, shimmering hair valiantly struggled to remain in her braid. Her brutally honest and unassuming manner of showing up 'as is' only made her more lovely, and the way she blinked at his bare chest with a follow-up flush to her face sent a surge of hot satisfaction in his gut.

Note to self — while with Katerina, go shirtless more often.

Kat ripped her gaze from his chest and raised her chin at a defiant angle, too late to fool him. "Paying up." She lifted a coffee cup and plastic bag from Growlers and Grounds. "I don't want to be accused of not making good on my deals." She shoved the coffee into his hand. "Nasty iced hazelnut macchiato with almond milk, as requested." Her expression of disgust was adorable, all scrunched nose and shudder. "You made no specifics on the pie, so you get coconut cream. No takebacks."

"There is no such thing as a wrong pie," he said solemnly. "Payment could have waited. I had no plans to track you down and demand payment with interest until tomorrow." But the fact she'd brought it tonight rather than delay made the blood race faster in his veins.

"All the more reason to deliver it now." She turned away.

"You surely don't expect me to eat this entire pie by myself?" He'd say almost anything to stall her, but in all honesty, inhaling a pie by himself was no problem at all. "So that's your plan, to fatten me up so I'll lose any physical challenge?" He added approval to his tone. "That's not an entirely bad plan."

"No one can play ping-pong after a donut hangover. I've absolutely confirmed that. And you've been duly warned." Her mouth curved into a small but very real, heart-stopping smile.

If he hadn't already been irrevocably lost to her, he would be now.

"Stay, Katerina," he said, somehow keeping the heat and need from his voice. "Have some pie with me." *Have whatever you want with me.*

She hesitated on the doorstep, and he held his breath. After a long beat, she finally said, "I haven't had dinner yet."

"Pie absolutely counts as dinner." As she frowned, he pressed his case, lifting the pie meaningfully. "This particular masterpiece of deliciousness encompasses all the food groups—grains, dairy and the versatile coconut is a fruit, nut and seed. *Bam.* Fruit group and protein covered."

"And more than enough for a seriously debilitating sugar high." Her attention drifted to the SUV parked at the curb, as if it held some answer inside the dark windows that only she could detect.

"Even better." He watched her waver without adding more persuasion tactics. As badly as he hoped she'd stay, no matter how short or long, the decision needed to be hers. When it came to spending free time with him—minutes without the competition infusing their six-week challenge—he refused to push her.

Her shoulders relaxed slightly, and he knew she'd made her choice, but she kept her boots planted on the doorstep, her gaze on the SUV. "I promised Gia I'd be nicer to her friends."

"I suspected charming Gia might include some unforeseen benefits, but more along the lines of discounts at the spa, not her playing the 'be nice' card on her older sister. After all the kerfuffle today, you must be famished."

"Only a lunatic would use the word 'kerfuffle'." She grimaced. "I mean that in the nicest possible way."

"No offense taken." He opened the bag and lifted the lid off the pie, releasing the sweet scent. Merciless, he waved it under her nose and slowly backpedaled into his house, luring her. "Excellent choice, Angel."

He didn't specify whether it was the pie or accepting his invitation to stay. Both were solid choices.

"Don't make me regret it, Farkos," she said, following. "I can rescind the nice card whenever I choose and, for God's sake, put on a shirt."

"I understand," he said as he closed the door behind her. "Not many people can bear this level of heat."

"I was more concerned about the burning in my eyes." She imitated his monotone and walked past him, moving deeper into his house. "Being nice to you might be beyond my capabilities, and dammit, I hate apologizing."

"I believe in you, Hellman." Having mercy on her, he grabbed the shirt he'd tossed on the chair and pulled it on. "How's the head injury?"

"Just a flesh wound. It's fine." Her sharp gaze flicked over his living room, undoubtedly cataloging a hundred different details that a normal human wouldn't, thanks to her training. He did the exact same thing whenever he entered an unfamiliar room, determining the locations of exits and potential entry points, searching for the smallest sign of danger or any innocuous detail that might seem out of place. It hadn't meant life or death to him yet, but that was a chance he'd never take.

Looking both fierce and lovely, Katerina fit perfectly into his hallway, and he swore the empty space sighed and settled, as if it had been waiting just for her.

She cocked her head toward the living room, where the record still played. "*Grease*?" The way she eyed him like he was some sort of bizarre circus creature was almost insulting. "Really?"

"Don't try to deny you don't know every word to *Hopelessly Devoted to You* and didn't sing along to Olivia Newton-John with your hairbrush in the mirror." He laid the pie on the small kitchen table. "I'll know you're lying."

"Please." She sniffed. "While that was going on in *your* bathroom, I was banging my head to Metallica. No wonder Gia is so protective of you. If Ian knew, he'd eat you alive."

Katerina leaned one shoulder against the wall, not quite entering the kitchen. An awkward undercurrent clearly tugged at her usual confidence. He got it. She was fresh from a long-term relationship, a marriage that had claimed her right out of high school. Hanging one on one with a man who was neither her husband nor one of her familiar co-workers must feel like her skin didn't fit quite right, and he'd made it very clear that he was attracted to her.

Chasing her away by moving too fast was not on the agenda, even though she'd looked at him—more than once—as if he might taste even better than the coconut cream pie on the table. He could live with that, for now.

"I celebrate my feminine side openly and my unashamed love for musicals is common knowledge." He dug a knife and two forks from the kitchen drawer, made sure they were clean and reached for the stack of paper plates. "And dancing... I'm legendary."

Laughter bubbled from Kat, short-lived and sweet. "Get out. Like the Twist? Or are we talking more about dance fever?"

When he turned, he found her a few inches inside the kitchen, the smallest of steps and yet an entire leap forward. "Anything and everything, Angel," he said, not letting on how much her smile sent tiny, electrical shockwaves through him. "I have three sisters, and they all took years of dance lessons. Guess who was their required practice partner?" He hooked both thumbs at his chest. "This guy."

She leaned a hip against the table, still smirking. "Bust me a move."

He gave her an insulted look. "Just because you brought me treats doesn't mean I'll perform on cue, Katerina." Sinking the knife into the pie, he cut an X through the meringue and crust. "Besides, dancing for you would be unfair. I'd blow your mind and we still have five weeks of challenges ahead. I'd feel terrible, winning like that."

"Such admirable sportsmanship."

"Indubitably." He landed a quarter of the pie on a plate and set it on the table. Solemnly, he presented her with a fork. "Let the feast begin."

"Dessert for dinner." She slipped into the chair and viciously stabbed her fork into the pie, a violation of pastry etiquette. "My mother would be appalled, not that it would be a new state of being for her when it comes to me, which is why I'm going to eat this whole thing, even if it makes me sick." She pressed her lips together, clearly she'd shared more than she'd intended.

"That's the spirit." But the hint of bitterness in her light words, the demolishing of her pie rather than appropriately devouring it, drove him to lower his fork and ignore the protest of his bottomless stomach. "Gia mentioned your mother made an unexpected appearance today."

"She did?" Kat paused in her pie abuse and stared at him. "You two are like a pair of little old ladies who meet for regular gossip sessions at the salon."

"Your point?"

"It's sick."

"Therapeutic," he disagreed mildly. "Feel free to join whenever you want."

"Hard pass." Tossing her fork aside, she leaned back in the chair and crossed her arms. "Just a warning—After spending more than a day with my mother, I grow fangs and my eyes take on a red glow. Since she's here for a week and insists on staying with Gia rather than getting a room at the hotel across town, my condition might not be reversible. If I hadn't spent my last twenty bucks on coffee and pie, I'd be the one across town in my own peaceful room."

Roman kept his expression bland to hide the ache left by the invisible fist that had just punched him in the gut. He should have known she hadn't come here tonight in an effort to get to know him better, because she couldn't stop thinking about him like he couldn't stop thinking about her or a desperate need to bask in his presence.

Bollocks.

He shoved a bite of pie into his mouth and let the sweetness ease the pain. Yet even in Katerina's rejection, she'd left fragments of hope among the wreckage. She could have found another place to go if she'd truly wanted to. She hadn't been required to inform him that her mother had come to town or that they weren't on the same wavelength. While it stung his ego that he was her last resort, a mere pawn in her quest to avoid her mother for as long as possible, he let the stab to his pride melt away. Katerina's ploy was an opportunity in disguise, handed to him on a golden platter and simply waiting for him to snatch it up and run with it.

"I happen to have a weakness for those of a snarly nature." He shrugged at her arched eyebrow, ignoring how his heart pummeled his ribs. "I have a proposal — and before you say no, hear me out."

"No."

The wicked sparks in her big brown eyes as she took a dainty bite of pie nearly knocked him flat. She was *playing* with him, and he didn't care what had driven her to his doorstep tonight, whether it was the begrudging fruits of a lucky win at the range or prolonging the wait before an unpleasant encounter. It merely confirmed the signs that had been popping up since she'd appeared weeks ago like an exotic woodland creature in a plastic sea. If he didn't tread carefully, slow and silent, he'd chase her off.

Like Irini.

He pushed the thought aside before it hooked him in the gut, focusing on the woman present, not the girl beyond his reach. Accidentally chasing his Angel away would severely damage the spark that had stirred with her arrival. He had to keep it nice and easy.

Roman shook his head in mock disapproval. "Now you're just being purposely disagreeable."

"It's my specialty." The barbs in her smile hinted at a deeper secret, one she was nowhere ready to reveal.

"Not from my viewpoint." He continued before she could process his meaning and protest. "I used to share this house with my father and sisters."

Kat rested her chin on her hand and nibbled at her pie, her expression disinterested. "Wow. That's amazing. Tell me more."

"So glad you asked. My father passed away three years ago."

She straightened and had the grace to look ashamed for her bratty behavior. "Sorry. That sucks."

He nodded, willing to endure the jab of pain if it meant she'd take him seriously for a minute, two if he were lucky. "My sisters lived with me here until recently. One got hitched, another attends college across the state and the other" — his throat tightened, but he forced the words out—"she's...away. Their rooms are all vacant."

She was watching him as if expecting more, and when it was clear he was through, she narrowed her eyes. "What you're saying is you have enough space for all your best dance moves?"

"Excellent observation." He rubbed his chin. "But not my point." Leaning forward, he held her gaze, alert to her reactions. "Gia's house has become crowded. I have space, lots of it. Think about it."

Kat stared at him, frozen, her fork paused in mid-air, halfway to her mouth. His offer had the capacity to tip their fragile relationship either way. She would either appreciate his generosity or kick his ass for being too forward, not that he expected anything romantic or sexual. 'Want' was a mile away from 'expect'. He'd never pressure a woman that way. Her space, her body, her choice, *always*.

But of course, she didn't know him well enough to get that. Maybe mentioning his empty house had been the wrong move, a risk that would come back to bite him.

The music in the other room ended. His father's ancient record player wasn't fancy, with an electronic arm to lift the needle. The scratch of the needle without any grooves made an uncomfortable *click-click-buzz, click-click-buzz* in the awkward silence between them.

"Give me a sec. I'll be right back." He scraped back his chair, hurried to the living room and flipped the record over as fast as he could.

When he returned to the kitchen, *Beauty School Dropout* playing behind him, Kat was gone.

Chapter Eight

The afterschool club building loomed ahead, dull against the bright morning heat of summer. Kat parked her SUV, rubbed her gritty eyes and yawned so hard that her jaw popped. Another night on Gia's sofa watching television until three in the morning reminded her that she couldn't function much longer this way, and a couch potato lifestyle wasn't conducive to the frame of mind she needed for training. She could blame her mother's visit for the couch cushions, but the restless night was all on Roman.

She pocketed her keys and slipped out of the SUV, hitting the locks and activating the alarm system. Leave it to another man to disrupt her sleep pattern, although what had kept her awake for days after her breakup with Vic had nothing in common with the sleeplessness induced by Farkos.

Roman. She'd known the second she stepped up to his house that it was a mistake, that she shouldn't have listened to the stupid voice in her head telling her to get the presentation of coffee and pie out of the way so she could kick the shooting range defeat behind her and focus on the future wins. So what if it was at an hour that some people might read more into a visit? She'd done it without any motive other than checking a bit of unpleasant business off her list.

But finding Roman without his shirt on had dumbed her brain down while forking through the rest of her body like lightning. Thinking had been impossible with all those lean muscles on display, and when he'd seduced her inside with the irresistible aroma blend of coconut pie and warm holidays, even the warning bells in her head hadn't been enough motivation to make her walk away. And once he'd lured her into his house, she'd been mesmerized, as if some dark magic had taken her senses eternally captive.

She smoothed a hand over her no-nonsense bun, needing a reminder that she retained control of at least one facet of her life. Roman had surprised her when she hadn't expected it, as if he practiced ways to push people off their foundations. Until the chance meeting at the public range a few days ago, every time she'd encountered him, he'd exuded a grim and unyielding devotion to justice, duties and his friends, both questionable and not. She wasn't sure if he'd hidden his dry sense of humor before or if she'd been too preoccupied to notice it, but now? Knowing he held an unapologetic love for musicals and dancing and had a body created for sin?

She swiped a hand over her face, trying to dislodge the image of Roman with his jeans slung low on his hips, the muscled ridges of his shoulders and ribs, the plane of his stomach, the sexy V leading to — she gritted her teeth — places she had no intention of exploring.

While with Roman, she seemed to revert into a hormonal sixteen-year old.

And did he seriously ask me to move in with him? Sharing space with him had 'bad idea' spray-painted all over it and sticking around to explain to him why was more than she'd signed up for. Walking out had been an easy solution. She'd only been there to deliver coffee and pie. Objective completed. There had been no other reason to stay.

She had *not* run away. She'd slithered off with a great deal of dignity.

The lingering Roman problem was why she was here, at the afterschool club, long before he was due to make an appearance. Today was her day off from firearms training and if she hung out with her mother all day at Gia's, she'd be in the cell beside Mr. Peters.

Troubled kids to the rescue. Who would've thought?

Dressed in her customary casual—jeans, T-shirt and purple Converse—Kat ventured inside. The door squeaked shut behind her and the quiet corridor held an air of abandonment. Maybe she was too early, but the gymnasium double doors were propped wide in invitation. If the club wasn't open for business, the building would surely be locked.

She marched through the hallway and stepped into the gymnasium. Clay and a young woman who hadn't been around the previous day spoke quietly in the corner. Only one kid slumped in the polar opposite side of the gym, snapping her gum, her gaze on an electronic game in her hands.

Valerie. Despite the fact that it was summer, she wore a black hoodie, black jeans and—*surprise, surprise*—black tennis shoes. Her shining black hair was again caged in two tight French braids.

Clay looked at the doorway and recognition lit his features, followed by a healthy dose of disbelief. "Katerina… You came back."

"So it seems." She slid her hands into her back pockets, an unfamiliar awkwardness sweeping through her. Without badges and guns, she was out of her element, and as much as she hated to admit it, having Roman's challenge as an excuse to come here had alleviated the weirdness. "I expected more kids. If you don't need help, I'll—"

"Oh no, don't leave." He hurried toward her, as if he might leap at the door to block her escape. "You just got here. The kids arrive at all different times. Trust me. We can always use your help."

She glanced at Valerie, who had yet to look up from her game.

Clay smoothly pivoted so his back was to the girl. "Valerie's always early," he said in a low voice. "She usually beats me here. I find her waiting by the door, giving me attitude for not being on time." He cleared his throat. "We always have both a man and woman employee or volunteer here at all times and never is one left alone with a child."

"Smart move." She nodded. Less chance of any claim holding up should a man be alone with a girl or a woman with a boy. Back home, she'd seen her fair share of those accusations and nothing good ever came of them. Even if they were a total lie, the stigma remained with the accused for life. People believed what they wanted to believe.

"The club has enough problems getting funding. We do whatever we can to avoid any situation that might scar our reputation. Roman's great with that."

An image of ripped abs and a dusting of dark hair streaked across her mind. She shoved it away and forced a smile. "I'm sure."

"The previous night with Mr. Peters was unfortunate." He glanced at her temple, which was nothing more than a scrape and bruise. She had a worse bump on her shin from the softball game. Obviously, Roman had informed him of both the incident and her 'life-threatening injury'.

"Whatever Roman told you about how it went down, I'm sure he exaggerated when it came to me and any so-called wounds. I'm absolutely fine." It wasn't hard to read the source of his worry. "No lawsuits here. Just keeping the peace."

Relief washed over his features and his shoulders relaxed. "Honestly, we wouldn't be operating without him. His efforts on behalf of the club are tireless, and no one is more invested in the kids than he is."

"You don't say." She managed to keep her smile pasted on.

"He truly *cares* about people, no matter their background." Clay shoved his glasses up. "You don't see that often in this world. People are more concerned about their own reputation and welfare than another's. When giving, there's that expectation of getting something out of it, whether it's a taxable donation, a mention in the paper or a thumbs-up from the community. It's not like that with Roman. He volunteers because he wants to. Period." The corners of his eyes crinkled as he smiled. "And now he brought you."

She almost mentioned their challenge, that being here yesterday had been more manipulation than voluntary, but an annoying sense of charity showed up, twisting her. "I didn't bring the paperwork with me."

"You're an officer and Roman invited you." Clay winked. "I'll take that risk for today. Be sure to bring the signed papers tomorrow."

She opened her mouth to say she wasn't sure tomorrow was any kind of certainty, but Clay abandoned her to greet a new kid walking through the door. Her hands still in her pockets, she turned toward Valerie. Roman had said the girl needed a female role model, but Kat wasn't a social worker. She hadn't taken any classes on how to deal with troubled kids. She wasn't even sure she was much of a role model. Sure, she poured one hundred and ten percent into her shooting and her job, but that hadn't exactly helped her in the relationship arena. Being strong didn't prevent failure or pain.

Valerie sniffed and slashed a hand across her eyes, erasing a tear.

Kat knew an angry cry on the verge when she saw one. *Oh, what the hell.* She set her shoulders. The worst thing that could happen would be the rejection of a teenager she barely knew. With the demolition of her marriage still ringing in her ears, what was a little more? She could handle it.

Valerie didn't look up at her approach. She didn't even twitch when Kat pivoted, slid to a sit on the floor beside her and leaned back against the wall.

"Hey." Kat drew up her knees and draped her arms over them. "What ch'ya doin', Gherig Girl?"

"*Trying* to have some alone time." Valerie's mouth set in a hard line and she stared into the game screen, totally brushing Kat off. "Can't you find someone else to bother?"

Kat frowned across the gym at the only other kid, who jumped up and down beside Clay like he'd eaten a bowl of sugar for breakfast. "You seriously expect me to hang out with that battery-operated thing over there?" She flicked her fingers in a dismissive gesture. "Give me a break."

The musical notes of *Donkey Kong* rose from Valerie's device and Kat couldn't help leaning in to watch over her shoulder. Competition in her family extended from the field to board games and everything in between. Much to her brothers' delight, she'd usually lose any video games that had to do with war — which was ridiculous, because her shooting skills should work the same on screen as in reality — but any old school electronic games? She rocked them.

Cartoon Mario bit it to a well-tossed barrel by his nemesis the gorilla and the death-music touted the loss.

"See what you made me do?" Valerie huffed and gave her a glare. "If you hadn't been breathing on me, I would have finally saved the princess. Do you know how many times I've tried to pass this level? Like a zillion."

"Sorry to disrupt your concentration." Kat kept a straight face. The glitter in Valerie's eyes had switched from tears to annoyance, which was absolutely worth the awkwardness of sitting beside a girl who clearly didn't want to share her secrets or emotions. She'd take irritation over the blues any day. "Want me to try? Maybe I can make it up to you by passing the level."

Valerie smirked, slow and scornful. "I could use a good snicker session."

Kat grinned as Valerie handed her the device. *Game on.*

It had been a few years since she'd played, and when she got Mario killed in the first minute, Valerie snickered.

"Laugh it up, Vee." Kat scowled and straightened, getting serious. No way would she let this girl watch her suck at *Donkey Kong*. "I'm just warming up."

"Whatever you say, Pageant Queen."

Ten tense minutes of flying fingers and mumbled curses at stupid digital gorillas passed with Valerie leaning in. For a girl who wanted her to lose, she seemed overly invested in each climb up a ladder, every jump over a barrel, hissing at close calls. But Kat hadn't completely lost her video game skills. With a final hammer strike, the gorilla fell from his landing.

"Yes!" Vee crowed, kicking her feet in the air.

"Take that, you filthy animal." Kat flexed her aching fingers. She hadn't remembered *Donkey Kong* being so hard to beat.

As Mario got his princess and the happy music of victory played, they grinned at each other.

"Pretty good for a runner-up." Vee held out her fist.

"No beauty contests, no regrets." Kat bumped her fist to Vee's.

Movement flickered at the gym's double doors as another person entered the gymnasium, too tall for a kid. Tingles of awareness drifted down her back. Roman walked inside, dressed in dark jeans, a black T-shirt and boots. His presence was like a light switch savagely flipped on, firing her flat-lined libido.

"Aw, hell," she muttered.

Vee gasped, her ebony, almond-shaped eyes wide in mock-alarm. "Don't let Clay hear you talk dirty like that." She straightened from her slouch and wagged a finger. "No cursing at the club." Her Clay impression was remarkable.

"That wasn't a curse. Hell's a legit place and I was simply expressing the sense that I'd suddenly fallen into it."

"I'll try that next time I slip and see if it flies with Clay." Following her gaze, Vee nodded sagely. "So, it's like that, huh? Typical boy likes girl and girl pretends to hate boy situation."

"I don't pretend." Kat sniffed. "And whatever I feel for Roman doesn't contain enough passion to be classified as hate. It's more...necessary tolerance."

"Oh. My. God." Valerie stared at her and snapped her gum. "You're crushing on Roman big time. I can't wait to tell him."

"If you mean 'crush' as in I'd like to pulverize him beneath my heel, then yeah." Kat shrugged, ignoring how her heart had decided to beat at an unhealthy rate. Somehow, she managed to keep her hands relaxed over her updrawn knees instead of giving in to the urge to jump up and ditch the afterschool club. If she did that, then both Roman *and* Valerie would chalk it up to the feelings she definitely didn't have for Roman.

Peopling was an exhausting activity.

"Whatever." Vee's sing-song tone suggested her opinion hadn't magically changed with Kat's explanation.

"Yeah, whatever." She growled. "No wonder you two get along so well. You're both WOBs."

Valerie gave her a gleaming, slit-eyed glare. "Watch it, Pageant. Insult me again. I dare you. Payback's a pig."

"Don't threaten me." Kat held her gaze, no backdown. "And WOB isn't an insult. It means someone who usually wears only black."

"Oh." Vee's hostile posture deflated and she shrugged one shoulder. "I'm down with that."

"What's he doing here so early, anyway? Doesn't he have to work or something?" With their training yesterday, Kat had assumed—wrongly, as it turned out—that he'd be working dayshift today. She had another basic training round on Wednesday with two other officers and more on Friday. Then they'd get to the fun stuff.

Why can't Farkos suck at shooting?

"Nah, he's always here Tuesday mornings for the groove-a-thon." Slipping her game into the pocket of her hoodie, Vee gave a little dance wiggle.

Kat groaned and thunked her head back against the wall. "I don't even want to know."

Valerie's mouth softened, her expression vulnerable as she looked toward the door, where Derick trailed a handful of other kids inside.

Talk about a crush. Kat considered ribbing her about it with the same vengeance as Vee had teased her and quickly discarded the idea. It hadn't been so long ago that she'd forgotten how it felt to like a boy and how devastating it could be when the secret came out into the open—especially if the boy didn't feel the same. If Vee and Derick were any level of friends now, the odds of that friendship surviving a romantic rejection were slim, a risk that kids usually didn't consider. And for someone like Valerie, who was passed from foster home to foster home? A brush-off could destroy her.

Nope, it was better to let crushes die a natural death than risk announcing them. Licking wounds in private beat public humiliation any day. *Been there, done that, wouldn't go back even if I could.*

Roman looked her way, pivoted and headed straight for her.

"Dammit," she muttered.

"That's it, PQ." Her smile sharp, Valerie stood. "Keep feeding me the ammo. I'll stock it up. Blackmail is always *so* useful." With that, she ditched Kat, giving Roman a high-five in passing.

Kat scowled at her back. *I never liked kids much anyway.*

Roman suddenly blocked her view, and as much as she wanted to ignore his presence, with all six-feet-three-inches of him looming over her, it was impossible. His midnight eyes glittered. "I knew you'd come back."

Before she could respond, he took Vee's place and sat beside her, much too close for comfort. His holiday spice scent and the warmth of his big body curled around her like satin ribbons, too luxurious to shake off. He stretched out his long legs and crossed his ankles, as if prepared to stay a while.

Refusing to give up any ground, she turned her scowl on him "Why aren't you at work?"

"My schedule is off, thanks to the rigorous and riveting firearms training for the next month or so." He clasped his hands over his belt. "And I'm always here on Tuesday mornings."

"Right. For the groove-a-thon." She scrunched her nose. "I heard too late to avoid it."

He eased an inch closer, his breath brushing her cheek. "The offer remains open for as long as you're around, just so you know."

"To dance?" Kat pretended to misunderstand in the hopes that he would go with it and move on. "Hard pass."

"Oh, you'll dance with me, Katerina," he said in a low purr that made the blood pound in all her secret spots. "That's unavoidable. But I'm referring to the offer to use one of the empty rooms in my house for as long as you want or whenever you want. No expectations, strings or hidden agenda, just looking out for a member of my blue pack. And feel free to bring pie with you whatever hour you want to swing by. Any flavor is welcome."

"There won't be any further pie from me." Lifting her chin, she did her best to look down her nose at him.

"That remains to be seen." His gaze drifted over her face to her mouth and lingered there. "So many future challenges to lose, so many bites of pie awaiting me."

Kat clenched her thighs together. Dammit, the way he said 'bites of pie' in his low, rough voice made the phrase sound like an indecent proposal. Maybe it *was*. With the way he still looked at her lips, as if torn between kissing her and daring her to do it, she had more than enough trouble focusing on all the reasons why even thinking about kissing him was the worst idea ever. He'd shaved recently, leaving his jaw smooth and highlighting his wide, expressive, very kissable mouth. She'd bet he wouldn't hold back like he did with his smiles. He'd probably throw his entire body into a kiss, his hands in her hair, his arm keeping her tight to his delicious chest, his hips pressed close, every inch of him invested in bringing her to a slow, steady burn—

"Hey, lovebirds." Valerie's voice cracked the spell cast by Roman and his mouth, releasing Kat from captivity. "Are we dancing this morning or not?"

Kat tore her gaze away from Roman and scowled. Vee looked down at them, one fist on her cocked hip, snapping her bubble gum in an annoyed rhythm. The girl wore an expression of utter disgust, as if she'd caught them making out, not just thinking about it. "I'm not dancing." She ignored the bedroom rasp of her voice. "Not today…not ever."

"Never say never, Angel." Roman's murmur fluttered along her nerves in a dark, sensual wave.

"I'll say it again. Dancing—not going to happen." Kat refused to look at him as he smoothly stood. Maybe not looking would render his mojo powerless. No man had ever manipulated her senses so easily. Before Vee interrupted, she'd been two seconds away from finding out if she was right about how he kissed.

Rescued by a hostile teenager.

Roman pivoted and leaned into her face, killing her resolve not to look. One corner of his mouth curled into that secret smile, full of mischief and knowing. "Thanks for the throwdown on dancing. I know exactly what my next challenge will be." He winked. "One full, guaranteed point to me, and all I have to do is ask you to dance."

Kat did her best Roman imitation with zero expression. "Take him away, Vee, before I hurt him in front of impressionable children."

"That would be totally worth missing dance hour." Staying put, Valerie's eyes shimmered, her smile vicious.

"What? Is that part of the club program, promoting and encouraging violence toward elders?" Kat shook her head and made a shooing motion with her hand. "Go. Leave me in peace. I'm trying to be a good role model here."

"I'm barely thirty." Roman notched his chin up, his tone offended.

"Dang." Valerie looked him up and down with a critical eye. "How do you have the energy to dance at that age? Shouldn't you be home in your recliner or something, watching game shows? You might break a hip on the floor if you're not careful."

A laugh broke free before Kat could stop it, and both Roman and Valerie looked at her with raised eyebrows. Was it so unexpected for her to laugh that when she did, it surprised people? Maybe she should change things up. "Show the whipper-snappers how it's done, grandpa. Bust a move, not a hip."

Snickering, Vee gave her a high-five.

Roman hooked his thumbs in his belt. "Is that a challenge, Katerina?"

That hint of mischief on his mouth made it to his eyes, giving them a wicked gleam, and all her humor died. He made her forget, too easily, that her marriage had officially ended only a day ago...considering Vic had surely signed after his surprise visit. She didn't need someone else—let alone someone who was already an expert at pushing all her buttons, both good and bad—getting inside her walls only to burn her down from the inside out.

Ignoring Roman, Kat popped to her feet and headed for the door. She sorely regretted accepting his quarter-point, mid-week dare. Enduring tonight would be enough of a challenge on its own.

Chapter Nine

Roman made it to Franny's Diner an hour before the appointed challenge time to set up, and by seven o'clock, he was eyeing the waiting apple pie tempting him from the table beside the computer and polygraph equipment. The back room at Franny's was perfect—small, intimate, reservable—and lit only by violet-scented candles in glass bowls. The aura hinted at romantic, but not enough to keep Kat stalled at the door.

He closed his eyes and relived the moment he'd had with her on the gym floor earlier, only a breath between them, an electric sizzle created by Kat overheating him. Time had seemed to stand still while she'd looked at him, her brown eyes soft and thoughtful, her pulse beating hard enough that it vibrated at the collar of her T-shirt. She'd been thinking about kissing him, he'd bet the entire contest on it, and it had taken every ounce of Farkos determination to remain still while she decided. As badly as he wanted to touch her, kiss her, merely breathe the same air, any contact had to be instigated by her. If he went wolf on her like the pounding in his veins demanded, he had zero doubt that she'd pulverize him, and that would be inconvenient all around. He liked his face and preferred all important body parts to remain in working order.

Maybe it was a good thing Vee had interrupted. If Katerina had kissed him, he wasn't entirely certain he'd be able to stop, even with the location and a young, impressionable audience. It probably would've got him put on club probation, and Clay needed all the help he could get.

He shifted on the chair and scrubbed his fingers through his hair, the sexual energy revived and swirling hot, needing only a memory. *Holy shiznit.* Kissing his Angel would be epic—whenever it happened—and tonight there would be no audience or interruptions.

The door whispered open, bringing in a delicious draft of fried onions, and he drew a silent breath, every inch of him on high alert. Katerina stood in the entrance, wearing washed-out capris jeans, a faded NYPD T-shirt and her purple Converse. She'd freed her hair from its earlier bun and it spilled over her shoulder in a low ponytail. Her gaze swept the room, and he suspected she'd documented every detail, from the drab wallpaper to the candles to the outdated tile.

The door clicked shut behind her as she fully committed and stepped inside. "Farkos."

He was immediately on his feet and had taken a step toward her before stopping himself. "Katerina. You're almost late."

"You said seven." She looked at her watch. "It's six-fifty-nine. I didn't see any reason to be early."

He could think of several reasons—so he could see her casual elegance, hear her husky voice, dream up ways of killing the distance between them—none of which he bothered mentioning aloud. If she thought for even a second that tonight's challenge was anything more than his attempt to get on the score board, she'd be gone.

"I arranged for pie, in case you're hungry." He tossed her a menu, which she caught nimbly. "If you need dinner first, Franny will fix you up."

She dropped the menu on the table as if it might bite her. "This isn't a date."

"Every day is technically a date."

"Don't be a smartass."

"And people eat food together all the time without any expectations. You don't have to make it weird just because you like me." He managed to keep his expression neutral as her dark eyes gleamed. Damn, he loved teasing her. She made it so easy.

"'Like' is too generous of a description, and this whole challenge situation is weird, so don't pin that on me."

"You agreed without any undue influence." He shrugged. "If there's any weirdness going on, it's of an equal amount between us."

She snorted. "Keep telling yourself that." Her gaze dropped to the polygraph equipment on the table and her mouth tightened. "That's one old-school lie detector you got there. How much dust did you have to brush off when you dragged it out of the nineteenth century?"

"It may be ancient, but it's functional."

"Get many confessions from it?"

"One or two." Actually, he'd never used it and only had a crash course the previous night on setting it up. Graywood outsourced a polygrapher from another agency — in exchange for some defensive tactics training, courtesy of himself — but Roman had sat in on a few interviews. Whether or not the polygraph had any bearing on the confessions was impossible to say. "Might even get three, depending on how it goes tonight."

Kat picked up the rubber tubing that was used to wrap around the chest to monitor breathing, stretched it and released. The strap snapped the table, an inch away from his fingers. "Whatever secrets you keep, I don't want to know."

He let his mouth curl. "Keep telling yourself that."

She flicked him a glance, her eyes glittering with either irritation or defiance — both, if he had to make an educated guess. "Everyone knows polygraphs are inconclusive, so what's the point?"

"It's for entertainment purposes only, obviously. If I wanted to forcibly extract all your mysteries — which would be far less fun than discovering them at leisure, by the way — I'd be more inclined to use the AVATAR."

He waited for her to either ask what that might be or acknowledge that she knew. Her gaze cool and steady, she lifted her eyebrows slightly, as if to say, 'get on with it, Farkos.'

"AVATAR stands for Automated Virtual Agent for Truth Assessments in Real-Time," he said. "It's more effective, but harder to cart around since the machine is life-sized. Not that Graywood has one, anyway."

"I know what it is." She didn't sound impressed. "What's the challenge? Twenty questions without any variables in the monitor for the win?"

He gave her a scandalized look. "I hate to even consider the boring contests you had growing up, if that's your idea of a trial. No, this isn't twenty questions, done and run."

"Of course not." She plopped into her chair, stretched out her long legs and crossed her ankles, angling away from him. "That wouldn't waste enough of my time."

He sucked in a breath. "Worthy bets are *never* a waste of time, Katerina."

She studied him a lingering moment, long enough to be a dare. "How do you do that? Keep an absolutely stone-still face, use a monotone and still come across as a smartass?"

"It's a gift, and if you want to know more, you'll have to accept."

"To put *you* under the polygraph?" She sat up straighter, her gaze more intent.

"The role is your choice, Angel. You may interrogate me, or I'll do the interrogating." He leaned back in his chair and watched the decision flicker across her face. It wasn't difficult to determine each pro and con as it filtered through her expressions. If she was the interrogator, it would imply that he intrigued her enough to want to ask him personal questions. On the other hand, allowing him the freedom to ask her about whatever he wished? That was the greater risk. Either way, no matter what she chose, he couldn't lose.

"This is a lot of work to go to for a lousy quarter of a point that won't even help you in the long run, since you have no chance of winning."

He shrugged. "You're worth the effort."

A flare of emotion erupted in her eyes, there and gone like lightning, and she rested her elbows on the table, the polygraph and laptop between them. Whatever that emotion had been, it had been the final drive in her decision.

Kat stretched her arm across the table, her wrists facing the ceiling. "Link me up."

"Magnificent." He rubbed his hands together, unable to contain his glee. Being under her scrutiny had given him all manners of fantasies, but having her at his delicate mercy? A thrill of anticipation danced between his shoulder blades. He'd have to be careful with his questions, of course, and not stir up her pain while extracting more of what he wanted — not Katerina the sharpshooter, cop, firearms expert or protective sister.

More Katerina Hellman, the woman.

He set the metal plates on her fingertips and secured them. "The rules are that each question has to be answered. No passing, no matter what. Refusal is considered a forfeit."

She sniffed. "Bring it on, Farkos. I have nothing to hide." As he reached to put the rubber tubes around her torso, she grabbed them from his hands along with the arm band to monitor her blood pressure and said primly, "I can handle putting these on."

"I never thought otherwise." But missing the opportunity to lean near her and strap her in was a true loss. He plugged in all the proper cords and got the laptop running. "Are you sure you don't want any fruit and pastry fortification before we start?"

Kat gave him a flat stare.

"There's no need to be hostile. Shall we begin?"

"Give it your best, quarter-point effort." Her smile was saccharine-sweet, but it still managed to wriggle beneath his skin and spark his senses.

"Is Katerina Hellman your true name?"

She paused. "I'm unsure of the answer."

Truth.

"My birth name is Katerina Jacqueline Hellman. I changed my last name to Hellman-Patterson when I got married but requested my maiden name back when the divorce becomes final. If the judgment has been signed, my name is Katerina Jacqueline Hellman. Otherwise, it's Hellman-Patterson." As she spoke, her words became more brittle. "Do you know how much longer it takes to write a hyphenated name? I wouldn't recommend it."

"Additional information is appreciated, but not required, and I'd never be so uppity as to hyphenate my name." He added the barest hint of sarcasm to his tone to ease the tension around her eyes. "For the record, I'm ecstatic you're shedding the extra name. Less complicated." Certainly less complicated for him. He'd never sabotage a marriage, not even for the woman of his deepest dreams and darkest fantasies. *Aka Katerina.* If she wasn't single — even if not romantically available, yet — he'd have to find several other hobbies to keep his mind and the long nights occupied.

After a pause, she nodded and released a soft breath.

He frowned at the screen and the different colored lines monitoring her responses. "It appears you've passed the first question." He lifted his gaze to hers. "Barely."

"These interviews are generally conducted with yes and no questions." She folded her hands in her lap and gave him a knowing look. "You've never done this before, have you?"

"I'm not the one being questioned...Katerina Jacqueline." He notched his chin up and leaned forward. "Even without the hyphenated surname, it's still uppity."

As if unwilling to let him be the only one who gained ground, she planted her palms on the table. "You want to see uppity? I'll let you read it on the sole of my shoe when it's up close and personal in your face."

He let the miniscule smile he'd been holding back slip free. "Threats, Angel? When you get all snarly, I know I'm getting close to some deep, dark truth that you don't want outsiders to see." He eased even closer, watching the sparks in her eyes, loving how she didn't back down a single inch. "But does keeping your own secrets close mean I can trust you with mine?"

She blinked, clearly taken aback by his question and yet too curious to dismiss it. Holding his gaze, she tilted her head, as if certain, unexpected realizations had suddenly clicked into place and she needed to process them and decide how to respond. Her scrutiny was like a hammer simultaneously cracking open his skull and ribs, exposing his entire being for her judgment. For her, he'd reveal it all, with no regrets.

A shiver stole through him, a sudden recognition of his own. *That* was why he was irreversibly drawn to her. She wasn't a person who spewed her soul to anyone who would listen. Her trust was a precious gift, one that deserved utter devotion and protection, and when she shared her secrets, it would be only to someone who she could entrust her heart and future to, her triumphs and failures, without censure.

He was the one to do that for her and the certainty of it rang through him like a bell, clear and undeniable. And flipping the table, asking her to keep his trust instead of the other way around, had been an inspired stroke of genius.

"What secrets?" she finally asked, her voice as soft as the candlelight.

"That wasn't the question," he said with equal quiet, unwilling to disturb the strange tranquility that had seeped into their conversation. "I have to know I can trust you."

"Is this like...the circle of trust?" No humor laced her tone and he understood the question beneath the light words. She wanted to know if he was messing with her, setting her up to fail, baiting her only to laugh later.

His chest tightened at the implication. Instead of defiance or annoyance, she'd chosen to crack open a door. It was only an inch, hardly a welcome and easily slammed whenever she wished, but it was a start. She searched for the smallest reason to trust him. He wouldn't blow it.

"Not a circle—a one-way street." *For now.* "I'm hoping you're the right person to help me with a sensitive and serious extracurricular activity. Nothing illegal," he quickly added as her eyebrow twitched. "But it's very personal and vastly meaningful."

"Is that why you've gone to such lengths to harass me?"

"Engage, not harass." He'd stopped watching the lines on the computer screen, his attention solely on her. "I couldn't simply trust you on instinct alone without some sort of validation. I needed to confirm you weren't a creampuff beneath the surface, that you weren't all talk and attitude." He continued through her soft snort. "Since complete honesty is the theme tonight, even though you're the perfect person to help me, that's not why I dared you at the range. Challenging you was the only way I could think of to get you to really see me."

"I've had absolutely no trouble seeing you, unfortunately."

"As someone more than Ian's lowlife friend? Other than another cop or the dude who got a lucky break at the range?"

"You *are* all those things," she muttered, her mouth twisting.

"But I'm more, and if I hadn't found some way for you to look beneath the layers, I'd still just be those things to you."

"Who said you aren't still just those things to me?"

"Am I?"

She hesitated for so long that his chest shuddered with each passing second, pounded to splinters by his heart. At last, she released a sigh that held an edge of defeat. "No, you're not."

He took a deep breath.

"You're something worse."

Worse. Not the endorsement he was hoping for. "That's not very civil of you."

Kat toyed with the hem of her T-shirt. "I'm figuring out what life looks like on my own. I don't need...extra complications."

"That's how you see me? As a complication?" Maybe he should be offended, but the way she said it hinted at a problem she wished she didn't have. In other words, she was attracted to him, interested, even when it would be easier if she wasn't. He nodded. "I can live with that, for now."

"Oh, I don't think that's ever going to change."

"It's the complicated things in life that make it fun."

"Maybe I'm looking for simple."

He almost smiled. "No, you're not. If you wanted simple, you never would have accepted my challenge. You never would have come to the afterschool club this morning and you certainly wouldn't be here with me right now. No woman who wanted a simple life would ever choose guns over gowns or law enforcement as a career. I'm sure she'd be a model or socialite instead." He winked.

"Hell." She pressed her lips together. "Gia talks too much."

"We're friends. That's what friends do. They talk about life and families. You should try it sometime."

"Hard pass. I know where you and Gia have your gossip sessions—while soaking your feet in rosewater and having your snaggle toenails filed down. If I go to the salon for even a haircut, my mom gets all teary-eyed."

"My toenails are soft and lovely and only require a good file-down every month or so, but we've digressed from the topic at hand. Can I trust you, Katerina Jacqueline Hellman?"

"Always." She met his gaze and held it. "Betraying trust is unforgiveable in my book."

The edge in her words conveyed a warning, a promise, and an icy prickle ran down his neck. Breaking her trust would result in a door slam. There'd be no going back, no second chances. The memory of meeting with the chief for the sole purpose of suggesting that Kat be brought in as the firearms instructor instead of adding it to his own workload flitted through his mind. A push without her knowing wasn't double-crossing, and if she hadn't wanted it, she could have rejected it.

"Then again, I could be lying," she added.

He didn't need to glance at the screen to gauge her honesty. Her brown eyes were guileless and watchful, an almost vulnerable glow daring him to choose whether he wanted to remain serious or go with humor. "Trusting anyone is always a risk. That's the beauty of relationships. Without taking a chance on someone, you'll never know what you might have found at the end of the rainbow."

"It's generally a huge pile of crap that sticks to the bottom of my shoe and the only way to get rid of it is with a pointy stick and a firehose."

"The odds are fifty-fifty that you'll find yourself knee-deep in a heap of poo." He leaned closer. "Or maybe every step will stir up butterflies, cause rose petals to drift from the sky in a perfumed rain and lure an army of kittens so soft that you'll self-combust at their cuteness."

Kat opened her mouth, closed it. "You're the strangest person I've ever met."

"Thank you." He let all the humor drain from his voice. "I trust you, Katerina. My gut tells me that I won't regret handing my secrets to you, and I always listen to my gut." He patted his stomach fondly. "In return, I promise not to push, persuade or trick you into any unpleasant substances. Any stepping will be of your own volition."

An expression flitted across her features, and he'd swear it was gratitude, as if it wasn't often that she was given the freedom to choose every step forward without any pressure, advice or opinions. She was so strong and independent that he couldn't imagine she'd let someone else influence her enough to do something she didn't want to do, but he got the need to want to make the people who mattered proud. His father's approval had meant the world to him, had given him the strength to continue in his footsteps.

"As you've proven worthy of my ancient polygraph machine—so far—I will entrust you with one secret." He lowered his voice to a hush and eased forward. As she imitated him, inching closer, studying his face, waiting, a thrill curled through his heart. There was no derision or distaste in her expression, only interest. "I spend my Saturday nights on the streets, connecting with homeless teens." He didn't want to scare her off with the fine print details of why he'd taken it on himself to help teens in need of food and shelter, a safe place to go, someone to trust, how every time he stumbled upon a homeless girl with black hair, his heart flatlined with hope.

Kat watched him, clearly waiting for more, for a dark, dirty tidbit worthy of her curiosity. As the silence stretched, she huffed. "That's not much of a secret."

"Slow down, girl. I have to set the foundation first. Revealing a secret is a delicate process. There's a balance to keep and—"

"Does your screen tell you how close I am to losing my patience?"

He gave her a steady look. "Just because you dazzle me with your shooting skills and get me all hot and bothered with a perfect takedown doesn't mean I'm simply going to spread out on the table and let you have your way with me." As a flush stained her cheeks, he resisted the powerful urge to follow up, simply to see what she'd do. "This is where the challenge truly begins, and here are the rules." He dropped his voice to a low purr. "Every time you look at my mouth, I get an extra quarter point."

As if the mere suggestion made her do it, her gaze flicked to his mouth and up again. The pink in her face deepened, and he couldn't deny the thrill that he had the power to make snarly, aloof, sharp-as-claws Katerina Hellman blush.

"Is that how these makeup sessions work? You get to make the rules up along the way?"

"Unless you stop me." He curled up one corner of his mouth, rebellious.

"Do you have a fae relative somewhere down the line? Is that where all these bargains and trickeries come in?"

"Insulting." He lifted his chin. "My blood is pure Romanian, not Celt."

"Gypsy genes then."

"Possibly. Stop with the distraction ploys, Katerina. Do you wish to forfeit or continue? You lose only a quarter point if you run away now."

She gave him a death glare, most likely due to his jab at her bravery. It was yet another quality he loved about her—her unwillingness to chicken out, even when the challenge got personal.

"I'm not intimidated by your questions, Farkos." Her intent focus remained purposely fixed on his eyes. "And not looking at your big mouth won't be a problem."

He let both corners curl.

While her jaw tightened, she didn't fall for the bait. "But that's it for making up rules. Twenty questions. If I don't answer—which won't happen—I lose the challenge and you get a quarter point."

"And every time you give the briefest glance to my mouth during the interrogation, I get another quarter point."

Her eye twitched and after a begrudging pause, she released an exasperated breath. "Fine."

"Deal." Lowering his chin, he gave her a sultry look. "Watch out, Angel. Here I come."

Chapter Ten

As Roman's crooked, mischievous half-smile curled to life—seen in Kat's peripheral vision, of course—a bolt of electricity rattled through her. She had the sensation that he'd subtly convinced her to step off a cliff into a freefall, that she'd made both the biggest mistake of her life and maybe the best, because whatever came next might be painful, but what remained on the other side of the aftermath had the potential to be incredible. First, she had to survive.

"Still feeling trustworthy?" His mouth twitched, *damn him*, and in her distracted state she almost forgot herself and looked.

"Nothing's changed in the last thirty seconds." But every hard beat of her heart contradicted her easy words. The public usually trusted her when she wore her badge—unless they were being arrested. Gia trusted her because that was what younger sisters did. When she had a gun in her hands and aimed at a target, everyone seemed to trust her, but that confidence stemmed from the bolster of titles or trappings, not because of who Katerina Hellman truly was as a person. The fact that Roman looked beyond all those details and left an open invitation to simply be herself, to be trusted and extend whatever she chose in return? It was both bewildering and strangely touching.

Not that there'd be any touching going on.

"Question number one." Roman watched her intently, waiting to pounce on any slip on her part. "Do you snore?"

"Like a logger with a monstrous chainsaw."

He glanced at the laptop screen, then back at her, and *tsk*ed. "Deceit at the outset is most disappointing."

"The deal we struck was that I had to answer the question, not that I had to answer honestly." She smirked. Bargaining was more fun when she managed to get the upper hand. She'd never tell Roman the thrill she got with his challenges, not knowing what to expect, what he might do. Playing fast and hard with her dad and brothers growing up hadn't been due to any sense of inferiority. She truly enjoyed keeping up with the boys. Most of the time, they had the better toys.

"This is a very serious investigation, Katerina."

"So, you start out by asking me if I snore?"

"It's important to know if it might be prudent to invest in earplug stock." He paused and double-checked the screen. "Which would be a no. Are you sure you don't want any pie? Interrogations make me hungry."

She shook her head.

He dragged the pastry in front of him and grabbed the waiting fork. "I get you all to myself, you luscious creature."

Kat pressed her knees together and hid a shiver. If he spoke to her in that same velvet tone, using those words, she might melt into a pool of butter. Stuck in the seduction of his voice, she watched him lift the fork to his mouth.

Roman paused and his gaze flicked to hers. "Quarter-point, Angel."

Hell. "You low-life, scumbag dirty cheater." Grimacing, she refocused on the plates and straps on her fingertips. "That's the whole reason you brought the pie, isn't it?"

"How dare you question my integrity? No one ever needs a reason to bring pie." He stuffed the bite in his mouth, chewed and swallowed. "But in this case, it helped."

The smirk in his tone tempted her to deck him, while the blood pounding hot and fast demanded she jump on him. She somehow managed to do neither. "Next question, Farkos."

He took another bite, watching her while he chewed slowly. "We didn't set a time limit on the twenty questions. I can go all…night…long."

The image of Roman shirtless, all those hard muscles on display, flickered through her thoughts. It was possible he wasn't exaggerating. No man naturally had those long, lean lines, but she wasn't about to ask him what he did to stay in shape. Her imagination was giving her enough trouble as it was.

"Some of us have to train with weapons bright and early and would prefer not to be sleep-deprived while doing it." She leaned forward and bared her teeth, making certain not to look at his mouth — his delectable mouth that now probably tasted like sweet, cinnamon-spiced apple pie. "Get on with it."

"No need to be pushy, Katerina." He set the fork down and stretched out his long legs beneath the table, brushing his calves against hers. "What would you have chosen as a career if guns and badges weren't involved — or are law and justice your passion?"

No guns? No uniform? The serious nature of the question threw her off balance. Besides the option offered by her mother — model, socialite, trophy wife — she'd never considered the alternatives. It was either do what she was good at or...she had no idea.

Thinking about doing something beyond the scope of her family's footsteps was like having the ground crumble beneath her butt. Why had she never thought about it before? She enjoyed shooting itself, didn't mind earning the respect that came with a demonstration, loved the thrill of hitting the target, but was shooting her passion? Making a difference in the world had been the ingrained teaching of her dad and brothers, and wearing a badge made community service part of the job. But there were facets of the position she wasn't crazy about. Justice mattered, but with each arrest she felt like a condemning judge — and she had no business determining the moral code of strangers. Every time she arrived too late to stop a crime or prevent injury to a victim, she left with the knowledge that she was powerless, another failure under her belt.

Not her favorite feeling.

But as much as people annoyed, enraged or exhausted her, she actually enjoyed helping them. It was the stopping on the road to assist with a mechanical breakdown or finding a lost kid who'd merely wandered away, escorting a motorcycle convoy through town while they traveled to the local hospital to hand out stuffed animals to children with terminal illnesses. Those moments were what drove her to keep going. Without a badge, she didn't see another avenue to get there. She didn't know how to do anything else.

Without her guns and badge, who would she be?

"I already told you about my wicked basket-weaving skills." She shrugged, playing off the empty pit that had formed in her stomach.

"And I told you, this was a one-way road. You don't know me well. I don't expect you to naturally trust me," Roman said, his dark eyes solemn. "But I want you to, and I hope one day you'll feel comfortable enough with me to speak freely, to be completely yourself." He released a breath and glanced at the screen. "Today, however, is not that day."

"I don't know, okay?" The words spilled out before she reconsidered the wisdom of going farther down this road with Roman, sharing discoveries and new fears. "I've never been anyone more than a sharpshooter or cop."

"I respectfully disagree. You've always been Katerina Hellman." The smallest smile twitched on his lips. "And you owe me another quarter point."

"Hell." She couldn't decide if he'd meant to trick her or if he merely refused to overlook even the smallest opportunity to gain the upper hand in their challenge, because his words rang with sincerity, undeniable. For reasons she couldn't comprehend, he didn't completely identify her with the career she'd naturally slipped into or the skills fostered by her father and brothers from a young age.

And she really had to stop looking at his mouth.

"We're even on the scoreboard now, Angel." Roman held her gaze, his eyes dark and deep as the night. The candlelight cast him in an unearthly glow, part shadows, part fire, and the blended scent of violets and pie and spices called her closer.

"A fluke," she murmured, her voice losing all its strength. If she reached across the table, touched his face, the rasp of stubble would slide beneath her skin — her fingertips tingled at yesterday's memory, when he'd been so dangerously close.

Tension danced between them, tight enough that her breaths came faster, sharp enough that her pulse raced. The silence stretched and gave her too much time to think. The unapologetic, open interest reflected in Roman's eyes didn't help.

She was used to ignoring how most men looked at her, judging her on appearance alone. They were easy enough to chase away with a curt word or two. But never had any man wanted to engage her for not only the skills she possessed, but also for who she was as a person. Never had a man put the trust ball in her court and left it there. And it had been a very long time since a man who knew her at all had looked at her the way Roman did now, as if she made the sun set and the stars fill the sky.

Infatuation... That was what was between them, something that flared to life and would burn out fast. As much as she tried to deny it, he'd awakened a part of her that had lain dormant, buried beneath a slowly dying marriage, the failed pursuit of happiness through a career and finding herself at the end of a decade nowhere closer to feeling...*right*.

She couldn't stop looking at his mouth, couldn't stop thinking about how he'd kiss — if he'd do it the same way he smiled — with only a fraction of emotion — or if he saved all the passion for his actions. Maybe she should just kiss him and get it over with, cure her curiosity and move on. Maybe they'd both hate it with equal passion. They could call their challenge a draw, she'd finish up her six weeks in Graywood without any further Roman Farkos complications and get back to life as she knew it, post-divorce.

Suddenly, the thought of finding an apartment to stash her minimal possessions in and returning to an existence that included her job with all the co-workers who'd chosen to keep Vic's secret instead of telling her left a chill in her bones. She loved helping people, was good at her job, but going back to a department where people trusted her less than a man who'd been unfaithful to her for months...?

"I have to know, Katerina." Roman hadn't moved, his elbows on the table, the laptop and all the connecting wires spilling her responses for his viewing pushed to the side. He watched her steadily, his expression set on his usual neutral.

She wanted to kiss the neutral off his face. "Know what?" Silently, she cursed how breathless she sounded. "You haven't met the question quota yet — "

"What you taste like." His voice, always rough, held a deeper rasp.

She went still, her heart threatening to punch through her ribs and escape. He hadn't kept his interest in her a secret, but he had to realize the likelihood that she'd shut him down. It was a pity she couldn't seem to find the willpower to do it.

"Then?" she asked, no longer in complete control of her words.

"Then I stop wondering." His attention drifted to her mouth and stayed there. "I stop driving myself crazy every minute, staying awake every night speculating on how silken-soft your lips are, because I'll finally know."

Kat sucked in a ragged breath. If she didn't take care of this fascination now, she'd be haunted by curiosity, tormenting herself with what-ifs.

Screw it.

Instead of answering, she planted her palms on the table and leaned forward, halfway out of her chair. When he remained completely still and his breath caught, she smiled, her mouth only an inch from his. She'd never let the power her looks seemed to have over the opposite sex go to her head, but knowing that she could knock Roman's socks off with only the implication of a kiss tempted her to reconsider.

"Don't say I'm never nice, Farkos," she said. "And this doesn't mean anything." She pressed her mouth to his.

As if he'd merely been waiting for her to make the first move, he immediately twined his fingers in her hair and cradled her face with his other hand, gentle with a touch of warning that if she tried to move away, he'd do his best to stall her. He stroked her jawline with his callused thumb while he waged war on her senses with his lips.

Kat closed her eyes, her arms wobbling beneath the onslaught, only holding up by sheer force of will. She'd intended to simply test the waters with the expectation that his kiss would leave her uninspired, one, done and over. Her kissing experience was limited to Vic. At seventeen, she supposed she hadn't been too hard to impress, and kissing Vic had been fine—fun at first, if not exactly physically overwhelming.

Kissing Roman... She had nothing to compare it to. His lips were soft and both coaxing and demanding, persuading her to surrender and promising she wouldn't regret it, and even as she told herself to stop, she couldn't bring herself to obey. Her body synced slowly to his, led by the pattern of each nibble of his mouth and teeth, and when he enticed her to open, resistance was futile.

Her blood heated with every stroke of his tongue until it trembled through her veins and pounded at every pulse point. His spicy-sweet scent pulled her closer, and before she'd meant to, she'd planted her butt on the table for better access to his warmth. One hand now free, she angled her torso enough to run her fingers through his hair and feel the rasp of stubble on his jaw. Whatever control she'd had completely dissolved, a willing slave to him as long as he continued kissing her.

His kiss was everything she'd hoped it wouldn't be and she had no idea how she'd deal with that once she figured out how to escape the spell he'd woven around her with his mouth, teeth and tongue.

"Angel," he murmured between one kiss and the next, pushing the laptop completely to the side. Never breaking the kiss, he dragged her across the table until he had her settled in his lap, caught in the polygraph wires and his strong arms.

Kat couldn't even care that one kiss had turned into another — or that letting it go on longer was a bad idea in a dozen different ways. Never mind that it had been so long since she'd been held as if she meant something that she was close to pushing away the past and future and simply living in the moment, holding on to the sensation of being wanted, of every nerve being brought to fiery life. That had nothing to do with it. She didn't mean anything to Roman and he didn't mean anything to her. Roman didn't know her, not really, and a kiss couldn't change that. As long as she remembered that, clung to it like a lifeline, she'd make it through the high he infused in her otherwise-reasonable brain.

He trailed kisses along her jaw to her throat, and she angled her head, unable to deny him access. She fisted his T-shirt with one hand and gripped the back of his neck with the other, afraid that if she let go, she'd float away.

"You're wrong, you know," he said against her throat, leaving a sting as he scraped his teeth over her skin.

Kat didn't bother answering. She didn't care what he believed she was wrong about, might even agree if he kept stoking the fire in the frozen wasteland of her body.

"This changes everything." He slid his hand beneath her shirt, his callused fingertips drifting over the bare skin of her back to the edge of her bra. "You'll still invade my dreams, but now it'll be about kissing you again." He wrapped her ponytail around his hand and eased her head back, gently controlling. "Having you here, in my arms... Convincing you to stay..."

Stay? Staying in Graywood wasn't an option. She wasn't here to make friends, to settle down or get close to someone, especially someone whose kisses should be a crime. With a single kiss, Roman had temporarily erased all her common sense. It wasn't infatuation. It was some kind of mental breakdown brought on by stress. She had to stop it while she still could.

Kat leaped out of his arms and off his lap. All the wires connected between her and the computer tangled her up, and in her attempt to break free, the pie tumbled to the floor. Roman caught the laptop as it fell and all the plugins jerked out, still attached to Kat.

Roman glanced down at the pie, its innards oozing from beneath the tilted tin onto the tile. "That," he said in a sober tone, "is a tragic fatality."

"You can have the extra quarter-point." Kat ripped off all the straps and wires and tossed them on the table.

"Katerina—"

Before she changed her mind and succumbed to the lure of his voice, she walked out. The pie hadn't been the only casualty of the night, and the taste of apple, cinnamon and Roman remained in her mouth like an inscription.

Chapter Eleven

"I sabotaged myself," Roman said the instant Gia settled into the salon chair next to him. He sloshed his bare feet into the warm, sandalwood-scented water as she removed her shoes. "I said too much last night, Katerina kissed me and I overreacted."

For half a second, Gia froze, one sandal in her hand, her blue eyes wide. The next half-second, she was in his face. "Kat kissed you?"

He slipped back into the memory easily, since he'd spent most of the moments between then and the present reliving Kat in his arms, her mouth on his, her hands in his hair, on his neck, his chest. Every place she'd touched had been imprinted with her signature and his lips would never be the same, still dreaming of her soft, supple skin that smelled like lavender and mint. The rest of him—all the spots she hadn't touched and left neglected—complained that they hadn't been claimed by her too, tight and needy.

Holy shiznit, she'd irreversibly drugged him with her kiss, and he was afraid she'd withhold the antidote just to prove to him she could.

"Yeah," he finally said, the word a tortured, wanting murmur. He met Gia's gaze. "She destroyed me. I may never recover."

Gia squeezed his face between her hands for a moment, laughing, then went about performing what had to be her happy-happy-joy-joy dance.

If he hadn't still been shell-shocked from the previous night, he would have joined in.

Spinning, waving her hands wildly in the air, she almost knocked over Sally, their faithful, quiet and no-nonsense pedicurist. Sally pointed a warning finger at Gia.

Sally ran a tight salon—no pastries, no backtalk and apparently no dancing.

"Sorry," Gia said, still smiling. She grabbed Sally's hands. "I was celebrating Roman being kissed. You can't really blame me, can you?"

She frowned at Roman, her dark eyes assessing.

"No need to look so surprised, Sally. Women often find me irresistible."

She muttered a word in Polish that sounded suspiciously negative and disappeared around the privacy screen between the salon foyer and customer chairs.

Gia flopped back into her seat and leaned halfway over the armrest toward him. "Tell me *everything*."

As much as he'd grown to appreciate his fast friendship with Gia—and how she'd managed to snake charm Ian's heart and inspire him to battle his demons—sharing details about her sister and all the things he'd like to do to Kat in private went beyond the scope of their relationship.

"She accepted my mini-challenge of the week, which happened to be a polygraph test."

Gia's eyes sparkled. "Did you make her confess?"

"You clearly have no sympathy for the trials your sister must endure to maintain her pride, do you?"

"Nope. None." She made an impatient gesture. "Don't hold out on me, Baconbits."

He gave her a level look. "I should have suspected Ian's negative effect on you. If you insist on calling me by a name sacred to bromances, be warned. I will find an appropriate retaliatory response."

"Stop stalling."

"To be fair, I'm not completely to blame for my actions. She kept glancing at my mouth in a most suggestive and unsportsmanlike manner."

"Using your man bits against you to throw you off your game." Gia nodded sagely, her chin on her fist. "That's a classic Hellman move. You should have expected it."

"I considered that possibility at first, but she continued to do so even after I added a quarter point penalty for every glance at my mouth, which I suspect is *not* a move taught by the Hellman clan."

"It could be her overarching challenge strategy — lose some percentage points to make you believe she's weak, only to turn around and smoke you when it counts." Tapping her finger against her chin, she narrowed her eyes. "What happened next?"

"The shameful and unanticipated Farkos defenses meltdown. I suggested that Katerina wasn't defined by her skills and she looked at me as if she'd hopelessly lost her Python and I'd just found it for her." He shifted in the chair, his body remembering all too well the effects of those brown eyes aimed at him, filled with such longing and fire. "Your sister then befuddled my thoughts and rationality with her Hellman sorcery, and I couldn't stop myself." He pinched his nose and released a long breath. "Rather than sticking to the challenge as planned, I made it very clear that I wanted to kiss her."

"And she kissed you instead of ripping you a new one and walking out?"

"Oh, she walked out—but not until after the kiss of the century." That kiss had scarred him for life. He'd never recover, ruined for any woman other than Katerina, because it wasn't simply the kiss that had destroyed him completely. Having her in his arms, a part of him that had been absent, a part he hadn't even realized he'd been missing, had suddenly made itself known. Now that he'd found her, he couldn't go back to the way he'd been.

With one kiss, she'd irreversibly altered him and he didn't quite see how his future panned out if she didn't feel the same.

"She kissed you," Gia said, her tone awestruck. "Roman, do you know what this means?"

"That I have better odds of beating Ian in the courtroom than winning even a slice of Katerina's heart before she leaves town." He sighed. "I know."

"Obviously not." She squeezed his arm. "I would have been dazed with admiration if she let you even get within kissing range by the end of your challenge, but she completely jumped that hurdle and went for the touchdown instead—on week one. You're a genius."

"As much as I agree with your sentiments on my state of ingenuity, I'm not following your rationale."

"Kat is incapable of being charmed. She blows guys off like dandelion puffs and smashes them beneath her boots as she walks away. She's so used to being seen as an object due to her looks, talent, occupation or some combination of all three that compliments don't affect her, even if they're sincere—especially when coming from a dude." She swirled her feet in the water, sending up a sweet, flowery draft. "But you, genius that you are, looked beneath the surface from the start. You've gone for her throat by casually accepting all the qualities other people usually make a big deal about. You've given her the freedom to be normal, to be herself with you and she rolled with it. Even if she won't admit it yet, you resonate with a piece of her that she doesn't let most people see. She wouldn't have kissed you otherwise."

Resonate. His skin prickled as if caressed by the hand of fate, a tug confirming his every step toward Katerina.

"Kat doesn't let hardly anyone get close to her, and even though she's feeling like she should retreat to her cage and snarl—cheating and breakups do that to even the toughest girl—she kept the gate ajar for you." Gia sipped her lime seltzer water, studying him. "She won't back out of your challenge just because she kissed you, if that's what you're worried about."

"Of course she won't. That's one of the reasons I find her irresistible. She doesn't allow any roadblock to stop her." The knot in his stomach since Katerina had walked out on him eased. Gia knew Kat better than anyone. He wasn't idiot enough to believe the road to his angel's heart wasn't still a rough and uncertain one, but Gia renewed his hope.

"Kat needs someone like you, Roman." She sighed and leaned her head back, closing her eyes. "You'll be perfect together."

He studied the relaxed lines of her lovely face, an echo of her sister's, with the same pouty mouth and slender nose. Confidence wasn't usually his issue, but the growing intensity of his feelings for Katerina was almost frightening. It wasn't so long ago that if someone would have told him his family would be scattered in a few years, he never would have believed them. Now, his father was gone, his sisters on their own, leaving him with an empty, echoing house and no one to share it with him. Getting his hopes up that he could convince Kat to stay in Graywood — with him — was a gamble with high-risk stakes. She could very well crush his heart and leave him twitching in the dust, forever crippled, like Ian had predicted.

But what was life without taking chances, especially for a shot at love, no matter how distant the target might be?

Roman closed his eyes, forced his shoulders to relax and laced his fingers over his belly, which reminded him with a grumble that he was overdue for an afternoon snack. "I didn't intend to fall for her so hard and fast. I don't deny she intrigued me from the very beginning, but when I convinced the chief to give her a try as the firearms instructor, I expected a slow-burn attraction, not my own demolition."

"Whoa, wait. Back up. You had something to do with Kat being hired?"

At the worry in Gia's tone, he squinted one eye open. "Chief wanted me to be the instructor, but, if I did, my other duties outside of the department would suffer. I'm not ready to sacrifice in those areas, so I suggested

Katerina, which was obviously an excellent recommendation." He shrugged. "The chief made the final decision."

Concern darkened the customary sunshine of her features. "Listen very carefully, Roman. Don't *ever* let Kat know you had anything to do with her being hired. It would be even worse than if she found out that I'm the one who nudged you into distracting her with the six-week challenge."

"Don't steal my thunder. I had the idea first. You merely encouraged it." The flash in her blue eyes spoke of storms and warnings. "It's not a secret that she's the best qualified for the position, and I didn't make the executive decision to hire her. It's not a big deal."

"It would be a ginormous deal to Kat if she thinks she didn't earn the job purely on her own merits or that she only got it because she was second choice. Trust me on this. Don't bring it up. *Ever.*"

He hated making promises he couldn't keep. He'd made one to his father—to keep his family together, his sisters close and connected—and at the time he'd believed he was capable of it. Not telling Kat that he'd suggested her as the right candidate for the firearms instructor seemed so trivial. How could she not believe she'd earned the right to teach firearms to a bunch of backwoods cops? He had been hoping to eventually get a gratitude cookie for it from his favorite sharpshooter, but if he dismissed the vehemence in Gia's voice and lost his chance at Kat before he'd won her heart...

"I don't like secrets unless they pertain to me." The alarm in Gia's eyes wasn't hard to read. She truly believed Kat would shut him down if she found out. He didn't think she gave her sister enough credit. "Maybe it would be best to casually tell her and get it over with."

"Do you want to keep all your body parts attached and in their appropriate places?"

"That would be ideal."

"Then keep your mouth nailed shut."

Sally breezed past the screen, nail file at the ready, and he leaned back to let her work on making his feet pretty. He refused to lie and couldn't promise to never reveal the tiny role he'd played in getting Kat on at the department. For now, though, he'd heed Gia's advice.

If she were wrong—wrong about kisses resonating and miniscule, meaningless secrets—no amount of challenges or good intentions would save him.

* * * *

The next few days slipped by for Kat in a weary blur of potato chips, restless nights and steamy dreams, a couple of basic firearms training sessions to more of Graywood's finest and hours of sidestepping certain people—aka Roman Farkos—by sequestering herself in the private firing range or hanging with Vee at the afterschool club at very specific, Roman-free times.

Both her rusty *Donkey Kong* techniques and her stealth skills were now honed to perfection.

Late Saturday afternoon, after an hour of spitting bullets and blowing up targets that did nothing to destroy her demons, Kat trudged up the steps to Gia's porch. The door opened before she made it to the top.

"Hello, dear." Looking pristine and proper in her white pantsuit, Caroline took her in with an assessing sweep. There was nothing worth approving. Kat's instructor's polo shirt and cargo pants were almost as dusty as her boots. Her bun had loosened into an untidy mass near her nape and she had every reason to believe that her face was smudged. Still, the tightness around her mother's mouth rankled her already-frayed nerves. "I have the distinct sensation you've been avoiding me."

There was no use denying it. "I haven't felt like having tea and crumpets while discussing the weather lately, mother."

"Don't be sassy, Katerina Jacqueline." Caroline stepped aside as Kat passed through the door, as if she didn't want to contract any dirt — or the disease of an imperfect daughter. "Will you be ready in time for our family dinner tonight?"

"Family dinner?" Kat pushed a stray strand of hair from her eyes.

"I sent you a text, dear." Caroline closed the door behind them. "Don't you have your phone with you?"

She did, but she'd turned it off because...peopling and avoiding said people and all tall, dark and annoying badges who destroyed her with apple-pie kisses had been her goal. She pulled her phone from her side pocket and turned it on. "It still blows me away that you actually texted me."

"A successful woman must keep up with current technology." Caroline lifted her chin and straightened her already perfectly detailed jacket.

Kat looked at her from beneath her eyelashes. "Texting came out years ago."

"Yes, well, I had hoped it was nothing more than a fad, but as it has proved its staying power, I adjusted my thinking."

"Keeping with the times." Kat couldn't hide a grin. "Good job, Mom."

"Thank you." Caroline's blue eyes gleamed with pride.

It wasn't that she disliked her mother or that Caroline was a bad person in any way. They simply didn't see eye to eye, and as they both possessed the stubborn Hellman gene, those differences and an unwillingness to bend didn't always make their relationship smooth or easy. Plus, in Caroline's eyes, Katerina could have done so much better with her life.

The definition of 'better' was up for interpretation.

"Awesome, you're back." Gia flounced from the hallway in a picture-perfect pink dress and matching stilettos, her makeup and hair fantastic, the glamorous daughter Caroline had always hoped Kat would be. She eyed Kat up and down and shook her head. "And so not ready for dinner."

"Since I only found out about dinner two minutes ago... Yeah. I'm almost ready."

"I don't trust your wardrobe selection skills, so I'll help. It'll be faster, and if we miss our reservations, Gregori's won't hold our table." Gia grabbed Kat by the wrist and dragged her away like a prisoner headed to the whipping post—with heavy feet and slouched in fear.

Once they'd made it to Gia's bedroom, she shut the door and pushed Kat onto the vanity stool. Kat scowled at her reflection in the mirror. She looked worse than she'd imagined, like a witch after a failed ride on her broom, tossed from the sky and landing in a heap of questionable substances.

"Here." Gia handed her a facial towelette, which was moist and smelled of cucumber or some other natural crap that was supposedly good for skin. "Clean your face while I fix your hair."

Kat obeyed and winced as her sister disentangled the band and bobby pins from her half-dead bun and freed her hair.

"Normally, I'd ask what was up with you, but I already have a good idea why you've been slouching around more than usual and demolishing the potato chip supply on a nightly basis." Gia took a brush to her hair. "Don't let your marriage to a vermin in disguise affect your future, and especially don't compare other men to that two-timing slimebag. Don't waste a single second letting what he did to you hold you back in any area of your life."

"I'm not." Kat closed her eyes and gave her face a good wipe down. "I won't."

Gia paused in brushing her hair and met her gaze in the mirror. "Oh, really? Then why did you kiss and ditch Roman?"

Kat scowled. *Son of a jerkface... Of course he told her.* "You two gossip like bored old men at the bowling alley."

"That's what friends do. They discuss things, especially important ones like falling for difficult older sisters and the kiss of the century." Gia nodded before she could say anything. "That's right... He used the words 'falling for' and 'kiss of the century' all on his own."

A flock of dragonflies took flight in her stomach. Had that kiss — that shocking, haunting, scary kiss that had completely scrambled her brain and seared her blood — left him as affected as it had her? Or had he simply said those words to Gia, hoping they would get back to her and soften her up?

Gia thwacked her on the top of the head with the brush.

"Ow!" She found her sister's gaze in the mirror again. "What was that for?"

"I know what you're thinking. Roman isn't playing you. He may be a bit off-center, but he's a great guy."

"Since he's friends with *Ian*, that's highly questionable — the great guy part, not the off-center bit. I've already figured out he's — "

"Limited edition," Gia said, a warning in her tone. "I adore Roman, and you promised you'd be nice to my friends, including Ian." She paused, as if a new thought had just occurred to her. "Sis, if you're playing Roman, if he's your idea of a rebound, you need to be honest with him."

"I don't use people, G." She gave Gia a frosty look. "But thanks for thinking the worst of me and being more concerned about your special man friend than your sister."

"Oh, please." Gia resumed brushing her hair. "I know you wouldn't intentionally use people, but breakups can mess with your head and emotions big time, and you aren't exactly one for examining all your mushy feelings."

Kat rubbed the towelette over her eyes to get away from the knowing stare aimed at her in the mirror. *No argument here.*

"I know you might not think you're ready to jump into the romance game and I don't blame you. Being cheated on sucks. But you'll never know what you might be missing if you don't take those extra-special chances that fall into your lap." Her smile turned wicked. "Or whose laps you're dragged into."

Kat's cheeks betrayed her, suddenly hot. "Roman Farkos has a big mouth." *A soft, delicious, amazing mouth that turns me into a mindless, wannabe sex-kitten.* "And what happened to the sacred rule of not kissing and telling? Is it outdated in today's twisted culture? No wonder this world is going to hell in grandma's handcuffs."

"He also isn't hard to look at." Gia grinned as she expertly wrangled Kat's hair into an elegant updo and pinned it into place. "Tall, dark and built for endurance."

Kat spun on the bench to face her sister. "Tell me something terrible about him."

Reaching around her, Gia selected a handful of makeup. She pinched Kat's chin to hold her still and tilted her face up. "Not everyone appreciates his strange sense of humor." She applied a brush to Kat's eyebrows. "I've never seen him pissed off."

"Not helpful." She needed some dark, dirty detail to destroy her fascination with him. Because that was all it was—a passing infatuation, or possibly even the rebound guy Gia had suggested, not that she had any prior experience with being dumped. Did rebounds usually strike so hard and claw inside the chest to snuggle up as if they belonged there? She couldn't deny that Roman made her feel...good, amazing—even while he pushed all her buttons. He looked at her as if she was his wish come true, with or without guns or badges or kick-ass takedown abilities.

Hell.

"Stop frowning and keep still." Gia popped open a mascara tube and leaned in to her face. She brought the brush to Kat's eyelashes and carefully applied whatever black goop mascara was made of. "He eats too much and his love for pie leans toward the obsessive."

Kat groaned as the taste of apple pie reawakened, triggered by the memory of Roman's tongue in her mouth. "Don't bring up pie. *Ever.*"

"O-kaaay." Gia straightened, studied her a moment and whipped out lipstick in a bright shade of red that Kat would use to paint a fire hydrant. "Roman will tell you whatever you want to know. All you have to do is ask him."

But asking him would open herself to questions she wasn't sure she wanted to answer. If she admitted she was even remotely interested in Roman, that would require letting him closer and past the trappings. What if he was disappointed in what he found? Without her career and proficiency with guns, she was the most boring person she knew. She sucked at social skills, she could count her true friends on one hand and preferred books over people most of the time.

"Brows, mascara, lips and we're done." Nodding, Gia approved of her quick-fire makeup masterpiece, went to her closet and began rummaging through it.

"Roman annoys me." She ignored her sullen tone. "He pushes all my buttons. He set me up and freakin' beat me at the range."

"I heard. Here. Put these on." Gia tossed her a shirt a few shades paler than the lipstick and a flirty, lightweight matching skirt that would be several inches too short on Kat's longer legs. "Where are your pumps?"

"In my bag." She waved a hand in the direction of the living room.

"Change." Making good use of the Hellman commander tone, Gia gave her a warning look. "I'll be back with the shoes."

Kat bent down and unlaced her dusty boots, kicked them away and dragged off her socks. The rug felt like heaven beneath her bare toes — her bare, *stinky* toes. She slithered out of her pants, grabbed a bottle of perfume from the vanity and gave her feet a healthy spray.

"The thing you need to ask yourself is," Gia said, sweeping back in with Kat's bag, continuing the conversation as if it hadn't paused, "did Roman's kiss make you feel anything?"

Like I wanted to drown in him and only come back up for air if the apocalypse hit. She shrugged and shimmied into the borrowed skirt, ditched her dirty polo and dragged Gia's shirt over her head. She sniffed her armpit and regretted it. "Ugh."

Gia threw some deodorant at her and watched as Kat disguised the fact that she needed a shower with the scent of baby powder. "If Roman's kiss had been only shrug-worthy, you never would have ended up in his lap."

Kat shoved her feet into the pumps Gia handed her with more force than necessary.

"When was the last time a kiss from your ex pushed any button at all?" At Kat's death-glare, Gia added with wide-eyed innocence, "Just sayin'."

"And this conversation is over." Kat marched toward the door and glanced over her shoulder. "Just sayin'."

If only she could shut down the storm Roman brewed inside her as easily as she did her sister.

Chapter Twelve

At the restaurant an hour later, Kat sipped her white wine and watched rain dribble down the glass of the restaurant window while her sister and mother chatted about another frivolous subject. Pretending to be interested in fashion or the latest gossip might make her snap. A classy restaurant and wine required classy behavior. That had been Caroline's warning before walking in, directed at her. Kat took a less-than-classy large gulp of wine. *I'm a Hellman, I can do this.*

The empty plate in front of her made her want to stop by the store and restock the potato chip supply on the way home. She'd never understood how the presentation of food could be more important than the taste or why a portion the size of her thumbnail dressed up in a few curlicued vegetables and drizzled with fancy sauce counted as a full entrée.

Her unwillingness to be unnecessarily hungry had been one of the first clues she wasn't model material. Keeping up with her brothers would have been impossible by existing on carrots and celery, and there was no way she'd be able to lift a few of her heavier guns, let alone hold them steady through the kickback.

A draft of cool air on her inner thighs reminded her to keep her ankles primly crossed and her legs pressed together, not sprawled out and relaxed like a normal person. She gave her sister a dirty look. Gia had tricked her into wearing the short skirt, distracting her with a Roman discussion.

I'm not thinking about him.

She rubbed at a new callus on her thumb, courtesy of the last *Donkey Kong* competition with Vee. The afterschool club would close in a couple of hours. She might not envy Vee's foster child life, but right now she'd trade places with her, no hesitation. A tiny smile formed. Caroline would freakin' *love* Valerie.

"Are you listening, Katerina?" Her mother's voice broke through her happy vision.

"I am now." She smiled thinly at Caroline's small head shake. "All the talk of scarves and jewelry drove me into a state of sleeping with my eyes open." She drained the last few gulps of wine and plunked her glass down. "Is everyone ready to go?"

Gia's smile was fake, her blue eyes wide, and Kat's mostly empty stomach somersaulted. The specific details of the mental message Gia tried to send weren't getting through, but she was familiar enough with her sister's expressions. Whatever she'd missed in the conversation was ugly-bad.

Caroline delicately wiped her clean mouth with the cloth napkin, a clue that she needed a moment to collect herself before speaking, lest her tone be less than ladylike. "To repeat myself, I found a house for sale around the corner from Gia's. I believe I might enjoy living in a small town."

Aw, hell. Kat cleared her throat. "But Graywood is so far from your friends and clubs, home, Bryan and Ben." *Dad.* Even though her own divorce was fresher, it was easier to digest than her parents not being together anymore. It felt so *wrong.* "Why would you even want to live here?"

"Besides the fact that both of my daughters are here?" Caroline said, her eyes blazing, a harsh contrast to her calm tone. "The community is small enough that people are more connected, more interested in each other and the needs of organizations. It's just the change of pace I've been looking for, a new place to reconnect, find new friends and causes — a home of my own."

Gia, playing the perfect daughter, reached over and gripped Caroline's hand in a show of support, her expression sincerely sad. Of all the Hellman siblings, Gia had taken their parents' divorce the hardest. Falling head over heels for Ian had softened the blow, but they all knew that love was fragile, so easily broken, stolen or lost.

Her throat tight, Kat took her mother's free hand and blinked back an irritating burn of tears.

Caroline smiled at them both.

"I'm sure Gia will appreciate having you near, Mom." Kat released her mother's hand and leaned back. "I'm not sticking around Graywood, though. Five more weeks and I'll be back home."

"And that is another subject I wished to discuss tonight." At Caroline's firm tone, Kat's blood went cold, then hot. *Perfect. Mom's turning me into her next project.* "You need a clean break too, Katerina.

Returning to life as it once was isn't possible. I don't like the idea of you working at the same department as Vickery. It won't be a healthy emotional environment for you."

Vickery. Kat resisted snarling. Only her mother had ever used Vic's full, ridiculous name. "I'm tougher than the average jilted spouse, Mom. I'll be fine."

"Fine is not good enough for a Hellman. I already made an offer on the house down the street from Gia. You will reside with me until you decide where you want to spend your future."

"Nope." Kat was on her feet before she'd even thought to move. "I'm *great* staying at Gia's."

"Gorging on potato chips instead of sleeping?" Caroline gave her a pitying look. "If not for yourself, think of Gia. You're being selfish, tying your sister down when she has only recently found Ian, and law school won't be easy. She doesn't need the extra stress, dear."

Kat went numb. Even though she suspected Gia hadn't said anything of the sort, maybe she *had* been taking advantage of her sister's generosity. Gia could always go over to Ian's place to be alone—and she did—but her presence limited any romantic times at Gia's own house. And maybe it was true that being in Graywood added stress to Gia's life. Gia would never lay that burden on her, but if she'd slipped even the smallest nugget of worry or complaint near Caroline, their mother's sensitive radar would pick it up.

"Mom! I don't think that at all." Gia shook her head, her golden curls swinging, her eyes apologetic. "Kat—"

"No need to explain, G." Kat swiped her hand through the air like a sword, sharp and fierce. She held her mother's unyielding stare. "I'm not moving in with you, Mother, but thanks so much for your never-ending confidence in my abilities, as usual."

Her mother didn't even blink. "Sit down, Katerina. We will discuss this calmly and come to a resolution."

"There's nothing to resolve and my calm is fraying at an alarming rate, so I'm going before I do something that might embarrass you." Without waiting for a response, Kat whirled away and sped through the restaurant. Caroline would never lower herself to chase her and would stop Gia with a 'give her some space to work it out on her own' speech.

Families could be a major knife in the patootie. *Stab, stab, stab.*

Cool, moist air washed over her as she barged out of the door of Gregori's. She took a moment to breathe it in, to calm the ire cutting at her control. Stepping from beneath the awning, she closed her eyes and lifted her face to the sky. The drizzle dampened her hair and skin, and beat by beat, her pulse slowed.

"Katerina."

Her name spoken so softly in Roman's gravelly voice at first seemed to be a rhythm in the rain, a secret escaped to whisper in her ear. Mother had been right on one particularity. She needed to get more sleep. Her subconscious was playing tricks on her.

Kat opened her eyes, blinked the wetness from her lashes and found her imagination hadn't been tripping after all. Roman had his lean going on against the brick wall of the restaurant, and from the state of his sopping hair and his black T-shirt clinging to his torso like a second skin, jeans dark with rain, he'd been there a while.

Her mouth went dry. It was useless denying the truth any longer. That lean was incredibly sexy, one hip cocked, thumbs hooked in his pockets, one boot crossed over the other. If it hadn't been sexy, she probably wouldn't have noticed at all. If she hadn't been attracted to him, she would've ignored him after day one.

Who am I kidding? Roman wouldn't have let her ignore him, not with all the buttons he insisted on pushing.

He watched her with his customary bland expression, his eyebrows raised slightly, but the flames flickering in his black eyes, as if he'd like to peel her clothes off with his teeth, kiss away her lipstick and keep on kissing her into the weekend threw her off balance. What was he even doing here?

"Your gossip buddy Gia is still inside." Her tone was more growly than she wanted, but a girl could only take so much pressure before she exploded. After her mom's demand to become her caretaker and roommate on top of her train-wrecked life, her emotions were set on ready-to-snap. Keeping a safe distance from Roman without acting out – or acting on impulse – might be beyond her control.

He didn't move. "Be that as it may, I'm here for you."

'*For you.*' Her stupid heart fluttered. "How did you know we were even here?" She pointed at him. "You better not be stalking me, Farkos."

"My social life may be pathetic, but I haven't resorted to stalking yet." He flashed his phone. "Gia posted it on social media."

"Big surprise." Kat threw her head back and sighed at the sky, squinting into the rain. *And that's how my sister got me killed.*

"Have a nice girl's evening out?" The hint of humor in his tone betrayed his neutral expression.

"Delightful." She bared her teeth at him.

"I need help." He straightened from his lean and slid his hands from his pockets.

"Absolutely you do. I heard there's a great therapist downtown. You might check it out."

His mouth twitched. "An investigation for another day, perhaps. It's about Vee."

"What about her?" A cold thread stitched through her ribs and she faced Roman squarely. "What's wrong?"

"She didn't go home." He swiped his hand over his short hair, spraying fine drops of rain. "Her foster parents called me rather than reporting it." He shrugged. "It's not the first time."

"You have an idea of where she went?" Kat gripped her purse strap tighter. There were so many options for trouble a kid could get into, whether they wanted to or not. She hadn't known Vee more than a handful of days, but a bond created over *Donkey Kong* was eternal. Besides, she liked Vee. Girls with bad attitudes needed to stick together, no matter their age differences.

"Maybe. Derick saw her walk off with another girl who makes a habit of hanging out with some hoodlums. They sometimes loiter at a boarded-up building near the edge of town. It was originally a hospital in the nineteen-hundreds, converted into a church, then used as a mental institute and abandoned after some scandal a decade ago. It has sat vacant ever since. Even though there's a locked, chain-link fence securing the grounds, kids always manage to worm their way inside."

"Hoodlums? Really? That's what you Graywood people call punks?"

"I prefer to call them ne'er-do-wells, but I didn't want you to think I'm weird."

"It's far too late for that, Farkos." She couldn't hide a small, evil grin.

"I meant weird*er*." His voice softened and raindrops clung like crystals to his ebony eyelashes. "Will you help me look for her, Katerina?"

Her humor faded as she held his gaze, brought back to the night of the polygraph when he'd asked if he could trust her. Her answer was the same now as it was then. "Always."

"Not that I'm complaining by any stretch of the word, but do you want to swing by Gia's and change?" His gaze swept over her, from her pumps to the short skirt clinging to her wet legs and the shirt that probably showed more of her assets than she wanted to. Usually, she wouldn't care, but the heat in his dark eyes would undoubtedly distract her. With Roman, distraction could be detrimental to her sanity.

"Good idea. My boots are better for kicking in doors and chasing down *ne'er-do-wells*."

"Perfect. I was merely concerned that your choice in footwear might hinder my investigation, not that the current state of your clothes takes my imagination to hot nights." His voice lowered an octave. "And all the ways we could make it even hotter."

Her body throbbed at all her most sensitive pulse points. *Hell.*

He headed toward a pickup that was more rust than green paint. "Try not to get dirty in my truck." He attempted to open the door, but it stuck. After a two-handed jerk, then another, it creaked open. Roman

172

bowed and twirled his hand, like a subject to his queen. "After you."

Glad for the cool rain to temper the sudden heat slithering through her, Kat slid onto the peeling plastic bench seat and kicked aside a muddy soccer cleat as he closed the door and jogged around to the other side. The interior smelled like him — sweet and spice, like a present waiting to be unwrapped beneath the tree. Or a pie, hot from the oven.

Don't think about pie. She'd never be able to think about pie again without having a vision of Roman.

Rain drummed gently on the roof of the truck and rolled down the windshield, gathering at the crack zigzagging across the entire length. A black, gothic cross hung from the mirror on a black chain that looked ancient. An eight-track player and AM-FM radio sat dark in the dash beneath a hula girl, who wobbled her hips gently to a song only she could hear.

Roman opened the driver's side and jumped in, his keys jangling. He slid the key into the ignition and paused, looking at her. "I don't allow just anyone to ride in Marta." He winked. "At least not in the cab."

"I'm feeling really special about that." She tapped the rusted glovebox. "Get this beast moving, Farkos."

He sucked in a breath and stroked the dash, as if petting a cat. "Do not be disrespectful to Marta," he whispered. "She's very temperamental."

"So am I."

"Then you understand how easily she could desert us in inconvenient places," he said solemnly and turned the key.

The motor rattled, not turning over.

"See what you did, Katerina? Now she's upset. You should apologize."

"I should walk." She grabbed the door handle. "I'd get there faster."

"She doesn't believe in us, baby." He was definitely talking to the truck. "Let's show her that it only takes a little faith."

He turned the key again and the junker coughed. "Come on, darling. Don't fail me." With a sputter, the engine roared to life, backfired and rumbled at a steady beat. Roman nodded at Kat. "What a beauty she is."

"As long as she doesn't die before getting us to Vee, I don't care how hard she was hit with the ugly stick."

"Take that back," Roman said in a monotone. "Marta was my father's. She survived driving lessons with me and all three of my sisters, has landed in uncountable ditches, endured several rear-enders and, despite having a few hiccups on a journey or two, she's priceless." He glanced at Kat, his expression serious. "It's Marta's character that makes her beautiful, not her rusty fender or dented hood."

The heat still tumbling through her veins pooled in her belly, and she forced herself to look out of the window rather than at him, because she got the distinct impression he wasn't talking only about his beloved Marta. The fact he wasn't swayed by outward appearances or besotted by kick-ass skills softened her edges. It was bad enough that she was physically attracted to him. She didn't need any more reasons to like him as a person.

Ten minutes later, in dry jeans, a sweatshirt and her combat boots, her damp hair still in the elegant twist Gia had created, Kat climbed back into Roman's pickup and shut the door — twice, to get it latched right. When

Roman didn't drive away, she glanced in his direction. He stared at her as if she were a stranger.

"What?" She refused to fiddle with her smoothed-back hair or whatever makeup might be smeared on her face, although she suspected Gia had used waterproof mascara.

His throat worked, pale against his black T-shirt. "I had the oddest idea that you should be wielding a sword just now. You remind me of a warrior queen ready to take the lead against an enemy army."

"You read too many books." She ignored the growing warmth in her face.

"Not possible."

True. And dammit, why did he have to love books too?

"I may enlist to be your general." He put the truck into gear and pulled away from the curb, wisely having left the motor running. 'Precious' did not necessarily correlate to 'trustworthy'. "Don't be surprised if I slip up and call you Xena."

"Then don't be shocked if I punch you in the throat." Not that she was offended to be compared to any warrior princess who destroyed. Xena kicked ass. "How far away is this warehouse?"

"Institute, technically, and it's only half a mile out of town. Close enough for anyone who wants to walk or bike there and far enough to be beyond the public radar." He glanced at her. "It's a perfect hideout for runaways, punks and ne'er-do-wells."

She gave him a narrow look. "Vee's not a ne'er-do-well."

"Not by nature." The dull light of the cloud cover and rain gave him an even grimmer air. "She doesn't have a support system to back her up, offer guidance or a kick in the butt when necessary, which makes her easy prey for anyone who pays attention to her. Her tough attitude can't stand up against the need to belong."

"Being a teenage girl is rough—all that self-doubt and hormones rolling around inside like a confidence-wrecking ball. There should be a mandatory class to teach girls that their value has nothing to do with someone else's approval or acceptance."

"That might be helpful to boys too. Next time you see Adara, you should mention it to her. She could probably work it into the curriculum."

Kat pursed her lips. Adara was the one friend of Gia's who Kat had always approved of—sensible, honest and a take-no-crap attitude. She'd been instrumental in keeping Gia from drowning and out of trouble after Joey had passed, taking on the role of protective older sister while Kat had been hundreds of miles away and unable to. For that, she'd always be grateful. Plus, Adara's bottom-barrel-dregs opinion of Ian almost equaled her own. *Absolutely sensible.*

"Are you going to give me a hint as to what to expect next week?" Roman's low, gravelly voice wove a harmony with the rain, all comfort and lazy afternoons, and Kat almost surrendered to the powerful urge to release her seatbelt, scoot close to his side and lay her head on his shoulder. When was the last time she'd even considered voluntarily leaning on someone else, let alone a man she barely knew?

Small town Graywood, stress and lack of sleep were twisting her rationality…obviously.

"I haven't yet decided who I'm choosing for next week." It wasn't exactly a lie. She'd been instructed to select the best two officers for intensive firearms training. Roman was an obvious choice. There was no other standout among the handful of Graywood badges, and she needed more time to see if one rose to the top. "With such a small department, the options are limited."

He glanced from the road at her, wearing the tiniest frown. "I was referring to our challenge, but this subject may be almost as interesting."

"You didn't know?" The chief hadn't mentioned anything about keeping quiet. "Chief Clifton asked me to gauge each officer and test potential candidates for more specialized firearms training at a later date." She couldn't hold back a little grin. "It's going to be some serious fun."

"What manner of bribery do you demand to choose me? My heart? Wait, that's already yours. My soul? My firstborn child? A lifetime of serving as your love slave? I'll pay anything, Katerina."

The air bottled up in her throat and she couldn't breathe. *'My heart...already yours.'* He had to be flirting, kidding around. There couldn't be any real meaning in the words. He didn't know that she was a slob, preferred to read supernatural romance over the latest literary bestseller or had shamefully failed her driver's test three times before passing. He didn't know that she sucked at being a wife, obedient daughter and most close relationships in general. If he knew all those things, he'd lose interest and walk away, no matter how much he admired her shooting and takedown skills.

Calm down. He didn't mean anything by it.

"Are you okay, Angel?" His rough murmur dragged her attention back to him. Roman glanced down at her hands, which were fisted tight in her lap.

She immediately relaxed her fingers and spread them on her thighs. "Just thinking about shooting." Somehow, she managed a tiny smile. "With really big guns."

"I love it when you talk dirty to me." His smooth tone didn't transfer to his eyes.

Kat looked away before she could identify concern or an even more uncomfortable emotion, because she wasn't entirely certain any longer if she preferred that he walked away. When Roman arrived on scene, she was never sure what he'd dream up or how he might surprise her in both big and small ways. And since he'd wheedled his way into her free time, her focus had slowly angled away from the lonely life she'd taken a hiatus from and retargeted on him. The way he looked at her, surprised her, kissed her... It was far more exciting than her marriage had ever been.

She wasn't ready to let this strange partnership between them go...not yet. Keeping her distance — she could handle it, could shut him down whenever she wanted. Besides, she still needed to destroy him in their six-week challenge, and she knew exactly what to bring to the table, something that would, with any luck, snuff out all burgeoning sprouts of fascination.

Relaxing, Kat kept her evil grin in check. If Farkos wanted to win the next challenge, he'd have to pay through the teeth.

Chapter Thirteen

Roman pulled his faithful truck Marta into the gravel on the side of the road and parked well beyond the fog line. He wouldn't want his baby to get struck while he wasn't there to protect her. "We're here."

Katerina squinted beyond the rain-spattered windshield at the surrounding trees. "If you've brought me out here to ice me, dump my body in the woods and clear the way to the firearms instructor job, fair warning… I fight back."

"And I suspect I'd lose that particular challenge." He turned the motor off, and in the following quiet, the rain a soft rhythm on the roof, guilt pinched him. The firearms instructor reference reminded him of the promise he'd begrudgingly given to Gia. As he'd told her, he'd merely suggested Kat as the perfect candidate. All the rest was up to her and Chief Clifton. When she learned of his tiny, insignificant part in her current role, there was no rational reason she'd be upset. He wasn't hiding anything.

The knot in his chest could dissolve at any time.

"The driveway is a few yards back." He nodded at the clump of oaks masking the mailbox and entrance to the property. "Hiking in won't announce our presence."

"You mean like the backfiring of an old pickup?" Kat grinned with a hint of malice. "Are you sure Marta will still be here when we get back, not towed away as an abandoned clunker?"

"How dare you? Marta is a town celebrity." He kept his tone flat, unaffected, despite the rise in temperature thanks to Kat's proximity, her lavender-mint scent, the mischief sparkling in her eyes. Whatever reservations she'd had after their kiss at Franny's diner, tangled up in wires, heat and hands, seemed to have disappeared, and he sent up a silent prayer of gratitude. More quickly than he'd imagined possible, Katerina had become very important to him, and if he'd driven her away by moving too fast, he'd be haunted by regrets. He was too young to have ties to another ghost.

Kat struggled with the dented passenger-side door, but before he could leap out and make it to her side, she managed to escape. She slammed the door shut with her hip. "I didn't lock it. Maybe someone will steal it, take it off your hands."

"Most unkind of you, Katerina, especially after Marta carried you here without any protest."

He turned and walked toward the driveway, his mouth twitching at her snort. The gravel, dark with rain, crunched beneath their boots and accentuated the country quiet. The institution grounds were within city limits, but the road leading in wasn't well-traveled and few residents lived in the vicinity, all the makings of a perfect place for someone who wanted to hide from the rest of the world. Kids weren't the only ones who frequented the deserted building—and that was what worried him most about Vee being here.

As Roman passed the rusted mailbox and drew beneath the sheltering boughs of the oak trees lining the drive, Katerina came up to walk beside him, her hands in the pockets of her sweatshirt.

"Do you do this often?" She glanced at him. "Track down kids from the club who run off?"

Every chance I get. "I'm the guy people call." As much as he wanted to tell her why, exactly, he devoted so much of his free time to helping out troubled teenagers, diving too deep into his own personal life might make Kat feel awkward. "Searching for wayward teenagers is my latest hobby."

"You have particular training in that area?" As they walked, her eyes were alert to the trees surrounding them, the driveway bending out of sight ahead. He'd bet she made note of each uneven patch in the drive and potential hiding spots on either side, where an enemy might lay in wait.

"Not precisely. It's more of a passion."

She glanced at him, clearly expecting more.

He hid a sigh. His strategy in earning Katerina's heart banked on laying himself open, handing her the trust card to use however she wanted. If that included baring his soul, he had to take the risk, even if the timing wasn't perfect. "My sister, Irini, is a runaway."

"Oh." Her mouth tightened, and he was thankful she didn't waste time or energy with sympathetic words that offered no solution. "How long has she been gone?"

"Six months."

"Damn."

Exactly the same word he'd used when Irini had screamed at him for some reason he couldn't even recall, proceeded to blame all her unhappiness on him—along with a few uncomplimentary names that lent a questionable light to his role as her guardian and brother, both of which she pegged as 'pushy'—and stormed out. He'd thought she'd blow off some steam, come back when she got hungry and they'd hash it out, hug and put the fight behind them. Instead, he'd lost her. She'd vanished from Graywood or hidden so well that not even the police force could find her. No matter how many nights he'd spent searching for her, speaking to people of all walks of life, roaming in nearby cities, he hadn't found a single clue as to her whereabouts.

His heart twisted. Irini had been seventeen when she'd left and would be eighteen in a few weeks, if she still.... He cut off the thought before it formed. She was headstrong, a rebel and a Farkos—certainly not a victim. Wherever she'd chosen to go, she was undoubtedly surviving.

"So that's your secret, the motivation for your extracurricular activity of strolling the streets in search of homeless teens." None of the typical bite clung to her words.

"Fine investigative work, detective."

They walked in silence for a time, the scuff of their steps and the rain's velvet patter on leaves a gentle backdrop to their journey. The city and all its problems seemed distant, untouchable, and with Katerina beside him, for a lingering moment, the world adjusted into perfect symmetry. He could get used to this—going into battle with her, facing the future together.

"I'll help you," she said into the quiet, her gaze fixed ahead, "on Saturdays. I have nothing better to do, and since you provided me with the one-way street badge of trust, now I feel morally obligated."

"No obligation." He stopped and waited while she paused and faced him. "It's more than a duty, Katerina."

She nodded, her dark eyes solemn. "I want to do it."

"Good." A tightness in his ribs loosened. "Gia will be relieved to know her potato chip stash may live until Sunday."

"No, it won't." Kat smirked and continued walking, and the constant weight of Irini's prolonged absence lightened somewhat.

The trees ended at a rusted iron gate, which was chained and locked. An eight-foot wire fence created to intimidate intruders stretched on either side and a crooked metal sign bearing the faded address on Shadowbrook Drive hung from one stubborn iron pin. Beyond, a glimpse of the institution loomed up within the trees, a monstrosity of boarded-up and broken windows, peeling paint and a sagging roof.

"Shadowbrook. That's not ominous at all. People actually choose to go in there?" Kat peered through the gate bars as if they belonged to a jail cell, not an entrance. "It looks like a horror-movie set. How many people have been murdered within those walls?"

"No one knows." He fished the key from his pocket. "Which is the beauty of it."

"Hell," Kat murmured.

As quietly as he could, Roman unlocked the gate and disentangled the chain from the bars. The hinges creaked as he eased it open.

"Really." Kat slipped through, her gaze on the sprawling building. "This is the portal to some netherworld pit. I'm sure of it."

She reads the best books. He hooked the chain through the bars and left the gate ajar. "Scared, Angel?"

"I'd prefer to be kicking in the door to a drug house with an unknown number of subjects inside." She reached beneath her sweatshirt, pulled her Glock from its holster and released a sigh. "Bring it on, ghosties and goblins, demons and hellhounds."

Laughter curled up from his chest and he couldn't hide a chuckle. "You are surely aware that bullets have no effect on supernatural creatures?"

"Not if they're silver." She frowned. "Or iron. Wood for vampires. You should have provided me full disclosure so I'd be properly armed and prepared."

"If a werewolf brings you down, I'll take the entire blame for it."

"No, you won't. First hint of fur I see, I'm gone at full speed. I only have to outrun you to survive."

"Charitable of you." He stopped beside her. "But for the record, I'd sacrifice myself so you could get away."

"Don't tell me that." A delicate flush crept over her lovely cheekbones, which were on full display with her hair pulled back in its elegant twist. "Then I'd have to go back to get you and would probably wind up with your fate—mauled with my throat ripped out."

"And waste my great and noble sacrifice?" Unable to resist, he traced a raindrop that had gathered at the corner of her mouth with his thumb. He didn't miss the catch of her breath. "I'd want you to live, Katerina. Fully and freely."

Her pupils dilated and her lips parted slightly as he caressed her full lower lip. The fact that she didn't shoot him was encouraging. She blinked rapidly and the spell was broken. Roman dropped his hand.

"I could live fully and freely as a werewolf too," she said, heading slowly toward the chipped and moss-covered concrete steps leading to the institution, the Glock in her hand, pointed safely at the ground. "Just sayin'."

"I'm sure you'd be just as lovely covered in fur."

Time had been unkind to the once-grand building, and since it had received no maintenance or upkeep over the years, it was mildly surprising that the roof hadn't caved in yet. There was no denying that stepping inside was dangerous. Three stories of unkempt rooms, abandoned items from when the institution had been operated and a bell tower that had dropped its bell years ago left all manner of booby traps and accidents waiting to happen.

Weeds and yellow grass choked the curving sidewalk, its pavestones cracked, some of them so badly that they were little more than jagged fragments slowly sinking into the soil. As they drew near, the shadow of the building crept over them, swallowing them in black.

"Vee better be here," Kat muttered, her voice tight, gun raised as she ascended the stairs with careful steps. "If she isn't, I'm going to destroy her."

"Poor girl. Either way, she loses." He stepped over a crunched beer can, its label long ago erased by the sun. "Of course, you'll have to catch her first."

Kat halted at the padlocked door. "Long legs do have an advantage."

He loved her long, shapely legs that were probably useful for other activities besides running, such as wrapping around his waist while he —

"Farkos." The snap in her tone destroyed his fantasy and her scowl kicked it into the dust. "Do you have the key to open the door or not? I do *not* want to still be in there when it gets dark. I didn't bring a flashlight."

As he revealed the key and slid it into the lock, he kept his surprising observations to himself. Katerina was truly nervous. It couldn't be that she was concerned about who might be lurking inside. A nest of drug dealers wouldn't slow her down, and as far as he'd seen, she wasn't a germophobe unwilling to play in the dirt. Anyone who had taken down Mr. Peters so hard wasn't worried about getting hurt.

He glanced at her as he unlatched the padlock. She gazed up at the broken windows of the third floor, her face pale beneath the moist sheen of rain. Her grip on the Glock was bone-white. Could it be the possibility of being in there when night fell that frightened her? *Holy shiznit.* Was fearless Katerina Hellman afraid of the dark?

"You could guard the outside, in case Vee takes off." Even as he said the words, he knew they'd be rejected.

"That would be pointless. The building is too big. I couldn't possibly watch all the exits." She straightened and sucked a breath in through her nose. "You're not going in there alone, Roman. You don't even have a weapon."

"Wrong, Katerina." He flexed his arms. "Didn't you see these guns in all their glory the other night at my house?"

"Nice weapons, but easily broken." She eased the door open, her focus aimed ahead, missing his tiny grin ignited by masculine pride. A compliment from Katerina. Whatever might happen next would be worth the price.

"How is it you have keys to this place, anyway?" she whispered as they entered the foyer. The dull throb of rain on the roof sounded like the echo of a thousand distant heartbeats in the emptiness. Dust layered the parquet flooring, the sweeping bannister granting access to the upper floors and what few glass panes remained. Bruised evening light slanted through the boarded-up windows and elongated shadows of equipment left behind. The space looked more like a hotel than a warehouse or medical facility, thanks to the short time it had been a church.

"The property owner grew tired of the department calling at inconvenient hours. He provided us a set of keys and unlimited permission to enter if we promised to stop checking in with him every time there was a report of suspicious activity."

"Brilliant." Kat nodded without looking at him, taking in her surroundings. "Legal harassment at its best."

"I knew you'd approve."

Colorful candy wrappers and a few empty wine bottles rested on the front desk hulking at the foot of the stairwell, free of dust, an indication of recent visitors. Roman checked behind the counter and found only more garbage.

The institution was the size of a small hospital, with nearly a hundred rooms and abandoned desks, beds, cupboards and equipment to offer concealment. A couple of teenagers could be hiding anywhere. If they wanted to find Vee before she knew they were looking and had time to run, their best strategy was stealth.

"Look." Kat elbowed him, and he followed her gaze. Footprints smudged the grime, aimed toward the stairs — recent, but it was impossible to decipher if they had been made that evening.

"Magnificent. Going up."

"Better than down to the basement." Kat eyed the giant cobweb stretching from the bannister to one of the pillars rising to the ceiling heights. As she moved forward, her boot collided with an object on the floor, which rolled with a metallic clink, glinting in the gloom. She bent and picked it up with a frown. "A strange find in an abandoned building."

The bullet casing in her fingers was a dull bronze, and from the lack of grime, it hadn't been there long. Finding brass was troubling enough, but the weapon using a bullet of that caliber was far from an innocent BB gun or hunting rifle.

"It's a 5.56 NATO round," Kat said, studying the casing. "Probably AR-15 or M16, which isn't the main issue. If the people who come here carry weapons, it's not safe for Vee — or anyone else — to be around." The words had barely left her mouth before she was headed up the stairwell, gun pointed, all fear swept aside, assuming full-out police officer stealth mode.

A bolt of heat shot through him, stringing him up tight. *She's the sexiest woman I've ever known.*

Roman trailed her, and it took every smidge of his substantial willpower to focus on his environment and not Kat's exceptional assets nearly at eye level. The stairs groaned softly beneath their feet, and the emptiness of the institution seemed to stretch with the silence and fading twilight beyond. The trail of footprints they followed continued up to the third floor. He wasn't about to inform Katerina that the third floor, back in its hospital days, had been the mental ward — which was an improvement from the basement, which had served as the morgue and now stored everything from shoeboxes full of outdated medical supplies to naked mannequins left behind by the defunct church's *Stitches for the Streets* group.

Kat paused at the threshold of the top floor and gave each dark hallway a cursory glance, allowing Roman time to catch up.

He leaned near her ear. "There are several wings with dozens of rooms. They all intersect, with a central meeting point at the bell tower. Should we split up?"

She fisted his shirt and dragged him around to face her squarely. "We are *not* splitting up," she snarled in a low voice. "Neither one of us have flashlights. You don't have a weapon. There's too much space." She held the bullet casing in his face. "It's too dangerous."

"I prefer to stay with you, anyway, Angel." Being so close to her, the heat of her hand on his chest, her clean, herbal scent filling his senses, her body a slender but solid force a bare inch away, it was only by some miracle that he resisted taking that step to kill the distance between them, pulling her into his arms and resuming where they'd left off in a tangle of wires and tongues.

Her lips parted slightly and by the way she looked at his mouth — *quarter-point penalty* — she'd turned onto the same track of thought. She drew a rough breath and cleared her throat. "We need to find Vee. Stop messing around."

"You're the one still holding on to me," he murmured, "not that I'd ever complain."

Kat looked down at her hand in his shirt, her expression surprised, as if she hadn't even realized she'd grabbed him. She released him as fast as she'd latched on to him, an unfortunate reaction. He would have happily snuck through every dusty and disturbing room in the institution with her holding on to him as if he was all that kept her grounded.

Roman smoothed out his T-shirt. As much as he wanted to stretch his time with her for as long as possible, Katerina was right. Finding Vee before dark would be ideal. "This way," he said, cocking his head toward the hallway to their right. "There are a couple of rooms that seem to be the favorite hangouts. We'll check those first."

Lifting her gun, her eyes shimmering in the gathering gloom, Kat nodded and followed.

Only a person without any sort of sixth sense wouldn't be at least mildly disturbed by the aura left inhabiting the building, as if the ghosts of long-gone patients still lingered with the ditched hospital beds and oxygen machines. And no, it wasn't creepy at all how a wheelchair lay in wait in the hallway ahead, parked at an angle, half in shadow.

"Hell," Kat whispered behind him. She stayed on his heels, the barrel of her gun pointed safely past his shoulder.

Many of the rooms were empty beyond the dust and grime of years, requiring no more than a quick glance inside to determine they didn't contain flesh and blood. Others needed more of an inspection behind beds with only bare mattresses, around machines draped in cobwebs and inside cupboards to ensure they were indeed unoccupied. The dead quiet that followed them suggested that, despite the footprints, they were utterly alone. None of the rooms where some of the braver homeless and thrill-seeking teenagers had loitered in before held any signs of recent activity. Even the children's ward held only its stash of broken, scattered toys. By the time they returned to the bell tower at the center of the four wings, the sunlight had dwindled to little more than shadows.

Kat lowered her gun, her jaw tight. "They must have left through another door or window." She still spoke in a hush, as if loud voices might carry to ears belonging to the unseen — and not necessarily human. "We would have seen or heard them by now."

As if triggered by her words, a scrape came from above — in the bell tower.

Roman leaned over the railing, looking up. A ladder with several missing rungs rose into the gloom.

"Vee wouldn't be that dumb," Kat whispered, following his gaze. "Would she?" There was another sound from the tower, and she cursed under her breath. "Remind me not to destroy her before giving her a big, sharp piece of my mind first." She grabbed an unbroken rung and began climbing.

As much as he wanted to play the hero, to protect Katerina by putting himself in the line of fire and her behind him, he resisted that urge. Noble intentions or not, she wouldn't appreciate the gesture. If she needed him, she'd let him know. He watched her careful climb, gripping the sides of the ladder from the bottom. In case she stumbled, he'd be there. If she lost her hold, he'd break her fall. He'd catch her, no matter what it cost him.

Kat made it to the top and disappeared into the gloom.

Several seconds passed in silence as he remained looking up, each one driving his heart faster, and only common sense kept him from racing up the ladder as fast as he could to make sure she was okay. There hadn't been a shot. If she'd been attacked, there would be noise. *Give me a clue, Angel.*

Finally, she peeked down from the heights above, her face pale in the shadows. "All clear. Vee's not here, but you should come up."

The hair on the back of his neck stirred. Willing his pulse rate to slow, Roman climbed into the darkness.

Chapter Fourteen

Four windowless openings high in the bell tower faced each direction, offering free access to the last sunlight and the cool air fragrant with rain. A few bird nests inhabited the tower heights, where the heavy bronze bell had once hung. It had fallen some years back, leaving a ragged, dangerous hole in the floor. Somebody had placed a few loose planks across the gash, and Roman couldn't imagine that the owner had done it, considering the unkempt state of the institution. The planks looked as old as the building itself.

As he stepped off the shuddering ladder and onto the floor, the boards groaned and shifted beneath his boots, and he paused, mid-step. The combination of his weight, mildew and decay may prove to be too much for the old tower. Carefully, he circled the hole at a safe distance, keeping close to the sloped ceiling as he maneuvered to where Kat crouched.

She looked up at him, her dark eyes flinty. "I'm guessing ghosts and otherworldly spirits don't require beds."

A stained, twin-sized mattress rested tight against the wall beneath one low, sloping rafter. On top of the mattress, a thin blanket tangled in a half-wadded ball, spotted with bird droppings and a stray feather. Food wrappers and smashed soda cans littered the floor. Glinting among the garbage was a used needle.

"Or fixes beyond fear." He hit the flashlight app on his phone and made a quick sweep, searching for more needles or any other evidence of drugs — used, hidden or otherwise. As the light drifted over the low beam above the makeshift bed, he leaned in closer. The post closest to the mattress appeared worn, as if something attached to it had rubbed at the wood, leaving gouges. He lightly dragged his fingertips over the smoothed track in the wood, a chilled hand clamping his nape. Not only had someone been in the bell tower, but they'd been held here, possibly chained.

And all he could think of was Irini, alone in the world, missing, no matter how hard he searched, gone because he'd pushed instead of letting go.

"Hey, Roman." Kat's soft voice pulled him back to the present. She looked up at him with something dangerously close to concern. "The residue in the needle should be tested. I doubt you'll get any viable fingerprints, but you could try. If I had some gloves, I'd take it with us." She huffed out a breath. "I guess we'll have to come back."

"I'll be back, but not necessarily for the needle." He handed her a pair of latex gloves from his pocket. This was probably the remnants of a temporary hideout used by a homeless person who'd managed to score some drugs—or maybe even a place Vee and her friends had used at some point. He resisted looking at the gouged wood again.

Kat gave him a peculiar look. "You don't carry a weapon with you off-duty, but you keep purple latex gloves in your pocket?"

"One can never be too prepared, Angel."

"Your idea of being prepared clearly isn't the same as mine."

"Another reason why we make a great team." He took a picture of the needle among the scattered cans and gave in to the pull to examine the scarred post again. "What is your professional assessment of this?"

"It's a secluded place with little chance of being found." She slipped on the gloves, carefully picked up the needle and dropped it into an empty soda can. "I'd say someone believed they'd scored. A quiet, dry, relatively safe place to lay low for as long as they wanted and do whatever they wanted while here without much worry of being caught." She stood, the can in her gloved hand. "And they were obviously right."

"What about this?" He shone the light from his cellphone on the worn post.

Katerina bent near, her brow furrowed.

From one of the floors below, feminine voices drifted up, followed by the laughter of two teenage girls who had no clue they weren't alone in an off-limits place.

Kat met Roman's gaze. "Now that I know she's safe, first I'm going to kill her, then I'm going to destroy what's left of her." She tiptoed toward the ladder, the can carrying the needle in her grip. "After that, she's getting a long, sharp lecture on running off and the dangers of being in abandoned places."

"I thought you were only going to kill her if you didn't find her here." Roman took pictures of the mattress, the floor and the post before following her.

"I lied." She paused at the head of the ladder and her smile held a hint of evil. "Let's surprise them, shall we?"

The chill on Roman's neck fell away. When she smiled like that, as if nothing could stop her, and woe to anyone who stood in her path, he was completely lost to her all over again.

Vee and her companion weren't hard to track. Their loud voices, laughter and an occasional shriek followed by a giggle echoed in the empty halls. Kat insisted on a quick stop at the children's ward along the way, where she selected an instructional tool or two. They halted on the second-floor landing and peered around the corner.

The glow of two flashlights bobbed closer, like laser pointers in the gloom. The growing darkness couldn't hide Vee's sturdy form and sleek, black hair in French braids. The girl walking beside her wasn't like Derick had described, and since Roman didn't recognize her, he doubted she resided in Graywood — at least not permanently. She carried a backpack on her slender shoulder, her dishwater-blonde hair a dull gleam. If Vee had left with one shady person and wound up at the institution with another, what had happened in the hours between then and now, and why hadn't she gone home or at least checked in?

Kat lifted a finger to her lips, signaling silence. Her face was flushed, her eyes bright — she was obviously enjoying putting her diabolical plan into action. She hefted the dusty, half-flat rubber ball she'd found in the children's ward and — evil grin on full display — tossed it gently into the hallway.

All talk and footsteps stopped, and for a split-second, the only sound was the slow, lop-sided roll of the ball over the grit lining the floor. Shrieks erupted, ringing to the rafters in an ear-splitting echo, and the drill of feet running the other direction completely camouflaged Kat's muffled laughter.

Roman watched her, straight-faced, as she doubled over and held her ribs with one hand, her mouth with the other. Tears leaked from her eyes. He waited until she straightened, her shoulders still shaking. "You're a fiend."

"I know! Did you see their faces?" She barely got the words out before she clapped both hands over her mouth and the humor routine started all over again.

Settling in to wait, he leaned one shoulder against the wall and tucked his hands into his pockets. Witnessing Katerina lose her composure — due to a prank on wayward teenagers, no less — was intoxicating and made him wonder about what other depths she hid from the world. That she shared this brief window into herself and what made her laugh felt like a minor miracle. It both warmed him and awakened a terrible yearning for more of her.

No, not *more* — all of her. He wanted to know everything, from her favorite flavor of pie to her darkest fear. He wanted to be the one she felt safe enough with to be completely open about her flaws and failures, dreams and triumphs. He suspected she didn't let many people into that space, which merely meant he'd treasure it that much more when he got there.

"We should probably track them down before they disappear. Don't you agree?" Roman pushed from the wall as Kat straightened once again, tears of laughter shimmering in her eyes.

"Sure," she said, breathless. "One second." She jogged around the corner and returned with the dusty rubber ball beneath her arm. "I may need this later."

"It's only now that I've fully realized how terrifying you are." He descended the stairs with her at a companionable pace. "And you don't even have your weapon out."

She slid him a sly look. "There's nothing more satisfying than blowing people's expectations to smithereens, with or without my favorite guns."

"Consider me duly impressed yet again by all that is Katerina Hellman."

Her smile faded, and he instantly regretted the words, true though they were. If he didn't turn the subject away from her fast, his odds of convincing her to stay with him longer tonight shrank to minimal. Pie had proved to be only semi-effective, and Katerina remained stubbornly unaffected by nearly all that was Roman Farkos. And peeling his shirt off right now would be too suspicious. Their next challenge wouldn't be until the following week, on her schedule, at her whim. He wasn't ready to let her go, and after examining the beam of the bell tower and the gouges possibly caused by a chain, the raw wound in his chest that had been there since Irini had left ached. He couldn't return to an empty house, consumed by all the terrible situations his sister might be in.

"What I wonder most is how Gia survived her childhood with three older siblings who raise hell and sip on fear for fun." At her responsive smile, he breathed a silent sigh of relief. "She seems quite mentally stable, all things considered."

"Until you insult her shoes." Kat's shoulders relaxed. "Then, watch out. She's the worst of the Hellmans."

While Gia had her own methods of taking people down, he couldn't imagine she could come close to her sister. "I appreciate the sacrifice you made in ditching your family dinner to come with me tonight."

Katerina snorted. "I'm sure Gia has told you that my relationship with the esteemed Caroline Hellman is complicated."

"Gia and I do have other discussion topics beyond you and your family." He added some insult to his tone. "Believe it or not."

"Not." She huffed out a breath. "Gia is the daughter mom always wanted, and Gia is so smooth and cute that she slithered out of the future mom hoped for her without any hard feelings or disappointment."

"Politician's wife, world-changing socialite, Miss USA?"

"Living the dream," she said flatly. "I'd rather be traipsing through a scary abandoned building full of ghosts and goblins with you than having a formal dinner with mother while choking over the doting-on-her-favorite-daughter any day."

"I can't decide if that's a compliment to my dazzling charm or a snub."

She canted her head, as if pretending to think about it, and when she looked at him, mischief sparkled in her eyes and his heart forgot to beat. "Maybe a bit of both."

"Half a flattery from Katerina?" He nodded. "I'll take it."

"Don't get used to it." The small smile she wore made his blood sing.

"Oh, I *will*. I plan to weasel more accolades and utterly deserved fawning until you can't help but pay homage to me."

Kat stopped suddenly, each boot on a different step, and pivoted to face him. "I don't know if Gia put you up to this or not and, really, it doesn't matter." In the shadows, her skin glowed, luminescent, and a few strands of sleek hair had escaped from her updo to frame her cheek. "I can't remember the last time I had this much fun...with anyone."

"Tonight isn't Gia's doing." He couldn't help himself. Roman stepped close and gently tucked her hair behind her ear. Keeping his touch light, he caressed her jaw and cupped her face with one hand. When she leaned into his palm instead of moving away, his pulse pounded harder, faster. "Whether or not you see it, you affect people, Katerina, and I'm not speaking of the skills you've practiced and honed over the years. You're not like Gia and I'm grateful for that. There are some types of people who are drawn to Gia and what she represents, while others, such as me —" he brushed his lips over hers once, soft and teasing, "respond to the brilliance in you. Value can't be regulated by the number of those people who are drawn to you, only the response. You don't have to be like anyone else to be perfect just as you are."

"Charming *and* a conveyer of personal wisdom? Be still my heart." Whatever snark she'd hoped to convey failed beneath the breathlessness in her voice and her glittering gaze fixed on his mouth. "But you were friends with Gia before meeting me."

The hint of vulnerability in her tone killed him. How could she even compare herself to Gia or doubt for a second how amazing she was on every level? "Not really. We formed a bond over our mutual admiration for Ian. She admires him in much different manners than I do, in case you're wondering." Since she remained within kissing distance, he pressed his mouth to hers again, lingering a second longer than before. "I knew from the very beginning that you weren't like anyone else."

"Because of how I look." Her statement was soft, hinting at a wound long ago scarred over, accepted and endured. "What I can do."

"I'd be lying if I said I wasn't insanely attracted to you physically, but it's deeper than that. It goes beneath your shooting skills and how seamlessly you flow from snarky beauty queen into television detective mode at the first sign of trouble — which, in and of themselves, would have been enough to interest me." He held her gaze. "What I'm going to say next might sound deranged and merely confirm your assessment that I'm off-the-charts weird, but the potential pay-off is worth the risk." Roman drew a deep, shuddering breath and released it. "The second you parted the sea of sequins and tuxedos last month at the Senior Center fundraiser, I was irreversibly undone. I'm not saying it makes any sense, because it doesn't. I wasn't expecting you and yet, at the same time, I recognized that I had been waiting...waiting for you, even while I hadn't realized I'd been waiting at all."

She pursed her lovely lips, eased out of his gentle hold and continued down the stairwell at a slow, thoughtful pace, while his heart hammered a ragged beat. He gripped the handrail and followed. In one fell, ill-advised lack of judgment swoop, he'd pushed her away by being too honest. *I'm an idiot.*

"You're right about one thing, at least," Katerina finally said. She glanced at him, her expression neutral. "Off-the-charts weird."

Roman forced his attention away from her and to the institution door. He'd never been the woman magnet Ian was or personably popular like Gia, and that had never bothered him. He ranked somewhere in the middle when it came to appearance, made friends easily enough and scored as much as he struck out in the romance department. But swinging and missing with Kat opened a pit in his stomach. Now that he'd found her, losing her was unthinkable.

They made it to the first floor with its desk and the once-upon-a-time grand foyer fallen into decay. Beyond their footprints and those of Vee and her friend entering, there weren't any more, which meant the girls had departed the way they'd come in — probably through the basement. No matter how many times the outside hurricane doors had been repaired, every time the department received a notification of suspicious activity, that was where the damage was usually found.

At the institution door, Kat spun again so suddenly that he bumped into her and had to grasp her arms to keep from knocking them both over. In regaining his balance, he wound up pushing her back against the door, his body flush with hers.

For a moment, neither one of them moved. Her heat seeped through his damp T-shirt and warmed his skin. Her sweet herbal scent filled his lungs, intoxicating, while the soft exhale from her lips brushed his chin.

"I promised Gia I'd try to be nice, so I was just going to say that I get where you're coming from, at least a little bit." She reached for his face, hesitated, and he held his breath. When she trailed his jaw with her fingertips, it took all his willpower not to close his eyes and simply savor the unexpected sensation of her touch. "You're a symbol of everything I don't want."

He blinked. *Not quite the confirmation I hoped for.*

"You're a cop—been there, regretted that." She watched her finger slide over his five o'clock shadow to his chin. "You're too much like my family members, turning even the simplest, most mundane tasks into a competition."

"Nothing wrong with adding a touch of excitement, is there?" His breath caught as she ran her finger along the curve of his bottom lip, bringing everything to aching life from his mouth to his toes.

"Just as wrong as wanting a moment of simplicity," she said, her gaze on his mouth. "This spark or competition or whatever you want to call it between us is simple, easily explained. It's fascination, brought to life in a moment and quick to end." Her dark lashes lifted and the heat in her eyes burned. "Maybe we should just" —she shrugged— "get it over with, out of our systems. If we go with it instead of fighting it, we'll resolve the situation faster and go back to business as usual."

Roman took her face between his hands and stroked her cheekbones with his thumbs. "My sweet, snarly Angel. We'll have to agree to disagree on this subject. Going back is impossible." Before she could reply, he pressed his mouth to hers and kissed her like it was a lazy Sunday morning, as if they had all the time in the world and he planned to take every second exploring how she tasted, the sensation of her body beneath his hands, her silken hair in his fingers.

He didn't care what she chose to call the heat between them—infatuation, lust, a minor switch in sanity — but she was wrong if she believed the emotions burning between them would fade or that they could ever revert to a casual, professional relationship, and he'd do everything in his power to prove it to her.

Chapter Fifteen

Kat closed her eyes, gripped Roman's damp shirt with both fists and held on for dear life. At the diner a few nights before, while he'd been interrogating her for his stupid competition, she'd thought he'd pulled out all the stops when he'd kissed her.

She'd been absolutely, one hundred percent dead wrong about that one.

Hell, he was magnificent, stealing her senses with only his mouth and controlling her in ways she'd never known were possible. Each slide of his tongue and gentle nip of teeth lured her deeper into his web. She was a willing victim, lost to his spell, even while a tiny part of her dazzled mind whispered that consequences awaited when she came up for air again.

Screw the consequences. She'd never responded to another human being this way—all sparks, fire and desperate wanting. Buried beneath it, a quiet hum rang deep inside, as if with Roman and in his arms was exactly where she was supposed to be. She slipped her hands around his neck and pressed closer, her body aligning with his from thighs to shoulders, a direct connection to his hardness and heat.

Roman groaned into her mouth and angled his head, taking the kiss deeper, and the thread of control she'd still managed to hold on to snapped. With a little jump, she wrapped her legs around his hips and clung to him like he was the one giant tree still standing in a raging storm. She wasn't surprised when he held her, strong and steady.

"Katerina." He said her name like a prayer, full of wonder, as he scattered lingering kisses along her throat, and damn it all if she didn't melt more under his adoration. "You destroy me."

No, not destroy. More like consumed, body and soul. She ran her fingers through his short hair and tried to catch her breath. All this time, she'd been shortchanging herself with Vic. Not once had her body roared to life beneath his touch. Never had she wholly surrendered to sensation, forgotten to worry if she might be using her hands wrong or if she should use more tongue and be softer, more feminine. Roman liberated her from a cage that she'd become far too comfortable with, a trap she'd been in so long she'd accepted it as unchangeable.

A scream from outside, distant and shrill, cut through the sensual haze, sharp as a sword. Neither one of them said a word as they separated and barreled out of the door, into the evening rain.

Still breathing hard, her gun out, Kat searched the grounds. The driveway was empty to where it curved out of sight. No teenagers were visible among the trunks and shrubbery of the overgrown woods. It was impossible to tell which direction the scream had come from.

"We should split up." Roman looked to the west, where the eaves met with the trees. He didn't wait for her answer, jogging away into the gloom, not that she was offended. He was right, and she didn't mind going solo. Being outside the walls of the institution gave her an irrational sense of safety.

There had to be another entry point in the direction Roman had disappeared, the same way Vee and her companion had fled, but if she was a freaked-out teenage girl, she wouldn't head into the woods as night descended, where all sorts of creatures could be hiding, waiting for an easy victim. She'd go for the road and civilization.

Keeping to a brisk walk, Kat's boots clicked a steady beat on the pavestones. Guilt curled in her gut, competing with the gasoline in her blood left by Roman's kiss. Maybe she shouldn't have pranked Vee. It had been so long since she'd even had the urge to be playful, to tease someone. Her freakin' ribs still ached from laughing so hard. She wasn't like normal people when making friends — her mark of approval included first sarcasm, then teasing — but if Vee wound up being hurt because of her prank...

Movement glimmered through the limbs and leaves ahead as Kat approached the chain link fence, ghosting out of sight at the road. Roman had left the chain loose and now the gate was ajar, an indication that someone else had come back through.

Kat picked up the pace. Hopefully, that person had been Vee, on the move and not writhing in a ditch somewhere with a broken leg — or worse. The needle, the bullet casing and the worn post in the bell tower rolled through her mind, pieces of a puzzle in need of solving. Whatever had recently happened in the solemn silence of the institution, it hadn't been good. Knowing that Vee had been anywhere near that scene made her chest constrict. Foster kids, especially ones who had never fit with the right family, were vulnerable to the dregs of society. Graywood was a small town, where people seemed more willing to socialize than hide behind their fences, but small didn't correlate with completely safe. There would always be vermin of the human type waiting to manipulate any opportunity.

She strode through the gate, leaving it open, and jogged to the end of the driveway. Walking on the side of the road, headed toward the city, a girl dressed all in black was hunched in her hoodie.

Relief washed through her, replaced by fury. "Valerie!"

Valerie spun, paused and, after a marked hesitation, trudged back toward her.

Kat slipped her gun in the holster beneath her sweatshirt and met her halfway. "What are you doing out here?" An accusing growl thundered in her words.

"It's a free country and curfew isn't for another three hours." Cocking her hip, Vee popped her gum. She looked Kat up and down, from her boots to the twist of her hair. "What are *you* doing out here?"

"Went for a long walk." Kat lifted her chin in challenge at the doubtful arch of the girl's eyebrow. "I like walking in the rain. It's my thing." Vee would probably put two and two together, but until she did, she wasn't going to cough up to scaring her in the institution. It would save her a ton of trouble if she remained wary of that place, even if it took a phantom or fake fright.

"Boring much?" Vee blew a pink bubble.

"Idiot much?" She ignored the girl's glare. "Usually, when people don't show up where and when they're supposed to, other people get worried. Some of those other people traipse out into the rain and dark, looking in ditches and unsavory places, hoping they don't find anything there."

Vee shrugged. "Don't get your panties in a knot because of me, Pageant Queen."

I'm seriously going to kill her. Kat counted to five, leashing her fury, before answering. "Leave my choice in underwear out of this. I don't like being unnecessarily worried about people I care for. There's this invention referred to as a phone. If you don't feel like going home, call me. We'll play video games and gorge on pizza until we figure it out."

"You don't care about me." Vee snorted. "You hardly even know me and I didn't sign up for the Big Sister program."

"Don't tell me what I do or don't care about, Gherig Girl." She leaned in, adding enough ice to her tone to freeze Valerie's eyebrows off. "Newsflash... Not everything's about you. Maybe you're not looking for a big sister, but as much as I love my baby sis Gia, she's the complete opposite of me, the perfect princess and daughter. Finding another girl that I actually get along with who is more into sports than dolls or purses? That doesn't happen every day, if ever."

Vee looked away. Her mouth pressed into a tight line, but her chin trembled.

"Do you really think I'd be out here if I didn't care? I could be sprawled on the couch eating potato chips, watching lame action movies and adding people who annoyed me to my hit list. I decided I liked you better than that, so here I am, looking in weird places for my *Donkey Kong* partner." She swallowed past the sawdust in her throat. "Worried about the second younger sister I thought I'd never have."

Vee stopped chewing her gum, and when she spoke, her voice was small. "Really?"

The vulnerability in her expression threatened to kill Kat, and it took all her effort to keep her voice steady, to not let on how deeply it struck home. She knew exactly what it felt like to be found wanting. "Hell yeah, really. Do you know how rare you are—a girl who won't take any crap, can show up the boys on the field and can almost beat me at Mario Kart?" Giving in to an uncharacteristic urge, she dragged Vee into an embrace and held her tight. "Don't go AWOL on me again."

For a second, Vee's arms went around her in a vise, then, as if realizing what she was doing, she struggled to escape. "Let me go." Laughter shimmered in her voice. "Freak."

"Punk."

Vee stuck out her tongue.

"Next free day, we're having a self-defense lesson. Do you know how many creeps could be out here? What they could do if they found a girl walking alone?"

"I can take care of myself."

"And we're going to make regular visits to the range. No arguments." Kat ignored Vee's annoyed expression. "You need to learn firsthand about gun safety and how very dangerous they can be. I prefer that you keep clear altogether, but it's better to know what to do if you come across one."

"Too late, PQ. Mr. Crocker, foster father number seven, is a range member. Family rules required a field trip to the range and a safety lecture that went on for so long I thought I'd die." Vee slipped her hands into her hoodie pockets. "I have zero interest in guns and I won't go through that craptastic information session again. You're not my guardian, so you can't make me."

"Don't be a brat, and I'd never force you to do anything. But I'm at the range almost every day if you change your mind."

The cadence and crunch of someone running in the gravel alongside the road pulled Kat around. Roman jogged toward them, and her mouth went dry. In the growing gloom, clad in black, he resembled Hades slipping free of the underworld to wage war, shadows curling and dancing around him.

A strange jolt rattled through her, a sense of déjà vu, as if Roman carried her destiny along with him, hurling it at her like an unstoppable spear. She watched him approach, frozen, torn between running away and flinging herself at him. If she held on to him, she'd have to deal with the fallout when he realized she wasn't what he thought and let her go.

"Valerie." Roman swept past Kat without slowing and plowed into the girl, lifting her off her feet and swinging her in the air. "You're safe."

Vee shrieked, a mixture of surprise and laughter, and pounded on his back. "You belong together. You're all freaks. Put me down!"

After another full-circle swing, Roman obeyed and stepped back. He was breathing hard, as if he'd sprinted for a mile, and his eyes glittered. "Sorry. Got caught up in the moment."

The coals still swirling through Kat changed, softening into warm and sweet. Roman truly cared about Vee. Finding her wasn't a duty to him, part of his job — whether or not he was technically on the clock. He hadn't used his free time to track her down for a sense of glory or future recognition at the department, maybe a letter in his file to give him a leg up in the next promotion. That had been Vic's MO — a façade of caring when he was more about being recognized as one of the good guys, a spike in his pride, a tool to use in moving up the power ladder with his sights set on lieutenant, captain then chief.

Roman wasn't even in the same category as Vic and that knowledge rattled the lock on her heart.

He placed his hands on his hips like a mother scolding her wayward child, and Kat might have laughed if she wasn't still dazzled. "What were you thinking, coming out here without telling anyone — ?"

"Save it." Vee lifted her hand in the universal sign for *shut your face*. "I already got the lecture from Cover Girl."

In an unusual display of facial expression, Roman narrowed his eyes. "I heard you scream."

"That wasn't me, and next time I'll call before going for a long walk in the rain."

Both Roman and Kat stared at her, waiting for the truth.

"Fine." She huffed out a breath. "I was hanging with a friend in the deserted building over there." She waved a hand vaguely in the direction of the institution. "We lost track of time. My phone died because I forgot to charge it the previous night. Satisfied?"

"What friend?" Roman asked in his monotone. He looked around, as if expecting someone to pop up from the ditch with a wave of greeting.

"No one you know." Vee snapped her gum. "Her friends picked her up and they had a stupid tickling match. That was why she screamed."

"Try me. I know everyone."

"She's not from Graywood, okay? And I don't have to explain anything to you."

"True." Roman shrugged. "But you will to Mr. and Mrs. Crocker and your caseworker, if they decide to involve her."

Vee's mouth hardened into a line. "Whatever. I just needed a bit of fun. Is that a crime?"

"Sometimes." Roman pivoted toward where he'd parked Marta. "Come on. I'll give you ladies a ride home."

"Ladies," Vee scoffed.

Kat slung an arm around the girl's shoulders and guided her forward. "Doyennes, thank you very much."

Roman faced them, walking slowly backward, and she'd swear in the dim light he almost smiled. "I was being polite and refrained from calling you both a very appropriate 'termagant'."

"I prefer 'vituperator'."

"You're both beyond weird." Vee made a face of disgust.

"Limited edition," Roman said solemnly, just as Kat said, "Thank you."

"Gross." Vee shrugged Kat's arm from her shoulders and increased her pace. "Get a room."

Kat didn't miss the hot glint in Roman's eyes as he met her gaze for a lingering moment then turned back around. Sharing a room with Hades in the flesh might not be the worst idea for a girl to get rid of a bad case of fascination, because no matter what Roman thought or how much he disagreed, the tension strung between them would never be more than temporary intrigue.

Not even a clarified moment of destiny could change that.

Chapter Sixteen

Waiting for the club to close, Kat sat beside Vee on the gymnasium floor and forced her hands to relax. Ten more minutes and she'd be alone again with Roman for their next challenge. She couldn't decide if the thrill traveling through her nerves was of anticipation or dread.

A little sigh came from Vee, and Kat followed her line of sight to where Derick and Roman played one-on-one basketball in the otherwise-empty gym. Their sneakers squeaked with every switch in direction and the rapid dribbling of rubber on wood echoed to the high ceiling, a constant auditory barrage. Crushing on an oblivious boy was some sort of life-orchestrated teenage-girl torture, even more painful for Vee, temporarily stuck in transition between tomboy and future doyenne.

Doyenne. Kat had learned that word from a female self-defense instructor at the academy on day one. Definition—a woman who was the most respected

215

person in a particular field—and that was after her teacher had kicked every single student's butt one after another, men and women alike. 'Doyenne' was a perfect description, and she hoped Vee would figure out it could apply to her, too, whether or not she won anyone's affection.

Roman threw the ball above Derick's skinny, outstretched arms and swished the ball through the hoop. Several days had passed since the institution, and doyenne or not, Kat still hadn't managed to push away the memory of Roman's hard, strong body pressing into hers, how the silken slide of his tongue had awakened every sense and left her wanting more, more, *more*. Kat pressed her knees together and gritted her teeth as her body throbbed in remembrance. She might be too far gone to help herself, but maybe she could be useful and save Vee some future boy trouble.

"Listen up, Vee." She gave the girl a light elbow jab in the ribs. "Just because Roman is kind of cute in a tall, dark and pale way, doesn't burn your eyes when you look at him and he makes you feel like you're the most important person in the world when he talks to you, it doesn't mean he's all that." She managed to keep both her tone and expression neutral. Roman's methods were rubbing off on her.

Vee gave Kat a look of horror. "Roman? Ewwww. Gross." She drew out the word, making it sound like *guh-ross*. "He's like fifty or something. Disgusting."

"Oh, right. Disgusting old man. What was I thinking?" *Rude*. Thirty was *not* the new fifty. Hell, she was only a few years from thirty. Kat returned to studying Roman, her blood heating another degree. 'Disgusting' wasn't even close. The nylon shorts and sleeveless black T-shirt he wore clung to his lean lines, leaving most of his muscles on display. She'd spent far too much time fantasizing about the kiss in the diner — and in the institution, backed up against the door, his heat and hardness turning her molten. Meanwhile, Vee had been dreaming of Derick...hopefully without as much detail.

Kat snorted softly. *We're both pathetic.* "If I were your age — and not as close to ancient — I might think Derick's not bad. He plays decent softball, even if he misses most of his shots at basketball."

"I guess." Vee shrugged, playing it cool.

"Take it from me," Kat said, keeping her voice low, "if you like a boy, sometimes you just have to come right out and tell him. Otherwise, he probably won't get it."

Vee frowned, her eyes narrowed, as if scheming how to best tell Derick that she liked him — probably by tackling him. She shook her head as a flush crept over her cheekbones. "What if he doesn't like me?"

"It's a gamble." Kat toyed with the shoelaces of her Converse, her own version of playing it cool. "If the feelings aren't mutual, it might sting, but then you know and won't waste more time on a worthless cause." She gave Vee another elbow-poke. "Besides, if he doesn't like you, he's an irreparable idiot. I mean, what's not to like? You're smart, sassy and pretty enough for any pageant. It's better to figure out his mental capacity sooner rather than later. Trust me on that one."

Vee folded her arms and slouched. "All boys are idiots."

"Good point."

They both fell into silence, each watching their own crush in action. Despite Kat's offer to help Roman out on Saturday to comb the streets for kids in need and maybe find some hint as to his sister's fate in the process, his usual partner had shown up. Instead, she'd spent her weekend doing her best to avoid Caroline and hanging out with Vee. She was surprised Vee wasn't sick of her company yet.

"If I was as old as dirt—like you," Vee grinned, malicious, "Roman might not be the worst choice you could make. At least he has all his teeth and doesn't require a walker."

"Are you absolutely certain he has all his teeth? He never smiles. I'm suspicious." But tonight, she'd find out for sure. Her challenge plan would make sure of it.

Vee frowned at Roman as he whirled around Derick, made another basket and slapped the boy on the back, merciless. "If he didn't have teeth, he wouldn't be able to eat as much as he does."

"Also true."

From the doorway, Derick's mother whistled at him and the ball game was officially over. Derick gave Roman a high-five and jogged out of the door. He paused and pivoted long enough to wave goodbye to Kat and Vee. When he was out of sight, Vee sighed again.

Perfect timing. The club closed in five. Kat had been counting down the minutes upon arrival, ridiculously excited to hit Roman with her challenge. That was the only reason her nerves were strung tight and giddiness threatened her control. *A crush, that's all it is between us—fun, explode and done.*

"Want a ride home?" Kat stood, held out a hand to Vee and heaved her up.

"I think I can handle the two blocks between here and there without getting lost or kidnapped." Vee pulled her hood up over her French braids and stuffed her hands into her front pockets. "But if anyone offers me candy from a windowless white van, no promises."

"Not funny." Kat joined her on the way to the door, hyperaware of Roman stowing the basketball on the shelf. "Stuff like that actually happens. If a vehicle slows down near you, go in the opposite direction."

"Seriously?" Vee's dark eyes gleamed in the shadows of her hood. "I'd be such a bad hostage that my kidnapper would pay you to come get me." She continued on, out of the door and into the hall, wriggling her fingers in farewell. "Call me if you're bored or need to escape Mother Hitler Hellman. Take it easy, Grandma."

"Punk." Kat grinned at Vee's back.

"Ready to go, Katerina?" Roman's gravelly voice pulled her around and —*son of a jerkface*— her pulse skyrocketed at his closeness, his spicy-sweet holiday aroma invading her lungs. "I'm all aflutter wondering how you're going to challenge me tonight. And since you agreed to food, the anticipation is killing me." He rubbed his flat belly. "I'm famished."

"All aflutter?"

"You know, in a dither." He kicked the gymnasium lights off. "But in a good way."

"I don't want to know where you get your vocabulary."

"I read the best books." He shut the door behind them and locked it.

"Do they have sword fights, hot heroes and supernatural creatures from the underworld in need of being destroyed?"

He looked at her sharply. "Have you been spying on me, Angel? If so, I approve."

"I'm not that desperate." *Yet.* And the fact that he *did* read those kinds of books dragged her an inch closer to doing something stupid. She kept going at a quick pace before she changed her mind, crowded him up against the wall and kissed him silly. She had a challenge to win and wouldn't let him distract her.

"You're going to love where I'm taking you." By the closeness of his voice, he'd caught up to her with his long stride. "And worry not — pie is included."

Kat couldn't hold back a little laugh, surprised how natural and easy it came. Not even two weeks had passed since starting the temp job in Graywood, dealing with Roman and already it felt like she'd been settled here for...ever. She slowed enough for him to kill the distance between them. Running was pointless, as he was providing transportation. Maybe it had been a sign of weakness to let him choose the location and bring food along, as if this were a real date, but she was having a hard time caring.

Fifteen minutes later — after a quick stop at Franny's diner, where Roman emerged with a picnic basket that undoubtedly contained some flavor of pie — Roman eased a sputtering Marta onto a narrow dirt road, rough and rutted. He stopped to unlock a crooked gate barring their path and hopped back in before continuing onward. Trees crowded either side, scraping against the windows and sides of the truck. Marta's paintjob left something to be desired, so she supposed he wasn't too worried about any damage.

The woods added a layer of darkness to twilight and Kat had the strangest sensation that they had drifted from reality into one of the fantasy worlds she loved to read about. Ferns and moss carpeted the space between the trees, gathering around fallen logs, moss hanging from bent branches like pale, scraggly beards. A dragonfly flitted past her window, glowing sapphire blue. As much as she wanted to ask where he was taking her, she didn't want to ruin the unexpected, fragile web of magic.

The road curved and the trees broke into a small clearing of grass and wildflowers on the edge of a small lake. Roman put Marta into Park and turned the engine off.

"We're here." He didn't make any move to exit, as if giving her a chance to let it soak in.

She'd been to lakes before, of course. Growing up in a big city didn't mean her family never went on vacation or spent an occasional summer weekend at a rented lake house. But this space was different from any resort or human-harnessed body of water. With the exception of the one-lane path leading in, there were no signs that people came here often, if at all—no trash or structures, only nature undisturbed. Pale light shimmered over the lake like glass on ice, highlighting a few insects skipping along its surface. The surrounding forest held secrets and shadows. Only the gently sloping bank where they'd parked had any grass to speak of, the others ending abruptly at the trees, eroding banks held up by a knotted braid of gnarled roots.

"It's even better up close," Roman whispered. He leaned near, one hand on the picnic basket nestled on the bench seat between them, pulling Kat's attention to him. His eyes glittered with unspoken words as he briefly looked at her mouth. Then he was out of the truck, the basket swinging from his long fingers, headed for the passenger side.

"Hell," she muttered to the emptiness of the cab, her resistance crumbling. She couldn't let him distract her, at least not until the challenge was over with another triumphant win in her column.

After two tries, Roman hauled the passenger door open and offered her his hand. "My doyenne." Humor gleamed in his eyes. "As you've rejected the term 'lady'."

"You're learning, Farkos." After a hesitation, she took his hand and hopped out. When he turned her hand over and pressed a kiss to the pulse at her wrist, her breath caught. She covered it with a scowl. "Distraction attempts are futile."

"Are you challenging me yet again, Katerina?"

"That's not a challenge. It's fact." She pulled free of his loose hold, ignoring how his skin sliding on hers sparked electricity in her nerves. "There's only a miniscule possibility you'll win today. If you surrender now, it will save some time."

"When it comes to you, Angel, I'll never surrender." Holding her gaze, he leaned close. He tucked a loose strand of hair behind her ear and glided his fingertips over her cheek, soft as butterflies, drifting to the corner of her mouth, and her heart kicked into a trot. "But if I lose, at least it won't be on an empty stomach." He headed for the grass.

Kat bit back a curse, following, her lips tingling at the denial. He was absolutely trying to distract her. Worse, it was working.

Bypassing where Roman tugged a blanket from the basket, she wandered to the edge of the water. Despite the sun being down, late July heat warmed the still air. Beyond a few chirping crickets from across the lake, a deep quiet shrouded the clearing, as if this truly was a world separate from the mundane struggles of life. She used to hate being alone, coming home after a long day of work, passing Vic along the way and finding herself in a cocoon of silence. She'd leave the television on just to fill the house with some noise, give the impression that she wasn't completely separate from everything and everyone. Every light in the house stayed bright and burning until morning.

She lifted her gaze to the sky, where the first star gleamed. All those years, she'd been lonely. Even married, surrounded by her family — both by blood and in uniform — she'd never quite fit. But here in this secluded place, with Roman, all her inadequacies and failures drifted into the ether. She should be terrified. Instead, she sat down, took off her shoes and socks and rolled her jeans to her knees.

The water was cool and refreshing on her skin. Smooth pebbles and mud cushioned her feet as she waded calf-deep into the lake. She took a deep breath and released it, so unaccustomed to the sense of peace that she barely recognized it.

"Katerina." Roman stood at the edge of the water and held out a beer bottle to her, luring her back.

They sipped in silence for a few moments, Kat with her feet in the lake, Roman a step behind her on the grass. The quiet lap of water pulled her deeper into the magic of the secluded location, and she had a sudden urge to lean back against Roman, let him wrap his arms around her and hold her until night had fallen — maybe even longer.

The whisper of sliding cloth made Kat glance over her shoulder and she swallowed hard. Roman dragged his shirt over his head and tossed it onto the bank. Holding her gaze like a new challenge, his eyes gleaming with amusement, he kicked off his shoes and socks with hers.

She'd resolved long ago to never put any stock in another person's outward appearance, but...*hell*. He was finely built and he knew it affected her. *The sneaky bastard.* She took a long draw from her bottle, the beer a balm on her dry throat.

"It's hot," he said, as if he needed to explain. "If shirts weren't required at the club, I would have taken it off earlier." He strolled past her only a couple of steps, the water rising to his thighs in an obvious drop-off. "To give you more glorious skin to ogle while I played basketball."

Kat sputtered on her beer and wiped her mouth with the back of her hand. "Your humility is impressive." She tossed the empty bottle onto the bank beside his shirt and their mingled shoes. "And staring, appalled by your corpse-pale skin glaring in the lights, isn't the same as ogling—"

She yelped as he swung her up and heaved her into the air. With nothing to hold on to, she plunged beneath the surface. Luckily for Roman, the water was deep enough that she didn't hit the bottom when she landed, but shallow enough that she found her footing fast. She burst up, gasping, her hair in her eyes.

Roman's laughter skipped over the water, echoing, and she could barely make sense of it. She'd never heard him laugh before, which hadn't been particularly shocking since he refused to smile, and she hadn't thought much about it. Now, she'd never forget it. The sound was so open and sincere that holding on to any anger at being both taken unaware and man-handled in the same second was impossible. It made her want to join in, to forget the rest of the world for a while and give in to happiness.

But he didn't need to know that.

"You're dead, Farkos." Kat swiped hair and water from her eyes and gave him her favorite battle stare — cold and bloodthirsty. It was somewhat satisfying when his laugh shorted like a failed circuit. She'd make him laugh again later. "Nobody throws me in the water, messes up my hair and gets away with it."

He was already dogpaddling away before she'd finished the sentence, and she couldn't hold back a grin. There was something empowering about the ability to make a strong, healthy, sexy man run away in fear.

And she was also a phenomenal swimmer. Kat caught up to him easily, grabbed him by the ankle and dunked him. The second he came up, she splashed him with every ounce of Hellman relentlessness.

Spluttering, Roman turned his back to her, trying and failing to shield his face. "Truce, truce!"

"Not a word in my vocabulary, Farkos." There was no keeping the glee from her tone.

"Drowning someone is a crime," he managed, "no matter the reason."

"Self-defense drowning — it happens." She didn't stop, enjoying the harassment more than she probably should. "Are you surrendering?"

"I surrender," he gasped, "under protest."

"Don't say I'm never merciful." She ceased fire, bobbing in the water up to her chin, grinning as he swiped water from his eyes.

At last, Roman blinked most of the moisture away and shifted to face her. "Vicious woman." His mouth curled on one side. "I like it."

The peace that had whispered to her since their arrival gathered around her, gently drawing her close. For the last five years, probably longer, she had immersed herself so deeply in her job that she'd barely taken time to breathe, let alone have fun. Vic had become more of a roommate and fellow officer than a source of companionship. Romance and emotional support had been nonexistent between them, and maybe that was partially her fault, but he could have said something, figured out another method to get her attention besides cheating. Filing for divorce before having an affair would have at least made it possible for her to retain some semblance of respect for him.

No more mulling over the past. She wanted this precious, unexpected moment to last as long as possible.

Kat gave Roman a halfhearted splash, and as he averted his face, she shifted to float on her back. The water lapped against her skin, cool and calming, and the sky was a clear lavender, broken by the first stars. Closing her eyes, she spread her fingers and imagined all the junk in her life draining out of her fingertips and sinking to the sludge at the bottom of the lake, where it would stay, forever forgotten.

"You look like a water sprite basking in the twilight, preparing for a night of revelry beneath the stars." Roman drifted up beside her, his heat caressing her bare arm. "Or mentally preparing to head into battle to single-handedly take on an army of orcs."

She laughed and a shard of her that had been cracked for so long shifted, piecing itself back together. "You *do* read the best books."

"I'm insulted you even questioned it for a moment." His spicy-sweet scent joined the outdoors aroma blend of water, grass and outdoors as he lowered his bare torso into the water, bring his face closer to hers. "*The Hobbit* altered me for life."

"Me too." She turned her head slightly toward him. Hell, he was delicious, all wet and glistening. "Since we're going full fantasy here... My turn." Kat righted herself but didn't move away. Her thighs brushed his as she gently treaded water, studying him. "You're like a dark fae from the underworld, rising from the realm where you reign to sow mischief on the surface."

"And find an unearthly human beauty to trick into returning to the depths with me at dawn." His voice was low and crushed velvet, his breath a caress on her chin. "I'd make sure there were no loopholes for you to manipulate into escaping."

"There's *always* a way out, if the heroine is clever enough." Her thigh brushed his again, nothing more than a slip of skin on warm skin, but it made her entire body tighten.

"Dark lords need love too." His gaze drifted to her mouth.

The need to touch him, to drift closer and slide her arms around his neck was like an ache, throbbing in time with her heartbeat. She wanted to feel the hard lines of his body against her again, explore every slope and angle of his back, shoulders, chest —

"I'm not one to disturb the peace, generally," he said, his voice rougher than usual, "and I usually don't care what level of heat my food may retain, but you may prefer your chicken alfredo to be at least halfway warm."

Kat released a silent breath as he drifted back toward the shore. *Down, girl.*

Chapter Seventeen

"Gia is such a rat." Kat followed Roman toward shore with a slow, easy breaststroke, catching up. "Spilling my favorite food to you."

"I'd be a fool not to take advantage of the opportunities that innocently present themselves to me." His tone was smooth and even, contradicting the devious gleam in his eyes. "I have garlic bread too."

"Damn you both." With a sigh, Kat splashed out of the lake and trudged to the picnic basket and blanket. The glorious aroma of roasted garlic and Italian food coaxed her onward. She nabbed a mini loaf of garlic bread and tore off a chunk. She moaned as she stuffed it into her mouth. "Heaven."

"Appropriate, don't you think, Angel?" Roman sprawled on the blanket like some half-naked deity waiting to be hand-fed grapes by his adoring horde of followers.

Water droplets clung to his skin and the sprinkle of hair on his chest — she forced her gaze to remain above his ribcage and refused to see how his wet shorts clung to his legs and hips. *Dark fae lord, indeed.* He'd already dished up pasta, chicken and salad on a plate for each of them, but if he believed for a second that she was going to feed him, he'd be greatly disappointed. That didn't mean she had to remind him to put his shirt back on.

"When do you plan to share the particulars of tonight's challenge? I have sustenance now." He lifted a fork wound with pasta as proof. "I'm fully prepared."

Kat sat cross-legged on the soft, fuzzy blanket and watched him devour his food for a minute, prolonging the anticipation. When he looked at her expectantly, she took another bite of bread and gave him her wicked smile.

He paused, mid-chew, then swallowed. "Do you even realize the thoughts that run through my head when you smile at me like that?"

Her mouth went dry at the flames in his eyes and she was thankful her bite was already down her gullet. "It's supposed to make you want to flee in terror."

"Not even close." His mouth curled up at one corner.

Hell, he was an expert at distraction. She needed a change of subject before she forfeited their competition right here, right now. The fact that he hadn't kept her occupied longer in the lake was a shocker. Either he was slipping or had decided to go the more honorable route for tonight's win. Neither one would help him.

Kat assumed her war face—lip curled, her coldest glare on him. "We're going to play a little game of 'Katerina says' and see how long you can go before you flub up."

"An improvised version of Simon says?" Roman sat up, one leg crooked, his arm slung over his knee, bread dangling from his long, capable fingers. Excitement glittered in his eyes, not the fear she hoped for. "And the rules?"

"If you follow my command without a 'Katerina says' before it, you lose." She smirked. "Simple enough, even for someone loaded down with carbs."

"I know how the game works, but, being devious myself, I'm suspicious of your intentions." He reached into the basket and plucked out two more beer bottles. As he popped the caps, he studied her. "There has to be a rule that you can't order me to do something I'm incapable of doing."

Taking the bottle he offered, she made sure her smirk stayed on, clear and steady. What she planned to ask him to do, at least the one she was most curious about and was a guaranteed win for her, was completely within his capabilities. She couldn't wait to see how he'd react. "I agree to your condition—or handicap, as it may be."

He went still and his nostrils flared, as if he could sniff out the trap she had set for him. Slowly, like a cat sneaking up on its prey, he set the bottle down and lowered his knee, copying her cross-legged position. Never breaking her gaze, he settled his big hands on his bare knees and nodded, sober and alert. "Very well, Katerina. Shall we begin?"

There were so many possibilities in this challenge, so many different directions she could take that it that she hardly knew *where* to begin. "Rub your belly."

"Pathetic." Roman sighed and shook his head.

Instead of wasting time, she went for his throat. "Katerina says smile."

He stared at her. "You're a villainess."

"Put up or shut up, Farkos." Anticipation tumbled through her. Either he'd forfeit or finally smile. Even if she had to work harder for the point, she'd win either way.

He took a swig of his beer and sucked in a deep breath. As if it pained him deeply, his mouth stretched into a close-lipped half-smile.

Sneaky bastard. Kat drew up her knees and primly clasped her hands on her jeans, which were still damp from the unwarranted dip in the lake. "Katerina says smile wide—with teeth—and hold it for ten seconds."

"You don't want to do this, I promise you." His tone was almost pleading, a useless ploy. There was no mercy in competition when a Hellman was involved.

"Absolutely, I do." She leaned back on her hands and flipped her ponytail over her shoulder, confident in her triumph. "You make it so easy to win."

"*Chara*," Roman muttered beneath his breath, and while she didn't know what the word meant, the way he said it was amusing enough. He bent his head and pinched the bridge of his nose. After a second, he looked up, defiant. "If you run, I'll chase you down. Don't say I didn't warn you."

"Don't be a drama queen."

He continued to stare at her, as if he could burn her into relenting with his black eyes.

"Five seconds until forfeit. Five. Four. Three—"

"Very well. I won't lose a point due to a natural genetic occurrence utterly beyond my control." His voice softened. "And I trust you not to misuse this information." Releasing a breath, he smiled, wide and open, baring all his teeth.

Hell...his teeth. Kat leaned forward. She'd considered all the possibilities of why he'd adamantly refused to smile—crooked or missing teeth, or even gold-capped in some regrettable gangster phase—but never had she imagined *this.* His teeth were white and straight, completely normal, except for his canines, which were peculiarly pointed—not wickedly sharp like an animal's...or vampire's, but enough to be easily noticeable. How had her tongue remained unscathed after kissing him?

"Get out," she breathed, reaching to touch one with her fingertip.

Roman shut his mouth and lifted his chin. "Ten seconds is up," he said primly. "Next command, if you please."

"You can't tease a girl with only a glimpse of a marvel then shut her down." She sat back. His neutral expression was clearly a guard against what he thought she might say, and she couldn't deny a hint of regret for pushing him. And it hurt a little that he was right to be on guard when it came to her. "Smile again."

He stared at her, unmoving.

"Katerina says smile for me with teeth again." She added a coax to her tone and used Gia's tactic of batting her eyelashes. "Please?"

"While I disapprove of your twisted and dastardly version of this game, you have discovered my weakness. I can deny you nothing." His pale, powerful throat bobbed. "I wouldn't willingly offer this to anyone else, on the off chance you were wondering."

She hadn't been wondering, but the way he'd said it, so sincere and tender, made her heart forget to beat. Then he smiled again, and her heart kicked back on, thrumming in all her extremities. It was a good thing

232

he never smiled. His mouth alone was dangerous enough to her rationality, but a full expression was unbearably magnetic, like a rare meteor shower. She couldn't look away for fear she'd miss a single second of something she might never see again.

"Mesmerizing, aren't they?" He'd reverted to his monotone, the one that gave nothing away and yet, now that she knew him better, revealed more than he probably suspected.

Kat fumbled for her beer bottle and forced herself to take a drink before responding, giving her brain a few seconds to recover and get back into the game. "What I'm most curious about," she said, her voice raspier than usual, "is how many people you've bitten."

Like that, his smile was gone, replaced by a very uncharacteristic, altogether bloodcurdling Roman Farkos glower.

"I had to ask." She widened her eyes, all innocence. "I don't suppose there are any reports of mysterious local maulings or bodies drained of blood, considering you work in the police department. Smart career move. I'm impressed."

"Now you know why I prefer not to smile." He drained his beer and tossed the bottle in the basket. "I had enough jokes growing up, and being of Romani descent only made it all the richer. That's not counting the fun fact that *Farkos* means 'wolf'."

"Life is so unfair." Kat sighed and shrugged at the sharp accusation in his gaze. "I'd kill to have a last name that meant wolf."

"That can be arranged," he said in a silky tone.

She ignored the flirty insinuation at a lasting, potentially permanent relationship. "If I had your teeth, I'd be using them as another weapon in my arsenal. Could you imagine how easy it would be to scare people off with those things?"

"While I appreciate the humor of the situation, you're not the one who has to live with them."

"We all have our greener grass, Farkos. I would have preferred to be shorter, less noticeable, an average Plain Jane, but whatever. You should really smile more." Before he could refuse, she added, "Or at least smile more for me."

Maybe she shouldn't have said that, shouldn't have been the one to ease his surprising insecurity, but seeing him want to hide any part of himself to avoid what other people might think about him rubbed a space inside her raw. He was better than most of the world, exactly as he was.

"Is that a 'Katerina says' command?" he asked in a voice dark with midnight promises. "I have to ask because I'm not sure my senses are working correctly. The most beautiful woman I've ever met—amazing inside and out, despite her occasional wicked streak— seems to be paying me a compliment rather than using my weakness to go for the kill and win another point in our competition."

She felt like a fraud. It would be great to truly be the person he thought she was—confident, strong, unstoppable—but that wasn't the whole truth. There were so many moments that she was nothing more than a pretender, an actor putting on the face of a woman who let nothing affect her and didn't need anything more than her career to make her feel as if she mattered. If she were good enough, perfect enough, maybe she'd figure out how to make it a reality. The loneliness of her years trying to figure it out on her own became a crushing weight. Her lungs seemed incapable of drawing a full breath.

"Katerina." Roman's rough murmur recaptured her focus, and when he smiled with teeth, it unraveled a net inside her. Words she'd never intended to share with anyone outside the department back home poured out.

"I punched Vic, while on duty. That's the main reason I'm on leave." She nodded, acknowledging his blink of surprise, his smile long gone. "He told me about the affair and I lost it, gave him a bloody nose. It was inside the department building, out of the public eye, no witnesses, which made it possible to keep it mostly hush-hush, but everyone at work knows, of course." Kat fiddled with a string on the hem of her shirt. "I haven't told my family. While on leave, I'm supposed to decide if I can handle working at the same department as my ex without any further incidents." She blew out a long, shaky breath. "Most days, it's not even a question. Then there are the occasional days where I'd rather play water polo with crocodiles while wearing a raw chicken around my neck than be anywhere near him."

Roman studied her in silence, remaining utterly still, as if he couldn't decide if he should say something or awkwardly creep away. The gentle lap of water and a lone cricket made a lulling backdrop to the gathering night as his pause stretched. If he wouldn't acknowledge her imperfection aloud, she'd do it for him.

"Amazing inside and out, aren't I?" She gave him a sharp smile.

"Was it worth it?" He leaned forward slightly, unblinking, his expression set on neutral. "Punching him?"

The tension in her shoulders loosened and she laughed. Leave it to Roman to look for the positive and dismiss the repercussions of assaulting a fellow officer, cheating ex-husband or not. "One hundred percent."

"Everyone messes up—even avenging angels. That doesn't make you any less amazing. It merely makes you perfectly imperfect." He flashed his fangs again and waved his fingers near his mouth. "You're in excellent company."

"Hell." Before she talked herself out of it, she touched his face, and when he grasped her hand and pressed a lingering kiss on her palm, unexpected tears burned her eyes. Somewhere along the way, he'd earned her respect, and she couldn't be anything less than honest with him. "I'll undoubtedly regret admitting this, but I like you."

His eyebrows went up. "As in *like*-like me?"

"You've been hanging around teenagers too long."

"Probably." He shrugged, holding her hand hostage when she halfheartedly tried to pull free. They both knew she could escape if she really wanted to. "Please continue. You were saying?"

Kat surrendered to his grip, to the comforting circles he made with his thumb on the heel of her palm. "I'm not looking for a relationship or romance. Half the time I'm not even sure where I'm going to be in a month. I never thought I'd be divorced or staying on my sister's couch in Graywood. I'm trying very hard to hold my life together and I can't focus on anything beyond that."

"But you can't resist liking me." He nodded, sober. "It's completely understandable."

"It's infatuation." Despite her resolve, her gaze drifted to his soft, sensual mouth. "I already explained that to you."

"And I reaffirm my right to agree to disagree." With a quick move, he lassoed her waist with one unyielding arm and dragged her into his lap. "I need to tell you a Farkos family tale, one that has nothing to do with inherited fangs."

"You've hijacked my challenge." She poked him in the ribs, needing to protest. If she let him wrest control away once, it was bound to happen again. He didn't need to know that she liked his arm around her, his heat against her, the rhythm of his heart a steady drum at her shoulder. "And all before pie."

"Then you should know how important this is to me, since I'm putting it pre-pie." His mouth twitched. "At an early age, my father told me never to worry that something was wrong with me or feel as if I'm missing out when my friends fall in love, get married or have kids while I remain single. He said it's a Farkos family curse to not fall in love."

Hearing his confession that he wasn't in love with her should have given her an enormous sense of relief, but it didn't. At all. He confirmed that the thing between them was lust, nothing more, nothing less, a fire that would burn out sooner rather than later. It was better this way—a fling that wouldn't get too deep or serious, easily ended when she left. So why was her throat tight?

Roman wrapped his free arm around her, too, as if he could anchor her to him. "That's not the end of the story, Katerina."

"Get on with it, Farkos." The growl she intended came out closer to a rasp. "I have a challenge to win."

"Our family doesn't *fall* in love. Love hits us, and when it does, we're completely conquered. After one glance at my mother, my father was irrevocably smitten. There was no going back, no trip, fall, get back up again. He was flat on the floor, done." Gently, he brushed her ponytail over her shoulder and followed the line of her collarbone to her throat, as if transfixed by the delicate bone. "That's exactly how it is for me with you. As much as I appreciate your outward beauty, your kick-ass skills, snarls and carefully guarded sweetness, that's all sugar on the piecrust. It's the combination of who you are that has smitten me beyond repair."

She stared at him and it took a few seconds to process his meaning. There was no way he was in love with her. Clearly, he was incapable of telling the difference between infatuation and real true love. "You hardly know me."

"I know that you're fiercely protective of the people you care about and are willing to tear apart suspicious attorneys and well-meaning law enforcement friends of said loved ones, if necessary. Not everyone appreciated or understood that, but I did. I'd do the same thing."

She snorted, anything to hide the way her stomach felt as if it was filled with a hundred excitable dragonflies. "You'd annoy the hell out of your sister's shady fiancé and his overbearing friend in a failed attempt to get them to leave?"

"'Overbearing' is a strong word, but if it meant doing the best by my sister, no matter what anyone else thought about me? Indubitably." He glanced at her scowl and his mouth twitched. "I know that you give one hundred percent to everything you do—no requests, no apologies."

"That's what a Hellman does." She gave him a superior look, trying to play it cool while pieces of her were twisting out of place. "But giving one hundred percent to my job meant minimal time for my marriage. Even though cheating is a scumbag move, I can't completely blame Vic for wanting more."

"I'm not Vic." He pressed a light, lingering kiss on her bare shoulder. "I'll never let you forget I'm here."

She shuddered at the sudden heat in her veins and suspected he was correct. Forgetting him would be impossible, especially with him constantly close. She couldn't imagine passing by him in the hallways with nothing more than a quick greeting and peck on the cheek before parting ways or reading in one room of the house while he watched football in the other, content with the arrangement.

"You're defined by more than your family name or what skills you choose to excel at, whether or not you have a natural inclination toward them." He lowered his voice to a hush. "I know you read good books, ones with warriors who battle hordes of *demonii* on a daily basis and will fight entire armies for his fated mate."

The warmth churning in her blood invaded her face. "Just because Gia tells you everything —"

"Some details are too sacred to gather from any outside source. I witnessed you reading in the hospital garden one day when Gia was still a patient."

"Spying is even worse."

"Not spying — a random Katerina sighting, which isn't the same at all." He dragged his knuckles down her forearm, triggering goosebumps. "I understand that you're not in the same emotional place as I am and I'm not asking you to be. I'll never push you into being something you're not. You don't have to be anything more or less than Katerina Hellman with me and I'll always respect that." His forehead wrinkled. "Whether or not you care about my opinion, that's a completely different topic."

She *did* care about his opinion and that was a problem she needed to fix right now, before she lost complete command of her senses. "I have an irrational fear of the dark that I can't always control." Carefully, she watched his face for any indication of shock or disdain, finding only patient curiosity. "When I was eight or so, I was playing hide and seek with my brothers. My parents had gone somewhere with Gia. I hid in the basement. Being insensitive dirtbag brothers that they are, they locked me in and thought it was hilarious. The lightbulb had burned out and I was alone, trapped and blind. I know — *now* — that it was only my imagination, but I swore something else was in the basement black with me. Sometimes, under certain circumstances, being in an enclosed space in the dark sends me back to that moment. I'm a freakin' grown woman who sleeps with the lights on."

There. Suck on that amazing Katerina Hellman fact, Farkos.

"My respect for your brothers just dropped a few pegs." He caressed her back, slow and stirring. "And I have no reservations about doing anything in full light." The suggestive tone of his voice left no doubt that whatever he was thinking of had nothing to do with sleeping.

Kat's heart jerked into a strange, fluttering dance. Revealing her failures and fears had no effect on his view of her. It was almost as if he wanted her more because of them. Her hands shook like they had when she'd flubbed up at the range and lost to Roman.

Lost to Roman. That was a precise description of the sensations barreling through her, as if she'd stepped off a cliff and toppled into a bottomless pit — all of her own free will. He had the alarming capacity to see through all her trappings, both discard and admire all the traits she used as an identity and look deeper, wanting that part of her she kept secret, that part that possessed all her wounds and failures and insecurities. And even with the wanting, he patiently waited for her to offer it up, as if it was his future and he'd wait as long as he needed to. Unlike every other person, he wanted all of her — the good, the bad and the hideous. The knowledge left her completely undone, destroying her remaining shards of prudence.

"Kiss me." Giving in to the urge he'd awakened in the water, she wound her arms around his neck.

He paused for a beat and canted his head. "Tricking me into losing the competition by tempting me to kiss you. That's hardcore, even for you."

"I guess you have to ask yourself one question." She leaned forward until a mere centimeter separated her mouth from his and closed her eyes, savoring the catch of his breath, the rapid beat of his pulse against hers. "What do you want more?"

Chapter Eighteen

When it came to a competition between kissing Katerina or not, Roman didn't need even a second to think about it. She was in his arms, her face lifted to his, waiting for a kiss, and he wasn't going to pass it up.

But since it included a loss, he would be taking his time, enjoying every moment and using every skill at his disposal to persuade her to make it last until tonight, the morning, next week.

Forever.

Slow and sensuous, he slipped his hand from the curve of her waist to her spine and trailed his fingers up, one vertebra at a time. Kat shivered, her thin, damp shirt doing little to hide the goosebumps that rose beneath his touch. When he got to her nape and her spill of wet hair, he used both hands to ease the band from her ponytail, freeing her long, glorious tresses to drape her shoulders.

"Better," he murmured, filling his hands with the smooth strands.

"Roman." She released his neck, pivoted to straddle him and grasped his face between her hands. "Katerina says kiss me...or else."

Win or lose, there was no denying her demand. He bent his head and pressed his mouth to hers. Katerina had glorious lips, lush and velvet-soft that he could spend an eternity worshipping. He trailed one hand beneath the clinging material of her shirt, exploring her back, and tangled the other in her silken hair. Her skin was warm under his palm, and as he moved, she opened her mouth, a small surrender that made his blood race hot and throbbing to every extremity.

As he deepened the kiss, the caress of her tongue on his tasted of beer, lemon and summer. He savored the strength and gentle curve of her body beneath his hands, the sizzling connection and growing energy between them, as if her soul answered his, even when she refused to acknowledge it with her words. When she squeezed his hips with her thighs and moaned his name—by accident or not—every cell ignited with liquid fire.

A wildness rose from a place deep inside him, and with an effort, he leashed the lust simmering in his every pore. This moment wasn't only about primal need, but recognition, acceptance and he needed to know that she wanted this—wanted him. He forced himself to ease back and brushed his lips over her ear. "Do you want me, Angel?"

Kat went still and swallowed hard. She trembled in his arms, as if fighting an inner battle. Acknowledging that she wanted him... There would be no retreat, not for either of them.

He held his breath, the heat strung tight through his body exquisite torture as he waited for her answer.

While he wanted her with every mote of his being, he wouldn't push her, wouldn't proceed without some confirmation that the connection between them was more than an extinguishable flame.

"Yes," she said at last. She leaned back and met his gaze, her pupils dilated, her mouth sweetly chafed from his kisses. "I want you."

Relief washed through him even as his chest constricted. She hadn't answered the question completely, not like he'd hoped, but where she denied full disclosure, he'd be an open book. "I'm yours, Angel, however you want me." He held her gaze. "So, take me."

She studied him, her slender thighs clamped around his hips. She flexed her hands on his shoulders, as if undecided whether to let go or hold on tight.

Roman leaned in and traced the tip of her ear with his tongue. As she shuddered, he whispered, "What are you waiting for?"

Kat locked her arms around his neck and kissed him with such desperation that every good intention of restraint went up in smoke and flames. With no real notion of how or when, he found her beneath him, the length of her strong, lean body pressed against him, her glorious mouth devouring his. With her heat surrounding him, her silent surrender a siren's call, going slowly would be a challenge.

Luckily, he loved a challenge.

As Katerina wrestled her shirt over her head, exposing the swells of her lovely breasts and the plane of her flat stomach, his heart stumbled. Since the moment he'd found her, his future had seemed to thread with hers, and he had no hope of disentangling his core. He was in love with her and every dream, every vision of what he wanted included her. It was up to him to prove to her that what they had together was far more than infatuation or a fleeting fire easily doused. And since she refused to listen with words, he'd have to resort to other available assets.

When she reached for the waistband of his shorts, he snared her wrist and placed her palm on his heart. Her skin was hot on his and the pulse in her fingers matched the rhythm beating in his veins. Slowly, he trailed his fingers along the velvet curve of her breast. He kept all the words he wanted to say — *beautiful, perfect, mine* — quiet in the hidden space of his spirit. When he drifted his fingertips down, her stomach quivered beneath his touch.

Katerina reached for his waistband again, her hand shaking, and this time, he didn't stop her as she slid her fingers beneath. When she touched him, desperate with a hint of shy, it felt like recognition at last.

Roman kicked free of his clothing, made short work of hers and, protection in place, pulled her tight against his hardness and heat. He crushed her mouth with his, surrendering to the storm of desire and longing raging through him. Beneath the first stars of a summer night, with crickets and gently lapping water a soft symphony surrounding them, he touched her, kissed her, teased her until she gasped and writhed beneath him in a silent plea for more.

And as he slowly possessed her, moved inside her, the flood of sensation offered by his Angel drowned him, leaving no part of him unaffected. This was what he'd wanted, what he'd waited for without even knowing it — the joy of giving pleasure to the woman who owned his heart, sharing her breath and body, connecting in the most intimate way possible as his soul melted with hers. She could deny the truth all she wanted, but there was no hiding the shimmering cord strung tight between them.

Together, they rose and fell, tangled in limbs and heat, and when Katerina moaned his name and shuddered around him, he followed her home.

* * * *

Kat eased out from Roman's arm wrapped loosely around her ribs and slid out of his bed. She didn't want to wake him just because she couldn't sleep. A dim glow from the hallway light filtered through the cracked door, and her breath caught at the sight of him sprawled on the dark sheets, his long, lean back a pale, powerful line in the gloom, those big, capable hands relaxed. Without any words, he'd adored her with his hands, mouth and body in a way that made it impossible to question how he felt about her, awakening emotions she'd never believed possible—deep, uncontrollable and consuming. The tryst at the lake had merely been the beginning, a surreal moment beneath the stars that had continued for another hour in the night water, cooling hot skin and stoking flames higher. Eventually, they'd made it back to his truck, an extra hour to actually make it to his house, which had extended to another moment against the wall between family photos, gradually moving to his bedroom...

Hell. She brought her hand to her tingling mouth. In all her years of marriage, never had sex been like *that*— life-altering, an undeniable connection between souls. Before, she'd never understood why other people called it 'making love' when it was just a physical, carnal act that was quickly over, then life continued as usual. Now, post-Roman, she absolutely got it.

And she had no idea how to handle it.

Kat snagged Roman's discarded T-shirt from the bedpost and pulled it over her head. It smelled of lake air and Roman, and the cool material on her bare skin reminded her of all the places he'd touched and claimed as his own. She smiled as she quietly shut the bedroom door. She'd done her fair share of claiming Farkos real estate too.

A lamp in the hallway kept the night at bay and the warmth in her chest expanded, flowing to her hidden corners. After her confession of her uncomfortable situation with the dark and basements, she suspected Roman had purposely left the light on for her. No other man, not even her brothers or father and certainly not her ex, would have been sensitive enough to acknowledge her fear, let alone do anything to ease it. Fear was meant to be faced and conquered, not coddled.

But another shaving of her heart curled free, settling at Roman's feet.

The carpet silenced her steps and she paused to grab her phone from the back pocket of her jeans, which were still crumpled in the hallway from where they'd been absently left earlier, only a stop along the trail of shoes, socks, shorts and shirts. She felt in the front pocket and sighed in relief as her fingertips brushed brass. She'd brought the bullet casing she'd found at the institution along to their challenge, intending to discuss her concerns with Roman, not become so distracted by him that her line of questioning derailed, crashed and was left behind in a burning, forgotten heap.

Kat wandered into the kitchen, flipped on the light and sat in one of the wooden chairs. Resting her elbows on the table scarred by years of Farkos family life, she slid her fingertips over the metal casing and the indentation she'd found on the bottom. Among the headstamp letters and numbers was 'LE' — marking the bullet as being manufactured for law enforcement only. Graywood officers didn't use these bullets. She'd bet her gun collection that whoever had dropped the casing played on the opposite side of the law.

Setting the casing on the table, she absently rolled it beneath her fingers, the barely-there friction of metal on wood lost in a clock's distant rhythm from another room. Stolen law enforcement ammo in an abandoned building, the signs that someone had been held in the bell tower, finding Vee and her friend there... It was possible they were all random, disconnected. But beyond the disuse and disarray left behind the institution walls, no evidence suggested a scattered timeline. Whatever had happened in the bell tower was recent, the casing itself was too shiny to be old, and Vee...

Teenagers searched for scares and things to do for kicks all the time, and the institution would be an obvious choice to any local, bored thrill seekers. But she didn't like what her gut was telling her — that there were no coincidences.

The soft pad of feet on tile alerted her to Roman's approach. She continued studying the bullet casing as he leaned down, slid his arms around her neck and pressed a lingering kiss to her shoulder, left bare thanks to his overlarge T-shirt. Kat closed her eyes and drank in every detail — the softness of his lips on her skin, the warmth of his big body at her back, his unique scent that she'd forevermore associate as part of her own, secret holiday. There was nowhere else in the world —

no other person — that could make her feel almost... perfect.

"I can't decide if I should be insulted that you have enough energy to get out of bed already or relieved that you're still here." Rough-edged with sleep, his voice was even more delicious than usual.

"My snooze schedule is off. I've been staying up until three, catching Z's most nights on a couch, not a bed." She shifted in the chair to face him. "My body doesn't know what to do with actual rest —"

The words dried up as she took him in. Bare-chested, black sleep pants he'd obviously dragged on while only half-awake, slung low enough she wasn't sure how they stayed on, and his hair remained tousled by her fingers. She pulled his face down to hers and kissed him, slow, with a promise of heat. "You," she said, breathless, "are the only man capable of making me forget what I was going to say."

He smiled for her, showing a glimpse of white teeth, and settled into the chair next to hers. He dragged her chair close, situating her legs between his splayed knees and sifted his fingers through her loose hair with one hand, picking up the brass from the table with the other.

"It's the one I found at the institution," she said. "The whole situation has been at the back of my mind, coming to a simmer. The headstamp is law enforcement. I don't like it."

"May I?" Roman tapped her cell phone. "The magic of technology may offer some answers or clues."

Since that had been her plan anyway, she entered her password and handed it to him. Those strong, capable fingers danced over the screen, and for a trembling moment she was back by the lake beneath the stars, slowly shattering beneath his touch.

"Six months ago," he read off her phone, bringing her back to the present, "there was an incident in Colorado — officer was shot, his gun stolen" — his pale throat worked — "during a human trafficking sting." He set the phone on the table, as if turning it off would erase the past.

"Crap." The image of the bell tower replayed like a movie in her mind, the details razor-sharp.

"For the last month," Roman said in a sober voice as he picked up the brass again and studied it, "during my Saturday night foot patrols, there have been rumors of a new group hanging around. A couple of local homeless kids have gone missing. They could easily have wandered to another area or decided to return home, but" — he met her gaze and pain shimmered in his eyes — "I don't like it, either."

As much as she wanted to assure him that Irini's fate wasn't tied to this, they'd both know she was lying. Instead, she shifted onto his lap, settled her head on his shoulder and held him.

He released a shaky sigh, wrapping his arms around her. "You don't know how much I've needed this." He kissed the top of her head. "Needed you."

Kat closed her eyes. *I've needed this too.* Her chest constricted at the admission and the keen realization that came on its heels, slicing her heart with scalpel precision. Following in the footsteps of her brothers, she'd gone with the unanimous decision to leave sappy hugs and vulnerable moments to the Gia-and-Mom club. Not even in her relationship with Vic had she relaxed enough to surrender to the small tug to be tender and unguarded. It was enough to make a girl think that maybe Roman was right about the savage, startling connection between them, that 'infatuation' was too tame a term to be accurate.

She stopped the train of thought before it chugged out of the station, not ready to ruin the moment with fantasies. Reality would show up soon enough. All the mush was probably due to the endorphins still raging through her veins, thanks to that which was Roman. If he ribbed her later about this moment of cuddling weakness, she'd blame it on bedroom aftereffects.

"Irini's choice to run... It's not your fault, you know." While Irini's fate remained unknown, she could at least tell him one truth. "Teenagers do stupid things." She snorted softly and ran her thumb over the ridge of a scar on his collarbone. "I should know, since I was still a teenager when I got married."

"That was a dumb move on your part." He huffed a laugh as she pinched him. "You should have waited for me."

She pushed away from him, held captive by his arms. "Maybe you should have found me first, Farkos."

"I wish I had," he said, his eyes softening and making her melt. "I know Irini's decision to cut ties was her own and that I can't control what anyone else does, but that doesn't prevent me from considering all the things I should or shouldn't have said or done and wonder what would have made a difference."

"Yeah." She sighed. "Life would be so much easier if we could control people."

"But not as much fun." His smile was short-lived. "The new faces in town? I suspect they're involved with the missing homeless kids."

Her gut agreed one hundred percent.

"That's why I decided to leave what we found in the bell tower untouched." He grimaced at the bullet casing. "For the most part. In case they return, I don't want them to know we've discovered the lair in the bell tower. I sent the syringe we found to the lab, but whether it's drugs or something else doesn't change that someone had been imprisoned there."

"And taken elsewhere." She cupped his face. "Irini has been gone for six months. These new players in town haven't been here that long, right? Don't make any assumptions."

He leaned into her hand and closed his eyes. "I'm trying not to."

"I know what will make you forget everything."

"Do you now?" Roman sat up straight, his eyes bright, and trailed his hand suggestively up her bare thigh, beneath the hem of her borrowed shirt.

Kat pivoted, straddling him, and kissed him suddenly, hard enough to distract him. She leaped off his lap before he changed her mind and, dancing beyond the reach of his grasping hands, she went to the refrigerator.

"It's a personal challenge, Farkos." She opened the refrigerator door and gave him a smirk. "To see what you love more—food or sex."

"How dare you present me with so impossible a choice?" He rose lithely from the chair, his eyes glittering. "If there's no way to win, it's not a challenge. It's down and dirty sabotage."

She shivered as he came up behind her and slid his warm, callused hand beneath the hem of her shirt and drifted up her ribs. "Then again, I might have miscalculated, considering the contents of your fridge." There was nothing in his refrigerator besides an apple that had seen better days and a carton of cream cheese. "This is pathetic."

"I have an idea," he whispered at her ear, making slow, sensual circles with his thumb on her skin. "I'll prepare my specialty — grilled peanut butter and banana sandwiches." He pulled her hair to one side and grazed his teeth over the lobe of her ear. It took all her willpower not to turn, drag him to the kitchen floor and have her way with him. "We can eat them in bed. It's an all-around win."

She sucked in a breath as he lightly bit her shoulder and licked the sting away. "Might be worth a quarter-point loss. I'll make the final determination afterward."

He spun her around and kissed her long and deep, leaving her flushed and dazed. His full smile was all wolf. "I promise you won't be disappointed."

Chapter Nineteen

As the sun made its first appearance on the horizon, Kat parked her SUV in Gia's driveway and slid out. Her steps were light as she trotted up the stairs to the front door. She couldn't remember the last time she'd felt so at ease, as if every mismatched note of her world had somehow settled into a smooth rhythm. She should be suspicious. Not once in the last decade or so had she woken up without at least one knot coiled tight in her body. A state of relaxation was too unfamiliar to completely trust.

Roman. He was the main ingredient in her life that was different, the one factor that had affected her in ways she'd never thought possible. As much as she wanted to continue to claim that her condition was mere infatuation, their relationship was far more complicated than a flame-and-fade situation. She wasn't sure who would wind up scorched and it was too much to believe Roman's version — that the quick spark between them could endure demanding careers and imperfections. The fact that she was starting to consider that he could be right was both terrifying and stunning.

Using the spare key Gia had given her, she unlocked the door and went inside. She quietly shut the door so she wouldn't wake anyone up and turned for the living room, where her travel bag was stowed.

"Good morning, Katerina."

At her mother's voice, Kat jumped, her heart kicking. Caroline sat on the couch, her legs primly crossed, her hands folded on her lap. While she was fully dressed in slacks and blouse, she appeared to have been there for a while.

"What are you doing up so early, Mom?" She was already sure she wouldn't like the answer.

"When a daughter doesn't come home, doesn't call or respond to text messages, mothers find it difficult to sleep." Her voice was polite, without accusation, but Kat was familiar with her mother's methods of conveying disappointment.

Kat dropped her keys on the end table and continued to her bag in the corner of the room. If she didn't need her work clothes, she'd leave before any damage could occur. "I'm not a child anymore, Mom. I don't need anyone to monitor my activities and I'm fully capable of protecting myself."

"I was merely concerned when you didn't come home last night and didn't answer your phone. That's all."

Nothing was ever so simple with Caroline Hellman. Kat rummaged through her bag for her khakis and department instructor shirt. "I had a date." Even as she said the words, she grimaced. She doubted her mother would give the green light to jump into the dating scene only days after her divorce, but since she'd never had Caroline's blessing anyway… "With Roman."

"Are you sure that's wise?"

Called that one right. She pulled her pants, shirt and clean underclothes from her bag. "Since when is wisdom required for dating?"

"Don't be waspish, dear. After separating with your father, I understand the emotions associated with a divorce. Getting involved with Roman so soon is both reckless and selfish. You're not ready for another relationship."

Kat took a deep breath and let it out. "One date does not a relationship make." She had no intention of sharing how fast and furious her feelings for Roman had hit. "I can handle my own social life without any interference, but thanks for the vote of confidence, as usual."

"What are you implying?" Caroline's voice took on an offended edge. "I'm concerned about you. No matter your age, that will never change. I am your mother. That's what mothers do."

All the peace that had surrounded Kat dissipated like dew beneath an unforgiving August sun. She tossed her clothes back into her bag and pivoted to face her mother. "Mothers are also supposed to support and encourage. And instead of judging me on every single facet of my life, it would be nice if once — just once — I got a thumbs-up from you rather than the underhanded disappointment."

"Spending the night with the first man who shows interest in you after your divorce or using Roman as a method to get back at Vic?" She shook her head. "I expected better from you, Katerina."

"I guess some things never change." Both fury and shame thundered through her and it was all she could do to grab her bag with shaking hands. She had nothing to be ashamed about and yet, no matter how many years passed, her mother's unrelenting disappointment still burned and pushed her down to when she was the girl who'd realized that she'd never be enough—the price she paid for being true to herself. "No need to wonder where I'll be." She marched past Caroline on her way to the door. "If I don't answer my phone, I'm either at Roman's or dead due to a stray bullet at the range."

"Katerina—"

She slammed the door shut before she could hear her mother's follow-up. No matter what she said, Kat had heard it all before.

* * * *

"I hope the spare room offer is still open," Kat said the second Roman opened the door.

Surprised to find her on his front porch again so soon, he barely had time to step aside, let alone answer. She brushed past him, apparently not needing permission—or, regretfully, a kiss—nearly knocking him over with the overstuffed duffel bag on her shoulder.

"If I had to spend one more minute with my mother, I would have committed murder." She glanced back at him. "If you repeat that, I'll deny it."

Roman didn't care what had brought her back. All that mattered was that she was here, in his house, smelling like a herb garden and filling the emptiness that had settled in the second she'd left. He shut the door, his heart beating at a ragged pace, as if this were a dream that would unravel with the light. "The offer is open-ended. Whenever you need it, I'm here for you." He added some silken heat to his voice. "And the room too, but, as you know, my bed is big enough for two. I'll even surrender a dresser, although I hate to put distance between me and my favorite T-shirts."

"It's not like that." She faced him in the hallway, squared off as if expecting a battle, and his temperature dipped a degree. "I need a place to stay. Gia's house is no longer neutral ground." She crossed her arms and gave him an even stare. "This has nothing to do with last night."

"And nothing to do with this morning?" He kept his voice low and stepped slowly toward her, unwilling to let her take their relationship backward. "Nothing to do with you wrapped around me, moaning my name – or the scratches on my back?" He pivoted, giving her a full look at his bare back, which contained solid evidence of her fingernails.

A flush crept into her cheeks and she lifted her chin, not backing down a single inch. "Nope. Nothing to do with any of that. I need my own room, my own space. Can you handle that?"

"Angel, you should know by now that when it comes to you, I'll figure it out." He cupped her face and stroked her cheekbones with his thumbs. "You're always welcome here with whatever strings or rules you want." He didn't miss that she didn't relax beneath his touch like she had before. "I'll never make demands of you...but I may propose a game or two."

He took her bag, then her hand and guided her up the stairs to the hallway of deserted bedrooms. She didn't try to pull free, a positive sign. "Pick whichever one you want, but just so we're clear…" Pulling her close, he kissed her slowly, with a hint of wicked, and she softened beneath him. "You'll always be welcome in my room, my bed, my arms, whenever you want."

She briefly rested her forehead on his chest, but quickly straightened, her gaze on the bedroom doors. "Which one has its own bathroom?"

* * * *

Half an hour later, Roman slid a grilled peanut butter and banana sandwich across the table to Kat, along with her own key to his house. She'd showered and dressed faster than any of his sisters ever had and still looked like a runway model in her khakis and department-issued instructor polo. He ignored the way she looked at the spare key as if it were an adder set to strike.

"This is going to be epic. Not only sharing the same space with you, but firearms training at the paintball arena?" He sipped his coffee, watching her take an impressive bite of the sandwich. "This has to be the best day in the history of ever."

"That's what you think," she said after swallowing. "Boyd's the one who needs more hands-on instruction than you, so we're double teaming. Us against you." She licked her fingers slowly, and his body tightened. "It should be a riveting session."

Roman leaned his elbows on the table and eased closer to her. "In case you've forgotten, this is a new week—a new challenge and my turn. I bet that even with the two of you against me, I'll still win."

"As thrilling as it would be to prove you wrong and kick your ego down to the level it belongs, this is a work session. I have to focus on improving Boyd's skills, not painting your ass in different colors." She smirked and stuffed more sandwich into her mouth.

"Don't pretend you're not obsessed with my fine behind, Angel. You can color whatever part of me you want with an entire rainbow of shades, but don't use that as an excuse. If you can't handle a split focus, simply admit it." He loved how her brown eyes sparked at the teasing accusation. "I won't think any less of you, ever."

"Once again, you're under the misapprehension that I care what you think about me." She flicked her fingertips in a dismissive gesture that did nothing to fool him. Despite her nonchalance, she absolutely cared about a lot of things. It made his heart stop, knowing that he was one of them. Whether or not she understood it yet, he suspected she never would have opened to him otherwise. She never would have spent the night in his bed and she would never be here right now, with him, devouring the one dish he knew how to cook.

He smiled at her, *for* her, as she'd asked him to do at the lake the previous evening. While he'd become accustomed to not smiling, it really had nothing to do with his teeth. People smiled for all sorts of different reasons and they weren't always sincere. When he smiled at Katerina, she'd never have to guess whether or not he meant it to be anything less than a sign that he was happy to see her.

She stopped chewing and gave him a suspicious look. "So that's how it is? You think you can distract me any time you want now by flashing your fangs?" She tossed the remains of her sandwich—nothing more than a scrap of crust—onto the plate and wiped her hands on the napkin. "Fine. Challenge accepted. Even while shadowing Boyd and instructing him, I'll still beat you in paintball without breaking a sweat."

Roman scraped back his chair and stood. "I was smiling merely to express that having you here with me, devouring my famous food creation, is how I'd choose every workday to start." As she rose as well, he came close, within range of her lavender-mint aroma, denying the need to touch her. If he did, they might be late to the paintball arena. Instead, he leaned near her ear and lowered his voice. "Every day off, I'd choose to wake up in bed with you wrapped around me—or me wrapped around you. I'm not picky."

At the slight catch of her breath, he smiled and headed for the door, his hazelnut-laced coffee and keys in hand. "Hurry up, Hellman. We don't want to keep Boyd—and my glorious upcoming win—waiting."

Chapter Twenty

The paintball course in Greenville, thirty miles from Graywood, turned out to be better than Kat had expected. It was situated on fifty acres and offered a variety of landscapes—from apocalypse to forest, gardens and forts—so many she'd had trouble choosing which one to reserve. They all looked like fantastic fun with guns, but they were here for training purposes, not entertainment. Going with practical, she selected the castle—and it had nothing to do with her love for fantasy. An officer needed to be prepared for any situation that might come up in a structure, whether or not it had turrets.

Turrets, as it turned out, had zero impact on Boyd. Crouched tight to the wall, Boyd behind her, Kat eased to the corner and peeked around. Roman hunkered behind a wooden blockade, his gaze set out of the window. Enough of him was visible for another shot. *Sucker.* A couple of green splotches marked his camouflage coveralls on the shoulder and knee, and purple paint had dried on his helmet, the only evidence of their hour-long session of Kat and Boyd v. Roman. The purple headshot had been hers.

Kat inched back and looked at Boyd. She made a hand signal, indicating that the enemy was ahead.

Boyd nodded and crept forward.

She grabbed his sleeve before he moved past and leaned close to whisper. "Remember what I told you," she murmured. "Focus only on the front sight of your weapon. Take a breath, hold it. Aim and release the breath after you fire."

The mask hid most of his face, but the contempt in his expression was clear enough. He jerked free of her loose grasp and crawled forward.

Misogynist. Kat counted to five before trusting herself to move. She understood a level of disbelief or distrust when it came to a stranger who had yet to prove themselves as legit. But to simply ignore solid advice from someone who clearly knew what they were doing — no matter their sex or other state of being — was stubbornly stupid. The splattered artwork all over Boyd's back and helmet should have been enough of a clue. Of course, no skills could be imparted without a will to learn.

Kat adjusted her belt and the remaining ammo. Maybe he thought he'd never need to use his gun in a small town like Graywood. That would make him even more stupid, and sharing her opinion wouldn't change anything. Worse, his stubbornness meant her failure as an instructor. If she couldn't convince some backwoods officers to listen and learn from her expertise, maybe she'd be better off opening her own paintball course.

It wasn't the worst idea she'd ever had.

Boyd eased his paintball gun around the corner, his eye at the sight. At least he held the weapon correctly and leaned as she'd shown him. The *pop-pop-pop* of paint pellets fired from his barrel joined the quiet.

So much for implementing any breathing techniques.

A spray of blue paint exploded against Boyd's helmet and he dropped back with a hiss. He clutched his head with his free hand, his eyes squeezed shut behind his mask. "Farkos, the bastard, shot me in the head!"

"Didn't notice." Kat couldn't keep the sarcasm from her tone. "More importantly, did you get him?"

"That would be a hard negative." Roman stepped around the corner, his weapon down. "Final shot. I win."

Kat couldn't deny it. While she had a single starburst on her chest, the evidence of Roman's victory was all over Boyd. He might as well have been wearing blue coveralls. *Lesson learned.* Never combine training with a student who refused to listen and a challenge from Roman. If she had been solo, the competition would have lasted for hours and, as much as she hated to admit it, winning wouldn't have been a sure thing. Roman was good—really good—which meant being selected to be the firearms instructor was even more of an honor. The department had someone as talented as Roman on their team and had decided to hire her anyway. It made dealing with students like Boyd almost worth it.

"My ear is ringing so bad I can't even hear out of it." Boyd kept his hand pressed to the side of his helmet, as if that would help.

"A real bullet would have hurt a lot worse." Kat straightened, keeping her weapon pointed at the ground. "I'm here to help you become completely comfortable with your weapon and more practiced at using it." She pinched the air. "You're this close to incompetence. I can't teach you if you won't listen to me. Where was your focus when you shot at Roman? Did you even take a breath before you fired?"

"Breathing is very important," Roman said in his monotone, his expression somber.

"I only have half of my hearing now and you expect me to listen to you?" Boyd lurched to his feet. "How many people have you shot on duty, Hellman?"

She'd pulled her weapon too many times to count, but she'd never had to shoot anyone, thank God. "None."

"Exactly. You expect me to learn how to shoot at people from someone who has only shot at targets?"

"As opposed to practicing on live people?" She snorted.

"The odds of actually firing my weapon at a person in a castle are none, and hitting a perp in the shoulder or leg would be enough to bring him down. I don't need to be a sharpshooter. All I need to know is how to aim and fire, and I don't need a pretty cop who can't cut it on the job to show me how to do that."

Kat was in his face before she'd even thought to move. "Take a good look at your suit and helmet. You wouldn't have to worry about bringing anyone down because you'd already be dead." She gave him her battle glare, cold and cruel. "And don't project your weaknesses on me. I'm freaking excellent at my job, too."

Boyd's eyes gleamed and his smile slipped over his face like oil. "That's not what Vic says."

She had him by the front of his suit so fast that he sucked in a breath. Fury colored her vision and rattled along her bones.

"Katerina." The warning in Roman's gravelly voice cut through the red haze, the only thing that stopped her from punching Boyd's helmet in the same spot where Roman had hit him with a paintball.

Boyd jerked away, his smile smaller, meaner. "You can be sure that I'll have some insightful statements to make on my comment card to Chief Clifton, Hellman." He picked up his paintball gun. "And I'm sure every agency will be interested in your level of self-control."

As he brushed past her, Kat closed her eyes and focused on her breathing. *Son of a jerkface.* Was that Vic's plan? To sabotage her here so the likelihood of returning home and still having a job was zero? Did he resent her that much?

"Hey." At Roman's murmur, she opened her eyes. Breaking the paintball ground rules, he had his helmet off. His dark hair was mussed and damp with sweat. "Don't let them get to you. Boyd is stuck in his ways and your ex... Well" — he shrugged — "he just sounds like a prick."

A laugh broke free, surprising her, and the anger that had held her by the throat only seconds before diminished to a tolerable level. She loved that Roman didn't reassure her with pointless comments about her skills, as if she needed the reinforcement. He hadn't confirmed Boyd's less-than-subtle indication that she was weak or incompetent. He didn't play the strong-man card and expect her to crumple or need a hug as she cried on his shoulder. Instead, he just backed her up, like an equal partner would. She loved that too.

Love. Her heart kicked—whether in a panic or excitement, she couldn't tell. But it didn't matter, because she didn't love Roman. She forced herself to study him, his solemn expression, the sharp intelligence in his dark eyes, the way he patiently looked at her with his head canted, as if he saw her as an enchanted queen slowly awakening from a spell broken by his kiss.

As if he already loved her and was simply waiting for her to figure it out.

Hell.

"We're technically off the clock, but there's still time for another game. I want to recapture a quarter-point." Mischief sparkled in his eyes. "The tire zombie apocalypse course is not to be missed." He pulled a canister of paintballs from his side pocket, tossed it in the air and caught it. "Unless you can't handle losing more ground to me? I'm counting down the days to shoot your Python."

"I shot you in the face already, but if you want more punishment, I'm your girl."

"Say that again," he said in a husky voice, easing closer.

"I shot you in the face." She kept her expression innocent, pretending to misunderstand.

"Don't make me tickle you, Angel." He nodded as she glared. "Oh, yes. Gia told me all about your very sensitive armpits." He stepped forward. "And that spot behind your knee, which I was told turns you into a mushy heap of giggles... I'm most inclined to witness that anomaly for myself."

"You wouldn't dare." She took a step back.

One side of his mouth twitched as Roman tossed his helmet aside, and it clattered on the stone. "Sounds like a challenge I can't refuse."

Kat whirled and made it down the hallway and onto the stairs leading out of the castle before the rapid pounding of his boots drilled behind her. Luckily, it was a Monday and there weren't many other people playing. She'd reserved full, exclusive use of the castle course, and the emptiness had added an excellent training element of tension while they'd been stalking each other. Now, without anyone to interfere, it became their personal playground.

She dumped her helmet beside a low wall and dropped her gun in a patch of grass, preferring to have her hands free. Roman gained on her, and without her helmet to muffle noise, his breathing puffed behind her, his steps loud and crunching on the gravel path leading between two massive cedar trees that marked the castle courtyard.

"You can't outrun me," he gasped. "Surrender now and I'll be merciful."

"Never!" Kat picked up her pace, her face hurting from an unstoppable smile. Blood sang in her veins and her breath rasped in her throat as she hurtled a ditch and ran for an outbuilding. She felt like she was a kid again, in a game of tag with her brothers, free of responsibilities with nothing but summer days and fun ahead.

But the man chasing her stirred her in ways that were nothing close to brotherly.

As she leaped onto a climbing wall and scrambled up, he caught her ankle. "Gotcha, Angel."

She kicked him in the chest with her other foot and laughed as he lost his grip and landed on his butt on the ground, looking dazed. "Think again, Farkos."

As he scrambled up, she jumped off the wall and raced into the hedge maze of the adjoining garden course. The moment the pathway split and turned a corner, she slowed her pace to a stealthy walk. The shrubs rose several feet above her head, enough to hide them both and prevent any cheating by jumping up for a view. Roman must have had the same idea. In the sudden silence, there were no footsteps to alert her to his whereabouts. She listened hard, keeping close to the shrubs, but not touching. Any sound might betray her location.

Kat walked at an angle, watching for any movement, both behind and ahead. She controlled her ragged breath until it evened out. Still, that ridiculous smile remained on her face, making her cheeks hurt. It was shocking how the right person could turn a crappy day into what would become fond memories. Vic had never figured that out—how to make her laugh when she didn't feel like it, how to lure her away from dark thoughts and moods. Maybe Roman was right and she'd sold herself short by not waiting.

Waiting for Roman.

Strong arms suddenly clamped around her, trapping her elbows against her sides. She was pulled tight against a firm, obviously male, body, so fast that she didn't have time to reach for the weapon she didn't have. Only countless hours of training—and a familiar, spicy-sweet scent—held instinct in check, and she resisted all the different methods of escaping and taking Roman down.

"Checkmate," he whispered in her ear, his stubbly cheek scraping against hers in a delicious friction.

Kat relaxed against him, still debating what would be more satisfying — showing him up or feeling him up. "Admirably sneaky. But we both know that if you were anyone else, you'd be flat on the ground, face in the dirt and gasping a surrender."

He swallowed, loud enough to hear. "So, you finally admit that I'm not in the same category as anyone else?"

The longing in his voice did something irreparable to her heart, and before she thought better of it, she turned her head and kissed his jaw, placing her gloved hands over his. "You're in danger of a smack down and that's what you want to know? If you're special to me?"

"Am I?"

Kat paused at Roman's question, a vulnerable, gentle inquiry into the pit of her emotions, dredging up what might belong to him. How special was he to her? When it came to relationships, gushing about what she did or didn't feel wasn't her style. Actions were up for interpretation and could be denied. Words weren't so easy.

"I usually don't let complications remain unresolved so long," she said at last.

He chuckled, his chest vibrating against her back. "Don't sugarcoat it. Tell me what you really think."

Her heart was suddenly beating faster and it became hard to breathe, even though Roman's grip wasn't suffocating. She could tell him that the last two weeks with him in the mix had inspired her to look deeper into who she was and what she wanted. She might offer up a vague summary of how her days hadn't been quite so dark with their challenge to look forward to. She could make a dismissive statement about temporary fun and infatuation and that she might miss him a little when it was all over. But none of those, while they held elements of truth, felt enough. She'd told him what she hadn't even been able to tell Gia or the rest of her family, and even in her worst moments, he saw underneath her layers and still wanted to know more. She might not be ready to solidify their relationship by giving it a name, but he deserved to hear that he mattered.

Turning in his arms, halfway surprised that he let her, Kat faced him. He had his neutral mask on, hiding his thoughts from most of the world, but she knew him well enough. Whatever she said next would impact him. As much as she practiced pushing most people back, being on display with her emotions was awkward. She planted her gloved hands on his chest, trapped between pushing and pulling.

"You're scaring me, Angel." One corner of his mouth ticked up, fell.

Good, because you're scaring me too. She released a breath, holding his gaze. "I don't know what you are to me anymore. You've gone from an annoyance to a complication to something undefined."

"Undefined in a good way, I presume."

"I don't know." She continued as his eyebrow twitched. "I can't—won't—make any promises that will end up broken, but I like how you've magically balanced a rough day and managed to make me laugh. And it's not just today. You seem to have a way of making me forget the crap."

"Unquestionably in a good way."

"You also have a way of making me forget common sense and rationality." She grasped for an explanation for her emotions, some excuse she could fall back on later to save her pride.

"I'm mind blowing." He nodded sagely.

"I should absolutely be putting distance between us." But when it came to Roman, practicality was powerless, leaving her to fend for herself...and she was losing.

"But you can't, because I'm magnetic." He grinned, flashing his adorably pointed teeth. "I believe we've found the proper definition."

"Annoyingly magnetic." She huffed a laugh of surrender. "Sounds legit."

"I believe we should explore this undefined area more." He lowered his head to her throat and pressed a lingering, open-mouthed kiss at her pulse. "Thoroughly. I refuse to remain confined to a gray area." He trailed his fingertips along her collarbone to the zipper of her coveralls, leaving a wave of heat. "Don't try to deny my magnetism. Resistance is futile."

"I'm choosing to go along with your plan." She closed her eyes as he gently bit her earlobe. "But make it known that if I wanted to, I could easily resist this thing you loosely call magnetism."

Roman straightened, his eyes hot and glittering. "That, Angel, sounds like a challenge I can't refuse."

He grabbed her hand and dragged her to the spot where he'd been hiding before surprising her, and it was easy to see how he'd caught her unaware. The hedge split in a way that made it impossible to see the opening until she was abreast of it. Roman relentlessly pulled her through a series of twists and turns until they arrived at the center of the maze.

A trio of birch trees, their trunks paper-white, towered above the hedge. A sundial and iron bench rested in a small patch of grass, surrounded by roses, white gladiolas and cosmos, giving the area an English garden vibe and a heady scent. The paintball cleanup crew must be amazing to keep the location free of splattered neon colors.

Roman had her backed against the tree in the next breath, trapping her in delicious possession with his lean body, erasing any potential protest with his mouth. He kissed her, slow and drugging, until her blood raced, her pulse throbbed in every secret and not-so- secret place.

She yanked at the fingers of her gloves, needing them off, needing to touch him, to feel his warm, velvet skin. The gloves dropped to the ground and she fumbled with the zipper of his coveralls, desperate to connect with his flesh. It was almost frightening, this power he had over her, coaxing her to willingly relinquish control. It was an act of trust, and the fact that she knew he wouldn't abuse or betray her weakness elicited a mix of terror and relief, because he tempted her to let him have his way — to trust him enough to open her heart, reveal her fears, dreams and all the cracks in between.

This won't last. How could it? It would be more her fault than his, letting their affair continue, knowing the end result. Eventually, he'd figure out she wasn't all that he thought, his infatuation would fade and she'd be back to being alone. Only, post-Roman, she had a feeling her pride would be more than bruised, and her heart? She'd be down for the count.

"You don't have to say you love me, Angel," he murmured between kisses. "Just be." He slid her coveralls over her shoulders to her waist, leaving her tank top free and her bare skin exposed to the air. "With me."

Her resistance disintegrated. If these fleeting moments were all she'd have with him, she'd be an idiot not to soak up as much as she could. Kat pushed his coveralls down his arms as she kicked off her boots and shimmied completely free of her paintball gear. In just a tank top and shorts, her department shirt and cargo pants left behind in the paintball locker room, she felt light and free. Or maybe it was the company. Either way, she was lost to the sensation.

The tree bark was a rough against her back, but she didn't have a mind to care with Roman's capable, calloused hands skimming beneath her shirt, his mouth exploring hers, and his hardness a dizzying friction against her. Touching him wasn't enough. She needed to be closer.

As if reading her mind, he hooked his arms beneath her legs and guided them around his hips. He rocked into her, and she swore she was ablaze — her skin, blood and every vital organ. Too much and not enough, she was completely at his mercy. She'd never been one to seek different and exciting places to indulge in carnal pleasure, but with Roman, the setting didn't make any difference. Outside, inside, at the lake, in the water, his house or a public paintball course, she couldn't refuse him. She slid her hand down, over the planes and ridges of his stomach, savoring every inch.

"Katerina." He moaned her name, as if it were a benediction, full of pain and hope, and nipped her lower lip. "I want you. Now. Here."

"Less talking," she growled, a wild need inside pounding, demanding to be eased.

He went still and his eyes widened slightly, which immediately sent her on high alert. She held her breath and listened. *Voices nearby, coming closer.*

"Crap," she muttered. She might be okay with getting down and dirty in odd places with Roman, but not with an audience. Planting her feet on the ground, she scrambled for her boots and coveralls while catching her breath.

The voices grew louder, indicating a group of people — at least four, both male and female.

"There's a nook in the maze behind us," Roman whispered, jerking his chin. "We can hide there."

"How do you know that?" But she was already following him, wincing as she stepped on pebbles, her socks not enough of a barrier to save her tender feet. Slipping on her boots would make the journey less painful, but that would require time she wasn't sure she had. She almost squeaked when Roman turned and swept her into his arms.

He grinned down at her as he strode for the hedge maze. "I come here a lot."

"Big surprise." She made her tone acid but wrapped her free arm around his neck. No wonder he'd been able to sneak up on her so easily. He probably had the hedge maze memorized just in case he could convince some sucker to accept his challenge.

Sucker had never been on her resume before. She'd completely bottomed out and it was all Roman's fault.

Inside the hedge walls, he deposited her in a spot that offered a filtered view of the tiny courtyard. Their unwanted company drew close enough to hear their conversation.

"Do you even know how to shoot this?" A male voice, not particularly deep. Kat would guess it belonged to a teenager or slightly older. "Safety off, aim at your target and fire. Anyone can do it."

Kat exchanged an amused look with Roman. *Tell that to Boyd.*

"I've played paintball before," responded a higher voice, feminine with a shot of sneer.

"What about the real thing?" A different, deeper, male voice asked, cool and confident. "Ever shoot a target? Another person?"

"Maybe." The single word was full of sass, while not committing to anything.

Why was that voice so familiar?

"While you've been stuck in 'maybe' land, I've iced three," the other male said. "*Bam-bam-bam.*" The brag to his words killed any credibility. Kat suspected the closest he'd been to shooting an actual human was in a video game.

The foursome came into view, and Kat's temperature dropped, despite the summer heat. Beside her, Roman stiffened. The two young men and one of the girls were unfamiliar.

The other girl was Vee.

Valerie and her companions all carried paintball guns, their safety masks flipped on top of their heads, camouflaged coveralls over their clothes.

Why isn't she at the club? Kat flexed her empty fingers. Even a paintball gun would be a comfort right now. While she wasn't one to judge on appearances, she couldn't dismiss what her gut claimed—that although Vee might not be in trouble at the moment, that condition could change with the wind.

The older of the two men, whose young face had a harsh edge, as if experience added years he hadn't actually lived, slid his hand over Vee's back in an almost possessive manner. The medallion of his bracelet glinted in the sunlight, silver twined with leather. "Don't worry. Shooting at Matt will cheer you up."

"I'll be your huckleberry." The other young man — Matt, apparently — twirled his paintball gun, trying a fancy move, and dropped it. As he scrambled to recover it, the others laughed. He wore an identical leather-bound bracelet as the other guy, and now that they were closer, details became clear of a circle center-punched by a cross and an inverted triangle. Kat couldn't imagine it was some sort of BFF token between the two.

"Fail." Vee sneered, the expression dimming her natural prettiness. "More like a gooseberry." She aimed her gun at the birch trees. A faint *pop* and yellow paint scarred the white bark. "I pretended it was *his* face." She dropped the barrel and swung it at Matt, making Kat wince. "You're right. I feel better already. Next time I think about listening to a traitor, I'll grab a weapon instead."

What the hell? Whether or not Vee wanted to, Kat was going to go all Caroline Hellman on her ass and they'd have that firearms safety lesson ASAP. Whose face did she want to shoot off? Her foster father, Clay, Roman?

The group wandered across the courtyard and to the far edge of the maze, headed for the castle.

"That's the girl Vee was with at the institution," Roman whispered, his focus on the young men and girls.

With baggy coveralls and helmet on, most details of the other girl weren't visible, but Kat noted what she could—skinny enough to look malnourished, deep undereye circles, a hint of bleached-blonde hair.

"We should say 'hi'." Roman's expression took an almost feral edge.

As he moved, Kat grabbed his sleeve, shaking her head. "We should follow them, keep an eye on Vee. She wouldn't be happy to see us right now." While it had been a few years since she'd been a teenager, that awkward age had left scars on her brain and she'd been enough like Vee to know that impressing friends would be more important than a couple of adults—and with this group, she suspected cops wouldn't be on the approved list. "Trust me on this one."

"Always." He motioned for her to follow him.

From a clandestine spot in the hedge, they had a good view of the castle grounds, and the group was active enough, chasing and shooting each other, that there was little downtime to worry about what might be happening to Vee. Watching her play, Kat couldn't ignore a twinge of pride. The girl clearly possessed some raw marksmanship talent to go with her athleticism, but that wasn't all that caught Kat's attention. The harsher of the young men shot with a skill and proficiency that spoke of hours at the range. He didn't hold his weapon as the other kids did, sideways like gangsters in a video game, and every shot he made was aimed at head, heart or knee.

Utterly merciless.

Eventually, Roman glanced at his watch. "I have to be on duty in an hour."

"I don't want to leave while Vee's here with these yahoos." She frowned as the marksman nailed Matt— twice—dropping the kid to the ground, clutching his head. Even with protection, those paintballs stung. "I'll find my own way home."

He hesitated long enough to mark his concern, then nodded. The fact that he didn't question her decision or try to change her mind only lodged him deeper into her heart. He squeezed her shoulder, his hand warm and strong, leaving an imprint on her skin. "Be careful."

She reached for his fingers, but he'd already turned away.

Kat watched the kids play paintball until they ran out of ammo. Then she stalked them back to the course headquarters, hounded by the bone-deep sense that something bad waited on the horizon, and if she made a wrong move at the wrong time, she wouldn't be able to prevent it.

As they crossed the parking lot toward a nondescript sedan, she made note of every physical detail of Vee's companions — the girl's track marks on her arm and shabby chic style, Matt's overgrown auburn curls and Iron Maiden T-shirt, the gun enthusiast's shaved head, snake neck tattoo and combat boots. They jockeyed for shotgun position and scrambled into the car, laughing like normal teenagers.

The instant the sedan peeled out of the parking lot, her stomach nosedived. She couldn't deny the sensation that she'd messed up by letting Vee go without at least trying to stop her.

The dust from the gravel settled and the hum of the accelerating vehicle dwindled into the distance, leaving Kat alone in the silence.

Chapter Twenty-One

The two-acre Graywood city park tucked between a mall and an apartment complex looked nice enough from a distance. Up close, the evidence of humans whose cares didn't include environmental upkeep became clear. Kat wrinkled her nose at the hint of sewer and garbage drifting on the summer air, the trash left behind by people who had no place better to go leaving apathetic stains beneath the trees. They'd spent hours walking, sightseeing the less refined spots in town, and despite Roman's easy conversations with the local homeless population, the sense of wasted time lingered like cigarette smoke in her clothes.

Kat crouched and shone her flashlight into a warped cardboard box tucked between a tree trunk and a rusted bicycle frame robbed of its wheels. The empty space stared back at her, echoing the raw hole that had formed in her gut after Vee and the paintball course. She hadn't slept well, either, the sense that she'd majorly screwed up and didn't yet know how haunting her thoughts, and telling Roman had tempted her by the hour until dawn. The fact that she'd actually considered sharing another fear with him...

Son of a jerkface. Sharing living space with him had been a reckless decision, made without fully considering the consequences. Every time she kissed him or he touched her, she temporarily forgot that they weren't a couple, forgot that she wasn't his. He wasn't her boyfriend or husband, not now or later. She had to regain control of herself before she slipped and couldn't break the fall.

"Comparable to the big city scene you're used to?" Roman's eyes sparkled. Dressed in faded jeans and a black T-shirt that clung just enough to hint at all those delicious muscles beneath, he still held an edge of watchfulness, and she suspected he had a weapon somewhere on his person, easily accessible should the need arise.

She brushed her arm against the weapon at her waist, tucked beneath her shirt. Always ready, like her. It was yet another quality about him that she lov —

Cold jolted through her, and she focused on the improvised tent made from a frayed tarp strung between two bushes. Walking around the more dangerous parts of Graywood as night fell with Roman was a better pastime than gorging on potato chips and gave her a welcome distraction from the man who was beginning to infiltrate every nuance of her life. But no matter what activity they were doing, every moment spent with Roman was a danger in its own — especially when the 'L' word decided to show up, unannounced and unwanted.

He'd said he simply wanted to be with her. Relationships were never that simple. They were messy, painful and full of disappointment.

"No one you've talked to on these excursions has ever seen Irini?" Focusing on work had been a viable remedy for the last decade, and she preferred discussing his missing sister to her own failure to manage her existence. Maybe it would ease the growing ache in her gut, the dead calm before an approaching storm she couldn't see.

"Oh, a few have pretended to have information — at my expense, of course." He kicked a pebble off the sidewalk and into the grass. "Nothing ever panned out. I prefer to believe that no news is good news."

Maybe, maybe not. She wasn't going to be the one to kill a single smidge of his hope. "Any news on who Vee's paintball partners are?"

He shook his head. "I'm beginning to question my investigative skills." So fast she nearly ran into him, he pivoted in front of her, forcing Kat to stop. "In case I failed to mention it earlier, thanks for agreeing to come with me tonight. It's hard." His throat worked. "Trying to remain positive when the odds are...ugly."

Whether it was his unexpected closeness or the vulnerability in his eyes, her ribcage squeezed, a definite warning. Step by slow step, he pulled her deeper into his world, and like the foolish human seduced by a fae, if she surrendered another inch, she'd never escape. She'd soften and he'd see her, really *see* her, and —

The sense that she tiptoed across an ice-covered lake as it cracked beneath her boots made her pulse flutter.

He caressed her cheek with the back of his knuckles, a tender, intimate act, and Kat swore the ground splintered under her soles into shards of ice. Any second and she'd be floundering beneath the frozen water, unable to breathe.

"There's no one else I'd rather have beside me searching for Irini." He paused, and the weight in that single disturbance in the silence rang like an iron bell in her ears. "Katerina, I'm—"

"It's obvious we're not going to find anything helpful tonight. The people who once stayed here are gone." She stepped back, out of his reach, ignoring how the loss of his touch turned her stomach. "I have a one-on-one with Boyd bright and early tomorrow and need to be sharp."

He stared at her, and she waited for the questions, the push for an explanation, a fight waiting to be triggered with just the right word. Arguments were so much easier to deal with than confessions and offered a valid reason to walk away, to put distance between them, the first step in an inevitable breakup. She lifted her chin in challenge—ready—and pretended her heart wasn't kicking and screaming.

Instead, Roman slipped his hand into hers and guided her back to where he'd parked his truck, as if he'd read her mind and refused to give her the easy out she wanted. As they walked, their boots on the concrete path kept a soft, easy rhythm. His fingers were warm and steady around hers, not the controlling stranglehold she hoped for. She could pull away easily enough—she *should* pull away. A strange sensation curled through her, disturbing because she couldn't decide if it was relief...or regret.

Kat sucked in a breath as they reached the truck and Roman released her hand to unlock the door. This moment was a crossroad, and Roman had made it clear that the next move was all on her. But no matter which path she chose, she was sure to lose. The real decision was what—if anything—she was willing to pay.

* * * *

Roman paced the pavestones of the secluded garden he'd reserved for the price of a future ride-along and pivoted at the gazebo decorated in strings of tiny lavender lights. He slipped his hands into his jeans' pockets instead of shoving them through his hair again and retraced his steps. He shouldn't be nervous. There was no reason Katerina wouldn't show. The note he'd left on the kitchen table contained the address of where to meet him, making it clear that this was a challenge appointment. She'd never admit it was a date.

A shudder ran through him. Over a week had passed since Katerina's decision to move in. Sharing the house with her had been an unexpected journey. They spent every possible free second together during the waking hours, but when it came to retiring for the day, they always said their polite good evenings and went to their respective bedrooms. Yet, every night, she'd slip into his room and beneath the covers like a midnight fantasy come to life, always gone by daybreak, back to her personal bubble in his sister's old room, as if she could pretend nothing ever happened between them in the darkness.

Most of those nights, he had the distinct impression that she didn't seek him out for the physical connection alone. She needed him as much as he needed her — simply to be with the one person who made life...*more* — deeper, brighter, richer. There were so many reasons why she'd be reluctant to make any confessions, all of which he understood. But he wished she'd do it anyway, to confirm that the fire between them was undeniable, far stronger, more crucial than a fleeting fascination.

Turning, he paused and faced the scene he'd created for tonight. Sycamores and ash made a loose barrier on three sides, their branches forming delicate lacework against the clear evening sky and tracing the stars like a dot-to-dot puzzle. Crickets made a soft symphony in the distance, and without any small-town noises, the quiet seemed hushed, as if the setting held its breath until Katerina appeared. Rosebushes bearing white blooms lined one side of the gazebo, capturing the gentle glow of lavender — Kat's favorite color — from the lights twined around the gazebo posts. Their delicate scent perfumed the warm air without any need for scented candles.

No challenge with Kat was complete without pie. A strawberry confection, straight from Franny's oven, sat on the gazebo railing beside tiny, portable speakers. A six-pack of microbrew nestled in the ice bucket nearby, her preferred frosty beverage.

Maybe it wouldn't matter to her that he'd gleaned all those favorite details from the time he'd spent with her, not Gia, or that he'd gathered them all in his awkward way of showing her how he felt.

Not telling her he loved her aloud was slow torture.

Roman resumed his trek over the pavestones and Irish moss, the stray fronds of a border fern whispering against his jeans as he passed. He couldn't push her into admitting that she possessed any deep feelings for him, and declaring how he felt would send her running. He couldn't ask her to stay, even though the thought of her leaving destroyed him. His only hope was to coax her with the meager weapons he had — dance moves, pie and her personal Kryptonite...his mouth. He wasn't afraid to use it against her.

Roman reached the gazebo, turned again and paused. Kat stood at the edge of the garden, and even knowing she'd show up on time, his breath caught at her beauty. Beneath the starlight, still mostly in shadows, she looked like a fairy queen bewitched by a mortal's snare. Her hair was long and loose, cascading down her pale shoulders and the strappy camisole the color of a clear lake. Even in casual capri jeans and flat sandals, she radiated elegance. Her lovely lips were parted, her eyes widened just a bit, and when she stepped forward into the light, her expression of wonder was undeniable.

Suddenly, he could breathe again.

"Seeing if you could surprise me better not be part of the challenge, Farkos." Her voice didn't hold any snap as she ambled toward him, looking from him to the corners of the garden, then back to him. "That would be low. Sneaky, but too low to be admirable."

"There's no such thing as 'too low' in competition." He met her halfway and they both stopped a foot away from each other. The fact that he almost smiled without thinking about it said a lot about the power she held over him. "Want pie first? And to be upfront and transparent, as to avoid any unjust accusations, it's strawberry. With whipped cream."

She licked her lips, and he almost popped his buttons. Only by some superhuman willpower did he resist the need to pull her into his arms and kiss her into forever. "I prefer to win before dessert." Kat shrugged. "It makes victory even sweeter."

"I admire your confidence." He surrendered to the urge to tuck her hair behind her ear and trailed his fingers along her jaw, her responsive shiver making his blood heat another degree. "But tonight will be a full point in my victory column, guaranteed."

Kat cocked a hip and curled her lip, giving him her disdainful look. "Bring it on."

"Thought you'd never ask." He leaned near, and when her attention drifted to his mouth, he dropped his hand before he reconsidered his sensible game plan, fell to his knees and begged her to be his anyway. "Stay right here."

Her gaze was a heated caress on his back as he walked to the gazebo. He called over his shoulder, "Feel free to ogle my assets as much as you want, Angel." He hid a smile at her incoherent grumble and stopped at the gazebo, where he'd set up his speakers and phone. His heart thrummed at an abnormal pace, too quick, as he put his challenge into action. *Can't Help Falling in Love* flowed through the quiet.

Pivoting, he found Kat with her arms crossed, her lip still curled. He made it back to her as Elvis crooned 'take my hand' and he offered his. "Dance with me for an hour, letting me lead when I want. That's the challenge." He lowered his voice. "I dare you to refuse."

The annoyance in her expression made her thoughts easy to read. She was stuck between a boulder and a tidal wave—her pride and her need to win. She'd vowed never to dance with him and reneging now would be a strike against her honor. But her hatred of losing made the choice a battle. He suspected he already knew what her final decision would be and yet a part of him hoped that—for him—she'd compromise.

She released a tight breath. "Dare accepted. I'm not dancing. You can keep your point, but I'll take the pie."

"No dancing, no pie, Katerina." He kept his tone soothing, velvet, unwilling to give up. He'd sacrifice his winning edge to have her dancing in his arms for an hour. "I promise I won't step on your toes."

"Do you *want* to lose our competition?"

"What I want, at least for this moment, is to dance with you." He eased closer, near enough to catch her herbal scent and heat. "I want you in my arms, your head on my shoulder as we sway to the beat. I want to feel your heart keeping time with mine, your breath on my neck. Any one of those things would be worth losing a hundred points."

Kat opened her mouth, closed it and swallowed. She looked to the gazebo and its twinkling lights, obviously avoiding his gaze. "You're going to have to settle for one point tonight."

"I thought you were a worthy opponent." His chest tightened, but he didn't lower his hand, leaving the offer open. "I'm usually not mistaken about people."

Her smile was sharp. "No one's perfect."

"Nothing beautiful in this world is ever perfect." The song ended, followed by *You Made Me Love You.* "It's not like you to give up without a fight," he said, all innocence. "Are you not getting enough sleep?"

A delicate flush invaded her cheeks. "My snooze situation is fine."

"It would be better if you woke up beside me every morning." He grinned with an edge of wolf as her blush deepened. "We've determined a lack of sleep isn't to blame for the brutal impairment of your competitive nature. Perhaps it's this." He pressed a kiss beneath her ear and trailed two more down her neck. "Or this?" As he slid his hand lightly down her hip, she shuddered but didn't soften her stance or touch him back. She didn't tip her head to give him better access to her neck or ear for nibbling.

"Don't," she whispered.

Immediately, he stepped back, beyond her personal space, and the tightness in his chest became a vise, slowly compressing. Her eyes were closed, her expression pained, and a wild sort of panic ignited in his heart. He was losing her and didn't even know why. "Angel, if you won't dance with me, talk to me."

A noise that could have been a laugh came from her throat and she opened her eyes. "You should know me well enough by now. I'm not much into meaningless chatter."

"Then make it meaningful." At her hesitation, he added, "Please."

She paused, staring at the gazebo lights, and Roman counted his rapid heartbeats while she decided. He couldn't force her to stay with him for a single minute, wouldn't want to, but the thought of her walking away, leaving an emptiness no one else could fill, left him cold. In a matter of weeks, she had irreversibly impacted his life, and even though she'd only been in his house for days, her absence would be more pronounced than his sisters with their own lives.

At last, she shook her head and turned back the way she'd come. "Really not in the mood."

"Then stay and have pie with me, no expectations." That vise in his chest became a desperate ache, a warning that if she left, she'd never return. "Hasn't our relationship moved beyond mere competition? Don't shut me down."

She suddenly whirled and faced him, her eyes flashing. "I came here for a challenge, not a conversation, meaningful, meaningless or otherwise. Since I forfeited, there's no reason to stay."

"I'm not enough of a reason to stay?" He couldn't breathe as she studied him, her expression unyielding. If she clung to pretending that he meant nothing to her, he could almost understand why she would. Their connection scared him too, but what they had together, what they'd found in each other—soulmate, partner, best friend—was worth any risk. Katerina wasn't one to let fear remain a roadblock. He could only hope she'd apply that practice to herself now.

"The last few weeks," she said in a trembling voice, "I've had the distinct sensation of dodging windmill blades equipped with razors. There have been moments of relief as I've realized I'm somehow not cut, but that relief fades fast because I know that I'll eventually wind up bloodied." She pressed her lips together and shook her head. "I like you more than I expected to, but that doesn't change the fact that my temporary job is almost over. I took it to prove to both myself and my captain that my divorce won't impact my skills, that I can work with anyone and remain professional."

"You *like* me?" The ache behind his heart sprouted barbs. "Our nights together... That's how you express *liking* someone?"

Kat shrugged one shoulder, her expression carefully neutral.

"You don't get to play the aloof card, Katerina. Not with me." He stepped closer, a dangerous edge in his emotions, and the wariness in her eyes gave him a stab of satisfaction. "You may find it easier to pretend that I mean nothing to you, that the nights in my arms didn't happen, but don't lie to me. Don't act as if you can't trust me, when we both know that's not true."

She folded her arms, not backing down, as usual. They stared at one another for a prolonged moment, neither one of them blinking. At last, she huffed. "Fine. I trust you."

"That's a start." He left the razor in his tone.

"Trust isn't the issue."

"You're correct. The problem is a lack of faith on your part. You're comparing me to everybody else you've ever met, everyone who has let you down or hurt you or told you that you're not enough." The shimmer of tears in her eyes told him he'd struck true. "I'm not them. I'm not Vic or your mother. I'm not Boyd or your captain, your brothers or father." He took the last step between them and cupped her face between his hands. "I'm telling you right here, right now, that I will always catch you if you fall. I'll always back you up. I might not always agree with you, but I'll never marginalize your opinion. And I'll always, *always* fight for you in whatever way you need."

She closed her eyes and moisture glittered at the seams of her eyelids. Still, she didn't lean her cheek into his hand or wrap her arms around his waist. Her spine was stiff, her arms and shoulders tense. Whatever war she waged, it was on the battlefield in her head, between two sides of herself. He was simply a casualty.

Gently, Roman kissed her forehead. "I'm not going anywhere, Angel. I refuse to push you into anything you're not ready for, but I'll be here for you. Until then..." He released her and stepped back. "You know where to find me."

Slipping his hands into his pockets, he walked out of the soft lavender lights and into the shadows, leaving his heart in Katerina's hands.

Chapter Twenty-Two

Kat parked her SUV in the one shady spot in the afterschool club parking lot and slid out. Two days after her dance challenge forfeit, she still reeled from Roman's reaction. No one in her life—not her instructors or mentors, friends or family—had ever left a decision completely up to her without any attempt at influence or manipulation. When he'd walked away, leaving her stunned with his open-ended invitation to forever, she'd swear the empty space he'd left behind had opened into a bottomless pit at her feet, waiting to swallow her up. And her heart...

She couldn't deny the possibility that he was right, that her lack of faith—her fear of being hurt, of being found deficient by the ones she trusted most—was the reason she couldn't bring herself to examine their connection for longer than three seconds. But Roman had never made her feel alone or apart. Even though their relationship was only weeks old, her gut told her she could trust him. She *did* trust him. But if she told him how perfect she felt whenever she was with him, uttered the words aloud, that would make her love for him real and give him the power to tear her apart.

Love. A hundred dragonflies took flight in her stomach. *Hell.*

The early summer morning calm didn't help her thundering heartrate and she stuffed her shaking hands into her jeans' pockets as she crossed the parking lot to the club building. The last two days, she'd purposely avoided Roman, needing time to mull over every detail of what he'd said, because the next step — *every* step afterward — scared the living hell out of her.

She flung open the afterschool club doors and entered the quiet hall. Her undefined relationship with Roman wasn't the only issue making it hard to sleep. Most of the officers at Graywood PD were enthusiastic and responsive, improving on their firearms skills. Then there was Boyd. Each session was another complaint on her comment card. The call into the chief's office to address their confrontation at the paintball course hadn't come...yet. But going by Boyd's smirk, it would be. He was simply biding his time. A single failure in such a small department would outweigh any success.

Even worse, more than a week had passed since paintball and Vee hadn't shown up to the club. She refused to answer any texts or calls. Roman had researched the emblem worn by Valerie's paintball partners, sent out queries to other agencies without any leads. Kat had gone so far as to drop in on Vee's foster parents, who claimed that she eventually came home every night. They seemed unconcerned about what she did with her time or who she hung out with, as long as she checked in. Reading between the lines wasn't hard. They were only worried about the monthly check they received from the government, not Vee herself.

Scumbags.

Kat entered the gym and her breath bottled up. As if she'd never been gone, Vee sat in the gym corner, hunched in her black hoodie and playing a handheld video game. Relief washed through her as she waved a welcome to Clay and went straight to Vee. She crossed her arms and proceeded to loom.

Vee didn't even bother to look up, tapping the buttons with her thumbs, complete concentration on the game.

When it became clear that looming had zero effect, she tried words. "Decided to come back and mingle with the peasants for a day?"

No response.

"What's up with the silent treatment?" Kat sat cross-legged in front of her and stared long enough for anyone to feel uncomfortable. Vee had some serious ignoring skills. "I thought we were friends."

She snorted, the first acknowledgment of Kat's presence.

"Friends don't ignore pages of texts or dozens of phone calls." Kat fought the urge to swipe the game from Vee's hands and throw it across the gym. "Friends don't go AWOL without at least a note."

"I don't do that to my *friends*," Valerie said, never taking her gaze from the screen. She pushed her sleeve up and silver glinted beneath the gym lights.

A cold ribbon curled in her belly. Vee was wearing the same bracelet as her scuzzy paintball partners, as if she'd become part of their club...or joined their gang.

Resisting the need to grab Vee's wrist and rip the offensive jewelry off, she tapped the silver emblem once and added some venom to her tone. "What's *this*?"

Valerie jerked her wrist away. Her eyes were black, poisonous flames. "My *real* friends are there when I need them. They don't tell me what I should or shouldn't do and they definitely don't give me crappy advice that blows up in my face."

Kat remained still, terribly aware of that invisible bottomless pit reaching for her.

"I'm sure it was easy for you, telling me what I should do to about Derick." She lurched to her feet with a sneer. "It wasn't like you had anything to lose, right? I was so dumb, trusting you when you don't even take your own stupid advice and tell Roman that you're in love with him. Keeping it real, aren't you, Pageant Queen?"

Stunned into silence, she could only stare as Vee flung her backpack over her shoulder and pointed in her face.

"Don't call or text me again or I'll file a stalking order against you." With those parting words, Vee hurried away.

Kat studied the stained gym wall without seeing it, stuck between shock and fury. She'd only been trying to help, to save Vee from the mistakes she'd made. If Derick didn't like her, it was his loss, and now that Vee knew where she stood with him, she could get over it and move on. Better a small heartache at the beginning than a heartbreak at the end. And calling her out, basically branding her a phony coward?

She rose, fury a scorching needle in her chest. What was the point? Vee had made it very clear that she preferred the company of hoodlums over her. If she didn't want their friendship to continue, Kat certainly wasn't going to push herself on the girl. She had her limits. As far as the people Vee chose to hang out with, Roman was perfectly capable of keeping an eye on them without her assistance. She hadn't come here looking for a friend, anyway.

People sucked, no matter their age.

She counted to five and turned toward the door. Vee had obviously left. Kat bit back a sigh. Stalking order or not, she should probably follow her, see if she hooked up with her shady friends. Even if their friendship had turned hostile, she never wanted Valerie to get hurt. And since Kristen, one of the female club volunteers, was here with Clay, she could leave for a few, no problem, except...

Clay frowned at some papers in his hand, and an unfamiliar man stood with them. Kristen looked in Kat's direction and the man came toward her.

"Katerina Hellman-Patterson?" he asked.

Hearing her married name on a stranger's lips was never a good sign. "Yeah?"

He handed her a paper. "You've been served."

"Marvelous." She scanned the summons as he made an exit. *Mark Peters v. Graywood Afterschool Club, a nonprofit corporation, Roman Vandilo Farkos and Katerina Jacqueline Hellman-Patterson.* She crumpled the papers in her fist. Being sued while on the job happened occasionally and officers had the benefit of the department's lawyer to take care of the litigation. But this... Her stomach tumbled. This lawsuit was a death sentence for her career. Once the captain found out—and he would—even if she explained the particulars in the most practical manner possible, his doubts about her self-control would deepen.

Her phone vibrated and she fished it from the side pocket of her jeans. *Graywood Police Department.* That rock in her stomach rolled again as she answered.

"Hellman?" At the chief's voice, she squeezed her eyes shut. "You have some free time this morning to chat?"

"Sure." By some miracle, her voice sounded normal. "What time?"

"How about now?" His even tone revealed no hint as to what the chat might entail, which was somehow worse.

"I'll be there in fifteen."

The ten-minute drive to the police department drifted by in a blur. Exactly on time, Kat settled into the chair in the chief's office and waited for the hammer to fall.

Kyle Clifton, Graywood Chief of Police, came from a law enforcement background. He'd risen in rank from cadet, when he was too young to be an officer, to a volunteer reserve. From there, he'd gotten his foot in the door when he'd been hired as a patrol deputy. Earning each promotion, he'd put in the time, learned every position of the department and gained the respect of his fellow officers and the community along the way. Kat had never met a more humble law enforcement officer in her life.

Which made this impromptu meeting all the more nerve-racking.

She sat in the chair he indicated, and even though he emerged from behind his desk and sat in the empty chair beside her rather than keeping the barrier between them, she couldn't relax.

"I won't waste time with pleasantries, which I'm sure you appreciate." He waited for her nod, his expression revealing nothing. "You still have another two weeks before the final demonstration, the before-and-after show where I suspect my men will prove that choosing you wasn't a mistake."

As much as she appreciated his confidence in her teaching, Kat kept her mouth shut. He hadn't got to the real reason for calling her in yet. She sensed that from a galaxy away.

"Nonetheless, it has been brought to my attention that you may have a personal conflict with one of my officers." He paused and studied her, as if waiting for her to voluntarily supply the name.

Hell, I have nothing more to lose. "Let me guess...Boyd."

He nodded. "I understand that Boyd isn't much of a go-getter and he's more stuck in his ways than some of my other boys. I suspected he might be resistant to you as an instructor, but I also expected your level of professionalism to handle it."

Her cheeks warmed at the censure. "You're right about all of it. I lost my temper after a long hour of going nowhere with him, then dealing with his contempt. I should have walked away instead of grabbing him by the front of his shirt and getting in his face."

The chief canted his head, looking thoughtful. "Well, I'm not so certain about that. Boyd would never listen to someone who's intimidated by him, but the fact that you manhandled him puts me in a hard spot. At the very least, I have to conduct a cursory investigation of his accusations."

Kat's stomach sank. An investigation would mean a letter in her file and a report back to her captain—another black mark, another reason why he shouldn't make her leave of absence permanent. Still, she was a professional, and as much as she'd like to throw a bitch fit, she refused to let Boyd destroy what remained of her dignity.

"I understand. No matter what you decide, I appreciate the opportunity to share what I know. For the most part, your officers have been great, and I hope

I've taught them at least a few new tricks." Somehow, her voice held steady. She stood as he rose from his chair and extended his hand.

"I have no doubt you've taught them well. As much as I wanted Farkos to assume the firearms training, I can't say I'm sorry that he suggested you take over instead." He winked and rose from his chair. "No matter what Boyd says."

Kat froze and the room seemed to close in on her, suffocating. "Roman suggested what?"

"I had no idea who you were or that you were in town until he mentioned it—with no small amount of manipulation, Roman style." The chief headed for the door. His voice seemed to come from a long tunnel, distorted and echoing. "He'd do almost anything to avoid additional duties until his pet project in the afterschool club settles. When he sets his mind on a goal, he goes after it."

She barely heard his words over the roar in her head. Roman had been chosen for the job and hadn't told her. All this time, he'd let her believe she'd been hand-selected, sought out, not a backup plan because he didn't feel like doing it himself.

Another man, another lie, another punch in the throat to remind her that she'd never quite be enough. She may have had to take the class twice to get it through her thick skull, but she'd just graduated with flying colors.

Chapter Twenty-Three

Generally, Roman checked in at the police department on a daily basis, whether or not he was on duty. Since Kat had joined part of his days and filled his house with new life, finding outside activities to fill the emptiness had become easy and he'd broken routine. But she'd been avoiding him and he had a solid reason to check in at the department. He'd sent a rough illustration of the symbol worn by Vee's new friends to a few other agency connections who owed him favors, and while nothing had panned out, he wanted to see if any information had come in. Then he was off to meet Gia at the salon to keep his feet pretty.

As he walked to his desk, past the chief's closed door, he glimpsed Boyd lurking by the dispatch office, probably because they always had donuts—not that he ever judged a man by the number of donuts he devoured. He turned on his dinosaur computer. As the email app worked at loading, he backpedaled to Boyd and the donuts.

"What's up with the chief being here on Saturday?" He jerked his chin at the chief's office. A table with donuts was just inside the dispatch door, and he took a pink frosted confection before Boyd got to it.

"Meeting with Hellman." Boyd dusted off a smattering of powdered sugar from the front of his uniform. "It was time."

The small smirk on his coworker's face killed his appetite, and he set the donut down without taking a bite. "Time for what? She has another two weeks before the training is over."

"I suppose that will be up to the chief, after he conducts his investigation." Boyd stuffed the rest of his donut into his mouth.

A knot formed in Roman's chest, dark and spiked, and a noise close to a growl rose from a place he usually reserved for uncooperative criminals. "What did you do?"

"Told the truth." Licking his fingers, Boyd's eyes gleamed with a triumphant light. "I bet you, like the rest of our department, didn't know that she was put on leave back home because she can't control her personal crap. I have a friend who worked with her, and when he found out she was temp-hired here, he told me what she'd done to him and warned me about her temper. It was my obligation to inform the chief of her outburst concerning me."

It took all of Roman's considerable self-control not to drag Boyd behind the building, toss him into the bed of his truck, drive him to the edge of town and drop him there, preferably in a sewer ditch. "I don't suppose this friend of yours is Vic Patterson?"

Boyd paused between licking his fingers clean. "Yeah, you know him? We were at the academy together, going on ten years ago. I hadn't talked to him for almost that long, but he must have heard I worked here and that Hellman was teaching firearms. You know how it is. We protect our own."

Roman counted to twenty, staring at Boyd while he did so and wrestling down a surprisingly strong darkness that suggested viciously rearranging Boyd's face. "Vic Patterson is Katerina's ex-husband as of a few weeks ago. He cheated on her and took her for every cent she had, which in my opinion justifies a proper fist to the face."

To his credit, Boyd actually looked guilty.

"*That* is why she is on a temporary leave of absence. Her personal crap is Vic himself, not any flaw in her skills, and as long as she's working here, you better believe I consider her as *one of our own*."

"I didn't know. I swear." Boyd lifted his hands in the universal sign of innocence.

The chief's door opened and Katerina walked out. Her lovely face was pale and she looked like she was on the verge of either breaking down or blowing up. When her gaze fell on him, he went cold. There was no reflection of the warm, funny and vulnerable woman he'd come to know, only the icy stranger he'd met at a masquerade ball weeks ago. She walked straight past him without saying a word, a queen done with niceties. He might as well have been Boyd — or not there at all.

"Katerina, wait." He hurried after her, but if she heard him, she made no sign of it. She barged through the doors and out into the parking lot, never slowing.

He caught up with her as she fumbled with her keys to unlock her SUV. "Angel, talk to me. Boyd told me what he did."

She whirled on him so fast, he almost took an involuntary step backward. "What Boyd did? How about what *you* did?"

This fury in her voice, the accusation in her eyes drove a knife through his heart. *Chief told her.* His stupid little secret, insignificant and meaningless to everyone except Katerina. He went for blasé, even as hairline cracks crept through his heart. "What did I do this time?"

"I thought being offered to train firearms was some sort of rainbow serendipity in all the crap, an opportunity to both occupy my time and keep my skills sharp while I was on leave, to show everyone divorce had zero effect on my job. It was perfect and I stupidly thought that maybe everything would turn out fine."

"It *will* turn out fine." He reached for an escaped strand of her hair to tuck it behind her ear, and she smacked his hand away.

"All this time, you knew it wasn't me the chief wanted as the firearms instructor." She pointed in his face, her tone slowly carving out his heart. "Boyd's behavior makes perfect sense now. Everyone else was fully aware that you were the preferred man for the job and rejected it. I'm only here because you needed a standby, a quick substitute, someone qualified enough to appease the chief so you wouldn't have to take on the extra duty."

"That's only partly true —"

She cut him off with a sharp swipe of her hand through the air. "If it was only the instructor position involved, a sting to my pride to protect the afterschool club, I could get over it." Tears shimmered in her eyes. "But you made it personal. Instead of telling me the truth, you played me."

"You aren't a game to me."

"Worse," she continued, as if he hadn't spoken, "even though I knew I shouldn't, I wanted to believe you. I wanted to believe that I was more to you than what I could do with a gun, that you were more interested in who I am than what I am, but relationships don't work like that, do they? If I don't fit inside the lines and keep with the expectations, it falls apart."

"Hell, Kat." How could she not believe he'd been completely sincere with her after everything? Or that he expected her to be anything more than herself? "You're *everything* to me. Don't you know that?" Risking her wrath, he stepped closer. "I didn't tell you about the position because you were obviously the best choice, whether or not it was initially intended for me. You're right about the serendipity, not only because your being in town was the perfect solution." Her eyes sparked like fireworks gone rogue and she fisted her hands, but since she hadn't attacked him yet, he held his ground. "I finally found you. I hadn't even known I'd been looking for you until that night. Every step I've taken with you since has merely confirmed what I already know. I'm unconditionally in love with you, *all* of you. If you had hooks for hands and couldn't shoot, that wouldn't affect how I feel in any manner." He tried for a smile that only made it to one corner of his mouth. "It would merely make it easier to beat you at the range."

All the passion drained from her expression and left it a blank, unreadable slate, as if she'd completely shut him out.

Everything inside him went numb. He preferred the anger. At least then he knew she hadn't slammed the door on him.

"I'm going home," she said as she stepped around him and opened her SUV.

"My house?" His heart pounded against his ribcage.

She shook her head.

"I never thought you were a quitter."

Katerina paused and the look she gave him could freeze blood and frost bones.

"We—us, you and me, what we have together— we're worth fighting for. Don't bail on me, Katerina. Fight back." His voice cracked. "Fight for *me*."

She slipped into the SUV seat without a word or a second look back, and he knew, deep to his core, there was no return for her. He'd lost her and no amount of pushing, pleading or challenges would change that. If she wanted to leave, he couldn't—wouldn't—stop her. Even if he threw a million truths at her, he couldn't force her to listen or believe.

As she shut the door and the engine sputtered to life, he stepped back and let her go.

* * * *

Maybe Kat should have texted Gia before showing up at her house, but she didn't want to risk leaving enough time for a family meeting to be called, and her fingers were shaking too badly to send a message that would make any sense. She unlocked the door and went inside without knocking.

"G? You home?" She tossed her keys on the end table and headed for the kitchen. When her mother appeared in the doorway instead of her little sister, coffee cup in hand, she almost turned around. Dealing with Caroline Hellman today was at the bottom of her long, long list of things that had gone wrong. "Hey, Mom. Why are you here? I thought you bought a house down the street?"

Caroline's gaze swept over her and she immediately retreated to the kitchen without saying anything.

No censure? No underhanded comment disguised as helpful? Kat hesitated before following. *This is it. The end of the world.*

Her mother poured a second cup of coffee, added a splash of caramel creamer and a shot of chocolate then handed it to Kat.

Slowly, she took it, staring at Caroline. This wasn't the end of the world. It was the loss of her sanity after one too many blows to her head and heart. Her mother always admonished her when adding sugar to anything.

"We may not always see eye to eye, but I'm still your mother," Caroline said, retrieving her own cup of straight black coffee, no additives allowed. "I know when one of my children is upset."

'Upset' didn't even come close to covering it, and she had no desire to discuss Vee's rejection, the investigation, Roman's heartbreaking betrayal or her own stupidity with her mother. Caroline's opinion of her was already low enough, and one more kick might break her.

Kat wrapped her icy hands around the cup and wished the heat could penetrate her chest. "I'm going home. I just stopped in to say my goodbyes."

"Is that the wisest choice?"

All the events of the day crashed down on her and she set her cup on the counter with too much force, sloshing hot coffee on her hand. "I don't need anyone's stamp of approval, Mother, and I learned at a tender age that I'd never have yours, so you can save your breath."

"Oh, darling..." Caroline laid her hand over her heart, as if proclaiming her innocence. "I've never fooled myself into believing that you especially wanted or needed my approval. You're my daughter and I love you, whether or not we agree on certain subjects." Tears—real, shimmering tears—filled her mother's eyes. "That will never change."

Kat sniffed and turned her attention out of the window, the unexpected display of emotion making her throat scratchy.

"All I ever wanted was to make you aware of the options at your disposal, that there were plenty of alternatives to law enforcement, careers that wouldn't put you into danger daily. I thought if I could convince you to simply give another profession a chance, you'd realize that."

"The same predators and scumbags inhabit every other career, Mother. The danger is simply different." She ran her finger absently over the smooth handle of her coffee cup. "Sometimes they're even worse because you don't expect the menace until it's already happened." Her heart constricted. Roman's secret may have been unexpected, but as angry as she was, she knew he hadn't done it to hurt her. Everything else he'd said in between would have been easier to digest if he'd disclosed that detail from the very beginning...and she would probably never have given him a second of her time.

I'm not thinking about Roman.

Kat forced herself to meet her mother's gaze. "I hated those uppity social events you used to drag us to, the way you glossed over my achievements and presented Gia like she was the one jewel of the family, leaving the rest of us in the background. Running in the opposite direction was an easy choice."

"Katerina, it was never *my* approval you looked for." Caroline joined her at the window. "Ever since you were a toddler, you wanted to be a part of whatever game your brothers played with your father, no matter how rough they were or how many times they made you cry. There were uncountable occasions I wanted to hold you close and keep you safe instead of allowing you to run with them." She sighed. "I knew from the start that I didn't have much of a chance at drawing you away, but I had to try. You always had more interest in their toy soldiers than any doll or cute stuffed animal."

"That's not true." Kat picked up her cup and took a sip, swallowing any hint of tears along with her coffee. "I still have Mr. Fluffy Pants in my closet."

Her mother looked horrified. "That ratty dinosaur your father won for you at a carnival?"

"Correction. I *beat* Dad at the ring toss for Mr. Fluffy Pants." Kat grinned, surprised she had it in her. "Best trophy ever."

Caroline's sniff held the usual amount of disdain, but the small smile afterward eased any sting. "I've always been very proud of you, Katerina," she said, her voice soft and rich with emotions she rarely expressed. "Even if we have different visions of what we want for your life, never doubt that I'm astounded by the achievements you've made, the strength and courage you've shown over the years and continue to exhibit on a daily basis."

The giant boulder in Kat's throat was hard to swallow down, the burn of tears impossible to hide. "Thanks, Mom, but you should know" —she sucked in a breath and let it out, along with a rush of words— "I'm on leave because I punched Vic, I probably won't get my job back, I'm being sued by a scumbag dad I took down at the afterschool club, my new friend ripped me a new one for giving her crappy advice and I found out that the only reason I'm the firearms instructor is because Roman didn't want it, so I broke it off with him."

There. It's all out in the open. She felt like a deflated balloon, all the air suddenly gone, nothing left but a shriveled, stretched-out shell.

"Oh, Kitty-Kat." Caroline wrapped her in a hug and held on tight, the act so rare that Kat stiffened in surprise. "You'll be fine. You're smart, strong and resourceful, and you'll always have your family in your corner."

Kat squeezed her eyes shut until the threat of tears receded and she could speak without cracking. "Kitty-Kat? Really?" She relaxed and wrapped her arms around her mother. "You've never called me that." Sighing, she rested her chin on Caroline's shoulder, not really minding the childhood nickname or the embrace.

"You'll always be my Kitty-Kat." Her mother stroked her hair like she had when Kat had been a girl, and it took everything Kat had not to let the tears free.

"I'm sorry, Mom, for believing I knew everything and for all the times I've been disrespectful. I'd name them individually, but that might take a year. I know you only want what's best for me, and even if we disagree, I appreciate that."

At her mother's sniffles, Kat bit her lip. Making her mother cry hadn't been part of her plan.

"I never meant to alienate you or push you harder than I should have." Caroline's tone strengthened. "But you know, it's never too late to start fresh."

"Mom!" Kat jerked out of her mother's hold. "We've covered this ground. I like what I do. Period. Not changing careers. If I'm not offered my job back, I'll find an agency that will take me."

"I wasn't speaking of careers, darling, even though I'd sleep better at night knowing you're not a walking target for criminals."

Kat gave her a suspicious look.

"And I have no need to rehash my opinion on your marriage to Vic."

"Thank God for small favors."

"Tone, Katerina. And I already knew about the incident with Vickery — all the family did."

Kat closed her mouth. "You did?"

"Your father knows everyone in the law enforcement world, and while I never condone violence, I can't say that I blame you for physically expressing your displeasure. I admit that in moments of weakness, I have also imagined a few choice acts to his personal... *appendage*, since I learned of his lack of character."

"Mother!"

"A mother has the right to protect her children." Caroline lifted her chin and her blue eyes flashed. "He hurt you, and as much as I believe laws should be adhered to, there should be additional penalties for those who break the bonds of matrimony. Severe penalties." Her eyes narrowed. "Unchangeable penalties."

Her mother seemed to have morphed into a creature Kat had never seen before, someone who might trade her expensive jacket and skirt for a black bodysuit and hood, slip into the night and exact her vengeance, no evidence left behind to trace the act to a mild-mannered, well-respected socialite. She suddenly had a new appreciation for Caroline Hellman.

"Clearly, I've been wrong about a few things." Kat sipped her coffee, not because her stomach was any less knotted or her future magically crystallized, but she needed a couple seconds to process this person who also seemed to be her mother. "All this time I thought I'd inherited my take-no-crap nature from dad."

"Language, dear, and you would do well to remember that your father isn't the only one who has steel in his blood."

Kat's small smile faded. Since her parents had divorced, beyond the initial family meeting when they'd announced their decision to separate, she hadn't talked — really *talked* — to either of her parents about it. Maybe Vee had been right in calling her a coward. By not asking for details, it protected the happy memories of her childhood, and she didn't want anything to tarnish what she'd believed had been a loving, if not always easy or perfect, family.

"Now that you're single again, do you ever regret it?" she asked quietly. "Marrying Dad?"

"Not for a single second." Caroline's voice was firm. "Even though we're going about our separate lives now, I wouldn't trade the years we had together or the family we made between us for anything. Each moment of pain or disappointment was always met by a triple amount of laughter and love." She studied Kat for a few seconds, as if she read an underlying motive for the question. "Every relationship is a gamble, darling. People will always eventually fail and hurt you, but when you find someone who recognizes your sharp edges, uncomfortable angles and cushions in between and still wants to walk beside you?" Her secret smile erased years from her face. "Hold on for as long as you can, even if it doesn't last forever. Those are the ones whose sunshine is worth the rain."

Kat sipped her coffee again, her throat tight, not that she had any wise response. Her mother's words jabbed the new bruises she bore from the morning, and if she thought about her insight into love and relationships too long, she might crack. All her emotions were too close to the surface, pushing for a release she didn't want.

"Don't compare our marriage with yours, Katerina." Caroline tapped her lightly on the nose. "Vickery wasn't right for you. Perhaps he was a mistake you had to make in order to grow."

The subject change gave her the lifeline she needed and she made a face. "I would've preferred a different method of teaching, one that didn't come at the cost of my bank account, house and a wasted decade."

"I know you don't want my advice, so I'll leave you with an observation instead." Her mother hesitated, as if choosing her words carefully. "Never in all the years you were with Vickery have I seen you be yourself—truly yourself—as you are when you're with Roman. Even at the hospital when you butted heads over Gia, I sensed something...different between the two of you."

Kat pressed her lips together and pretended to study her coffee, all her restless emotions coming to a barely contained simmer.

"I followed you, after you walked out on our family dinner at the restaurant."

She looked up, surprised.

"You were so upset after my suggestion to move in with me that I didn't want to leave any unpleasantness between us," Caroline explained. "When I saw you and Roman together, I waited beneath the awning. I heard how he spoke to you, like an equal, partner, friend, someone he admires deeply." Her eyes twinkled as she rinsed out her mug and placed it in the dishwasher. "He's quite the male specimen, isn't he? Especially in a wet shirt."

Kat choked on her coffee. *Who is this woman and what has she done with my mother?* "Eavesdropping, Mother?"

"No, dear. Simply regarding from afar." Caroline briefly squeezed her hand in passing, headed for the door. "I'm sure you'll make the right decision."

Chapter Twenty-Four

Half an hour after watching Katerina peel out of the police department parking lot and out of his life, Roman numbly finished rolling up his pant legs and sloshed his bare feet into the tub of warm water. As an added kick to his gut, the aroma of lavender-mint wafted up, courtesy of Sally. The downfall to quiet pedicurists was the fact that they overheard conversations and remembered small details, such as the mention of the soap scent used by the woman he loved.

He leaned his head back and closed his eyes. How the hell was he supposed to operate with a fractured heart?

He'd thought he was doing the right thing by not pushing Katerina or trying to influence her decisions, especially when it came to loving him. Maybe he was an imbecile, because he'd believed that she'd eventually realize they needed each other in a way that no innocently withheld information could break. Instead of strengthening the bond between them, his plan had backfired.

Annihilation complete — love, dreams, a future with the woman he required to be whole, all turned to dust. Worse, rather than showing Kat how much he adored her, he'd hurt her, destroyed an already-fragile trust and driven her away when he wanted to keep her forever. He'd offered her his heart and she'd chosen to walk away rather than work through the ache, unwilling to admit that their relationship, the life they could have together, was worth any battle or injury.

He'd taken the risk. Now, he paid the price.

"You're here early." Gia kicked off her sandals and plopped into the chair beside his. She turned to him and her smile faded. "What's wrong?"

Everything. "Katerina discovered the firearms instructor position was meant for me."

"Crap."

"I told her I'm in love with her."

Gia sucked in a breath.

"She's going home."

"Roman, you can't let her leave." She gripped his forearm, her blue eyes ferocious. "Use whatever trick or manipulation you need to, but don't let her go without hashing it out. Once she's gone, she won't come back."

"Hashing anything out is impossible when one party has no desire to do so." His voice rasped, brittle, as if he'd been sick for a week. "She made it very clear that our relationship is not worth the effort or risk to her. I have to respect her decision."

"You're not her scumbag ex," Gia growled. "She knows that. Convince her. Give her a solid reason to stay."

I thought I had.

315

He shook his head, the tightness in his chest threatening to snap his ribs. "I'd disco dance with the devil and buy him pie afterward to keep Katerina here with me, but the choice is hers to make without my influence." Every instinct demanded the opposite, that if he could simply see her again, speak face to face and explain after she cooled down, that he'd find the right words and she'd see the situation through his eyes. But that had failed horribly with Irini and, instead of convincing her to stay, she'd chosen to stay lost.

Lost. The thought of losing Katerina forever felt like an iron anvil to his chest, but in this instance, he knew he was right. She'd been prodded and pulled enough for one lifetime, pushed in opposite directions with the implication that if she didn't succeed, if she revealed any weakness or was less than her best, she wouldn't be loved. She'd learned to guard her heart against a world that judged her for everything besides the person she truly was. He refused to be like everyone else.

"I've made it very clear to her what I want, Gia. I won't do her the dishonor by telling her that I know what's best for her. She'll eventually figure out what she wants, what she's willing to take a chance on." He scrubbed a hand over his face, the last few nights of no Katerina and no sleep weighing heavy on him. "All I can do is hope that it's me."

Tears shimmered in Gia's blue eyes. She leaned over the chair and awkwardly flung an arm around his neck. "Oh, Roman, she'll choose you. That's not even a question." She eased back and smoothed his shirt. "You are, after all, a limited edition."

He could barely drum up his usual humor. "Not everyone appreciates awesomeness as much as you and I do."

His cell phone buzzed against his hip and he scrambled for it in his pocket, his heart skipping like one of his dad's old records. Maybe Kat had calmed down and wanted to talk. Boyd's number on the screen was a disappointment. He answered with a sigh.

"Boyd."

"Farkos. Upfront, you left your email open."

Unsurprising. After Kat had abandoned him, returning to the office hadn't even crossed his mind.

"As I went to shut it down, a message popped up and I couldn't help but read it," Boyd continued.

"As much as I enjoy having my privacy violated, if you want to take advantage of the male enhancement offer that managed to slip through the spam filter, I'd never stand in the way. You don't need my permission."

"Hilarious. There was a match on that symbol you sent out, that weird circle-cross-triangle conglomeration."

Roman shot from his chair, splashing water everywhere as Gia protested, causing Sally to peer in with a threatening frown. "And?"

"It's connected to a human trafficking ring. There was a big sting in Colorado, but apparently there are branches scattered all over the States. Want the info sent to your personal email?"

His phone buzzed with a text from Lars, the other deputy on duty.

Suspicious activity reported at the institution. Want to take it?

He texted back, all his senses on high alert, his focus narrowing to the call.

On my way.

* * * *

After the unexpected conversation with her mother, Kat retreated to her happy place to work through her troubles—ripping holes in targets with her favorite firearm at the range.

For a few glorious seconds, the power of her Python in her hands filled the gaps in her heart and smoothed out her boiling emotions, leaving her to focus only on the bullseye being demolished down range. She fired the last bullet, popped the cylinder and loaded it again as fast as she could. Without the gunfire and target to concentrate on, the thoughts returned.

'Every relationship is a gamble, darling.'

She pushed the cylinder tight, aimed and pulled the trigger. Her weapon shuddered, vibrating through her hands and arms, clearing her head and heart.

Empty of bullets again.

'I'm sure it was easy...telling me what I should do. It wasn't like you had anything to lose, right?'

The mere memory of the accusation in Vee's sneering voice sliced violently through her defenses. Her hands shook as she reloaded. She couldn't seem to take a full breath. The Python came alive in her hands again, but the momentary peace shattered with each shudder of the target.

'We—us, you and me, what we have together—we're worth fighting for. Fight for me.*'*

Kat set her gun down and braced herself on the counter, her shoulders heaving. Would Roman want her to fight if he knew the full truth of who she was?

That if stripped of her gun and badge, she was nothing special?

She clenched her jaw, but the trembling didn't stop. Most days, she didn't have it together at all and relied on a practiced performance to fool the world. Beneath the confidence was a girl who had never quite fit right anywhere, a girl who still sometimes feared what might lurk in the dark, a girl who was self-conscious about her stinky feet.

Pressing her lips tight, she lifted her gaze to the skyline. What would Roman think if he knew that she was more selfish than generous, that she often shut people out completely just to survive? Would Roman still want her if he knew she'd been lonely all her life, so deeply afraid to let anyone close enough to see her — really see *her* — that she'd chosen alienation over the possibility of being rejected? Revealing all her imperfections, truly being vulnerable with someone only to be discarded as deficient terrified her more than being outshot at the range, judged by family and peers or losing her job.

'I'm unconditionally in love with you, all of you.'

She wished with all her soul that she could believe that.

Kat closed her eyes, unable to see through the tears as a sob from the pit of all the pain she kept so deeply buried racked her entire body. She'd trade every bit of her sharpshooting skills and relinquish her badge to have it be true, to know without any doubt that Roman's love for her was real, unstoppable and would be strong enough to endure the ugliness and mundane.

'It's a lack of faith on your part.'

Roman's earlier words arrowed through her, hitting her straight in the heart, and she sucked in a breath as if she'd been physically struck. Several times, she'd told him she trusted him, and not once had he given her a reason to doubt him. Blaming him for not telling her about the instructor position had merely been an excuse to put distance between them, to protect herself...while he'd done the opposite. He'd offered up his exposed heart, trusting her not to destroy it.

Kat covered her mouth with her hand. Vee had been right. She expected everyone else to be vulnerable while she sat on the sidelines and gave advice she didn't have the nerve to practice herself. She'd let a damaged teenager shut her down when she should have been fighting back.

Fighting for the people she loved.

Hell. I love him. But did she have the guts to tell him, to open up and let him see all of her, knowing it could backfire today, tomorrow or ten years from now?

And now I can add 'coward' to my resume.

She pivoted and leaned her butt against the counter, wiping her eyes. As she shifted, a bullet rolled beneath her boot. Club members were supposed to clean up after themselves, collect duds and brass, toss their targets or carry them out upon departure, but there were always a few who slacked. *Jerks.* Taking a shaky breath, she picked up the dud bullet to throw it away and paused. The green ceramic tip was a dead giveaway for a highspeed projectile meant to penetrate flesh, bone...and protective vests. She flipped it. The primer was dented, confirmation that the bullet was a dud, and the headstamp — her heart stopped. *LE.* They were the same initials as the brass she'd found in the institution, marking it as manufactured for law enforcement only. Graywood PD was the only law

320

enforcement who practiced at the range and they didn't use this ammo.

The details were too much to be coincidence — the report of a human trafficking sting gone bad, the officer shot and stolen gun, finding the casing at the institution and its match here, the gouges on the post in the bell tower...

She turned the bullet over in her fingers as a coldness settled in her bones, the same premonition that had taken hold of her when she'd found the first brass on the dusty floor of the abandoned building. She pocketed her find and hurriedly searched the bay for any more clues, finding nothing out of the ordinary, but the chill didn't leave, and shooting her Python had lost its charm, its power of peace gone.

Her heartbeat pulsing a wicked rhythm all the way to her fingertips, Kat tossed her carton of ammo into her bag, placed her Python in its case less carefully than usual and snapped the case closed. She grabbed everything and ran for the range office, ignoring the curious look of another range member.

The office was empty of other people. On a whim, she dumped her duffel by the door and went to the sign-in book. She trailed her finger along the list of members who had used the same shooting bay in the last few days, not sure what to look for. Names scrolled by, none of which she recognized, not that she expected to. A criminal probably wouldn't bother checking in properly, let alone sign a roster, but if there was anything that might tip her off —

Shadowbrook. She paused, her fingertip beneath the name. *Shadowbrook*. Why was that ringing every warning bell? Whoever it was had visited the previous day at eight in the evening, only a few minutes before dark, when any office employee and most members would have been gone. Shadowbrook had added a crude design to each 'o' in the name, a cross through the middle with an inverted triangle.

Hell. It was the same design as the bracelets worn by Vee and her shady new friends. She swallowed hard. Shadowbrook had been a guest, brought by...

Valerie.

Shadowbrook. Her stomach dipped as she put it together. That was the street name hanging from the institution's gate.

I need to tell Roman.

Before she could follow up on that thought, her phone buzzed in her bag. She fished it out and the name on the screen made her ribs constrict around her heart.

Vee.

She picked up immediately, no greeting. "Are you okay?"

Valerie's sob was enough of an answer.

"Where are you?" Kat was already out of the door. "I'm coming for you right now."

"I did something stupid." Vee's whisper made the small hairs on Kat's arms stand up straight. "I'm in trouble and I don't know what to do."

"We'll figure it out together." Kat ran toward her SUV. "Just tell me where you are." Even as she said the words, she already knew what Vee would say.

"The abandoned institution on Shadowbrook Drive." Another muffled sob came from Vee. "Please hurry —" Then silence.

Kat didn't bother trying to call back as she flung open the door to her SUV. Instead, she dialed Roman.

The voicemail picked up on the second ring.

"*Farkos. I'm busy. Leave a message and if I find it worthy, I'll get back to you...when I'm not busy.*"

The voicemail signal seemed to take forever to beep.

"It's Kat. Vee is in trouble. She's at the institution." She paused, the weight of the bullet casing in her pocket heavy and solid. "I'm ninety-nine percent sure she's with the people who possess the stolen ammo." *And deal in selling humans.* "I'm going there now." Her throat closed up, making it hard to breathe, let alone speak. "I'd feel a lot better if you were with me."

As she tossed her bag into the passenger seat and climbed in, the truth dug roots inside her heart, too deep to ignore. In all practicality, she should have hit nine-one-one first. Instead, without even considering it, she'd called Roman. True, he knew all about the institution and what they'd found there, saving her the trouble of explanations, but that wasn't why she called him first. She trusted him, wanted him with her as both backup and support. She just...

Wanted him beside her, always. And instead of trusting him to love her, holding on to him, she'd let him go.

Kat screeched out of the parking lot, tapping her fingernails on the steering wheel as the automatic gate crept open. The second it was ajar enough for her SUV to squeak through, she gunned it.

She'd only made it a quarter of a mile when a new realization hit her. Roman wasn't on duty. The only reason he wouldn't answer his phone would be because he'd turned it off, and the only reason he'd turn it off was because he was doing something sly, such as sneaking into the institution. And he wouldn't know that Vee was there, in trouble, with people who had no problem with shooting cops.

Fear, blizzard-cold and debilitating, blasted her heart. She couldn't lose Roman, couldn't lose Vee, not when she'd just figured out how much she needed them both.

Chapter Twenty-Five

Kat pulled her SUV off the pavement more than a hundred yards short of the Shadowbrook driveway leading to the institution. Marta was parked in the same spot as when they'd been here before, and Kat forced herself to release a tiny breath, to ease the tension stringing her muscles tight.

Dammit. Roman was here. The slim hope that he'd turned off his phone to enjoy a coconut crème pie in complete peace splintered. It wasn't that she didn't trust Roman's capabilities — there was no one else she'd rather have as backup — but she'd prefer that he hadn't beat her here and unknowingly strolled into a viper's nest alone.

Alone because I ripped into him and walked away.

Instead of heading straight down the driveway, Kat worked her way toward the fence through the trees lining each side of the pavement. The first time she'd been here, she hadn't been concerned about potential surveillance. Tracking a runaway teenager in an abandoned building was a completely different scenario from invading a den of criminals bearing weapons — and her friends' lives might be on the line. Security cameras could be anywhere, planted by anyone, but they'd more likely be aimed at the driveway than random woodland and would absolutely cover the main entrance. As much as she wanted to hurry, she had to do her best to make sure her arrival came as a surprise. It was their only hope.

Kat avoided the gate and paused at the fence line to scope it out from the shelter of the woods. The chain was unlocked, loosely wrapped through the iron bars to keep the gate closed rather than secured, confirming Roman's presence. Her heart rate kicked up another notch.

Please don't let me be too late.

She climbed the fence as quickly and quietly as she could and dropped to the grass on the other side. Pulling her Beretta from the holster at her hip, her gaze on the glints of glass windows and weathered boards peeking between the branches, she crept forward. Her boots were silent on the moss and she ignored the scrape of branches on her bare arms, every sense locked on the institution ahead. At the edge of the trees, she forced herself to pause again to study the front exterior. The quiet hummed along her nerves. Nothing moved, and if there were cameras mounted, they were well-hidden. The main entrance was closed, and whether or not it remained locked was impossible to determine without trying the knob.

Walking through the front door wasn't going to happen.

When Vee and her friend had fled after being pranked, they hadn't used the front door, which meant there was another accessible entry point that might not be as carefully guarded. Even though it would take precious minutes, if Roman was already inside, barging in wouldn't help him or Vee.

Keeping to the trees, she circumnavigated the building, studying every window and door for any movement or sign of another living being. The sense of being watched stayed with her like a hand on the back of her neck, and she refused to acknowledge the source. If she couldn't see it, it was her imagination, nothing more.

She'd made it all the way to the back of the sprawling building before finding anything potentially useful. She crouched behind the thick trunk of an oak to take a closer look. A rusted drainpipe that had seen better days snaked up to a broken window on the second floor. Maybe she could climb it without dying...but if anyone happened to notice her, she'd be a sitting duck, completely exposed and vulnerable.

Beneath the pipe were the old-fashioned double hurricane doors leading to a basement. A chill curled down her back and lodged in her heart, and she kept going.

Kat made it all the way back to the front. All the other doors had been nailed and boarded shut. There were no ladders or random objects to use in reaching the upper floors. It was either the drainpipe...or the basement.

Already, she'd wasted too much time.

After making sure there were no visible cameras or other devices that might alert anyone inside that she was there, she broke from the protection of the trees and hustled across the overgrown lawn. Her back pressed to the wall, she holstered her gun and grabbed the pipe.

The rusted metal screeched and crumpled beneath her grip, useless. Climbing it would be impossible.

Which left her only one option.

Her throat dry, she dropped her gaze to the hurricane doors a few feet away. A padlock secured them together. One side was crooked, as if the hinges could be loose. Kat wiped her clammy hands on her jeans. With only her cell as a flashlight, she'd be solo , in the dark with the unknown.

But Vee and Roman were in there. Not going in wasn't a choice.

Kat crouched and fumbled with the door handles. The hinges squeaked, and she immediately stilled, listening hard, her heart hammering. When no sign of detection came, she tried again. Despite being crooked, everything held against the steady pressure of her pull.

Dammit.

Gritting her teeth, Kat wiggled the handles. The solid wood shuddered but held firm, and she didn't dare try to force her way in and make too much noise. She sat back on her heels and studied the doors some more. Rust discolored the hinges and none of them were missing, but...she leaned forward. On the crooked side, one hinge had scrapes on it, as if it had once been pried open. Carefully, she wiggled it.

The hinge popped free, and when she lifted the corner of the door, there was just enough space to squeeze through, certainly enough for a teenage girl.

If Vee is brave enough to go in this way, I can do it too.

She took a deep breath and slid into the darkness. When her boots hit concrete, she whipped out her phone and turned on the flashlight app, shining the light at the descending stairwell and door below. She made it down the stairs and grabbed the doorknob. It turned, unlocked, and she forced herself to open it.

A draft of stale air, the scent of dust and mold familiar from her previous journey inside the institution, drifted over her face. Silhouettes and shadows met the glow from her phone, a maze of furniture, storage trunks and boxes blocking her way. Amateur paintings, as if created by wobbling hands and warped minds, leaned crookedly against one wall. A naked mannequin stood among the artwork, watching her with unseeing eyes. Past the mannequin, a wooden stairwell rose into the darkness.

Kat ignored her racing heart and shaking hands. *Just stuff, nothing that can hurt me.* Purposefully keeping her gaze averted from the mannequin and disturbing artwork, the cool metal of her weapon a comfort in her grip, she entered the basement. She stepped over boxes filled with mildewed paper and black-speckled clothes. A layer of debris and grime grumbled beneath her boots with each careful step. She counted her breaths, controlling her fear.

Breathe in.

A scuttling came from the corner near the paintings, and the hair on her arms stood on end. She didn't look. The sound wasn't made by a human and her prey wasn't mice, insects—or anything beyond flesh and blood.

Breathe out.

She tracked the light from her phone and pretended nothing else existed except the glow at her feet guiding her to safety. There wasn't a wheelchair covered in spiderwebs or an empty crib dull with age. The unframed paintings of screaming faces and twisted landscapes she passed were merely canvas and colors with no meaning. And the mannequin —

From the corner of her eye, she caught movement, and no amount of experience, rationality or steady breathing could control the tide of complete and swamping fear rushing over her. Kat surged for the stairs and scrambled up as fast as her long legs could go. She reached the door, dragged it open and leaped through, slamming it behind her, quick.

The noise echoed through the institution like an alarm.

Crap.

Breathing hard, her heart a war drum beating against her ribs, she scanned the hallway for potential hiding spots. She hadn't explored the first floor with Roman and had no idea what, if anything, remained in the rooms. Maybe anyone who heard the door slam would think nothing of it or would shrug it off as the sort of noises that came with abandoned buildings. She could only hope it had warned Roman that he wasn't alone, not endangered him further.

If he was still okay.

He has to be okay.

Waiting around to see if anyone came to investigate wasn't part of her plan. She slipped out of her heavy boots and hurried away from the foyer and main stairwell, moving farther down the corridor on stockinged feet. The rooms she passed were all empty, with no place to hide, not even closets. When she got to the end, a noise came from around the corner, the stealthy scrape of soles on tile.

Someone was coming.

Kat set her boots down, pressed tight to the wall and aimed her weapon at the corner, chest high. If she fired, she'd give herself away — and endanger both Roman and Vee. But they could already be in trouble and dying wouldn't help them at all. She kept her focus on the corner. The silence stretched, long enough that she wondered if her imagination had been stuck in overdrive from being in the basement. She waited a few more seconds.

The barrel of a gun appeared around the corner, followed by...

Roman.

She instantly removed her finger from the trigger, lowered her weapon and slumped, her entire body trembling.

He approached her carefully, quietly, his dark eyes wide. "Katerina." His voice hardly even counted as a whisper, and if he had been more than a foot away, she doubted she would've heard him. "I didn't expect to find you here."

"I got a call from Vee," she murmured. "She's here, in trouble."

He nodded and drew close to her ear. "They're on the third floor by the bell tower. I texted Boyd for backup, but he must be out on another call. They have a scanner, so they know where Boyd is. They'll know if dispatch calls anyone in."

If they'd found him first... She swallowed. This wasn't the time for soft emotions and fears. "We've got this, Farkos." The familiar rush of adrenaline steadied her and sharpened her mind. "How many are there?"

"Three. Two of them are the guys from paintball."

The young men wearing the same leather bracelets that Vee had had on her wrist that morning — the wannabe punk and the killer with the shaved head. She could guess which one had been Vee's range guest and used Shadowbrook as his name. He was the one who needed to be taken down first.

Voices echoed, drifting nearer.

"This way," Roman whispered and ghosted back the way he'd came, headed toward the voices.

With nowhere else to go, Kat grabbed her boots and followed. He led her toward the basement door, and her skin pebbled with cold. She'd rather face an entire army of criminals, empty-handed, before going back into the basement. But he turned into the room right before the basement and dragged her inside. He pointed at the wall and a built-in cupboard she'd missed in her hurry to get away from the basement as fast as possible. Roman opened the cupboard doors.

It was an oversized dumbwaiter, large enough for them both. So, this was how Vee and her friend had escaped to the basement without using the main stairwell.

He pulled her in with him and silently shut them into darkness. Being pressed against his warmth and strength, his spicy-sweet scent surrounding her, she could suddenly breathe again. The sensation of being slowly lifted made her grab onto his waist. There were a thousand things she wanted to say to him but couldn't, and for the first time since meeting Roman, it wasn't her own issues stopping her. Instead, she laid her head against his heart and just held on.

When he wrapped her in his arms and laid a lingering kiss on her forehead, it felt like forgiveness, acceptance and forever all wrapped together. Before she could whisper any of the things she was dying to say, the dumbwaiter stopped and Roman carefully cracked the doors, searching the room beyond.

He opened the doors all the way and stepped silently out, his alert gaze on the exit. Kat set her boots down in the dumbwaiter. They both paused and Kat listened through the silence, attuned to any sign of nearby intruders. After a moment, he waved her forward as he crept toward the doorway and sidled up to one side.

Kat peeked into the third-floor corridor from the opposite side of the doorway, her Beretta at the ready. She met Roman's gaze.

Hallway is empty.

He made a hand motion, one direction then the other. *Let's split up and take them from each side.*

Kat nodded, and when he handed her a set of handcuffs from his side pocket, she gave him her evil grin. *Let's do this.*

They went in opposite directions, and damn if she didn't love him more for trusting her enough to be his partner, to know what to do and when to do it, no matter who took the lead. At the corner, she glanced over her shoulder just in time to see him slip around the bend. *Be careful.*

Considering they'd heard voices on the first floor and there were three dirtbags in the building, according to Roman, that left one currently alone with Vee. With any luck, they could take him out and get Vee to safety before the other two returned.

Kat came to the corner before the bell tower. Holding her breath, she peeked out. The guy with the shaved head, the one who was a superb shot on the paintball course, stood squarely in front of the ladder leading to the bell tower, an AR-15 at the ready. *Son of a jerkface.* Vee must be in the tower.

The next moment, Roman appeared around the corner, his hands in the air, two armed men directing him forward.

A chill coursed through her blood.

"Found our mouse, Luke." Matt, the other punk from the paintball course, bared his teeth as he poked Roman in the back with the barrel of his gun. "Told you I heard something."

"And I told you to keep your eye on the monitors." The sharpshooter with the shaved head—Luke, apparently—aimed his weapon at Roman. "We could have taken care of this problem before it *became* a problem."

"I object to being referred to as an 'it'," Roman said in his monotone. "Where's Valerie?"

"So, you're the one she called." Luke's lip curled. "Playing hero wasn't a smart move, especially for some kid that nobody wants. She's not worth dying for."

Yes, she is. Kat drew a silent, steadying breath. The two men behind Roman both relaxed their holds on their weapons. From what she'd witnessed at the paintball course, Matt was more likely to shoot himself in the foot than hit an actual target. Luke may have his rifle aimed at Roman but shooting in that position would endanger both of his cronies, and should something happen, it would take that extra millisecond for them to lift and aim.

Anything could happen in that millisecond of unpreparedness.

Vee was safe in the tower. Matt was a terrible shot. The other young man was an unknown factor. Considering who Roman was and the fact that he undoubtedly knew she was watching and would respond, she was willing to take those odds.

Carefully, she pulled one of her extra cartridges from her pocket and pried the top bullet out. She lifted a prayer—and tossed the bullet at Luke.

The second metal plinked on tile, he spun her way, already shooting as he charged.

Kat didn't have time to see if Roman had successfully used her distraction or not. She ducked as wood paneling splintered where her head had been, then she was sprinting hard. If he had a clear shot, he wouldn't miss. She had to be faster than him, smarter.

She skidded around the corner, her socks sliding on the gritty tile as another bullet struck the banister, spraying the wood in a shower of sharp needles. Kat jumped down several stairs, hurled herself onto the curved banister and slid down. Next time she saw her brothers, she'd give them each a high five for all their stupid contests growing up and always letting her join in. Halfway to the first floor, she leaped off and hit the ground running.

Luke's steps echoed behind her, roaring in her ears as she raced for the one place in the building that offered any amount of cover, the one place she could set up a quick defense, the one place she had zero desire to return to.

She flung the basement door open and flew onto the stairwell just as gunfire exploded and bullets sprayed the tile and doorjamb. Pain blazed across her shoulder—whether a direct hit or a ricochet, she wasn't sure and couldn't take the time to assess. Kat bit back a hiss. She'd counted the shots fired and as much as she'd like to believe Luke was out of ammo, she wouldn't bet her life on it. He seemed the type to be prepared with another full cartridge on his person, ready to go.

Descending into darkness, she scrambled over boxes and twisted artwork to the hulking water heater in the corner beneath the stairs and huddled behind it, far enough away from the mannequin that she couldn't see its creepy, watchful eyes but had a partial view of the stairs. Kat willed her breaths and heartrate to slow, keeping her Beretta aimed at the stairwell.

Luke scrambled in and paused at the top of the stairs, the landing boards creaking beneath his weight. Dust drifted from above, onto Kat's head. From his viewpoint, she could be hiding anywhere below, and being on the stairs would make him an easy target. If not for the stairs blocking her aim, she could hit him clean and clear from her location.

Gunfire exploded. Wood splintered, boxes shuddered and paper drifted like confetti as Luke emptied his weapon in an arc. The fast click and clatter of a cartridge being ejected and falling to the ground, another click and more gunfire followed. Kat crouched lower and covered her head as bullets ricocheted off the water heater, *ting-ting-ting*, then went quiet.

The sudden silence ached in her ears and his careful, creaking steps down the stairs drowned out her breaths. He surely hadn't been stupid enough to use all his ammo, but she needed confirmation. Carefully, she pulled a loose shell from her pocket and peeked through the inch-wide slat between the staircase and the water heater.

Luke descended the stairs in a crouch, his shaved head glistening in the shadows, his weapon sure and steady in his hand. His eyes flashed as he scanned the chaos of furniture and storage boxes. It was only a matter of time before he realized she wasn't dead or injured in the maze of boxes and furniture. He'd check behind the water heater, beneath the stairs, and if he still had ammo, it would merely be a matter of who was the fastest shot.

Kat kept her grip on the Beretta loose and ready, her pulse thrumming fast, as he disappeared from her view. Her shoulder throbbed and from the way her shirt stuck to her back, she knew she was bleeding. Grit and loose paper crunched beneath his shoes. He was coming closer. If he turned at all, he'd notice the water heater and the crawlspace. If he had another full cartridge, the odds of a stray bullet catching her were good. She had to distract him first.

Easing around the water heater, holding her breath, she peeked out. He was directly in front of the water heater, his back to her, gazing at the door leading outside.

Beside her, something in the gloom near the floor moved. At the same time, the basement door squeaked shut, as if pushed by an invisible hand, drowning out Kat's sharp inhale as a rat scurried across her foot.

Luke whirled toward the stairs with a soft curse

As Kat tossed the shell across the room, the mannequin watched with dead eyes. The bullet center-punched its plastic forehead, making it shift on its stand before clattering to the concrete floor. At the foot of the stairwell, Luke aimed at the mannequin and pulled the trigger.

Click. He pulled the trigger again, his eyes wild. *Click, click, click.*

He dropped the AR-15, pulled a Glock from his waistband and pointed it at the mannequin.

As bullets riddled the mannequin's head, Kat calmly shot Luke's weapon hand.

He shrieked and dropped the pistol. As it clanged to the concrete floor, he clutched his bleeding hand to his chest.

Kat let her evil grin fly free. *My best shot so far.* She stepped from behind the water heater. "Hands on your head, darling."

Instead of obeying like a good criminal, he turned and raced up the stairs.

She was on his heels and took him down at the stairway landing. It wasn't her fault he hit his head on the tile as he fell and knocked himself silly. Before he regained full consciousness, she handcuffed him to the water pipe at the door, made a quick pat down of his person, relieved him of his three knives, cell phone and plastic baggie holding a questionable substance, and managed to leap out of the way when he rudely kicked at her.

"Your rights will be read momentarily," she gasped, turning toward the main stairwell. Roman and Vee were still up there, facing the unknown.

"You can't leave me here," he called after her. "I'm bleeding." A note of panic entered his voice. "Something's *down* there."

"Yeah, rats. I hear the scent of blood makes them go into a feeding frenzy." She grinned over her shoulder. "You'll be fine."

Her smile widened at the string of curses that followed her, all aimed at her distinguished personage. She turned the corner without slowing. With Luke's muffled voice behind her, the quiet again fell around her, giving her no clues as to the fates of her friends. Kat climbed the stairs quickly, her stockinged feet silent, her gaze set on the floors above, weapon ready.

As she reached the second floor, a crash and a curse from a room down the hall drove her to full speed.

Kat passed the doorway of the children's ward, glimpsed someone moving inside and latched on to the doorjamb to keep from slipping and losing her balance. She squared up, steadied and leaned into the doorway.

Roman dragged one of the guys across the floor by his arm. The man's wrists were handcuffed behind his back, his nose bloody, and the footprint on his face told a story of its own. She stepped aside as Roman hauled the man past her to the banister. The man didn't protest as one wrist was uncuffed and secured to the railing. He slumped to a sit and hung his head between his knees.

"Well done, Farkos."

"You're bleeding."

"Just a flesh wound."

His mouth tightened as he headed for the stairs. He lifted his gaze to the third floor and whispered, "One more to go."

Matt. Shouldn't be much of a problem.

They ghosted up the stairs side by side and neither said a word as they split off in different directions. Now that she knew Roman was okay, all her thoughts went to Vee. If she wasn't okay, too, she'd handcuff Luke in the depths of the basement, close to the mannequin, who was probably already seeking vengeance for the loss of its head.

Rats or not.

She heard Matt before she saw him.

"If you don't hurry your sniveling ass down the ladder, I'm going to give you something real to cry about. We have to go *now*." Metal on wood cracked, echoing in the emptiness. "You heard the gunshots.

You know Luke doesn't miss. No one's coming for you and if we're late for the pickup, you're the one who'll regret it."

You wish, scumsack. Kat sidled up to the edge and glanced out. Matt stared up the bell tower ladder, his gun aimed at Vee, who slowly, shakily climbed down.

Kat's heart clenched. If Valerie slipped, she'd topple through the hole made by the heavy bell that had already fallen to its death years ago. Making a move now might endanger Vee, but if she waited for her to reach the ground, she'd be more likely to be used as a shield or hostage.

Taking a breath, she stepped into the open. "Freeze."

A glimpse of dark hair across the way told her Roman was in position.

Matt swung wide with his weapon, firing wildly, and Kat dove around the corner. With a screech, Vee scrambled back up the ladder and disappeared from sight as her captor dropped the gun and bolted toward the west wing. Roman gave pursuit, passing by in a dark blur. Their rapid footsteps echoed and faded into quiet.

Kat stuck her Beretta into its holster and ran to the bottom of the ladder. "Vee, it's me. It's safe to come down. We've got them all secured."

"Not quite," said another voice behind her, followed by the distinctive slide of a firearm being cocked. "Hands up."

Slowly, she obeyed and faced her assailant.

Chapter Twenty-Six

Kat froze with her hands up, her heart pounding, as Mr. Peters, Derick's father, gazed back at her from behind the barrel of a freakin' machine gun. How he'd gotten the weapon didn't matter. Whether or not he'd ever used a weapon in his life, he wouldn't miss her, not with that monster.

If he shoots, I'm dead.

"Because of you and Farkos, I lost custody of my son." His eyes gleamed. A bump remained on the bridge of his nose from the face-plant he'd taken on the gym floor, courtesy of her tackle. "Finding you here, though?" He wiped at the sweat trickling down his temple. "It's far more rewarding than any potential lawsuit win, because I get to watch your face close up as you lose everything too."

All the heat drained from her blood. Death stared back at her and there were no words that would change his course, nothing she could do to escape her fate, and all she could think about was that she hadn't told

Roman she loved him. As Mr. Peters tensed, the firearm aimed at her chest, she prayed that Vee would remain out of sight and Roman would hear the blast and know he was still in danger.

The shot boomed, deafening.

Despite Kat's resolve to stare down her killer until the last possible breath, she squeezed her eyes shut on instinct. The pain she expected didn't come, and she opened her eyes.

Mr. Peters writhed on the floor, groaning and gripping his leg just below the knee. Behind him, Boyd drew near, looking slightly stunned, the smoking gun in his hand still aimed at Peters.

Boyd kicked the machine gun out of reach and met Kat's gaze. "Just so you know, I *meant* to shoot him in the leg. It's at least a fifty-yard shot from the end of the hallway and I still hit my mark." He winked. "I recently had a great firearms instructor."

Kat narrowed her eyes at him. "Did you just wink at me?"

"What? You want a formal apology?" Boyd grunted as he proceeded to handcuff Peters.

"Nope."

She breezed past him to the ladder and climbed up without calling to Vee. The girl was probably scared out of her mind, in shock, and seeing a friendly face would be better than hearing a familiar voice. When she reached the landing with the angry gash in the flooring and the band-aid planks, she found the mattress and trash, but no Vee. Kat lifted her gaze and sucked in a breath.

Vee had climbed the sketchy-looking wooden pegs leading to the very top of the bell tower and stood on a narrow ledge. She held on to the post with one hand

and leaned over the emptiness, her focus set on the horizon, as if she'd gone up there to think about the wonders of the world…or to contemplate jumping.

She's going to jump.

"It's okay now," Kat said, easing her way around the hole in the flooring — the hole that Vee would fall through if she let go. "You can come down. You're safe."

"Adults in positions of authority always say that," she said without looking down, her voice as flat as Roman's. "But it's never true, not really. 'Safe' is the gloss that hides reality just long enough to make important people feel better about themselves. It doesn't apply to me." She wiped her nose with her free hand, and Kat tensed as her black tennis shoe slipped a centimeter. "Anyway, it will be easier for everyone if I'm just…gone."

"That's a bunch of crap." Kat gripped the tower pole directly below Vee, her gaze locked on the girl. "It wouldn't be easier for Clay. Who would blackmail all the language offenders if you were gone? Roman would be devastated to lose his all-star first baseman, and no matter what Derick did or didn't say, he'd miss you keeping him on his toes. *I'd* miss you. No one else will play *Donkey Kong* with me."

Tears rolled down Vee's face and dripped from her chin, landing on Kat's boot. "Derick, Luke, my foster parents, everyone… They're all pretenders. They like me as long as I give them what they want, be *who* they want, but the second I backtalk, resist, or say something they don't like?" She shook her head slightly, her sleek, black hair rippling in a breeze Kat couldn't feel. "No one can hide their true colors forever."

An ache throbbed in Kat's heart, a hard, sharp pain. She was as much of a pretender as anyone else. "You're probably right about that. People suck—always have, always will, some worse than others—but then there are the few that suck a little less, the rare individuals who make getting out of bed in the morning worth the effort."

Vee glanced down at her, then turned her gaze back to the horizon. "I'm a duty to you, a pity project. Don't pretend I'm more to make yourself feel good. Don't lie so you can be cheered as a hero for saving the stupid, troubled foster-care girl. The second I'm down, you'll eventually bail. I've been alive long enough to know that's how it works."

Throb, throb, throb.

"I've never had a hero complex, and real friends don't bail. They might walk away when they're angry, but when it comes to the real issues, the stuff that counts, they always have your back."

While completely true, her words weren't enough to sway Vee. Her expression remained unchanged, desperate, hopeless. Kat couldn't take the easy way out by hiding behind a sassy comment or attitude, not this time. She was acutely aware of Roman slipping up behind her.

"Do you know how long it's been since I've made a real friend?" She didn't wait for Vee to answer, didn't dare stop speaking for fear her voice would give out. "Forever. When it comes to making friends, I stink because—" She swallowed, her throat like sandpaper, rough and dry. Her hands shook and a strange echo rang in her ears.

Vee was looking at her now, her fingers white strips on the bell tower pole, her face smudged and wet with tears.

You can do this. "I stink at making friends because," her voice had lost all its confidence, tiny and trembling in the quiet, "I'm terrified that if they get too close, they'll realize I'm not an especially nice or interesting person. They'll discover I'm not worth their time and certainly not their effort." A sob broke through, breaking her last words. "They'll decide all my flaws outweigh any good qualities and move on."

Roman eased beside her, but she didn't wipe away the tears blurring her vision, wetting her cheeks and dripping onto her shirt. This confession was for him as much as it was for Vee. They both needed to know the truth.

"Beneath my shooting skills and badge, I'm a mess. I'm proud and selfish, lonely and miserable, stubborn and a bit on the mean side. It's taken me twenty-eight years to figure out that life isn't measured by accomplishments, but in the people we affect and who affect us right back. Relationships are a gamble, there's no denying that. But the people who matter? They're worth every step of the game, win or lose." Kat sucked in a ragged breath. "You're one of the few people who matter to me, Vee. Nothing you've done or will do has the power to change that. Everyone screws up. I promise I won't walk away." She looked up at the bell tower, where Vee was a smudged, watercolor outline against the heights. "I can't bear to lose you."

Either of you.

Blindly, she reached for Roman's hand, and when his fingers wrapped around hers, warm, strong and solid, the ringing in her ears ended. "Please, come down. Stay with me."

"With us," Roman added in a rasp. "Stay with *us*, Valerie. No bailing, *ever*."

Vee remained still for several heart-pounding seconds, long enough that Kat's fingers ached from gripping Roman's so tightly. When Valerie moved, Kat jerked, ready to try to catch her as she dropped, but instead of jumping, she slowly climbed down, one wooden peg at a time. The second she was within reach, Roman grabbed her and clutched her tight as she trembled. A siren wailed in the distance, and Kat released a long breath.

"Group hug, Angel." Roman fisted her shirt and dragged her against him, into his strength and heat, his holiday scent.

Kat wrapped her arms around them both and closed her eyes.

Home.

"Yo, Farkos," Boyd called from below, his voice strained. "A little help here?"

Roman released them. "Can you handle yourselves without me for a few, doyennes?"

"We'll manage." Kat slung her arm around Vee and pulled her against her side. "For a few."

He gently brushed a tear from Kat's cheek with his thumb, and the tenderness in his expression threatened to unravel her more. Roman quickly turned for the ladder, saving her any further display of uncontrollable emotions, and swung down like a practiced fireman. His voice drifted up, joined by Boyd's as they dealt with Mr. Peters, leaving her to focus on Valerie.

"If you ever do that to me again, Gherig..." She huffed a breath. "Just, don't do that to me ever again, okay? I prefer to avoid entering abandoned institutions through their freaky basements."

Vee went still then eased away, her eyes wide, her face puffy from crying and glistening with tears. "I thought you were terrified of basements."

"Freakin' right I am, but going through that hellhole was the only way to get to you." She swiped at her nose. "If I never see another mannequin again, I'm fine with that."

"This is going to be reported to human services, isn't it?" Vee slumped. "Hello, next foster home, where each one is worse than the last."

"I've been thinking a lot in the last few hours." Kat swallowed the lump in her throat. Saying the words aloud would make them real, no going back—and she was willing to take that risk. "I've been thinking about my future, what I want, who I want in it. I know I'm not perfect or easy to deal with. I eat a ridiculous amount of potato chips and watch too many B-rated action movies. I have high expectations of both myself and others." She planted a hand on each of Vee's shoulders and held her gaze. "Despite all that, I think I'd rock at being your foster parent, especially since you already have the necessary qualities of being a Hellman. You're stubborn, sassy and aren't afraid to take the field." That knot in her throat returned, softening her voice. "What do you think?"

"For real?" The unguarded hope in Valerie's eyes made her chest constrict.

"Affirmative. Going through all the red tape will probably take some time but—"

Valerie was suddenly squeezing the breath out of her.

Kat choked out a laugh and held Vee tight. "I'll take that as a stamp of approval."

"I guess that would be okay." Sniffing, Vee stepped free, trying—and failing—to appear unaffected. She lifted her chin at a jaunty angle. "I'm not usually a hugger, so don't get any ideas."

"That's perfect. Neither am I. Are you through messing around here? We have statements to give, dirtbags to put away and a formal foster parent process to start."

"I ain't the one dilly-dallying with small talk, Pageant Queen." Appearing fully recovered, Valerie turned for the ladder, and as she headed down, Roman's gravelly voice drifted up, the best music ever.

One prong of her future had been set into motion, but she still had a competition to win and she wasn't about to lose now.

* * * *

Midnight had come and gone by a few hours before Roman stumbled into his empty house and shut the door behind him, enclosing himself in dead silence. Katerina's SUV wasn't parked outside, not that he was surprised in the least. Her confession in the bell tower had been raw and deep, and she undoubtedly needed time to process all the elements she'd unearthed to both him and Vee without his interference.

Today had been a victory for local law enforcement. No one had died. Kat's injury had been a simple bullet graze, fixed with stitches. Vee was safe. Luke had confessed to shooting the Colorado cop and agreed to tell them everything, as long as it was away from the institution basement. A raid on the human trafficking organization was set to occur at dawn. Mr. Peters, it turned out, had been the local contact for finding potential victims and referring them for a fee. He'd been responsible for pointing Luke toward Valerie, information that would undoubtedly affect his flimsy lawsuit. Matt and the other young man involved would likely be regretting their decisions while in the company of their new roommates behind bars.

From what he'd heard, prison could be cozy in more ways than one.

He leaned back against the door, weary, his heart heavy, even with the success of the day. Despite how many criminals he took down, how much illegal activity he assisted in stopping, not having Katerina waiting at home to share his day, to balance him, fill his heart, simply *be* with him? The emptiness threatened to cave his chest in.

She'd offered no information as to any decision she'd made, and he'd been too busy at the department to ask her — not sure he would have, anyway. She knew how he felt about her. Pushing wouldn't change how she felt about *him*, and he refused to read anything into her actions or words at the bell tower. Danger and adrenaline made people do and say things they later regretted after the dust settled and emotions faded.

As Roman trudged into the kitchen, the void curled around him and squeezed.

Then he saw it on the kitchen table — a plain white card stuck between the salt and pepper shakers — no envelope, no writing on the outside.

Carefully, he eased the paper free and opened it. Katerina's sparse handwriting flowed across the white space.

Challenge
Date and time: Tomorrow eight p.m.
Location: The lake

Roman stared at the words, his pulse pounding abnormally fast. 'The lake' needed no further specification, but he wished he knew if she'd chosen that location to set him up for success or as a favorite spot to ease the pain of a chapter drawing to its end.

Chapter Twenty-Seven

Rain tapped gently on Marta's metal roof and dotted the windshield as Roman pulled onto the rough semi-road leading to the Farkos family property and its secluded lake. The overgrown canopy of oak and fir shielded against the shower and the sudden silence pulsed, eroding his fragile peace. At eight o'clock sharp, he parked Marta behind Katerina's SUV and hopped out, his heart in his throat.

He'd taken an unusually long time choosing his clothes, shaving, wondering if he should bring one weapon or two. In the end, he'd kept to his usual jeans, black T-shirt and boots, leaving all firearms behind. If she wanted their last challenge to be with guns, she surely would have mentioned it, and it was far too late to try to pretend to be something he wasn't.

When he got close to the front of her SUV, he stopped in his tracks. Kat leaned against the grill. Instead of her usual ponytail or no-nonsense bun, her long, glorious hair was swept up in an elegant design that had Gia's signature on it, courtesy of the sparkling hairpin of flowers. She wore a simple sundress the shade of twilight that brushed against her bare knees and, in place of boots, glittering sandals accented her freshly painted toenails. Her natural beauty, always breathtaking, destroyed the fragile hope he'd held on to all day. She'd never dress up for their final challenge, certainly not to impress him.

His ribs became a strangling cage. She was leaving and wanted to do it in style, just to show him she could.

Unable to draw a full breath, he forced himself to move until he was close enough to catch her herbal scent, a scent he'd come to associate with home, into his lungs one last time. He'd never be able to stomach lavender or mint in his footbath again.

"Punctual as always, Farkos." The way she fiddled with the seam of her dress pocket merely confirmed his suspicions. She was nervous and probably wanted to get the unpleasantness over with as soon as possible.

"I'll make this easy and put you out of your six-week misery. I concede. You win. There's no need to prolong it." It was the right thing to do, to let her go instead of push, but damn... A dull knife stabbed his heart, leaving the bloody, broken bits at her feet. He couldn't stand losing her. Not fighting felt so very wrong.

"So you can tell everyone that the only reason you lost our challenge was because you chose to?" She shook her head. "I don't think so."

All the emotions he'd been fighting to keep in check so he wouldn't drive her away surged up like an exploding volcano. If he was going to lose her anyway, he'd do it like a true Farkos — fighting for what he knew was right.

In one quick step, he trapped her against the car, his hands braced on either side of her, his face inches from hers. If she wanted to, she could push him back, send him to the ground with a splash of spilled blood for his effort, but he was beyond caring. "What do you expect me to say, Angel? That after tonight's loss I want another shot at a few extra fraction-points that won't do me any good in the long run? That even if I win tonight, I ultimately lose because you're taking your Python with you when you go?"

Kat stilled, her dark eyes wide and watchful, as if he was a bomb she had to handle with expert precision and any sudden move might set him off. That assessment wasn't wrong.

"After Irini, I didn't want to make the same mistake. I've done my best not to push you, to give you dozens of reasons instead to stay without being demanding. I've given you space and time to make your own decisions without my influence." His ragged breath stirred the loose curl framing her face. "But denying what we have together is a lie. Pretending it's nothing more than infatuation is you disillusioning yourself and protecting your heart. I'm not any of those people in your life who have made you feel like you have to be perfect to be loved, that if you fail or come in second place that you're any less of a person, cop or otherwise, and I'll be *damned* —"

Kat covered his mouth with both of her hands and asked quietly, "Are you done?"

He pulled free from her loose hold. "Not even close."

With a little sigh, she dropped her hands.

"If you think I won't remember every moment we've spent together, that I won't memorialize each smile and laugh, the glorious moment you knocked Peters off his feet, how your nose crinkles when you shoot or the way you look so vulnerable and ruthless and lovely all at once, you're gravely mistaken."

Tears gathered in her eyes, but she made no effort to shut him up again, and he refused to let her pity deter him from telling her everything he'd held back in a pointless effort to convince her to stay.

"Maybe it was a mistake to stand on the sidelines like a hopeful bystander, waiting for you to let me fight for you, but I'm through with that. I'll fight to be your permanent backup every step of the way, no matter what roadblocks you put in my path." He cupped her face between his hands, as if he could anchor his life to hers by mere touch alone. "Love isn't judgment or keeping score. Love can't be tallied and measured. It has no rules and doesn't always need time or experience to exist. Sometimes it just hits, like thunder or a lightning strike, and there's no possible way to avoid it. You can deny what we have if you choose, Angel, but that won't erase its imprint. If you leave, I can't stop you, but know that I'll be right here, waiting, hoping for you to come back to me, because you're the only one—ever—who has made me want forever."

She averted her gaze and her lower lip trembled. When she looked up again, the tears had vanished and the same woman he'd met at the masquerade ball reappeared—icy, determined and looking like she wanted to kick someone's ass.

Everything inside him went numb. He'd offered her his entire heart, his future and forever, and she was still walking.

"You're not allowed to forfeit this challenge, Farkos, not after all the effort I put into it." With one finger, she pushed him back and straightened from the SUV. "If you can make up the rules as we go, so can I."

Before he could protest, she grabbed his hand and tugged him relentlessly toward the clearing and the lake beyond. As the trees broke, raindrops misted his skin and hair, cool in the fading summer heat, so much like the moment they'd walked together down Shadowbrook Lane the first time that his heart ached. He dropped his attention to the grass shimmering in the waning light. No matter what he did from here on out, every step would be tangled up with memories of Katerina.

As she let go, Roman lifted his head. For the second time that night, he halted in his tracks. He'd been too distracted by Katerina and his emotions to notice the lights that had been mostly hidden beyond the trees. On the shore grass, slender poles had been set up to create a frame for uncountable strings of tiny lavender lights. The glow danced on the water's surface, adding an unearthly touch. A boombox rested beneath the arbor beside a pie and a six-pack of beer, all covered by clear plastic to protect them against the rain.

Kat pivoted, facing him. "From my count, you're a full point behind. This is your chance to break even." She pulled her phone from her dress pocket, pressed a button and *Hopelessly Devoted to You* flowed from the speakers. In invitation, she held her slender hand out to him. "Dance with me, if you dare."

Everything inside him threatened to shatter. If he was to have one last memory with his Angel, to memorize how she felt in his arms, a few minutes to replay over and over after she left, he preferred the lingering pain rather than not having the memory at all. His hand shaking, he placed it in hers.

Her smile, sincere and unfettered, made his breath catch, and when she pulled him beneath the lights, slipped her arm around his back and laid her head against his heart, he knew he'd never recover from Katerina Hellman. Surrendering, he held her tight, rested his head against hers and let Olivia Newton-John add to his agony, let the rain soak into his skin like the love he'd never expected to find, the love he'd already lost from the beginning.

Too soon, the song ended, and as the silence pressed in, Katerina straightened.

"Don't," he whispered against her hair, his voice breaking. "Not yet. I'm not ready." *I'll never be ready.*

Apparently feeling more merciful than usual, she acquiesced and let him hold her a while longer. "We have a serious problem now, you know." Her words were muffled against his damp shirt. "We're tied. No respectable challenge ends on a tie."

His throat was too tight, his heart too broken to argue that her count was off. He was ahead by a point and a quarter. It didn't feel like a victory.

Not releasing him, she lifted her head and met his gaze. "So, I was thinking about extending it... permanently."

With raindrops clinging to her lashes, hair and skin like crystals, she looked like a wicked fae prepared to cast a curse...or grant a wish from the deepest hollow of a heart. Vulnerability lurked beneath the challenge in her dark eyes, and he could hardly dare to hope he'd heard her right.

"I meant every word yesterday in the bell tower." That openness in her eyes shadowed her tone, softening her husky voice to a lull. "The way you look at me, how you make me feel..." She bit her lip. "I'm terrified that I won't live up to your expectations, that I'll find out long after I've fallen madly and completely in love with you that you've discovered the truth about me and leave."

"No, Angel—"

"Let me finish." Her tone was sharp enough to make him shut his mouth. "I haven't sugar-coated anything when it comes to my downfalls, so this is on you as much as it is on me, Farkos. It's too late for retreat and, after some unexpected wisdom from a surprising source, I came to a decision. I'm willing to descend into the relationship basement and stay in the darkness as long as it takes…if it's with you."

The blood pounded in his head, muffling her voice, but one word rang loud and true. *Stay.* "You're staying?"

Frowning, she eased back and studied him. "You seem extra obtuse tonight, so I'll be very clear. Despite my best efforts, you managed to slip beneath my defenses with your twisted charm." She glanced at his mouth. "And maybe the way you kiss had an irreversible effect on my rationality, but more than that, from the start, you saw…*me.* Somehow, you make all my imperfections perfectly okay."

Tears filled her eyes again, and before she could wipe them away, he grabbed her hands. He didn't want her to hide anything, not from him. He lifted her fingers to his mouth and gently kissed them one by one.

"I'm not Irini. I can't be pushed into anything I don't want to do, but I'll never disappear without an explanation. I don't have my future figured out, but I don't want to go back to a place where I don't fit in, especially when I've figured out where I do belong."

She released a shaky breath. "I belong with you, if you still want me."

"Angel." He cupped her face and peppered kisses on her face — nose, brow, cheeks, chin, unable to contain the pure joy expanding his chest. "Always. Forever. Here, with me, is right where you belong. Whatever comes at us, we'll handle it together, you and me."

"You, me...and Vee." She gave him an almost shy look, as if uncertain what his reaction might be. "I applied to be her foster parent."

If he hadn't loved her completely already, he'd be there now. "You do realize that's going to ruin a good portion of your self-descriptions. Your reputation is ruined. We're going to be an *amazing* team, the three of us."

"You have no idea what you're signing up for," she said, laughing as she slung her arms around his neck.

"I know exactly what I'm doing." He kissed her, a slow, deep, soul-changing promise to love her unconditionally, to fight whatever battles came at them, a vow of together forever, come what may. When he released her, her mouth was soft, her cheeks flushed and her eyes a midnight sky filled with stars.

"I'm finally convinced. You know what you're doing." Her smile curled around his heart and held him close, and he didn't need her next words to know how she felt, but *holy shiznit*, they were glorious to hear. "I love you, Roman Farkos...and I brought pie. Want some?"

He smiled for her, fangs and all. "Every single bite."

Epilogue

A week later, bright and early on Sunday, Kat walked toward the firing range office, her Python case in her hand. Roman had texted her earlier, saying he'd meet her there, since a call right before shift change had held him up—which was fine with her. It meant she could choose her favorite firing bay. She wasn't afraid of losing, but a Hellman never overlooked an opportunity to add an edge.

She opened the office door and paused, her stomach tightening. Boyd stood at the register—with Vic.

"Hey, Hellman." Boyd dropped the pen and slapped a 'visitor' nametag on Vic's shirt. "Keeping my shooting sharp. Aren't you proud of me?"

"So proud," she said, imitating Roman's best monotone, and set her gaze on Vic. "Quite the distance to travel for target practice."

"After all the bragging Boyd did about his first-class instructor and how it saved everyone's lives in a recent shutdown, I needed to experience his improvement firsthand." Vic's blue eyes flashed as he slung an arm around Boyd's shoulders. "We're old academy buds. Weird coincidence, isn't it?"

"Almost as weird as my old academy bud calling me up after decades of no contact." Boyd winked at her, sly. "Despite all the crap I gave Hellman, she still managed to teach me. All my bragging is completely on point. You'll see" — he punched Vic in the arm, hard — "Bud."

The door opened on a draft of holiday-scented air and Roman walked in. Dressed all in black, tall, menacing and sexy, he looked like the angel of death ready to pass sentence. "Sorry I'm late." He leaned down and kissed her, soft and lingering. There was no way he'd missed Boyd and Vic standing only a few feet away, but his gaze was all for her. "Wait long?"

"Just got here."

"I'm all aflutter with anticipation," he said, deadpan, as his attention dropped to the Python case in her hand.

Vic glanced between her and Roman and a knowing glint entered his eyes. "Good luck with that, Farkos."

As if only now realizing they had company, Roman pivoted. He leaned one shoulder against the doorjamb and folded his arms. "Boyd." He nodded and those dark, dangerous eyes went to Vic. "I don't need luck."

"Trust me, you will. Enjoy her warmth while you can." Vic smiled at Kat. "It won't be long until she returns to a frozen wasteland."

Kat's grip on her gun case became a stranglehold. She had so many possible replies to that. She couldn't decide on one quickly enough.

"If a man isn't capable of keeping a woman warm," he said in his monotone, his expression revealing nothing, "that isn't her issue. It's his." He opened the door and held it open for Boyd and Vic. "Happy shooting, boys."

It took all her willpower not to smile like a fiend. Even better, behind Vic, Boyd did it for her. *Damn*, small towns were magnificent, and after Boyd demonstrated his new-found firearms skills, she doubted Vic would be invited to return any time soon.

"Just trying to help one of the brotherhood." Vic straightened, as if righteously offended.

Keeping his stare on Vic, Roman wrapped his arm around Kat's shoulders and pulled her close.

A tic worked in Vic's jaw, and after a beat, he headed for the door. He walked out in silence. Boyd followed with a wink, still wearing his mean smile.

Kat gave Vic's back the appropriate one-fingered salute and faced Roman. "I didn't need you to defend me."

"I know." He leaned in and kissed her softly, sweetly. "But I'll always be your backup. Did you convince your ex to show up in an attempt to distract me from our challenge?"

"*Pfft.*" Kat marched to the register, signed up for her favorite bay and dropped the pen. "Don't make up excuses for when you lose, Farkos."

"I love it when you talk tough." He opened the door for her and followed her out. As they walked down the gravel road to the farthest bay on the range, he exhaled, long and slow. "I got a call from Irini on the way here."

Kat halted in her tracks and faced him. "And?"

"She's okay. That's all she wanted to say over the phone." His throat worked and moisture glistened in his dark eyes. He then flashed his teeth in a mega-watt, full-fanged smile. "We're meeting for coffee tomorrow."

"Roman, that's phenomenal!"

"My thoughts exactly." He wiped his eyes as she slid her arm around his waist and pressed her cheek to his heart. After a moment, they continued walking together, slower. "Guess what else I found out before leaving the office?"

"The donuts with the powdered sugar have raspberry filling?"

"I've tested that theory on uncountable occasions, and it has proven to be true eighty percent of the time — but that isn't the news. The sting was a complete success — all the kids recovered, the dirtbags taken down and enough information gathered to cripple the ring, if not demolish it."

"Good." Kat curled her lip. "Scumsacks."

"There's more." He glanced at her and his mouth twitched, a sign that whatever news he had was particularly exciting. "Chief applied for a grant some weeks back for a school resource officer and has someone particular in mind to fill it."

Even as her heart rate jumped, hopeful, she shrugged. Graywood's department was too small, too underfunded to afford another officer, and she'd already begun compiling a list of nearby agencies to check for openings. Getting another offer at Graywood PD would be a miracle.

"Us." His black eyes gleamed.

"Us?" She paused outside the door leading into the shooting range bay. "I suck at dealing with kids."

"He was notably impressed by how you dealt with Valerie." He wriggled his eyebrows. "As he should be. But even better, the grant includes afterschool clubs. It pays the salary for a police presence and positive influence at the club. While a phenomenal start, it's not the ultimate fix—but accepting would require a sacrifice from you."

She folded her arms and waited for the bomb to drop.

"You'd have to accept part-time as a patrol deputy, might have to take down a few dirtbags, throat-punch the occasional ne'er-do-well, work at the same department as me and—"

Kat jumped on him and kissed him, hard, only letting him go when the laugh in her throat demanded to be free. "Stop pressuring me. I'll think about it."

One side of his mouth curled up.

She pushed into the bay, set her case on the counter and opened it. Her Python shone from inside, waiting to redeem her from their last shocking loss. Roman settled in next to her with his favorite Glock, and he began filling the mag with bullets, his black eyes glittering with mischief.

Her heart swelled, threatening to burst from her ribcage. No, her loss at the range had been the ultimate win.

Kat picked up her Python and gave the love of her life an evil smile. "You're not going to beat me this time, Farkos. But if you're really, really nice, I may let you touch my Python."

"You stole my line." Then he kissed her and it felt like the sweetest victory. It felt like forever.

Want to see more like this?
Here's a taster for you to enjoy!

Anywhere and Always:
Falling for the Tycoon
Aurora Russell

Excerpt

The sky was a perfect unending blue, clear and brilliant, its beauty rivaled only by the magnificent expanse of bright aqua ocean and baby-powder-fine sand. It had always been Annelise's dream to see the Caribbean, and she knew she should have been happy. Ecstatic. Wasn't she still here, even if she was alone? But, instead, she just felt empty. Detached.

She'd cried her tears. So many tears. For weeks. Wondering what had gone wrong to make Kyle decide to walk out on their life together, ending their wedding and honeymoon plans abruptly. Wondering what would come next. Looking at the space where his toothbrush used to sit next to the bathroom sink, looking at the empty space in the fridge where the special espresso he loved had always been kept, she'd felt a gnawing, painful ache in her chest, raw like a sucking wound. She'd sobbed into her pillow, worried she'd alarm the neighbors in the condo above. Her hot tears signaled the end of not just a seven-year-long relationship, but also of her dreams for the future. She'd cried so much she'd gone numb.

She'd managed the chores of daily living—making food, getting dressed, going to work and to the store—but she'd felt like an imposter, like some zombie trapped inside the body of the vivacious, happy, hopeful woman she'd always been. She'd looked in the mirror and it had scared her. But still, nothing moved her anymore—not sadness, not anger, not understanding or judgment. Nothing. When the reminder from the travel agency had come through as an alert on her smartphone, the hot swell of anger had been as surprising as it had been fleeting. That spark was what had led her to do the crazy thing she'd done. Just to feel something, anything, she'd decided to take their honeymoon. Alone.

Logically, the decision had been clear. She should go—two weeks in a remote section of the Yucatan Peninsula, staying at an exclusive hotel right on the beach. It was a two-hour-long ride in a Jeep on bumpy roads through the jungle to get to the collection of luxury cabanas, perched right at the edge of a wild natural preserve. Quite a journey, but it was supposed to be worth it. This was her dream trip, and it was almost entirely paid for already...and non-refundable. When they'd booked it, she hadn't even had a nanosecond of concern about that portion of the terms and conditions. The idea that Kyle would have chosen not to go would have been laughable to her on that long-ago morning. After seven years of blissful love, she'd thought she'd known him inside and out. She had never been more wrong.

The decision to come had been more complex. Could she handle the possible emotional roller-coaster of going on what was supposed to be the romantic trip of a lifetime by herself? Was she crazy to risk putting herself through a possible ordeal of 'what-ifs' and 'might-have-beens'? But when she'd looked down at that small phone screen, slightly smudged from her fingers, and had again seen the hollow, eerie eyes in her dark reflection, she'd known. She was going to go. Her best friend, Marina, was the only one who seemed to understand and support her decision. Everyone else just looked at her like she'd lost her mind.

She hadn't been able to muster much enthusiasm for the packing, but still, even just knowing that she was packing to go had made her feel a little less frozen. Instead of staring at the same walls where she'd hung pictures with Kyle, or sitting on the same couch they'd spent several happy hours picking out at the furniture store, she would escape — or so she'd thought. But of course, she couldn't ever escape. Not really. She couldn't run away from herself.

So here she stood, looking at the prettiest view she'd ever seen, hands-down. The warm breeze ruffled her hair and the air held the delicate scent of tropical flowers mixed with the tangy salt of the ocean. Even the sound of the waves lapping onto the soft sand was exquisite. Soothing. And she could appreciate it all, but only in the abstract. Here in paradise, she was still frozen. Annelise sighed and turned, determined to keep walking until she began to thaw, even if it was just a little. Maybe seeing the jungle would help. She'd read there were even toucans. She sighed again, more heavily this time, trying to feel a glimmer of her usual optimism. Marina's voice replayed in her head, encouraging her. And with Marina's own past sadness, her advice meant even more.

'Go on, girl,' her friend had said. *'Don't let that man take one more day of your life. You have too much in you left to give. Go wild! Do anything and everything because you never know what's around the corner.'*

With those words in mind, Annelise doggedly continued, sinking her heels into the softer sand farther away from the waterline. It truly was incredible to be alone in such an unbelievably beautiful spot, and she hadn't seen another soul all day. She turned her face to the water again as she walked, watching as the sky lit up into a symphony of purples, pinks and oranges as the sun began to dip toward the horizon. Without warning, she fell over something large on the ground, landing squarely on a warm, hard object, which gave a startled grunt.

She scrambled up as quickly as possible, but not before she pressed up against the length of a tall, muscular man. He was warm and smelled of the ocean and the wind — and also a bit spicy, like some of the more exotic seasonings used in the local dishes. As she brushed herself off and stood as swiftly as she could, she just had time to realize that he smelled...incredibly good. *For someone I apparently fell on like a ton of bricks. Smooth. Real smooth, Annelise.*

"I'm so sorry!" she apologized, feeling a hot blush rise from her hairline to her ears and even onto her chest. She knew her cheeks must be flaming.

The stranger, dressed only in faded board shorts that might have been red once but were now a washed-out salmon, was covered in sand. It dusted his tan, muscular chest and sprinkled his dark-brown hair. He might have looked silly if he hadn't been... Well, the only words that sprang to her mind were 'unbelievably gorgeous'. No, that wasn't true. She also thought 'scrumptious' and 'hot as hell'. Mentally recalling herself, she realized he hadn't responded to her apology.

"Do you speak English? *Español*?" Annelise hoped he spoke at least a tiny bit of English, because her

Spanish was abysmal. "Oh my gosh, did I hurt you?" she continued, worried.

The man sat up with a little shake, and his mouth quirked into a wry smile, making his dark eyes crinkle at the corners. "No apology needed. I must have fallen asleep. I'm fine. No harm done. Although"—he gestured at the empty beach—"it was an unlucky coincidence that you should choose this one spot to walk onto." His accent sounded French, and his tone was compelling as he spoke, inviting her to share his amusement, not only at their situation but also possibly at life in general.

Annelise felt an unfamiliar smile tug at the corners of her lips. "I'm so glad you're not hurt. And 'unlucky' should be my middle name," she answered, the words out before she could recall them. It was totally unlike her to talk about her personal life with a complete stranger. Alone. On a deserted beach. *Totally* alone. She took an unconscious step backward.

The stranger didn't look as though he'd been lying in wait to trip unsuspecting tourists, though. He looked as if he belonged—and as if he was mildly interested in what she was saying. If he'd looked too interested, she might have shut down, but instead, she found herself answering the questioning quirk of his dark eyebrow.

"I've...had a bit of a setback recently in my personal life," she said. It was the understatement of the century.

"Sounds like it was a bad one. Do you want to talk about it?" he offered, as if it were the most natural thing in the world, just two strangers watching a Caribbean sunset and talking about their personal lives. It suddenly occurred to her that he was the first person besides the unobtrusive security guards that she'd seen on the private beach this entire trip. She'd actually begun to think she must be the only guest at the cabanas. Her thoughts turned suddenly suspicious.

"What are you doing on this beach? It's supposed to be private and definitely a no-trespassing sort of place." Her mind turned to the prominent guns she'd seen the security guards carrying, and she wasn't sure if she was trying to intimidate or warn the stranger.

The white of his smile on his tan face was stunning in the sunset. "Thank you for the warning, *chérie*, but I am a guest here…in the owner's cabana." He gestured with one long, muscular arm and Annelise noticed a path she hadn't seen before, leading to what looked like a giant house. It was much larger than her own spacious cabin.

"Oh, right. The owner's French, isn't he?" Annelise answered, trying to recall the details she knew of the resort. She'd learned about it from her colleague, and the owner was a big-time client of the financial services firm where she worked.

"French-Canadian," the stranger corrected, raising his eyebrow again, "but I'll let it slide just this once."

"Sorry…I know there's a big difference," she hastened to apologize. Great, she'd now offended a close friend of a client who could get her fired.

The stranger shook his head. "I was teasing. I'm not so easily offended," he said, bending up his knees and wrapping his arms loosely around them before motioning toward the soft-looking hollow next to him. "Care to join me? You can't beat the view."

Again, his offer was casual. Careless, almost. But somehow that put Annelise at ease when she hadn't been remotely at ease, anywhere, in months. He had a beautiful voice, dark and rumbling, deep and masculine. It was a good match for his tall, broad frame.

"You've already been on top of me. Is it so bad to be next to me?" He waggled his eyebrows in an exaggerated way, and the bark of laughter that escaped her shocked her so much that she put a hand to her mouth. She sat down more out of shock than anything else.

"I...can't believe you made me laugh. I haven't...felt like laughing in months." She spoke her thoughts aloud, almost forgetting she wasn't alone. Strange, but she felt such an instant camaraderie with the stranger that she already thought of him as a sort of friend.

Home of Erotic Romance

Sign up for our newsletter and find out about all our romance book releases, eBook sales and promotions, sneak peeks and FREE romance books!

About the Author

C.J. Burright is a native Oregonian and refuses to leave. A member of Romance Writers of America and the Fantasy, Futuristic & Paranormal special interest chapter, while she has worked for years in a law office, she chooses to avoid writing legal thrillers (for now) and instead invades the world of paranormal romance, fantasy, and contemporary romance. C.J. also has her 4th Dan Black Belt in Tae Kwon Do and believes a story isn't complete without at least one fight scene. Her meager spare time is spent working out, refueling with mochas, gardening, gorging on Assassin's Creed, and rooting on the Seattle Mariners…always with music. She shares life with her husband, daughter, and a devoted cat herd.

C.J. Burright loves to hear from readers. You can find her contact information, website details and author profile page at https://www.totallybound.com